THE FIFTH QUARTER

MIKE DAWSON

:01
First Second
New York

:01

First Second

Published by First Second
First Second is an imprint of Roaring Brook Press,
a division of Holtzbrinck Publishing Holdings Limited Partnership
120 Broadway, New York, NY 10271
firstsecondbooks.com
mackids.com

Library of Congress Control Number: 2020919611

Our books may be purchased in bulk for promotional, educational, or business use.
Please contact your local bookseller or the Macmillan Corporate and Premium Sales
Department at (800) 221-7945 ext. 5442 or by email at
MacmillanSpecialMarkets@macmillan.com.

FIRST

EDITION

First edition, 2021
Edited by Mark Siegel and Samia Fakih, with assistance from Rachel Stark
Cover design by Kirk Benshoff
Interior book design by Mike Dawson and Sunny Lee
Printed in China by 1010 Printing International Limited, Kwun Tong, Hong Kong

Drawn digitally using a Wacom Cintiq tablet, colored digitally in Photoshop

ISBN 978-1-250-24418-5 (paperback)
10 9 8 7 6 5 4 3

ISBN 978-1-250-24417-8 (hardcover)
10 9 8 7 6 5 4 3 2

Don't miss your next favorite book from First Second!
For the latest updates go to firstsecondnewsletter.com and sign up for our enewsletter.

BY ART
WE LIVE

For Orli

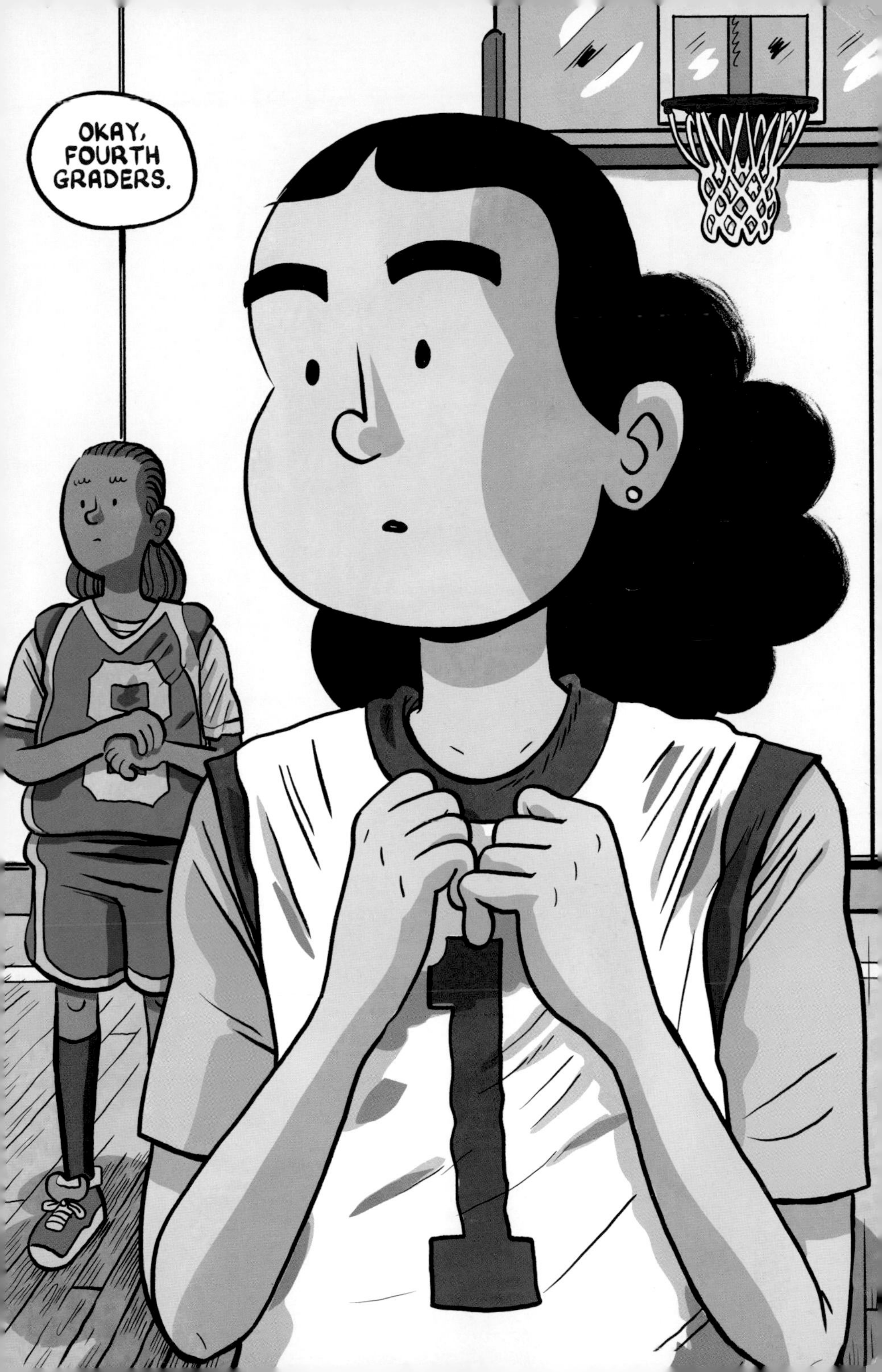
OKAY, FOURTH GRADERS.

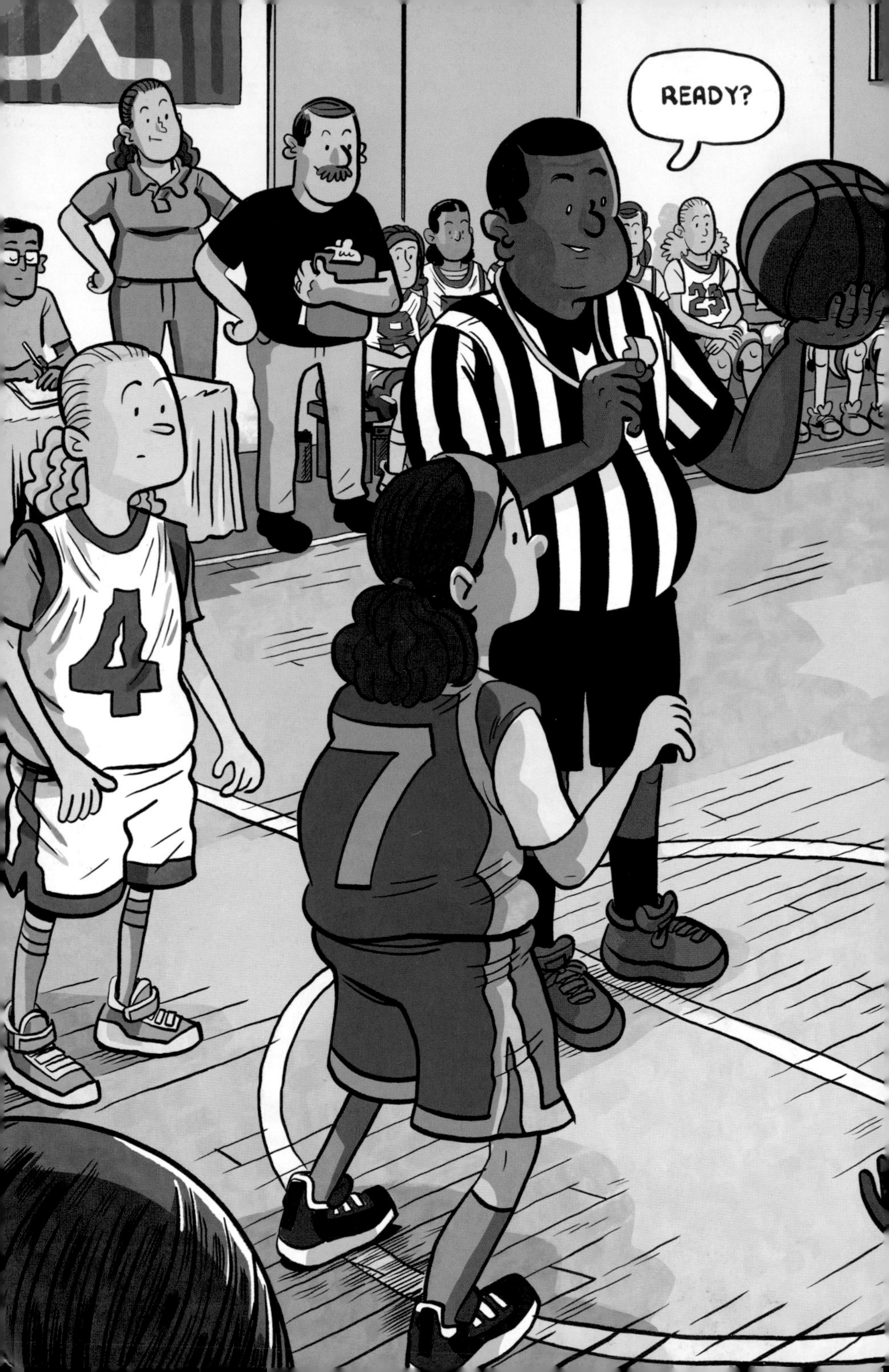
READY?

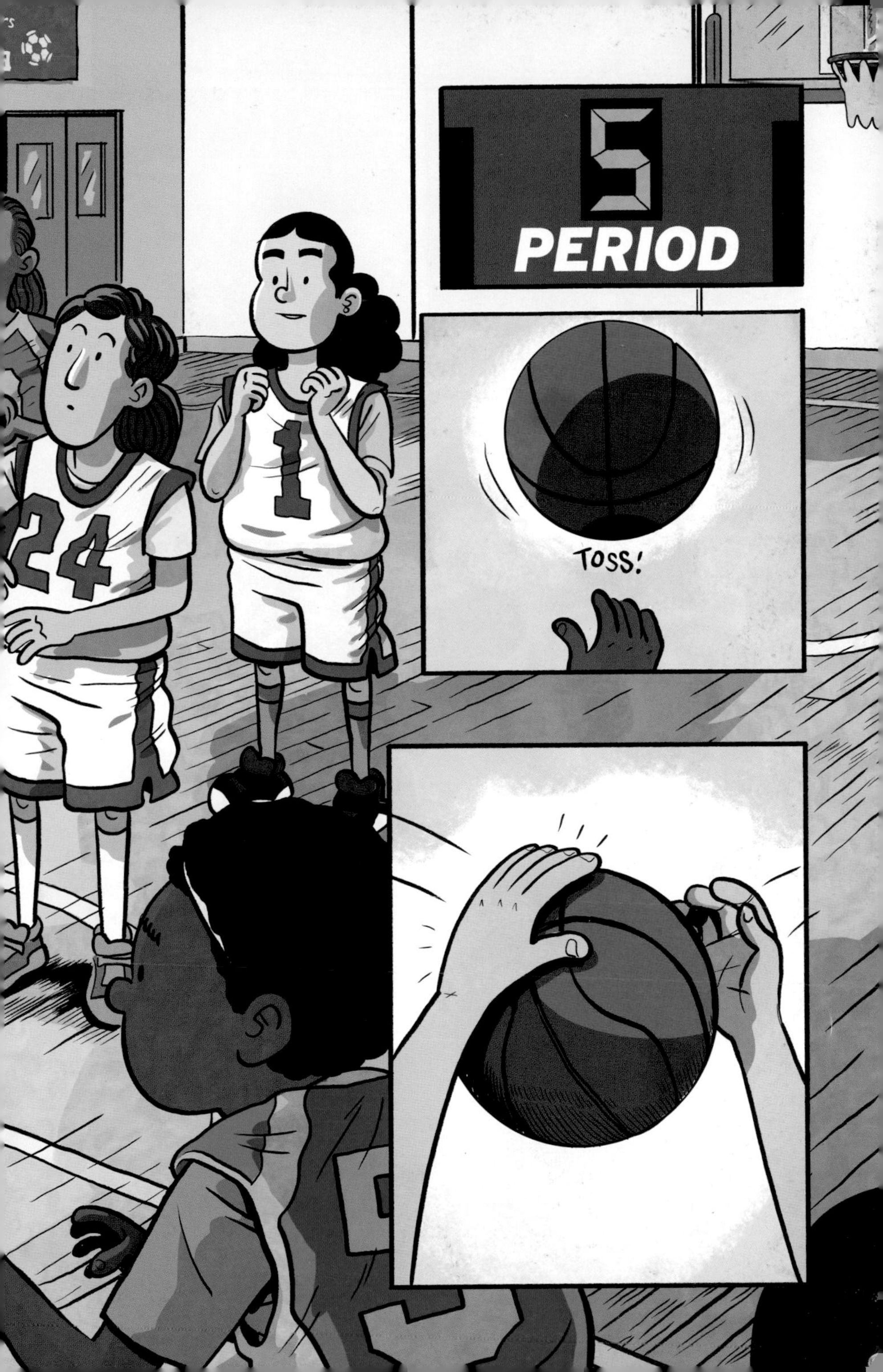
5
PERIOD
TOSS!

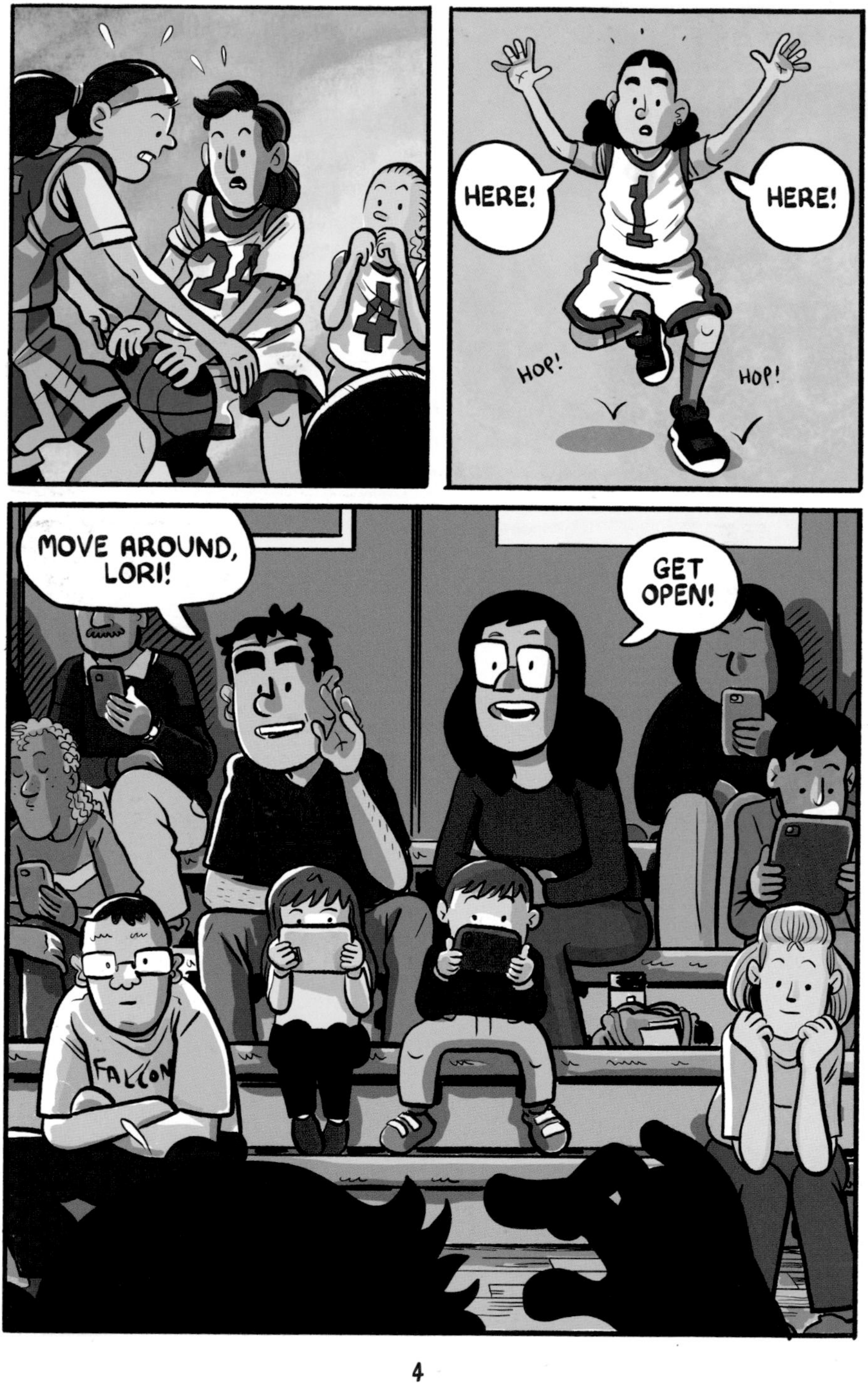
HERE!
HERE!
HOP!
HOP!
MOVE AROUND, LORI!
GET OPEN!
FALCON

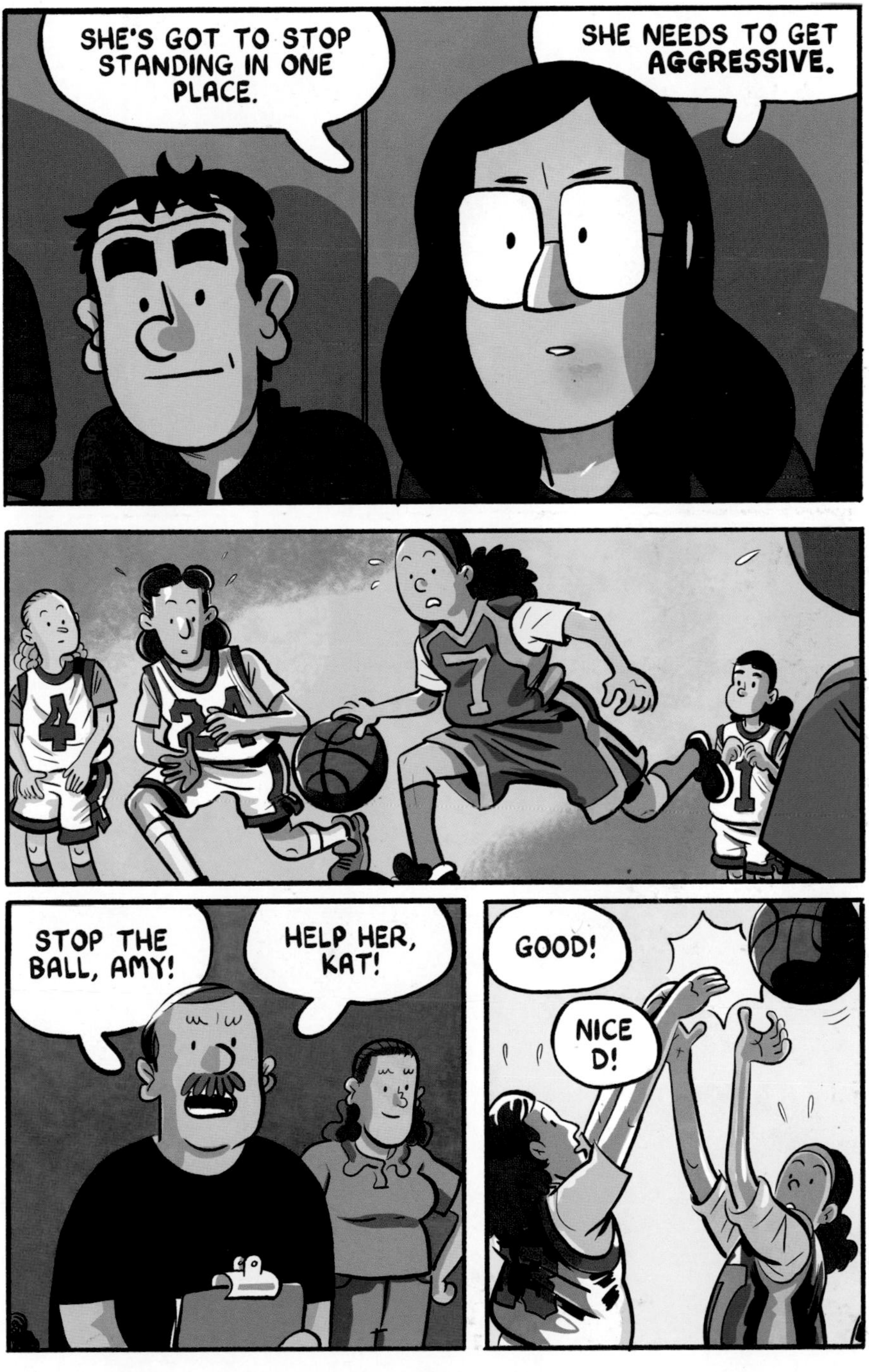
SHE'S GOT TO STOP STANDING IN ONE PLACE.
SHE NEEDS TO GET AGGRESSIVE.
STOP THE BALL, AMY!
HELP HER, KAT!
GOOD!
NICE D!

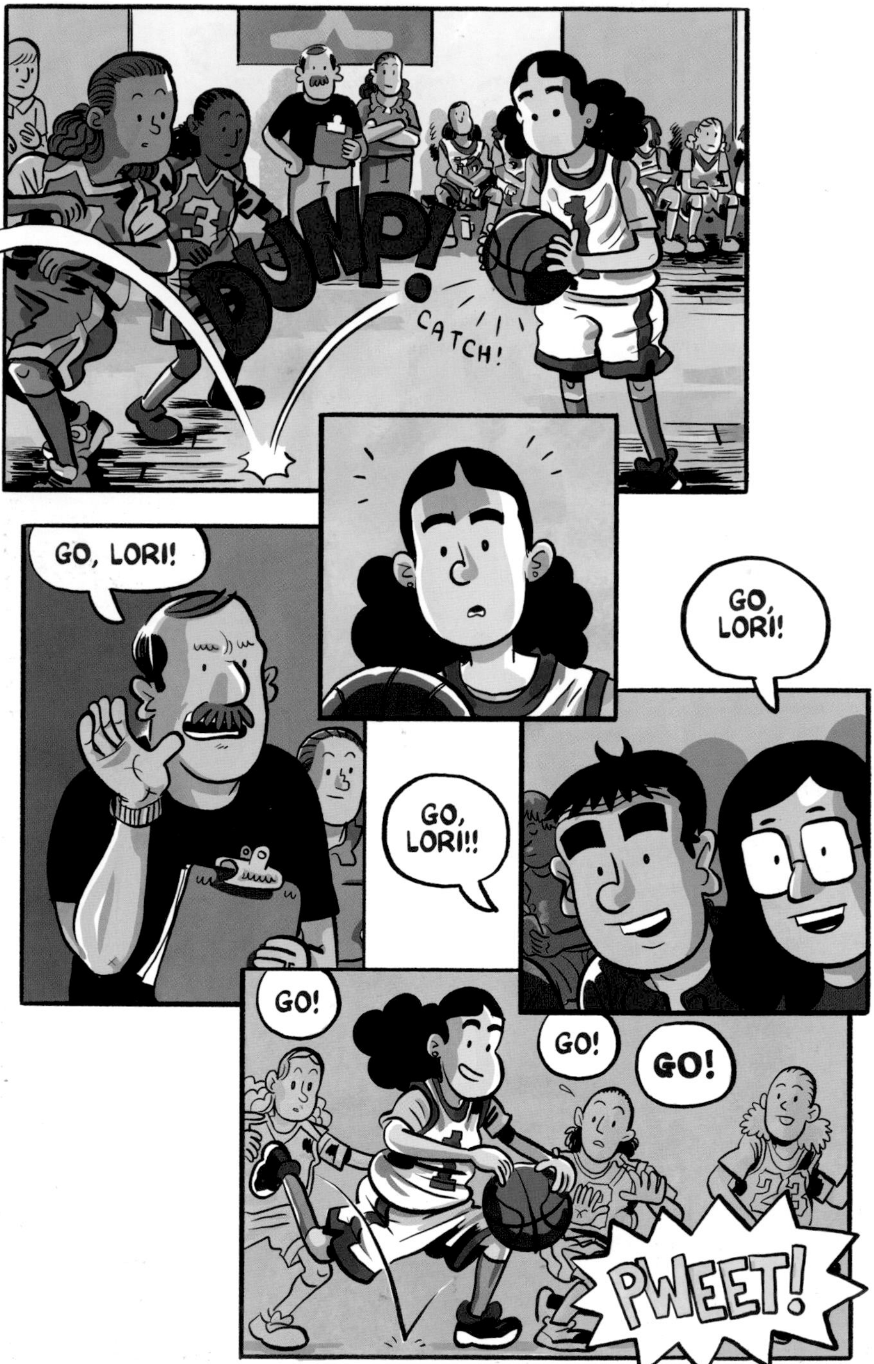
DUNP!
CATCH!
GO, LORI!
GO, LORI!!
GO, LORI!
GO!
GO!
GO!
PWEET!

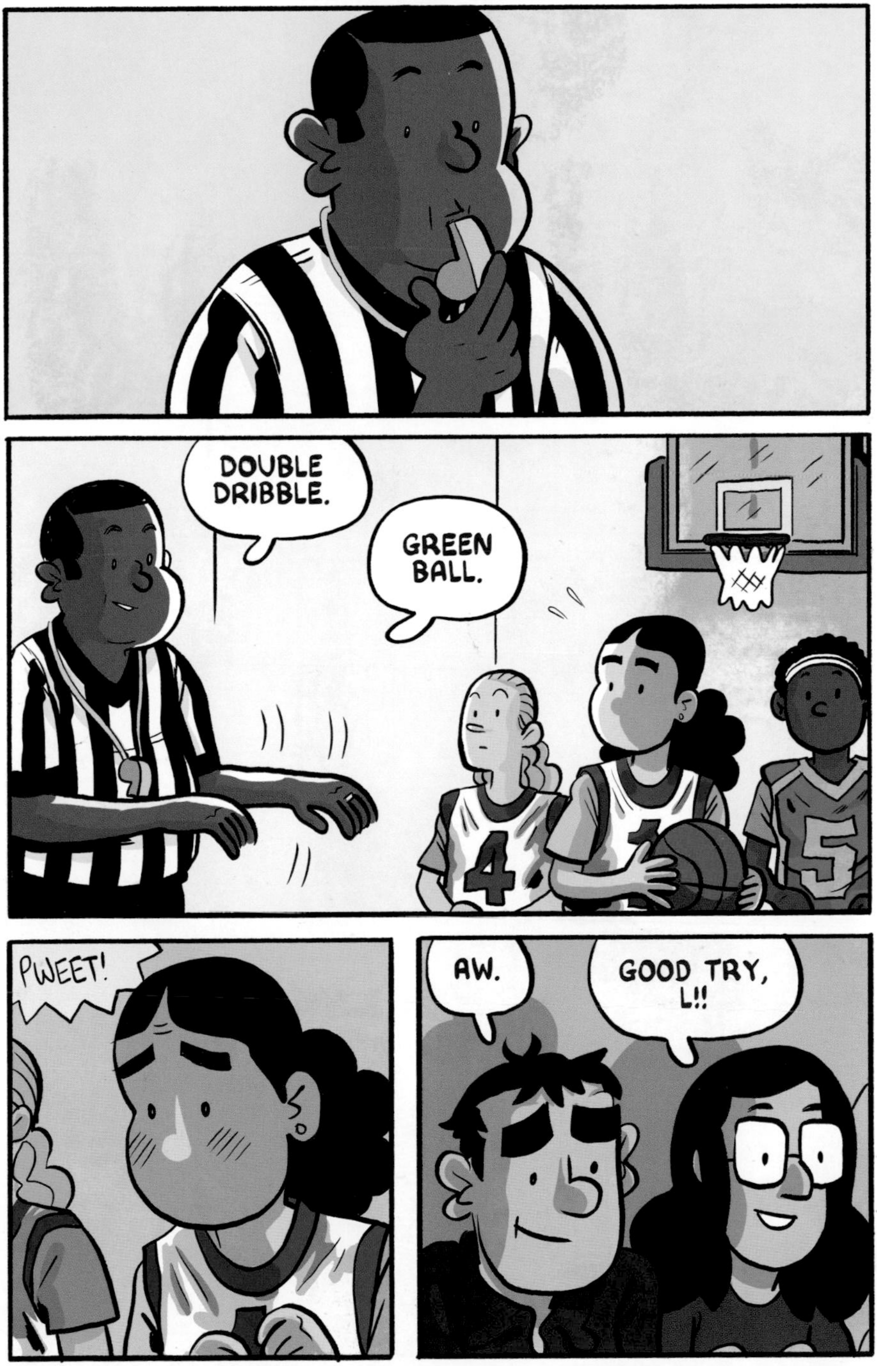
DOUBLE DRIBBLE.
GREEN BALL.
PWEET!
AW.
GOOD TRY, L!!

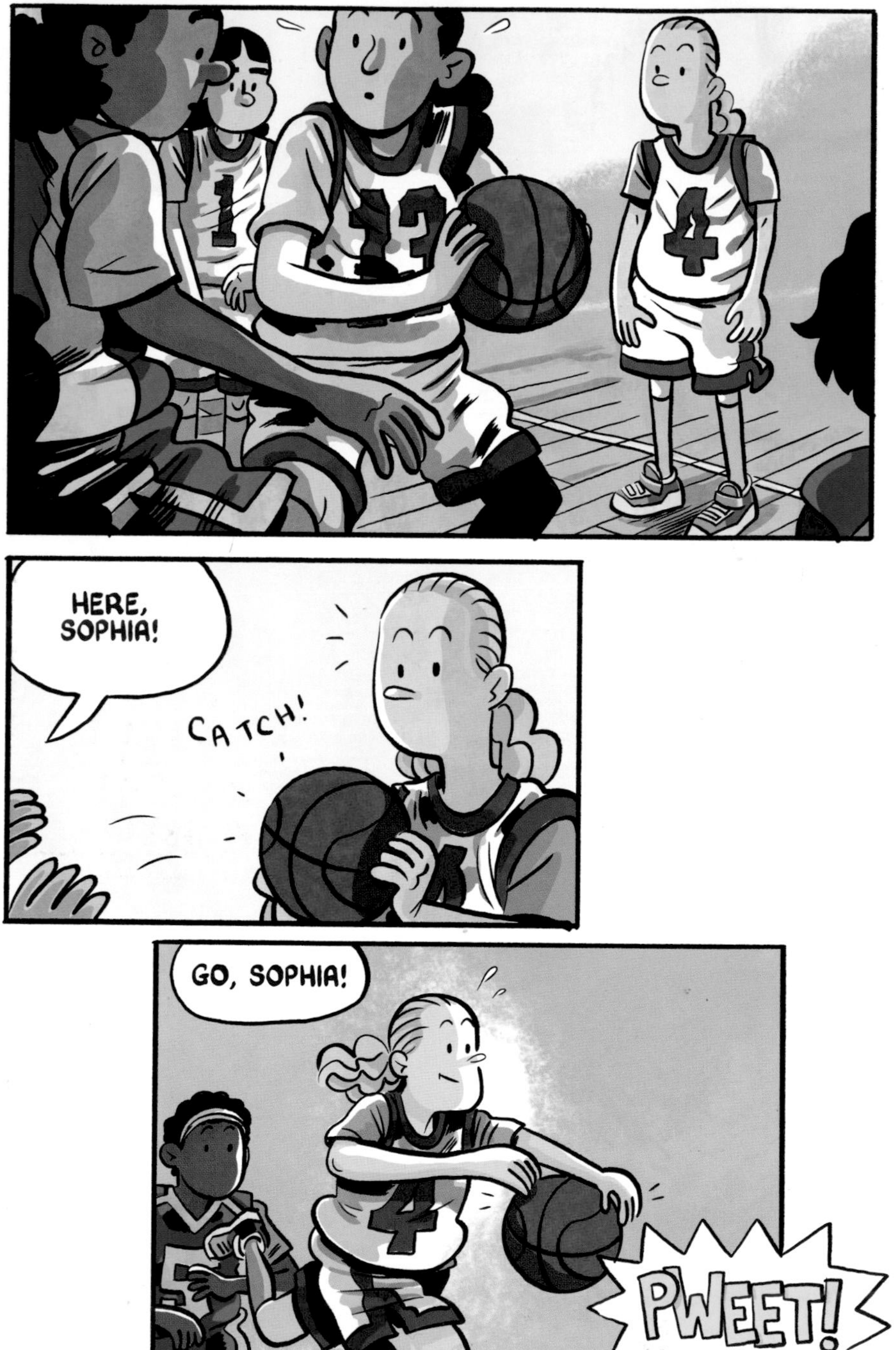
HERE, SOPHIA!
CATCH!
GO, SOPHIA!
PWEET!

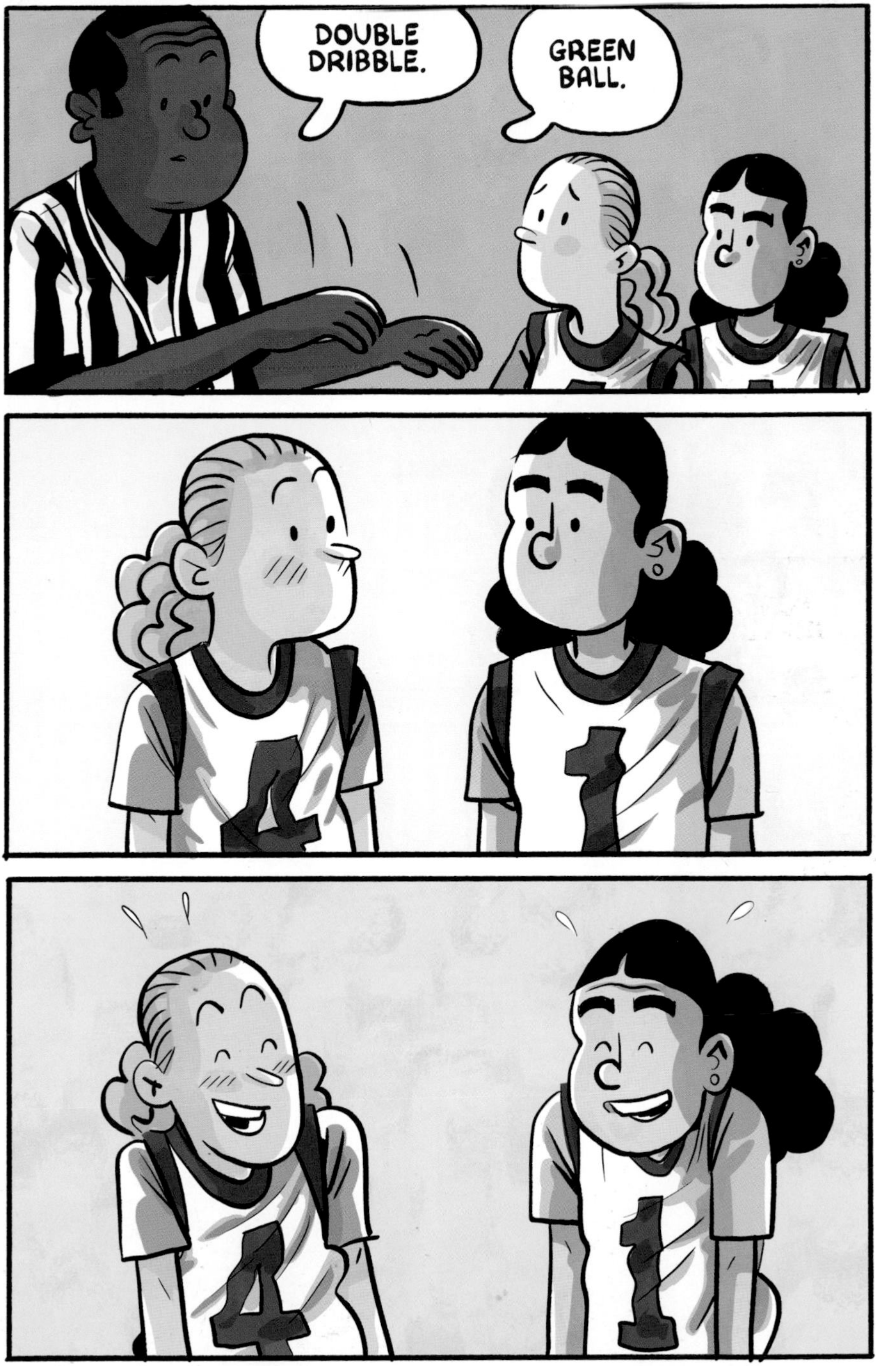
DOUBLE DRIBBLE.
GREEN BALL.

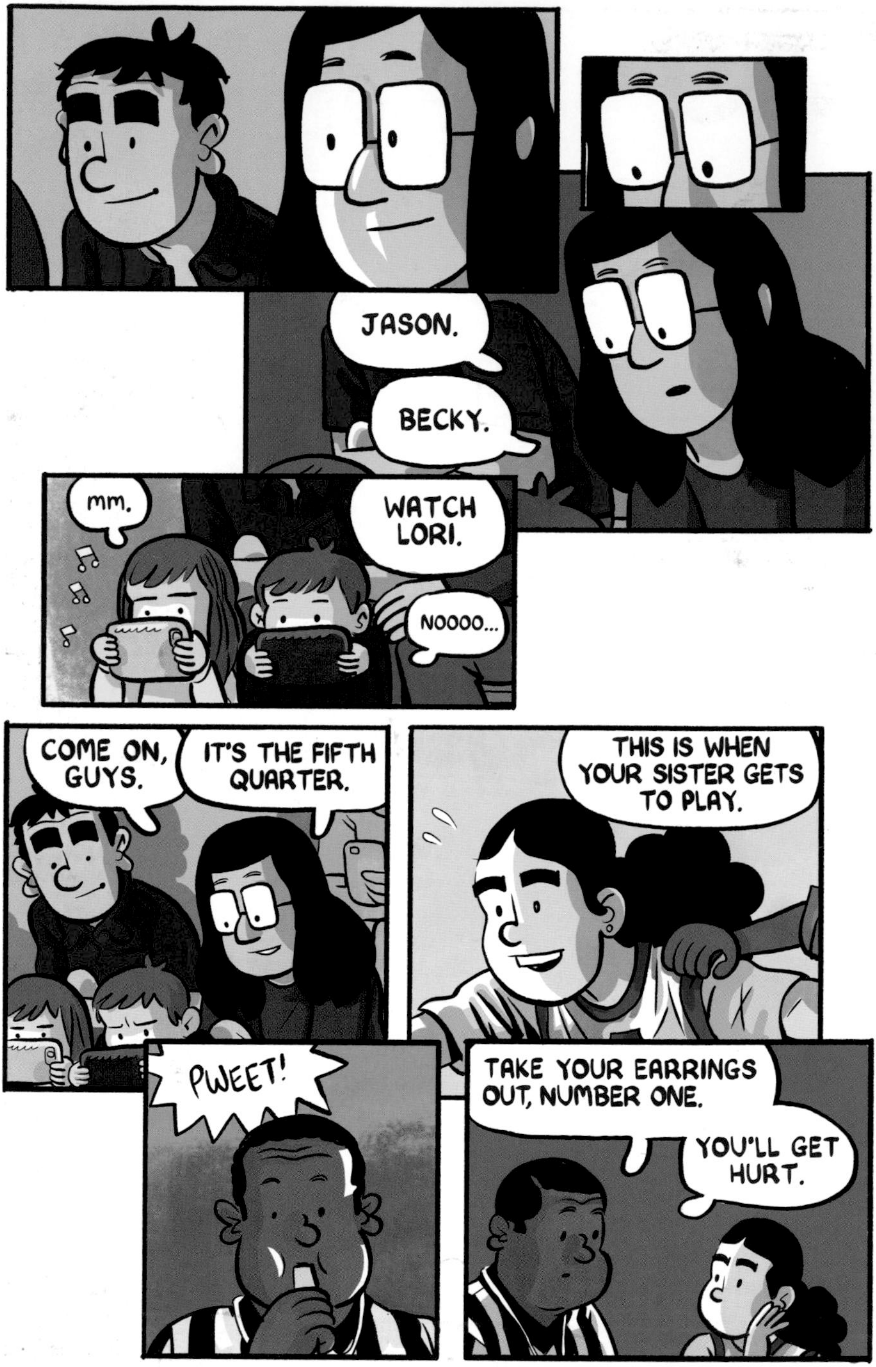

JASON.
BECKY.
mm.
WATCH LORI.
NOOOO...
COME ON, GUYS.
IT'S THE FIFTH QUARTER.
THIS IS WHEN YOUR SISTER GETS TO PLAY.
PWEET!
TAKE YOUR EARRINGS OUT, NUMBER ONE.
YOU'LL GET HURT.

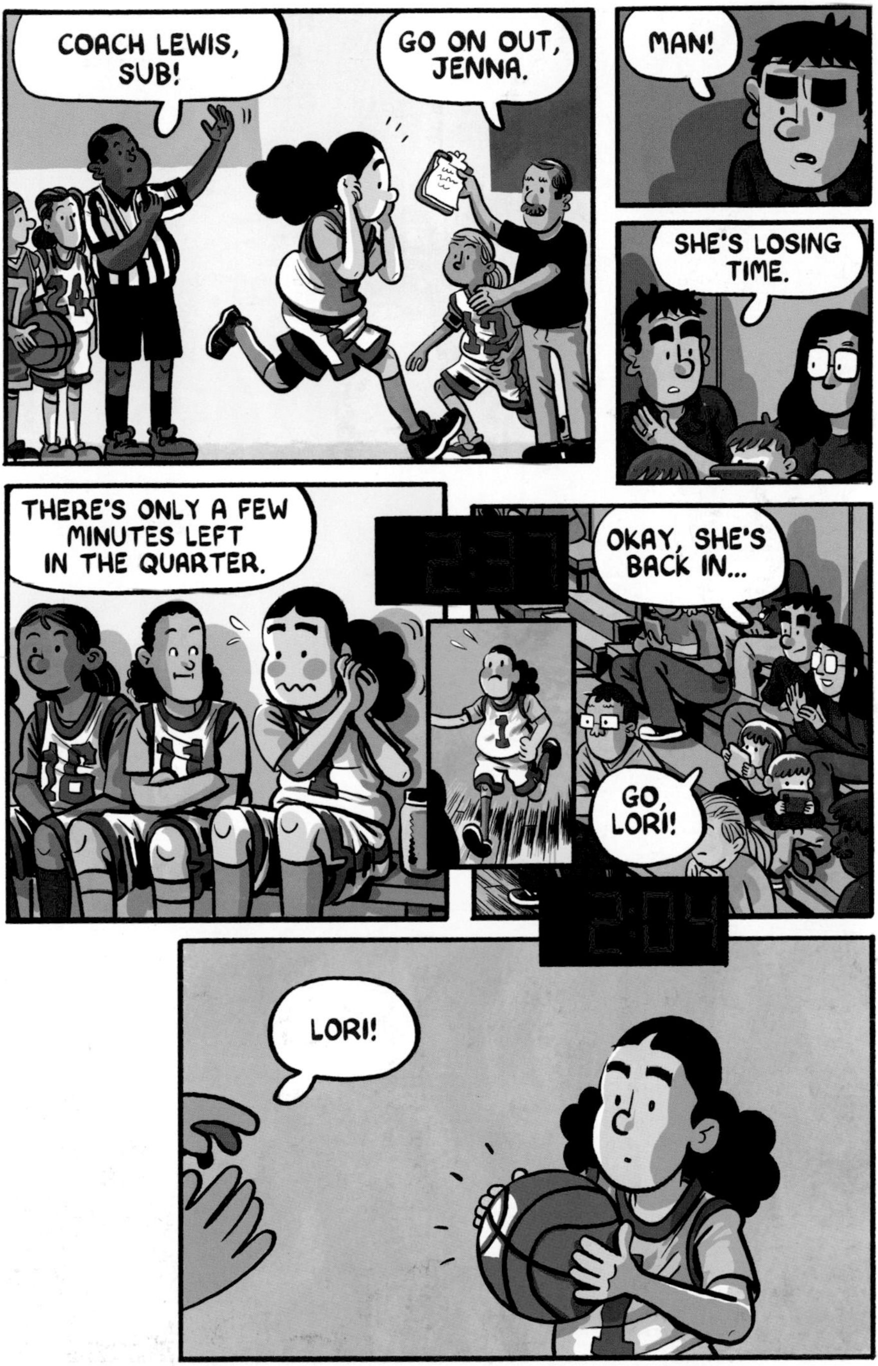
COACH LEWIS, SUB!
GO ON OUT, JENNA.
MAN!
SHE'S LOSING TIME.
THERE'S ONLY A FEW MINUTES LEFT IN THE QUARTER.
OKAY, SHE'S BACK IN...
GO, LORI!
LORI!

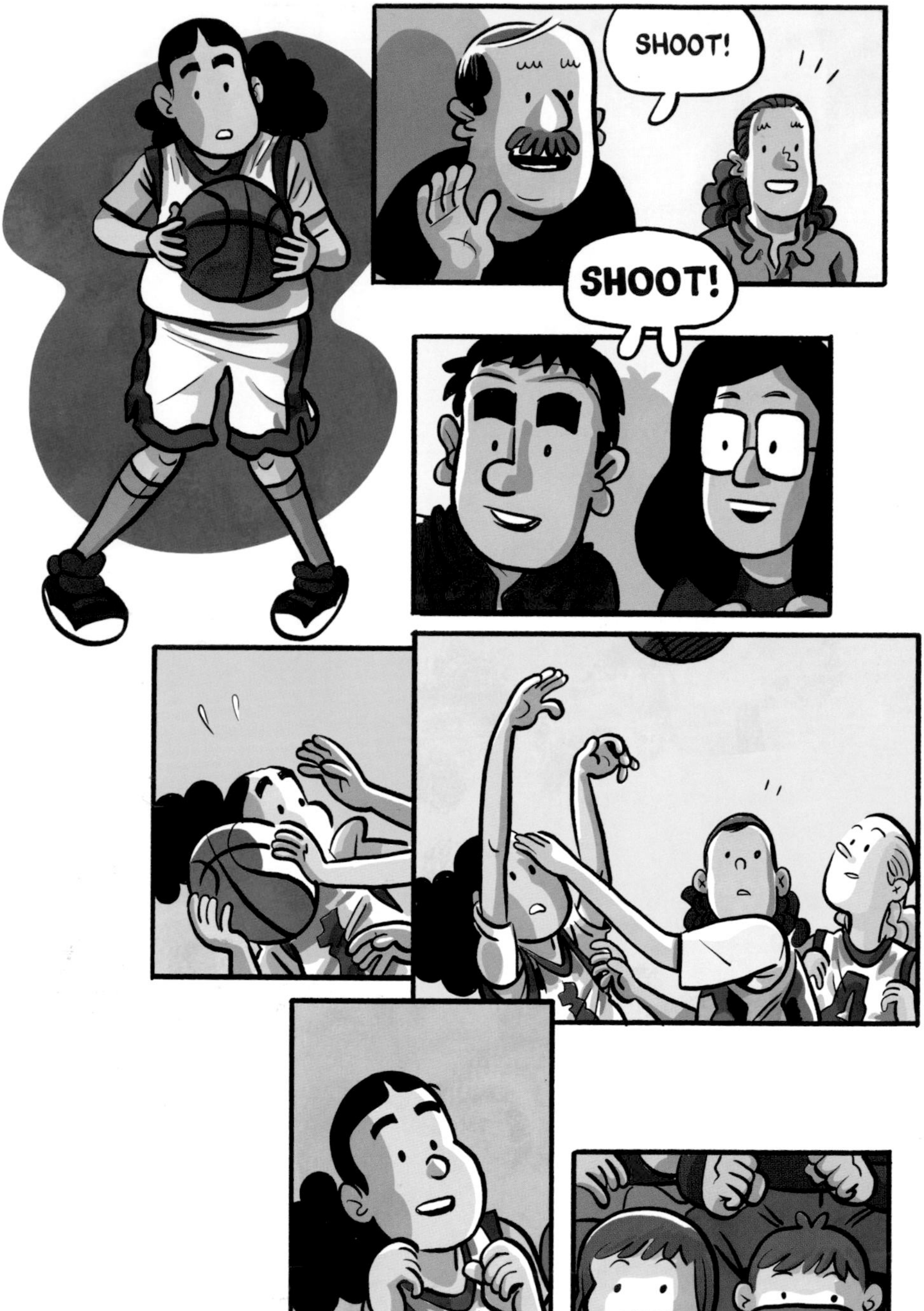
SHOOT!
SHOOT!

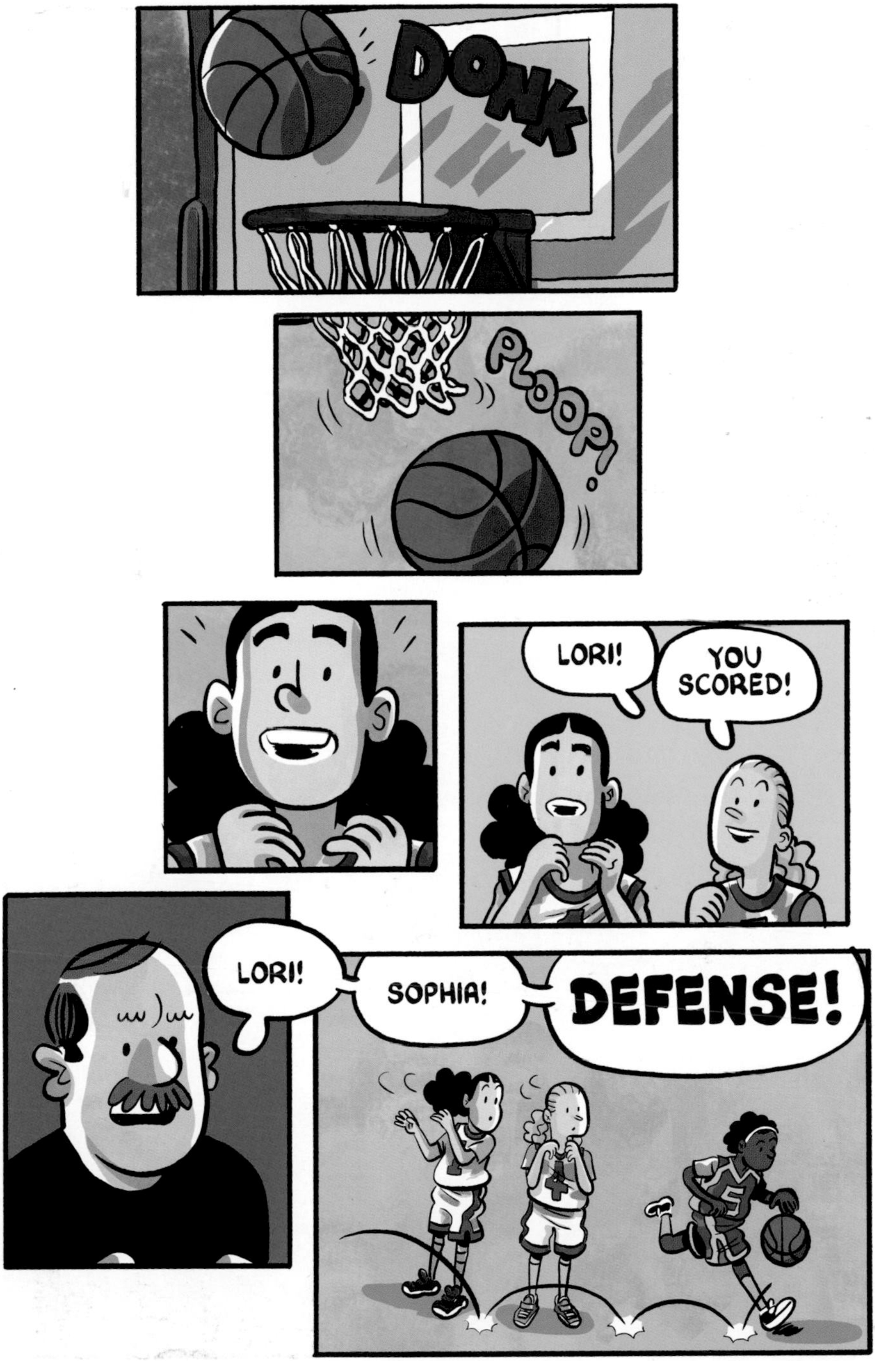
DONK
PLOOP!
LORI!
YOU SCORED!
LORI!
SOPHIA!
DEFENSE!

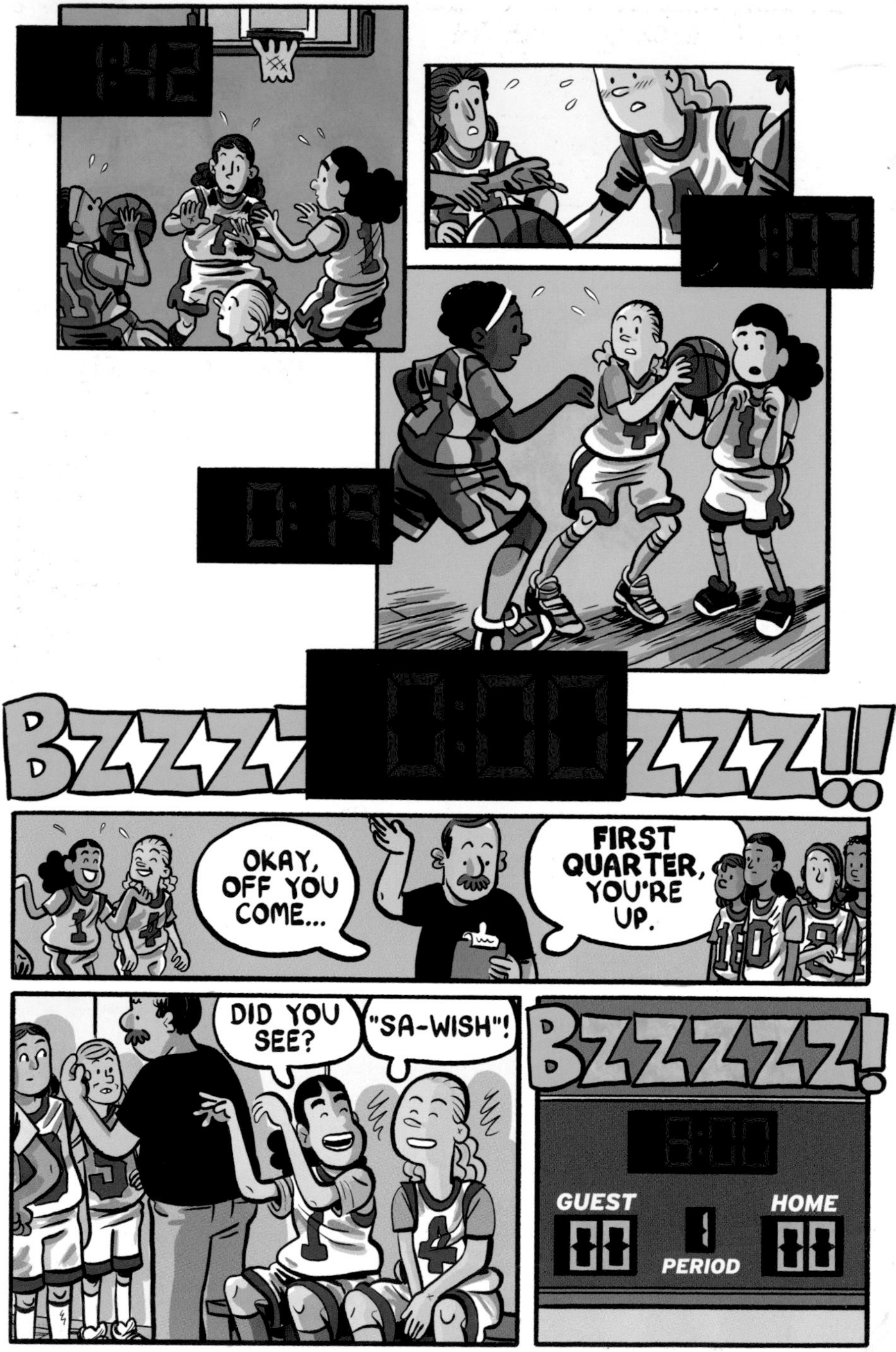
1:42
0:19
BZZZZ 0:00 ZZZZ!!
OKAY, OFF YOU COME...
FIRST QUARTER, YOU'RE UP.
DID YOU SEE?
"SA-WISH"!
BZZZZZZ!
GUEST
HOME
PERIOD

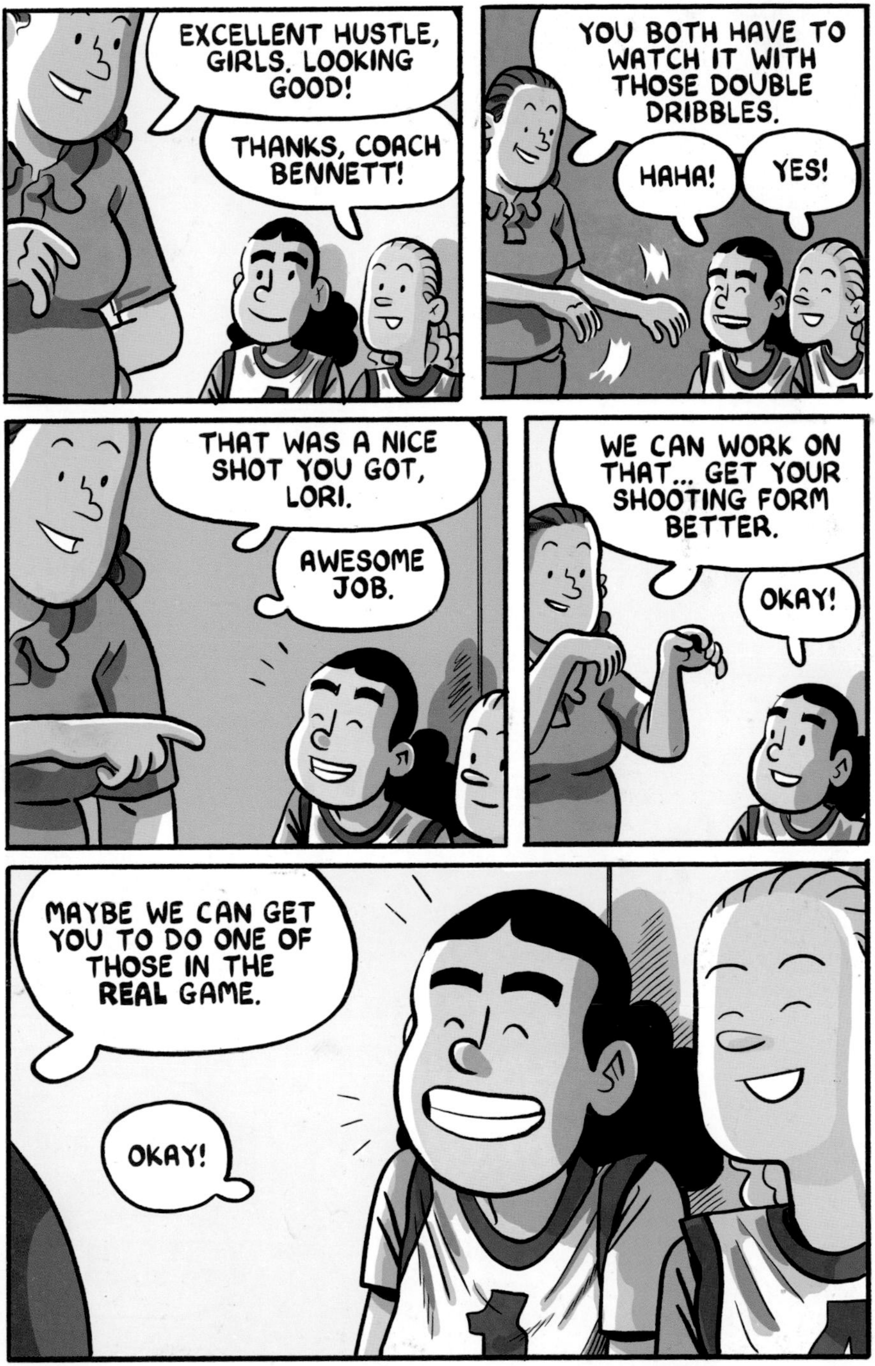
EXCELLENT HUSTLE, GIRLS. LOOKING GOOD!
THANKS, COACH BENNETT!
YOU BOTH HAVE TO WATCH IT WITH THOSE DOUBLE DRIBBLES.
HAHA!
YES!
THAT WAS A NICE SHOT YOU GOT, LORI.
AWESOME JOB.
WE CAN WORK ON THAT... GET YOUR SHOOTING FORM BETTER.
OKAY!
MAYBE WE CAN GET YOU TO DO ONE OF THOSE IN THE **REAL** GAME.
OKAY!

BLOMP!

HOME 00 → HOME 02

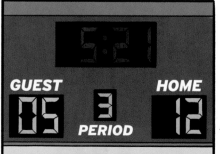

GUEST 05   3   HOME 12
PERIOD

OKAY...

LORI, SOPHIA, AND KAT—

GET READY TO SUB IN.

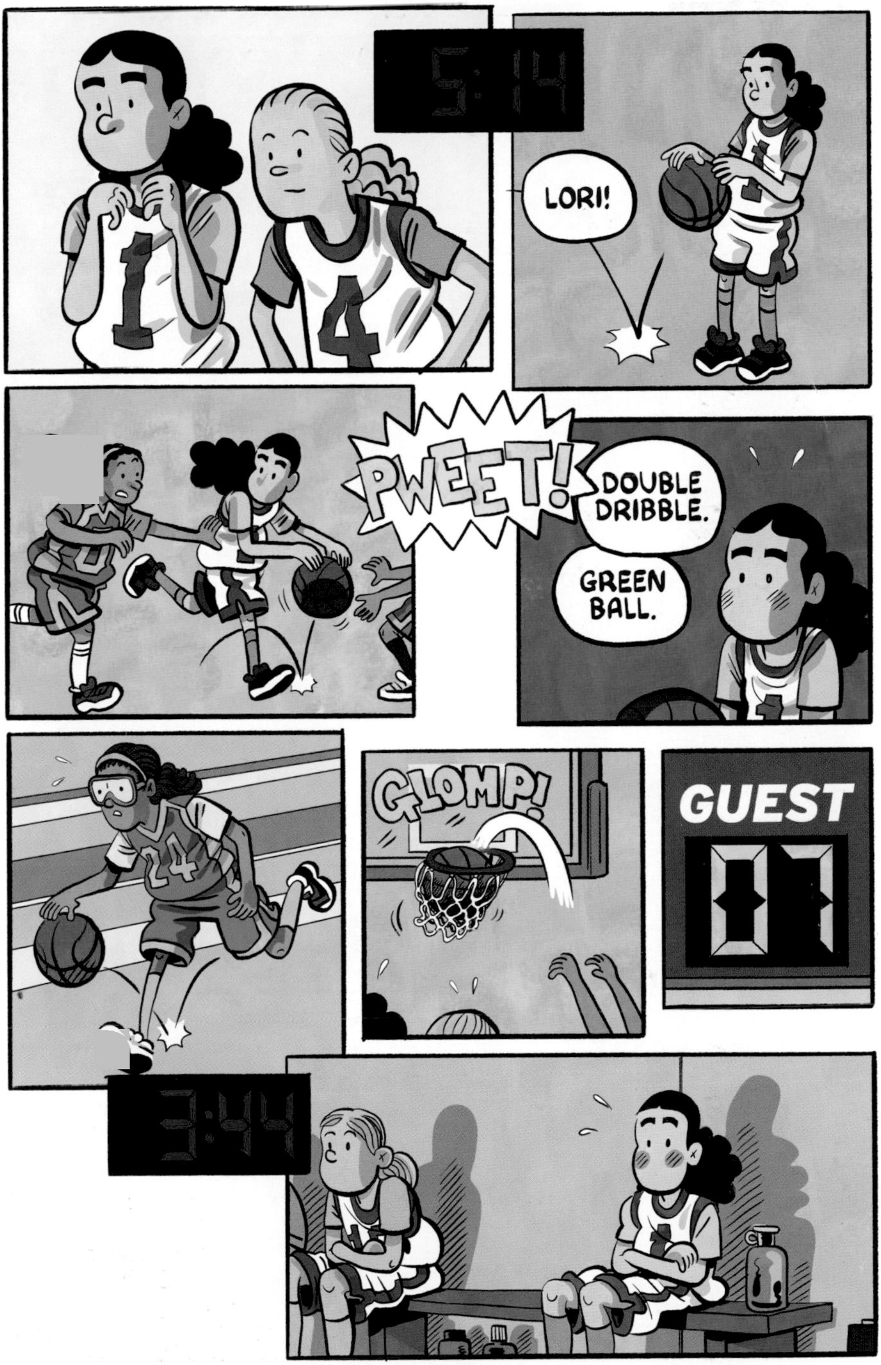
5:14
LORI!
PWEET!
DOUBLE DRIBBLE.
GREEN BALL.
GLOMP!
GUEST
3:44

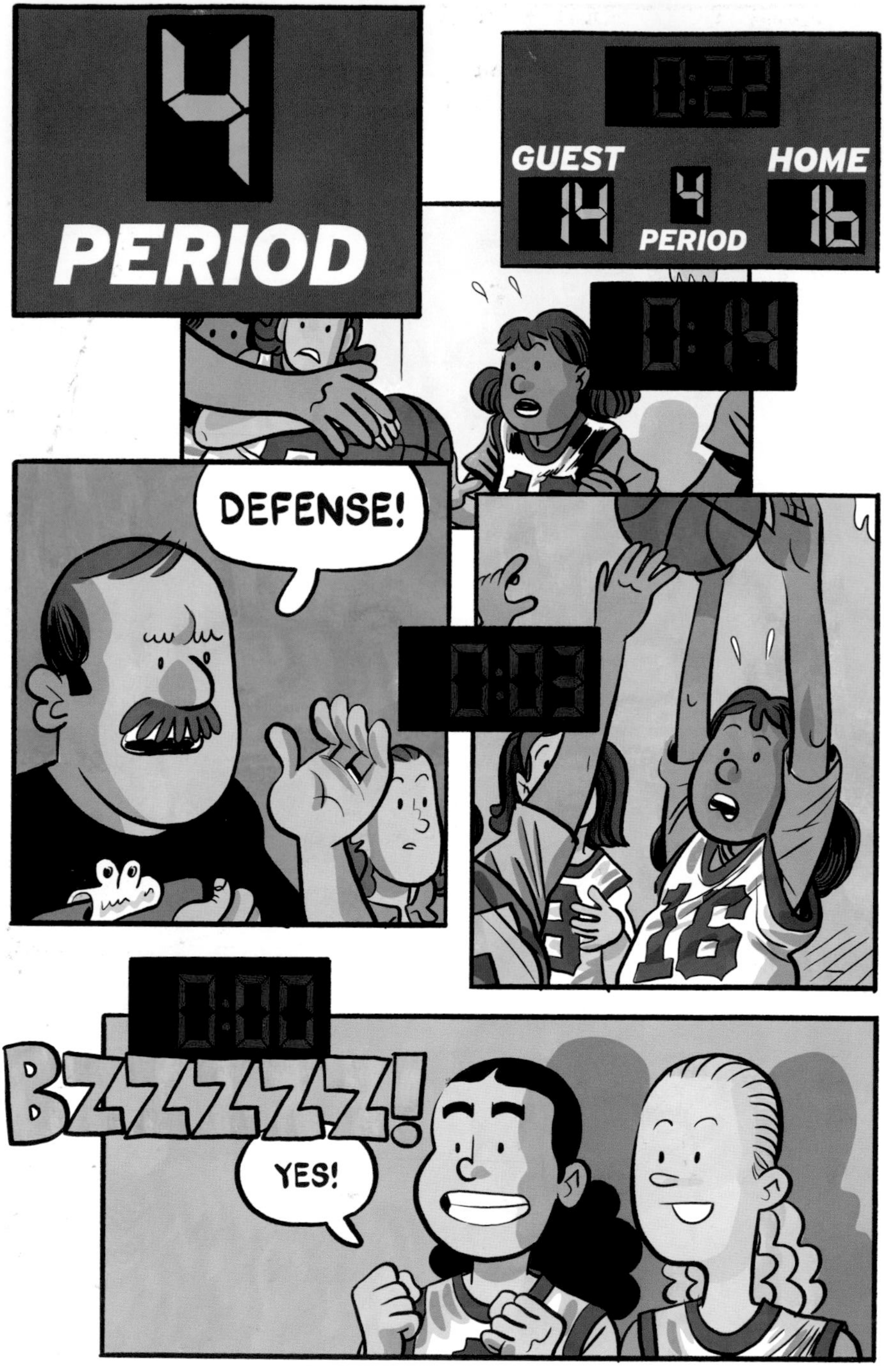
4
PERIOD
0:22
GUEST
HOME
14
4
PERIOD
16
0:14
DEFENSE!
0:03
0:00
BZZZZZZZ!
YES!

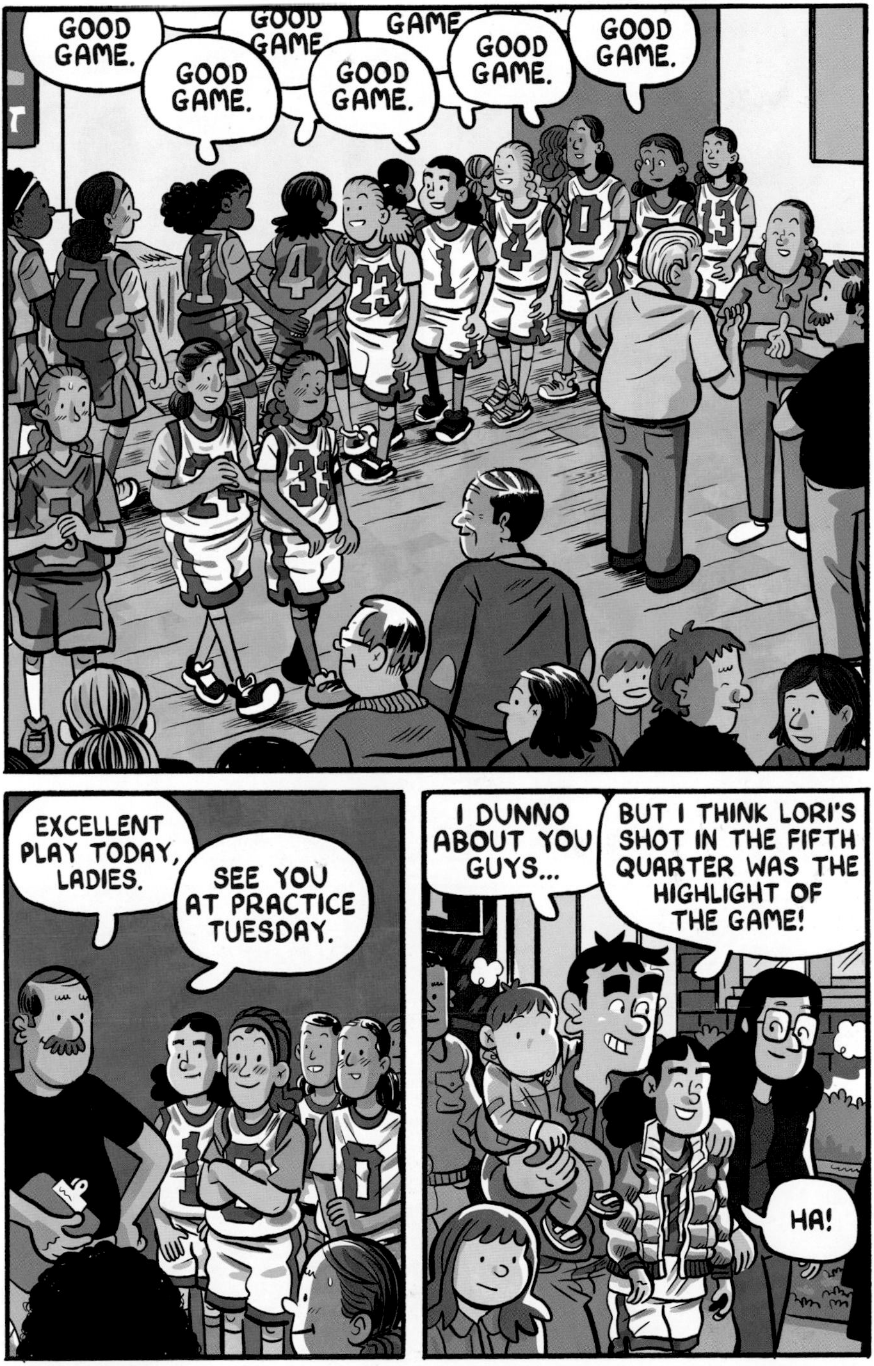
GOOD GAME.
GOOD GAME
GAME
GOOD GAME.
GOOD GAME.
GOOD GAME.
GOOD GAME.
GOOD GAME.
EXCELLENT PLAY TODAY, LADIES.
SEE YOU AT PRACTICE TUESDAY.
I DUNNO ABOUT YOU GUYS...
BUT I THINK LORI'S SHOT IN THE FIFTH QUARTER WAS THE HIGHLIGHT OF THE GAME!
HA!

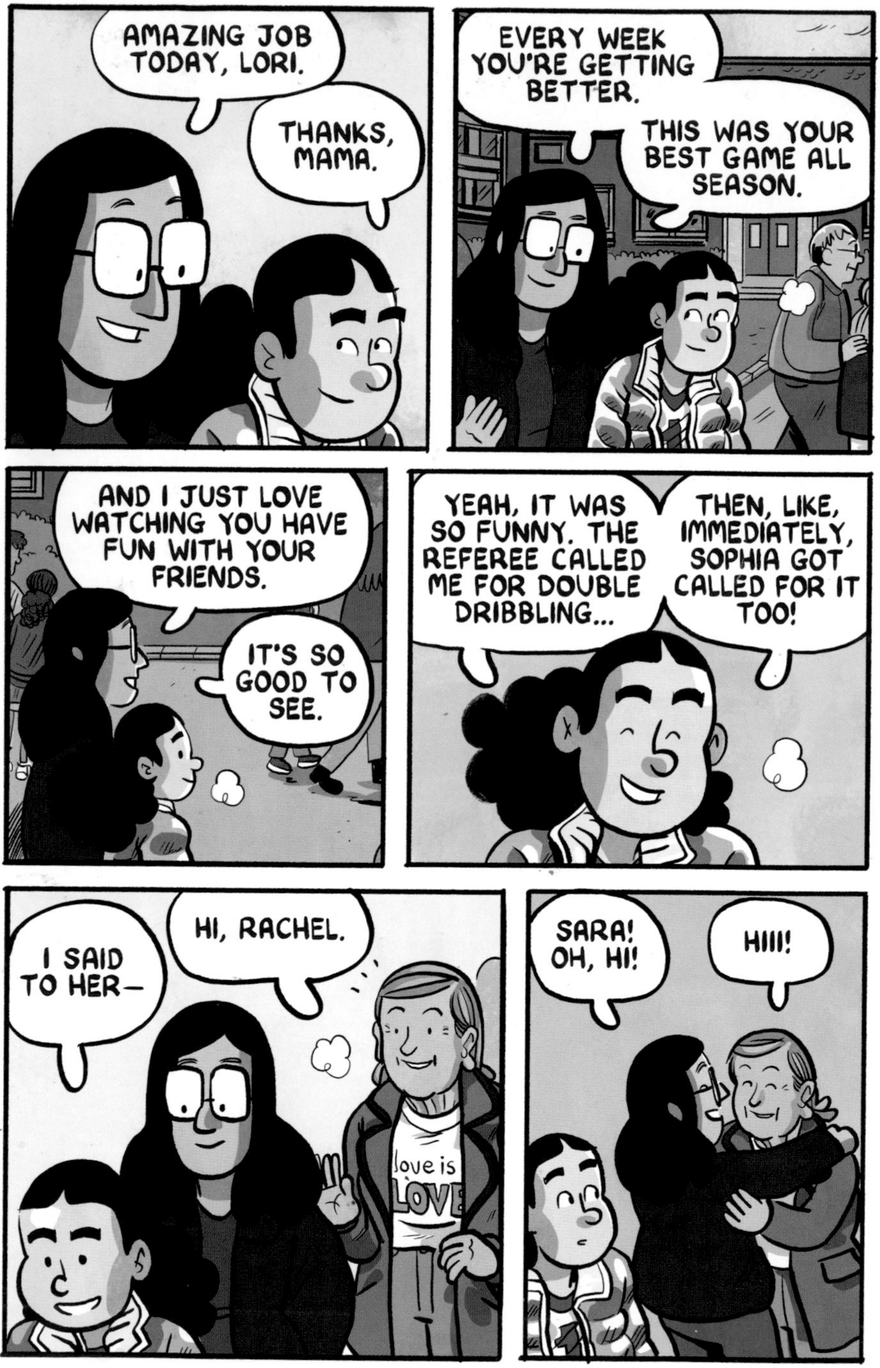
AMAZING JOB TODAY, LORI.
THANKS, MAMA.
EVERY WEEK YOU'RE GETTING BETTER.
THIS WAS YOUR BEST GAME ALL SEASON.
AND I JUST LOVE WATCHING YOU HAVE FUN WITH YOUR FRIENDS.
IT'S SO GOOD TO SEE.
YEAH, IT WAS SO FUNNY. THE REFEREE CALLED ME FOR DOUBLE DRIBBLING...
THEN, LIKE, IMMEDIATELY, SOPHIA GOT CALLED FOR IT TOO!
I SAID TO HER—
HI, RACHEL.
love is LOVE
SARA! OH, HI!
HIII!

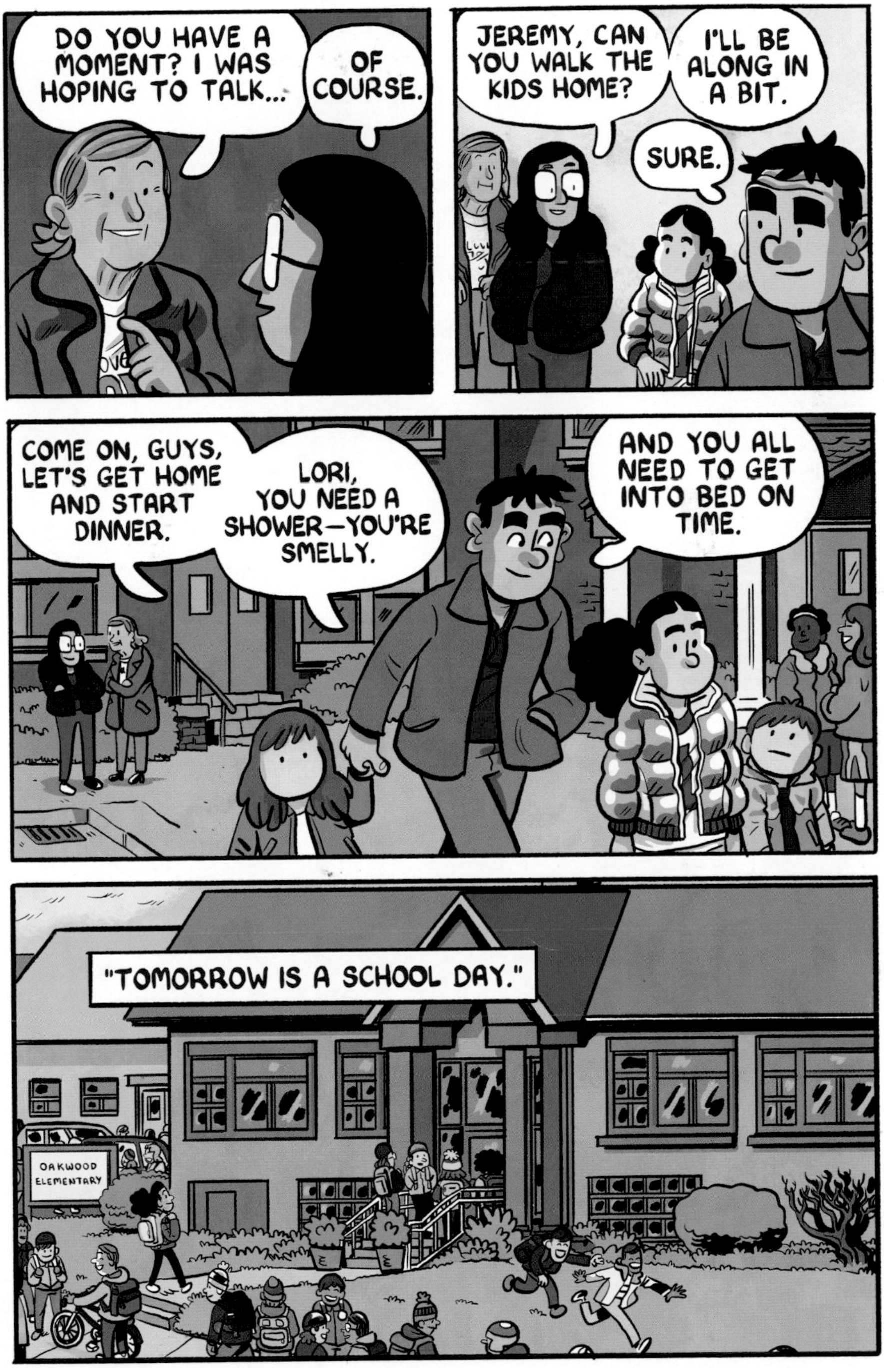
DO YOU HAVE A MOMENT? I WAS HOPING TO TALK...
OF COURSE.
JEREMY, CAN YOU WALK THE KIDS HOME?
I'LL BE ALONG IN A BIT.
SURE.
COME ON, GUYS, LET'S GET HOME AND START DINNER.
LORI, YOU NEED A SHOWER—YOU'RE SMELLY.
AND YOU ALL NEED TO GET INTO BED ON TIME.
"TOMORROW IS A SCHOOL DAY."
OAKWOOD ELEMENTARY

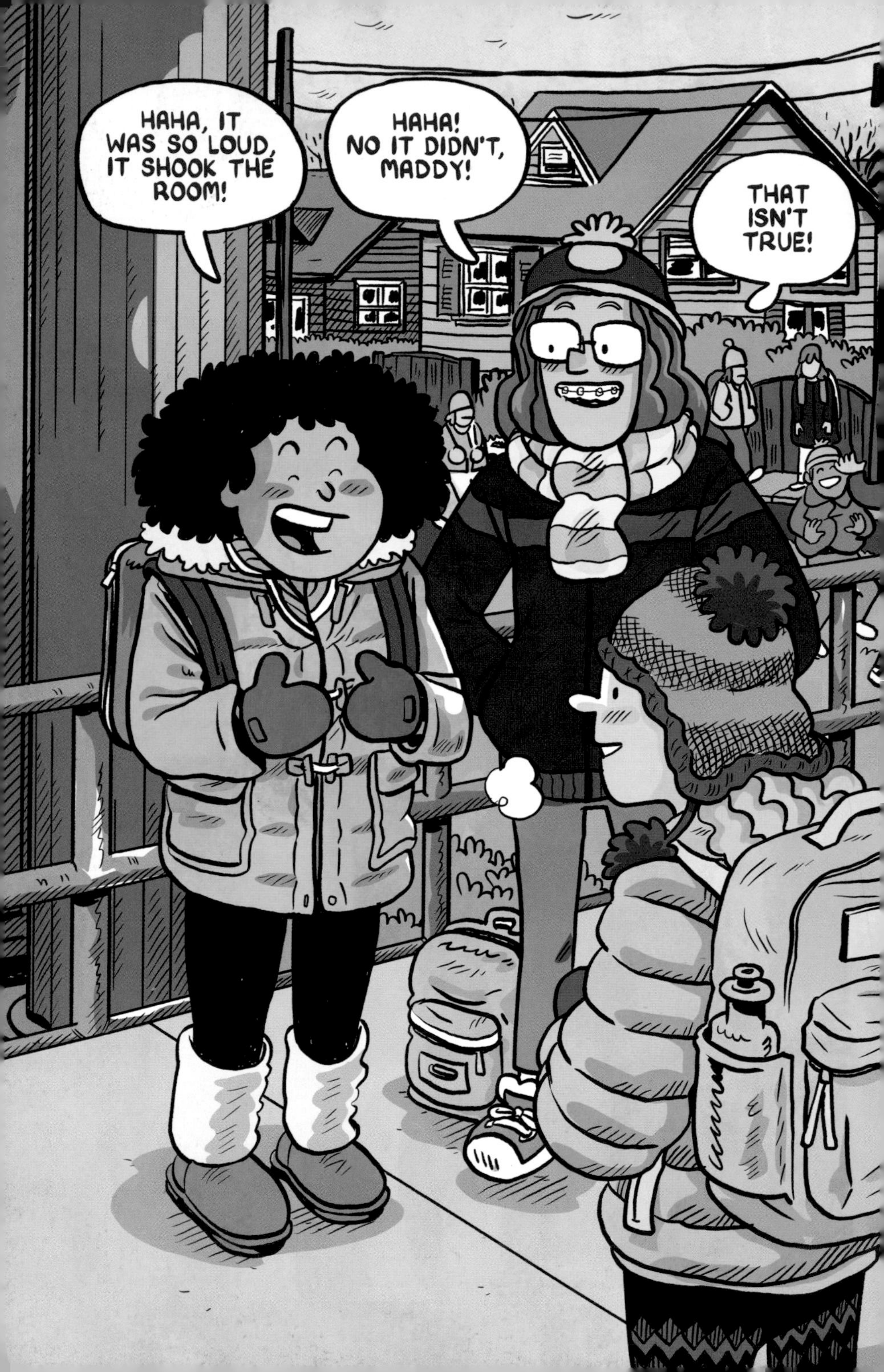
HAHA, IT WAS SO LOUD, IT SHOOK THE ROOM!
HAHA! NO IT DIDN'T, MADDY!
THAT ISN'T TRUE!

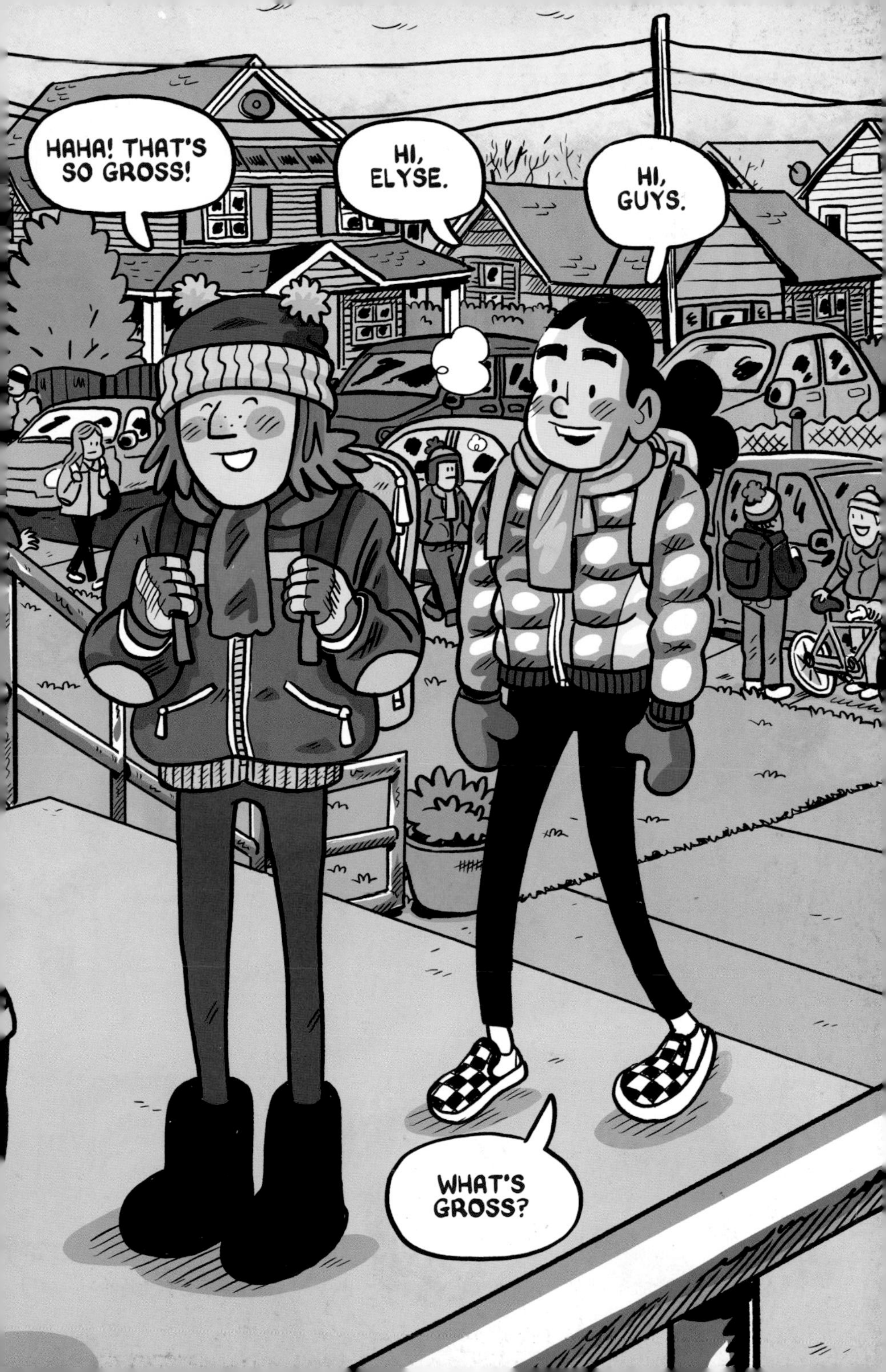
HAHA! THAT'S SO GROSS!
HI, ELYSE.
HI, GUYS.
WHAT'S GROSS?

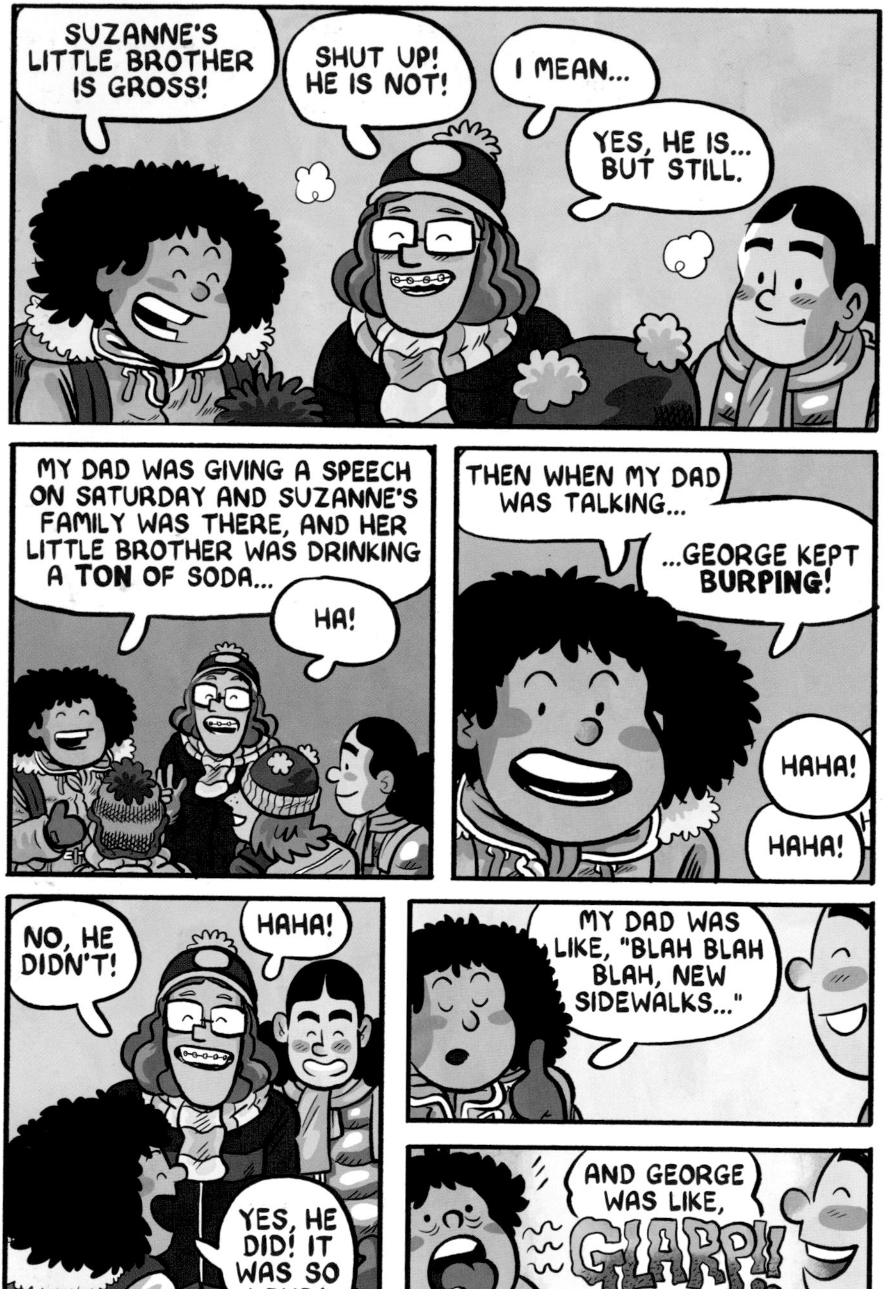
SUZANNE'S LITTLE BROTHER IS GROSS!
SHUT UP! HE IS NOT!
I MEAN...
YES, HE IS... BUT STILL.
MY DAD WAS GIVING A SPEECH ON SATURDAY AND SUZANNE'S FAMILY WAS THERE, AND HER LITTLE BROTHER WAS DRINKING A TON OF SODA...
HA!
THEN WHEN MY DAD WAS TALKING...
...GEORGE KEPT BURPING!
HAHA!
HAHA!
NO, HE DIDN'T!
HAHA!
YES, HE DID! IT WAS SO LOUD!
MY DAD WAS LIKE, "BLAH BLAH BLAH, NEW SIDEWALKS..."
AND GEORGE WAS LIKE,
GLARP!!

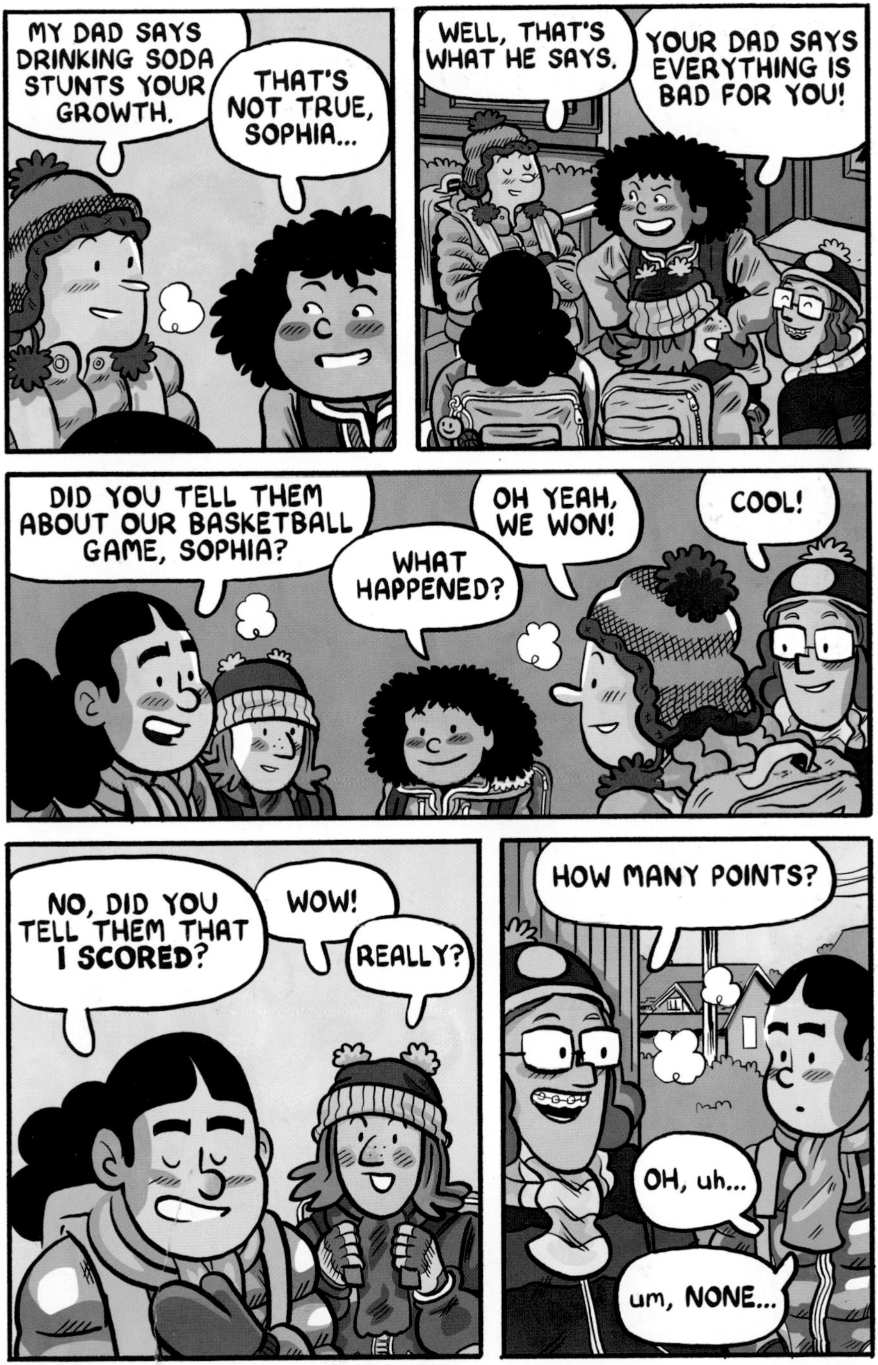
MY DAD SAYS DRINKING SODA STUNTS YOUR GROWTH.
THAT'S NOT TRUE, SOPHIA...
WELL, THAT'S WHAT HE SAYS.
YOUR DAD SAYS EVERYTHING IS BAD FOR YOU!
DID YOU TELL THEM ABOUT OUR BASKETBALL GAME, SOPHIA?
WHAT HAPPENED?
OH YEAH, WE WON!
COOL!
NO, DID YOU TELL THEM THAT I **SCORED**?
WOW!
REALLY?
HOW MANY POINTS?
OH, uh...
um, NONE...

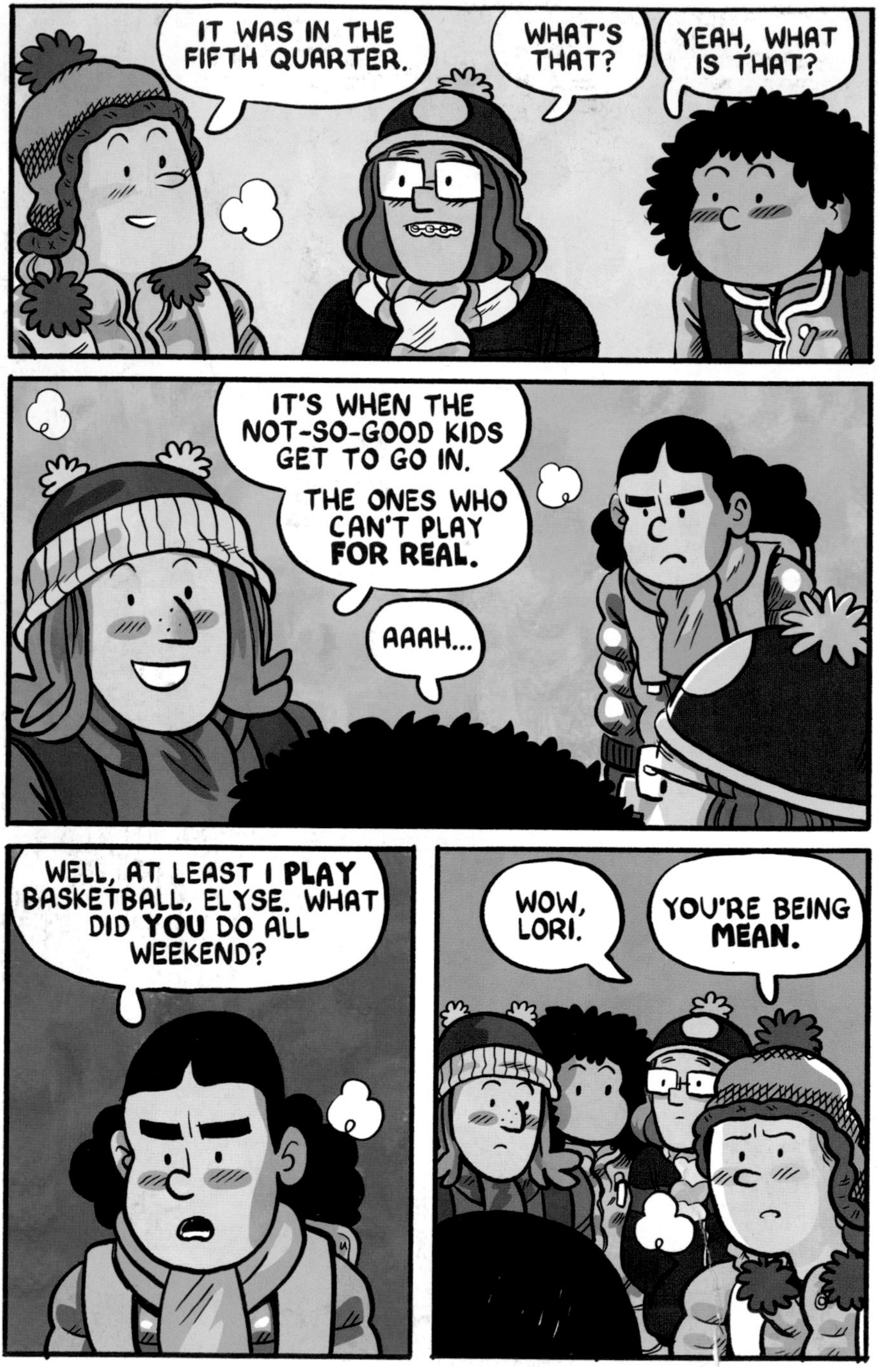
IT WAS IN THE FIFTH QUARTER.
WHAT'S THAT?
YEAH, WHAT IS THAT?
IT'S WHEN THE NOT-SO-GOOD KIDS GET TO GO IN.
THE ONES WHO CAN'T PLAY FOR REAL.
AAAH...
WELL, AT LEAST I PLAY BASKETBALL, ELYSE. WHAT DID YOU DO ALL WEEKEND?
WOW, LORI.
YOU'RE BEING MEAN.

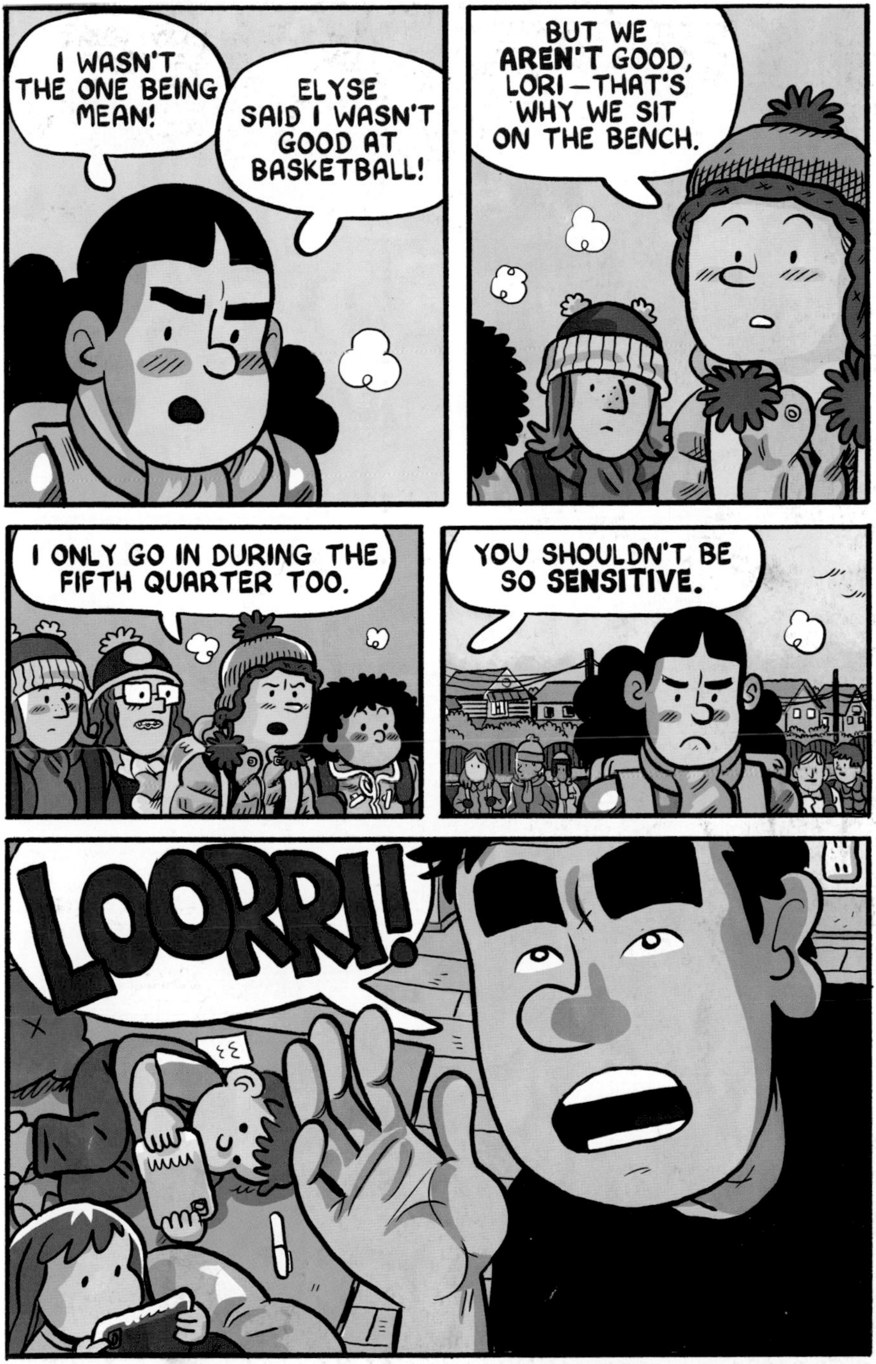
I WASN'T THE ONE BEING MEAN!
ELYSE SAID I WASN'T GOOD AT BASKETBALL!
BUT WE AREN'T GOOD, LORI—THAT'S WHY WE SIT ON THE BENCH.
I ONLY GO IN DURING THE FIFTH QUARTER TOO.
YOU SHOULDN'T BE SO SENSITIVE.
LOORRI!

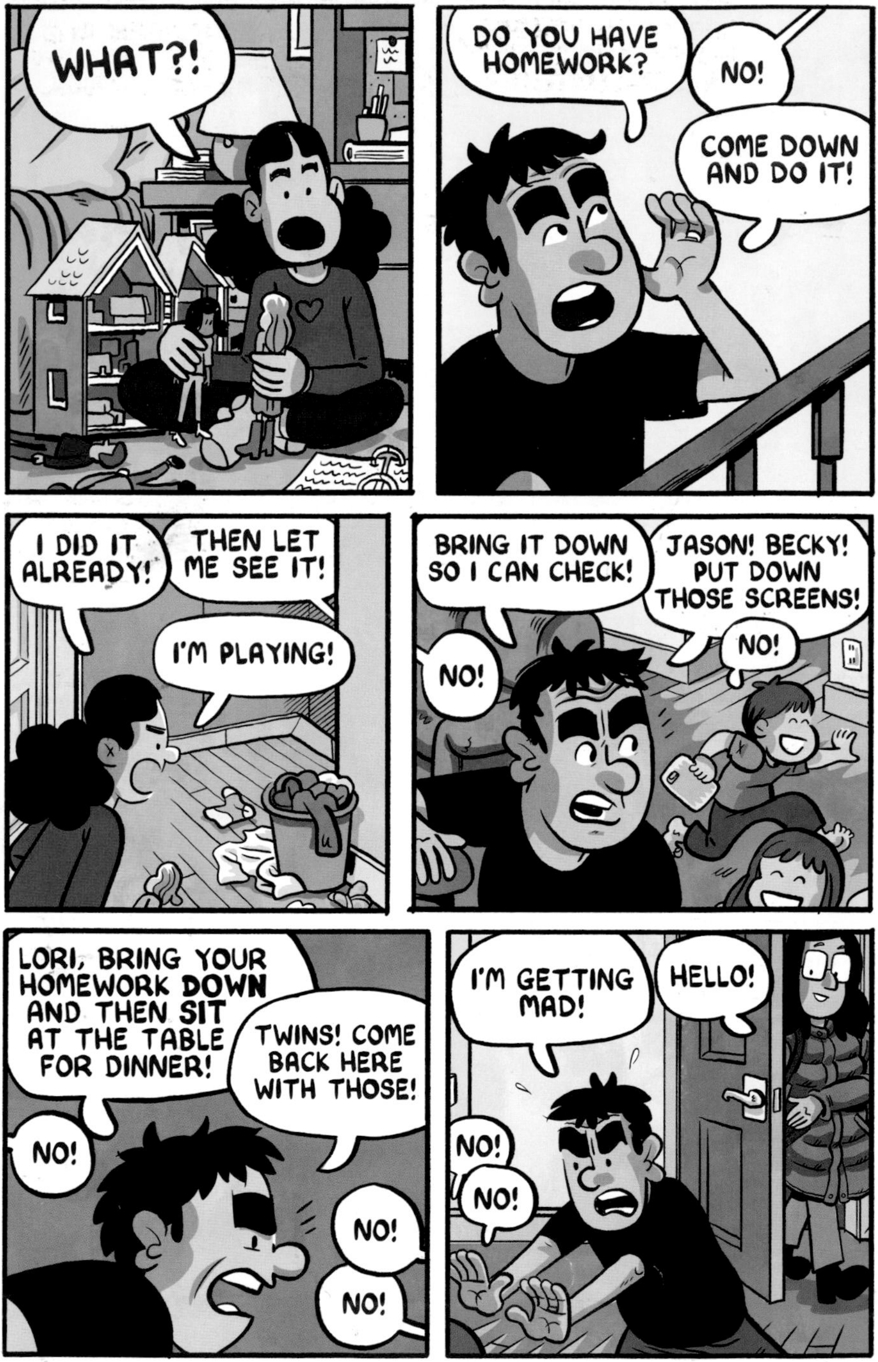
WHAT?!
DO YOU HAVE HOMEWORK?
NO!
COME DOWN AND DO IT!
I DID IT ALREADY!
THEN LET ME SEE IT!
I'M PLAYING!
BRING IT DOWN SO I CAN CHECK!
NO!
JASON! BECKY! PUT DOWN THOSE SCREENS!
NO!
LORI, BRING YOUR HOMEWORK DOWN AND THEN SIT AT THE TABLE FOR DINNER!
NO!
TWINS! COME BACK HERE WITH THOSE!
NO!
NO!
I'M GETTING MAD!
HELLO!
NO!
NO!

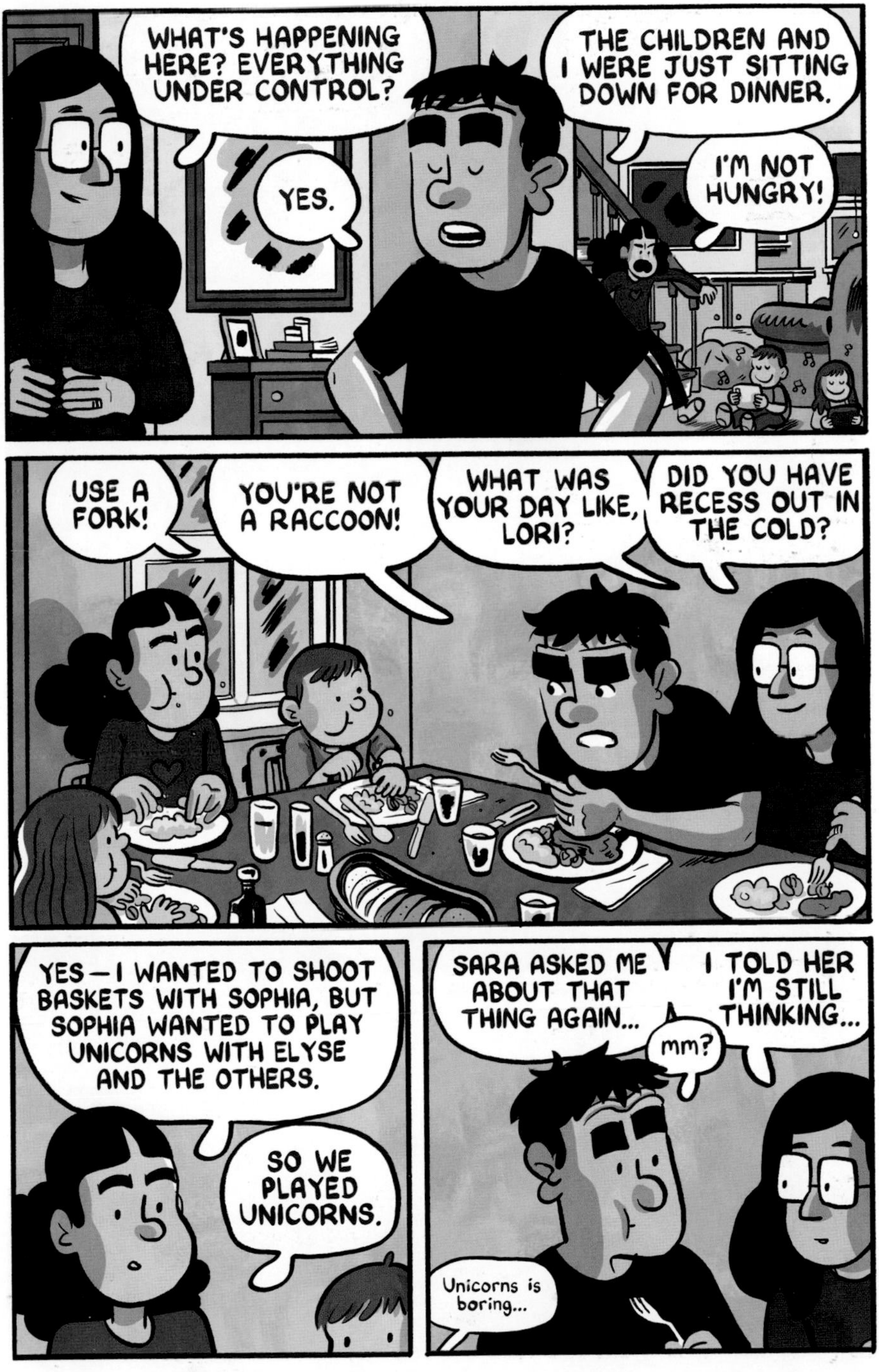
WHAT'S HAPPENING HERE? EVERYTHING UNDER CONTROL?
YES.
THE CHILDREN AND I WERE JUST SITTING DOWN FOR DINNER.
I'M NOT HUNGRY!
USE A FORK!
YOU'RE NOT A RACCOON!
WHAT WAS YOUR DAY LIKE, LORI?
DID YOU HAVE RECESS OUT IN THE COLD?
YES—I WANTED TO SHOOT BASKETS WITH SOPHIA, BUT SOPHIA WANTED TO PLAY UNICORNS WITH ELYSE AND THE OTHERS.
SO WE PLAYED UNICORNS.
SARA ASKED ME ABOUT THAT THING AGAIN...
mm?
I TOLD HER I'M STILL THINKING...
Unicorns is boring...

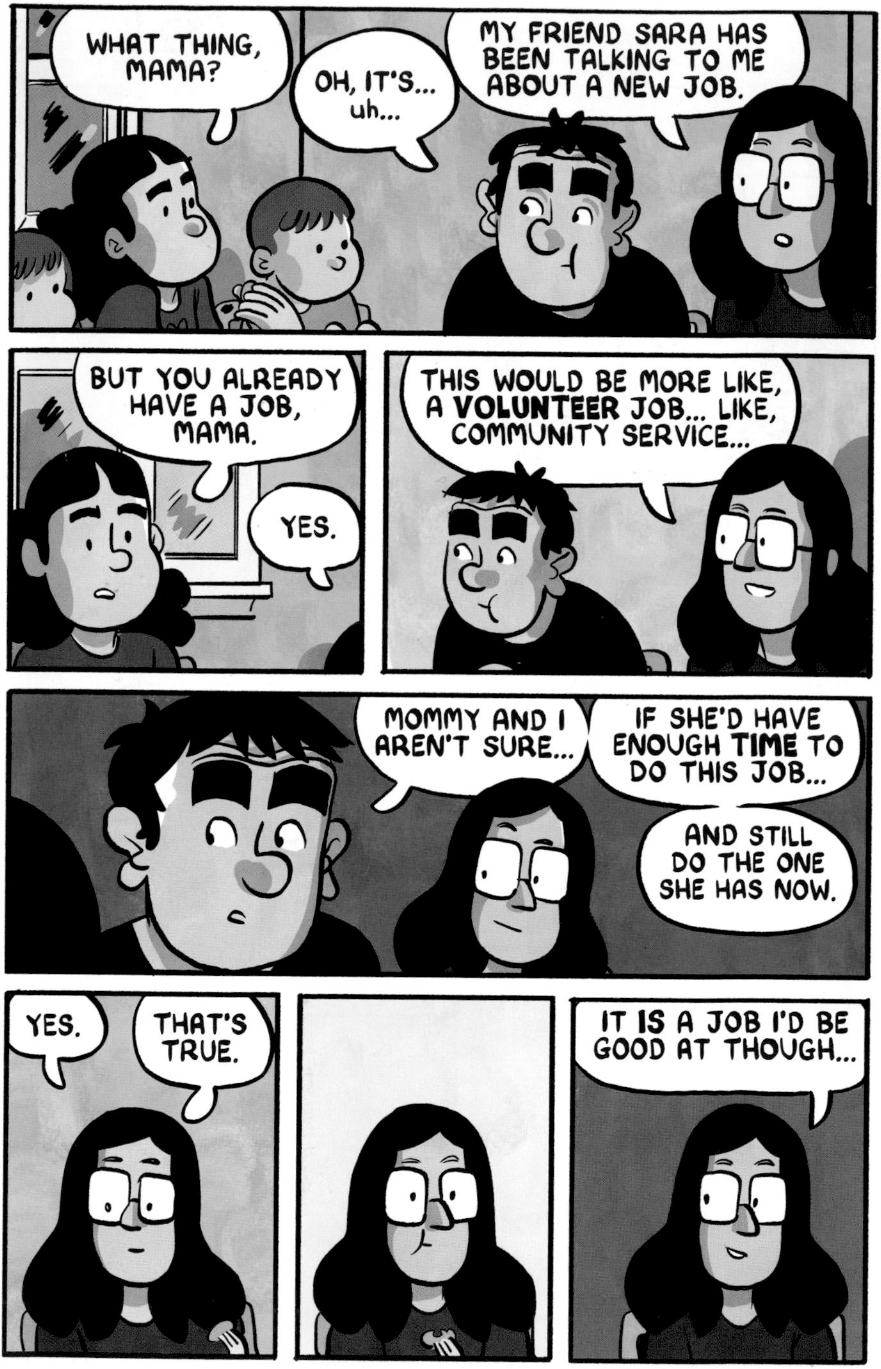
WHAT THING, MAMA?
OH, IT'S... uh...
MY FRIEND SARA HAS BEEN TALKING TO ME ABOUT A NEW JOB.
BUT YOU ALREADY HAVE A JOB, MAMA.
YES.
THIS WOULD BE MORE LIKE, A VOLUNTEER JOB... LIKE, COMMUNITY SERVICE...
MOMMY AND I AREN'T SURE...
IF SHE'D HAVE ENOUGH TIME TO DO THIS JOB...
AND STILL DO THE ONE SHE HAS NOW.
YES.
THAT'S TRUE.
IT IS A JOB I'D BE GOOD AT THOUGH...

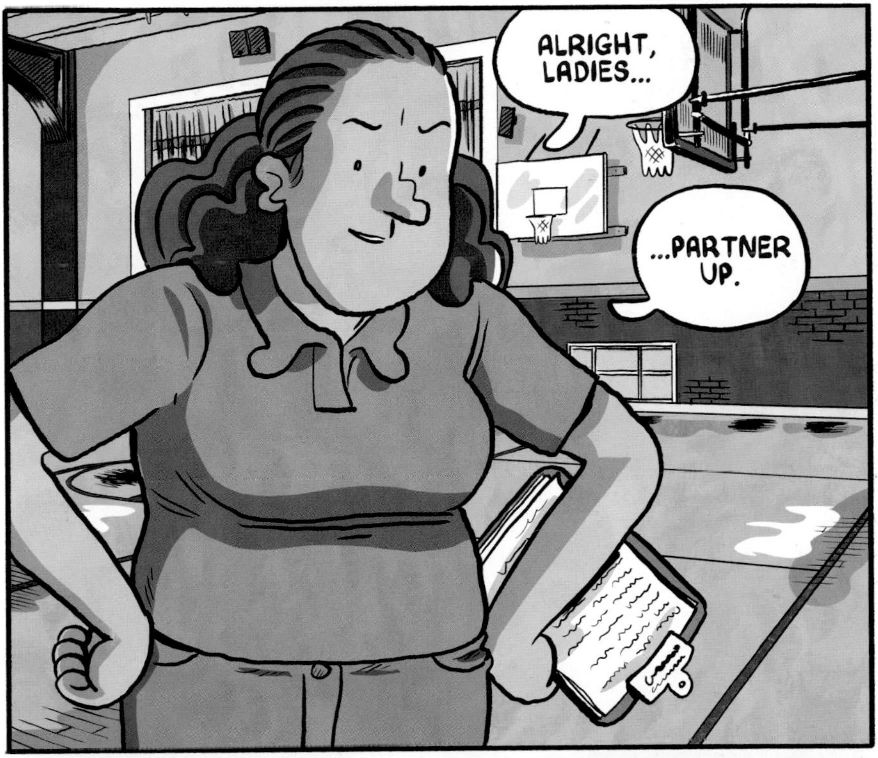
ALRIGHT, LADIES...
...PARTNER UP.

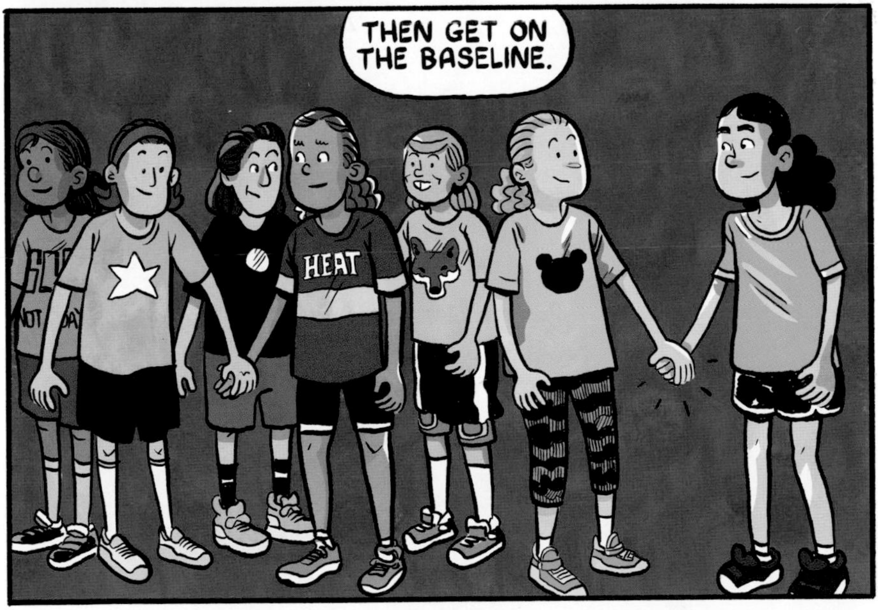
THEN GET ON THE BASELINE.
HEAT

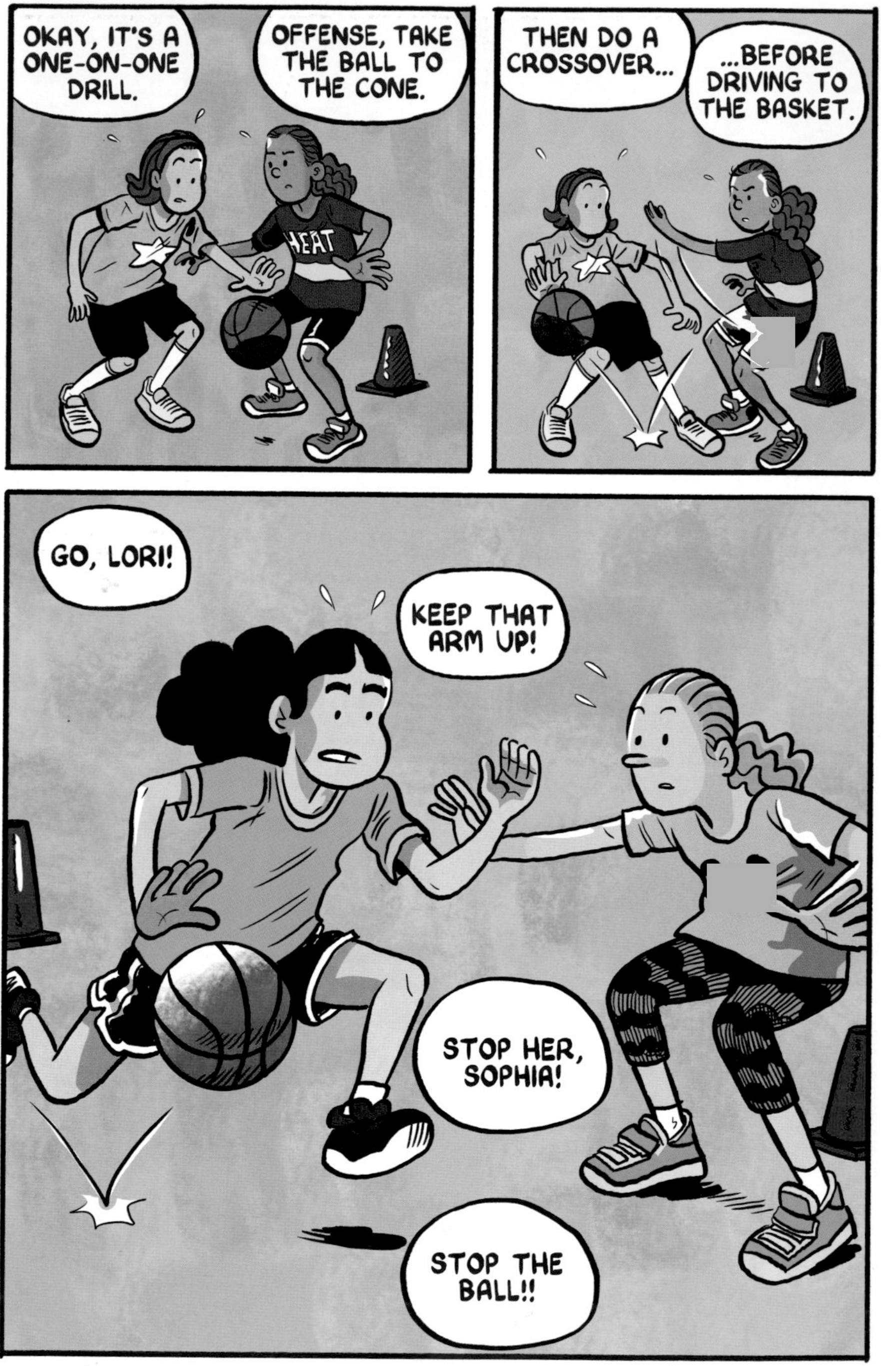
OKAY, IT'S A ONE-ON-ONE DRILL.
OFFENSE, TAKE THE BALL TO THE CONE.
HEAT
THEN DO A CROSSOVER...
...BEFORE DRIVING TO THE BASKET.
GO, LORI!
KEEP THAT ARM UP!
STOP HER, SOPHIA!
STOP THE BALL!!

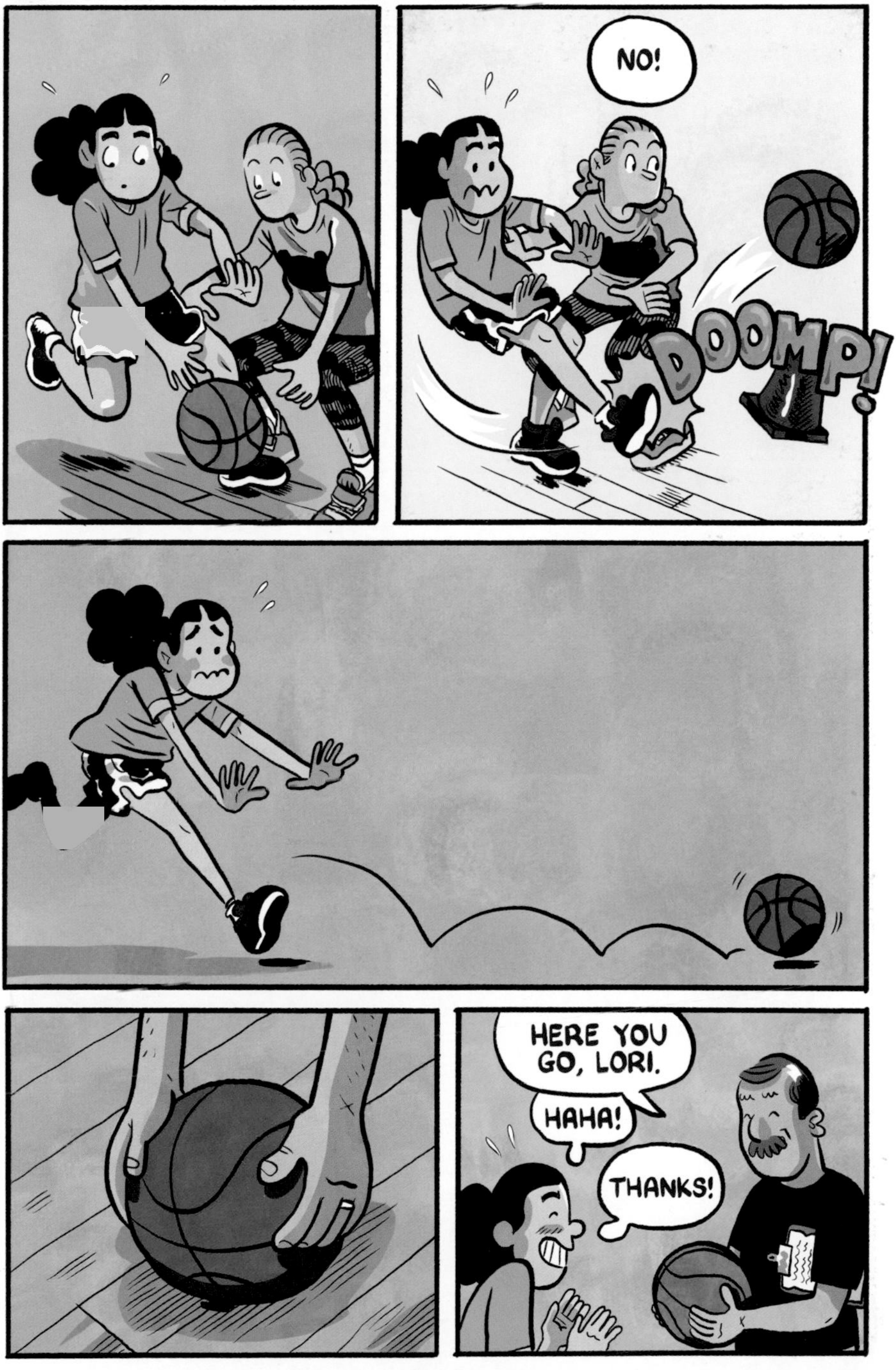
NO!
DOOMP!
HERE YOU GO, LORI.
HAHA!
THANKS!

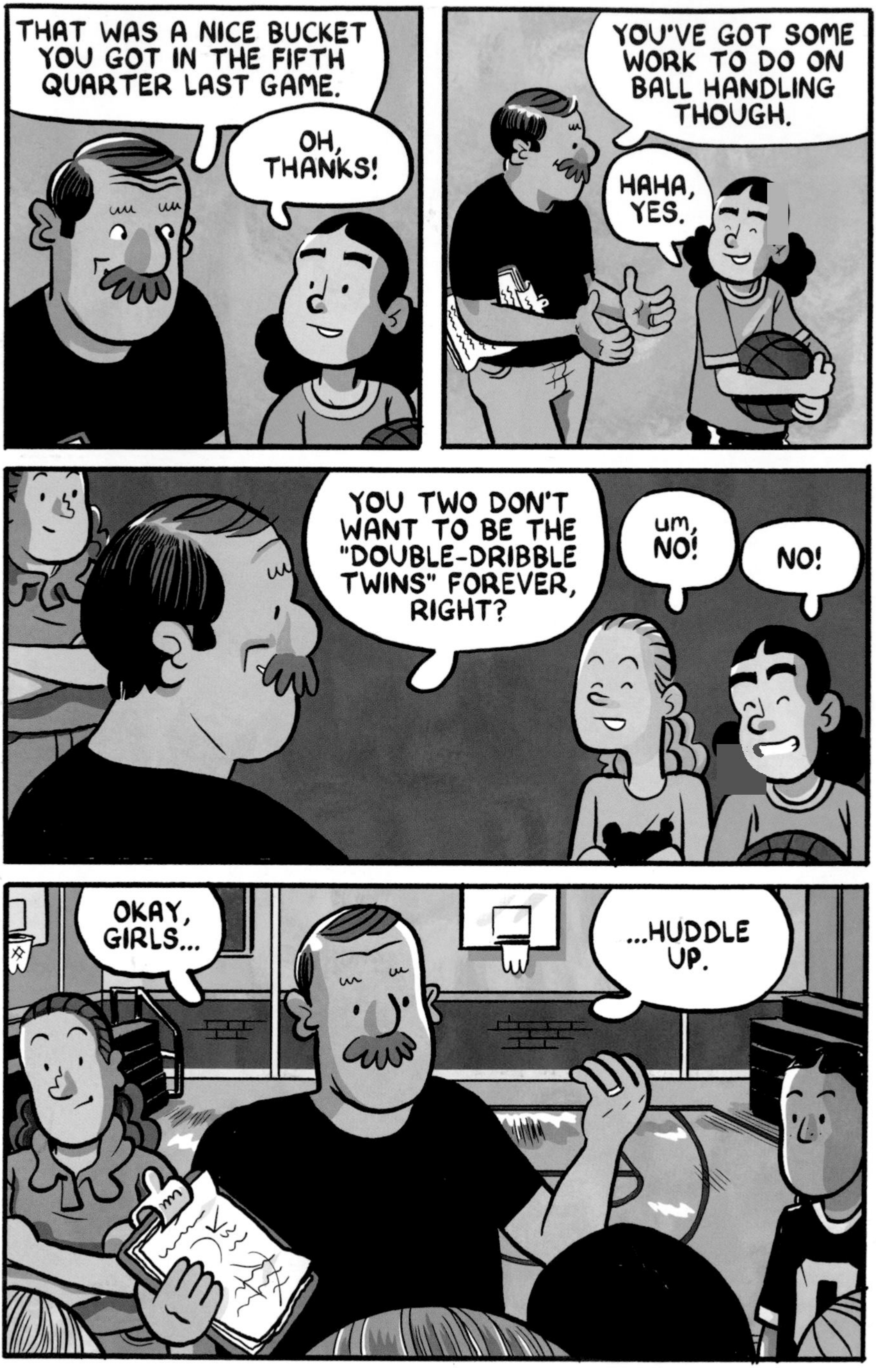
THAT WAS A NICE BUCKET YOU GOT IN THE FIFTH QUARTER LAST GAME.
OH, THANKS!
YOU'VE GOT SOME WORK TO DO ON BALL HANDLING THOUGH.
HAHA, YES.
YOU TWO DON'T WANT TO BE THE "DOUBLE-DRIBBLE TWINS" FOREVER, RIGHT?
um, NO!
NO!
OKAY, GIRLS...
...HUDDLE UP.

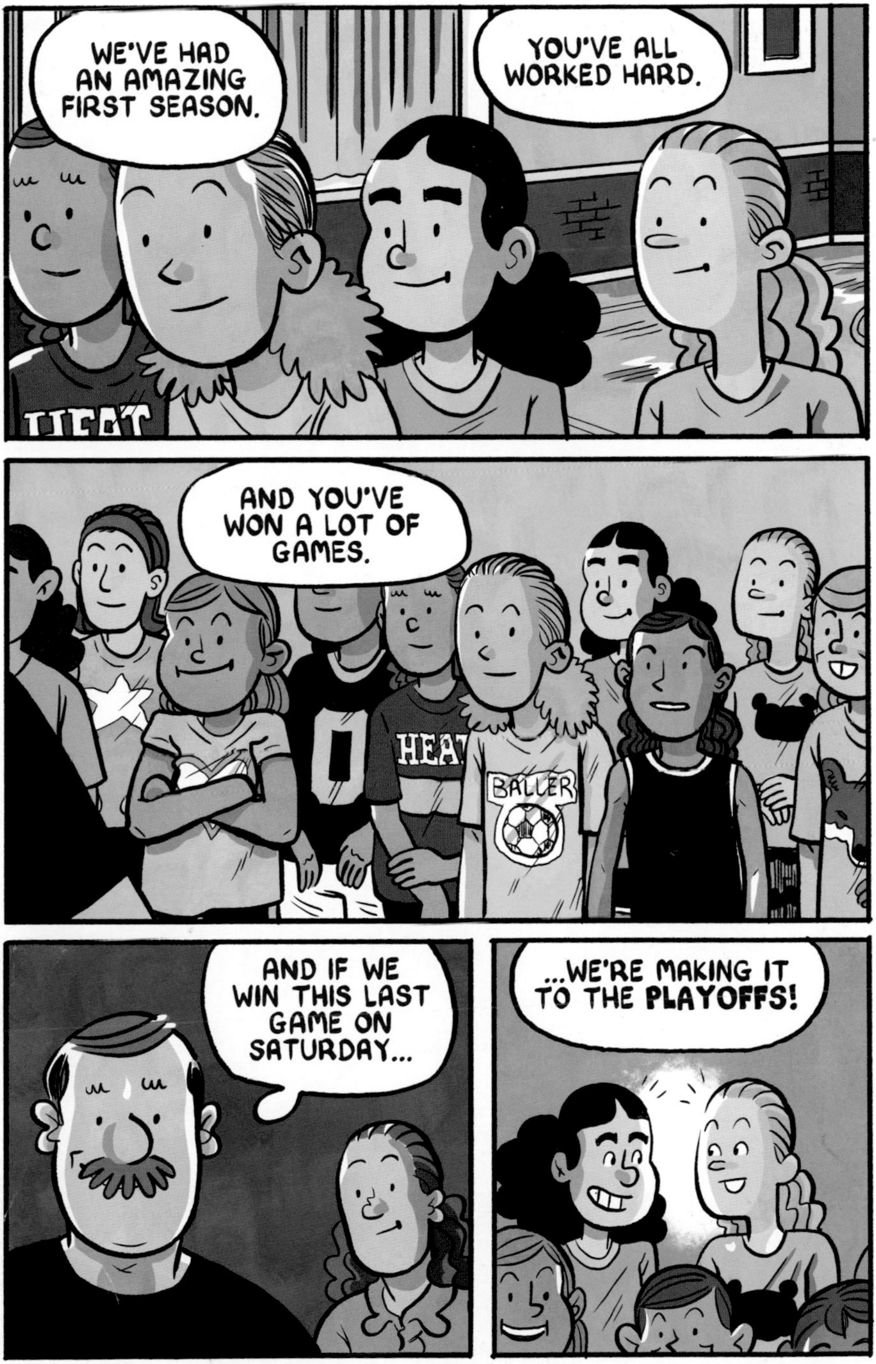
WE'VE HAD AN AMAZING FIRST SEASON.
YOU'VE ALL WORKED HARD.
HEAT
AND YOU'VE WON A LOT OF GAMES.
HEAT
BALLER
AND IF WE WIN THIS LAST GAME ON SATURDAY...
...WE'RE MAKING IT TO THE **PLAYOFFS!**

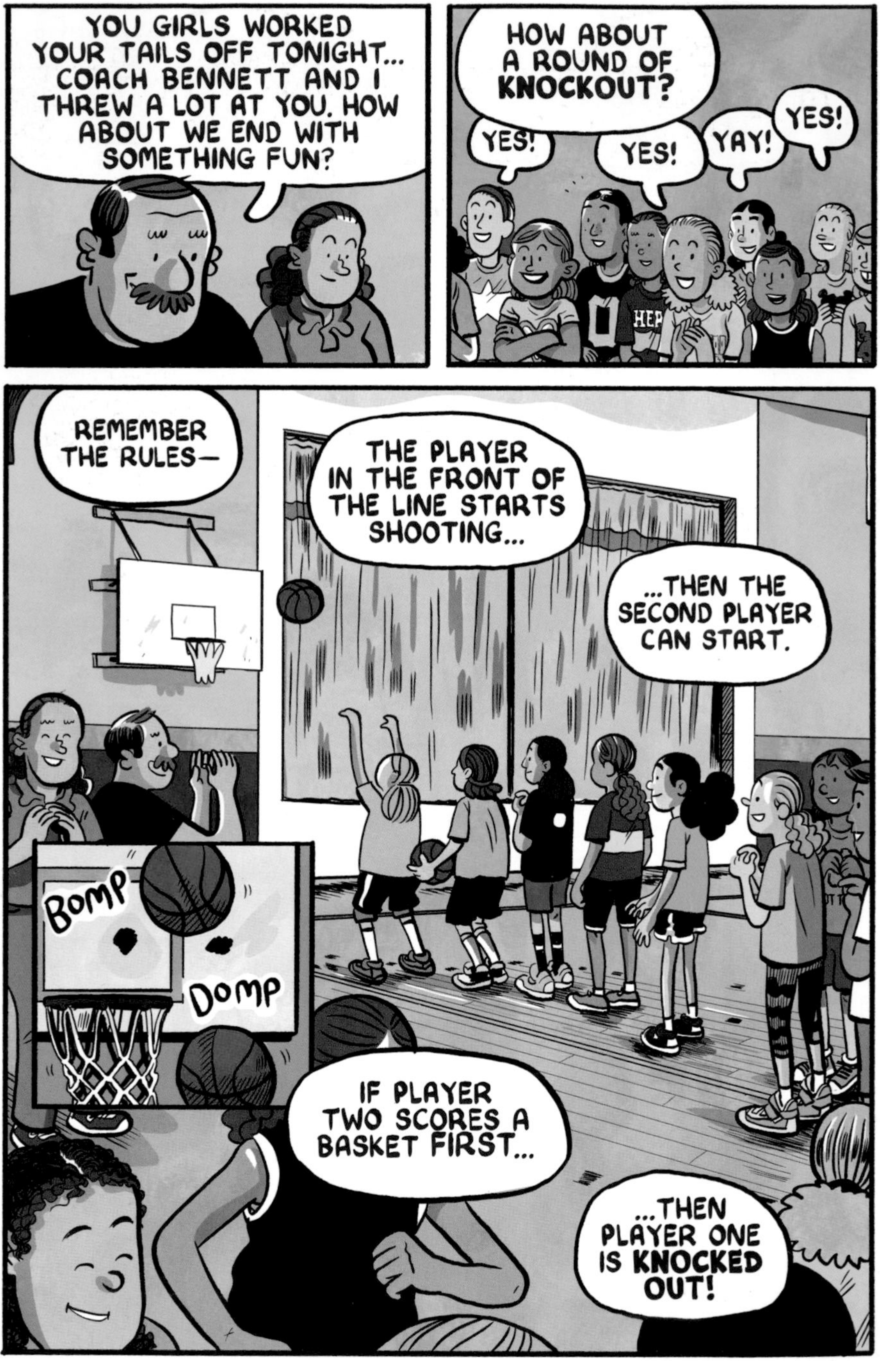
YOU GIRLS WORKED YOUR TAILS OFF TONIGHT... COACH BENNETT AND I THREW A LOT AT YOU. HOW ABOUT WE END WITH SOMETHING FUN?
HOW ABOUT A ROUND OF **KNOCKOUT**?
YES!
YES!
YAY!
YES!
REMEMBER THE RULES—
THE PLAYER IN THE FRONT OF THE LINE STARTS SHOOTING...
...THEN THE SECOND PLAYER CAN START.
BOMP
DOMP
IF PLAYER TWO SCORES A BASKET FIRST...
...THEN PLAYER ONE IS **KNOCKED OUT**!

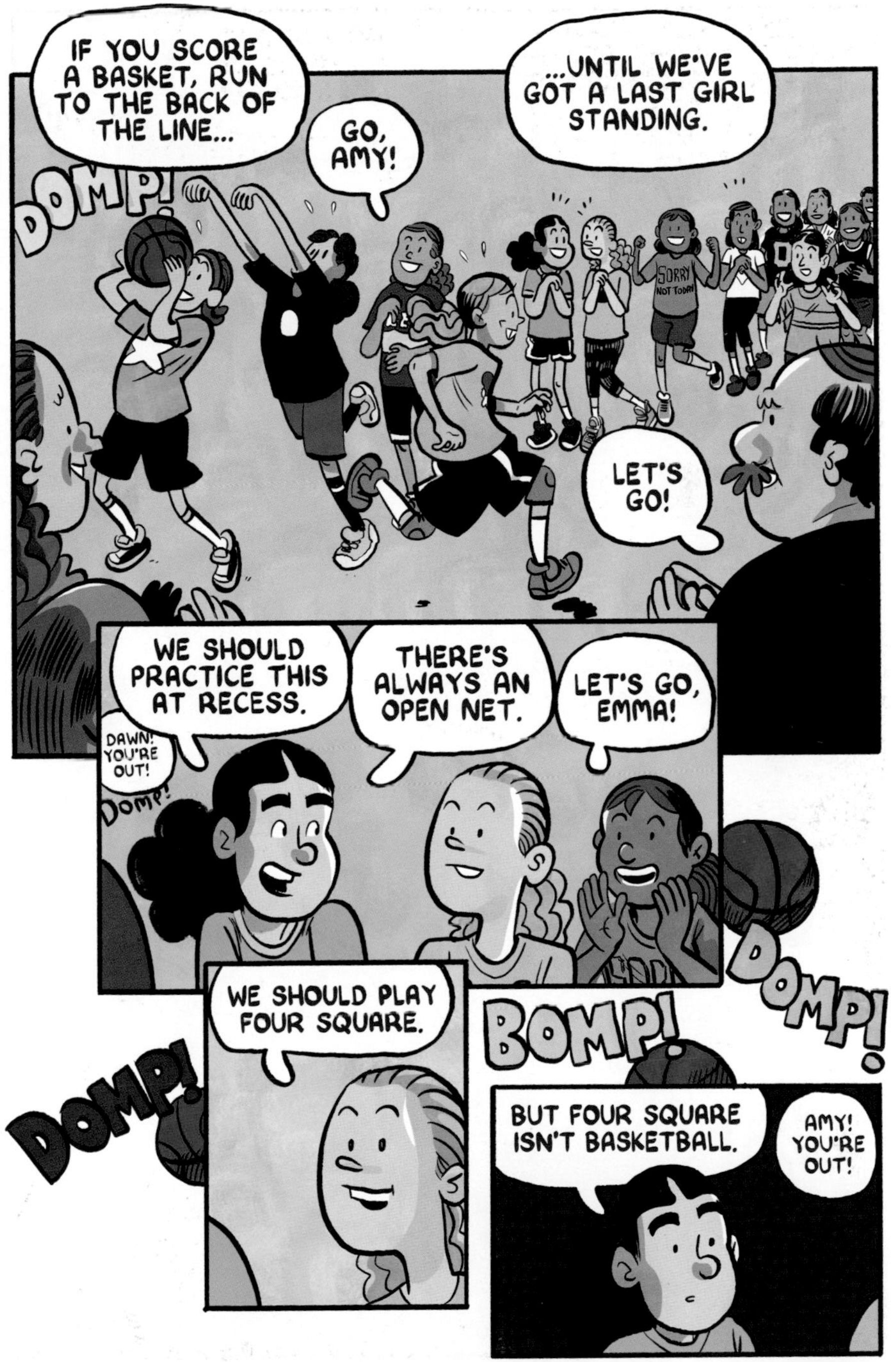
IF YOU SCORE A BASKET, RUN TO THE BACK OF THE LINE...
GO, AMY!
...UNTIL WE'VE GOT A LAST GIRL STANDING.
DOMP!
SORRY NOT TODAY
LET'S GO!
WE SHOULD PRACTICE THIS AT RECESS.
THERE'S ALWAYS AN OPEN NET.
LET'S GO, EMMA!
DAWN! YOU'RE OUT!
DOMP!
DOMP!
WE SHOULD PLAY FOUR SQUARE.
BOMP!
DOMP!
BUT FOUR SQUARE ISN'T BASKETBALL.
AMY! YOU'RE OUT!

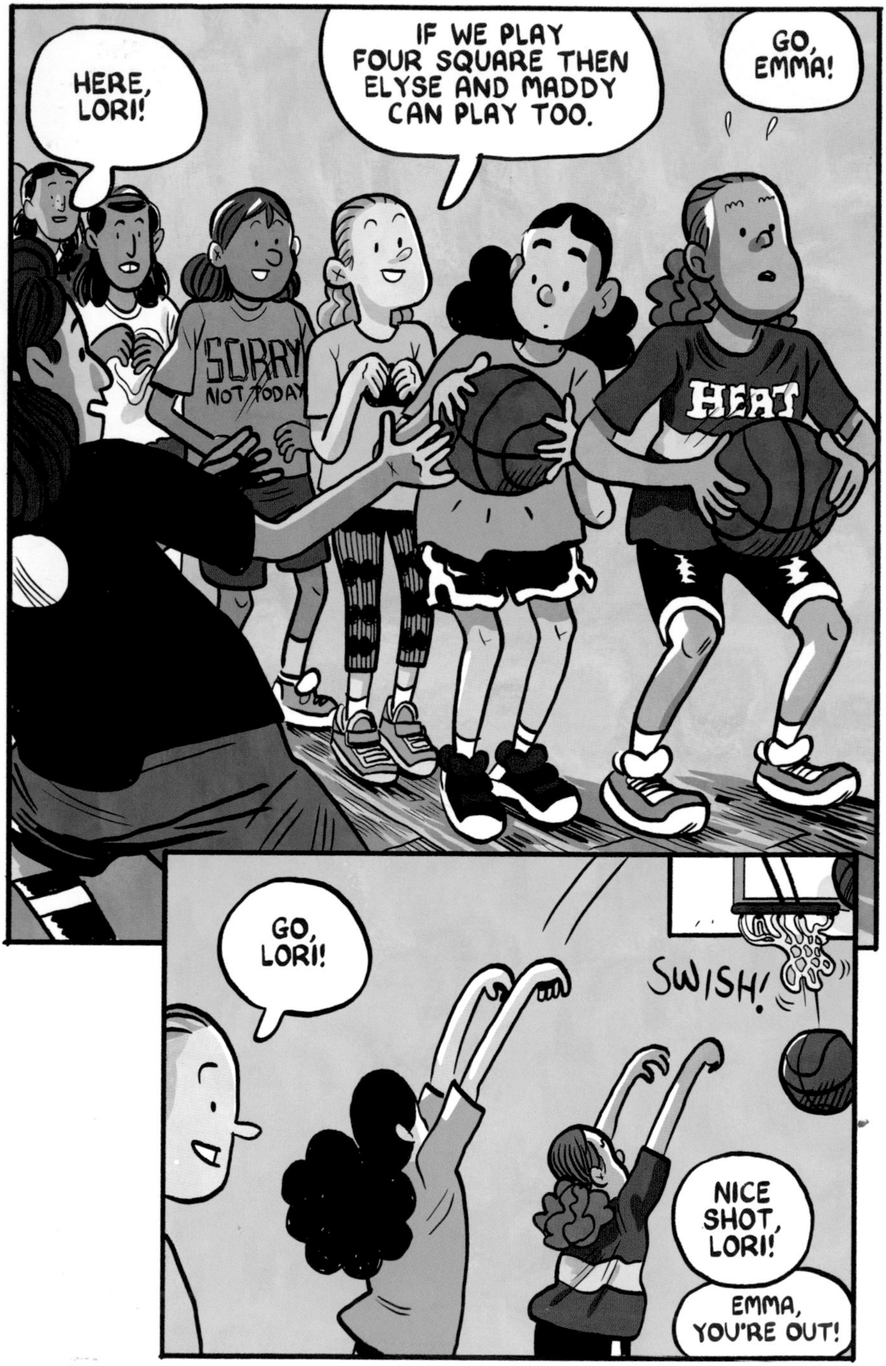
HERE, LORI!
IF WE PLAY FOUR SQUARE THEN ELYSE AND MADDY CAN PLAY TOO.
GO, EMMA!
SORRY NOT TODAY
HEAT
GO, LORI!
SWISH!
NICE SHOT, LORI!
EMMA, YOU'RE OUT!

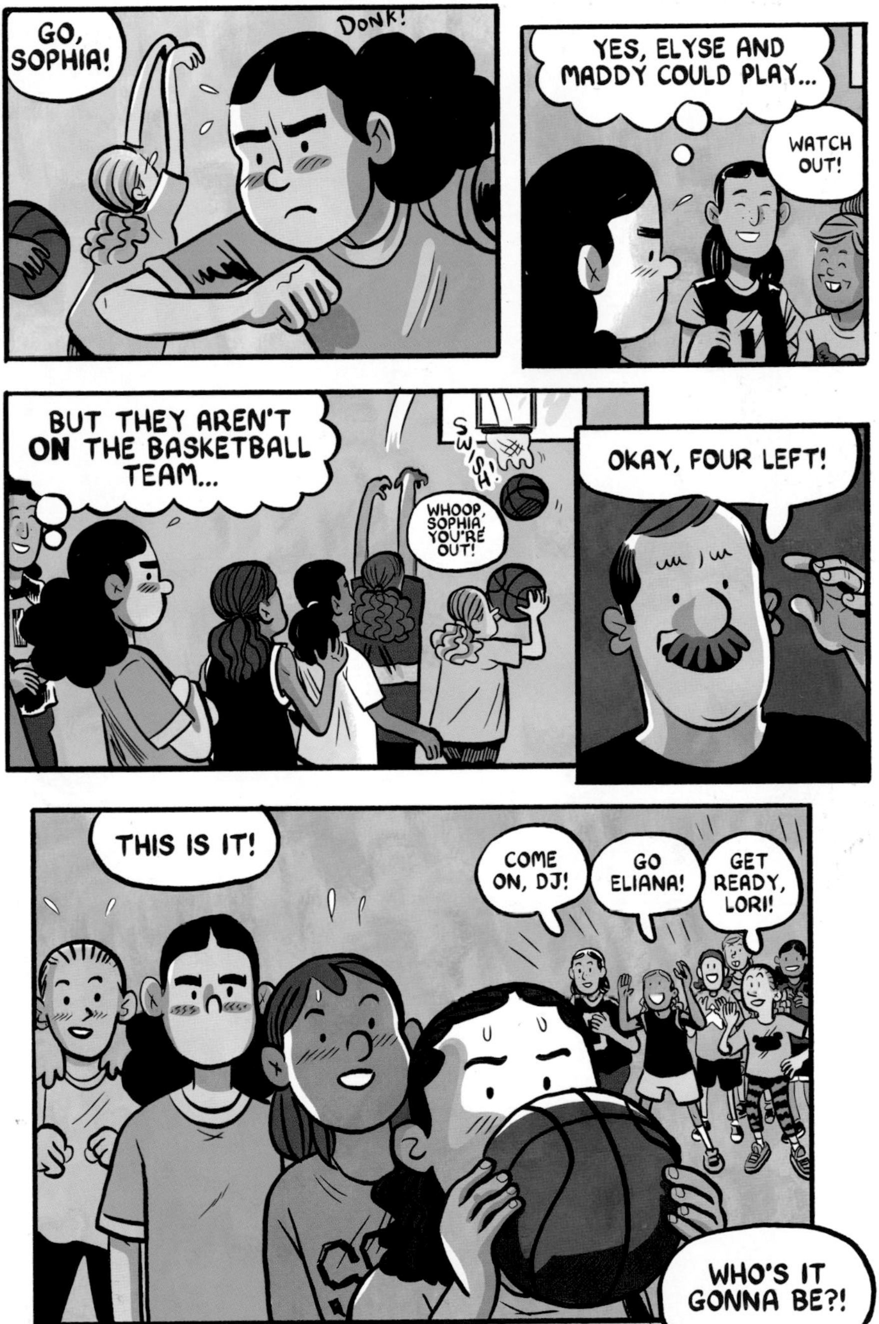
GO, SOPHIA!
DONK!
YES, ELYSE AND MADDY COULD PLAY...
WATCH OUT!
BUT THEY AREN'T ON THE BASKETBALL TEAM...
SWISH!
WHOOP, SOPHIA, YOU'RE OUT!
OKAY, FOUR LEFT!
THIS IS IT!
COME ON, DJ!
GO ELIANA!
GET READY, LORI!
WHO'S IT GONNA BE?!

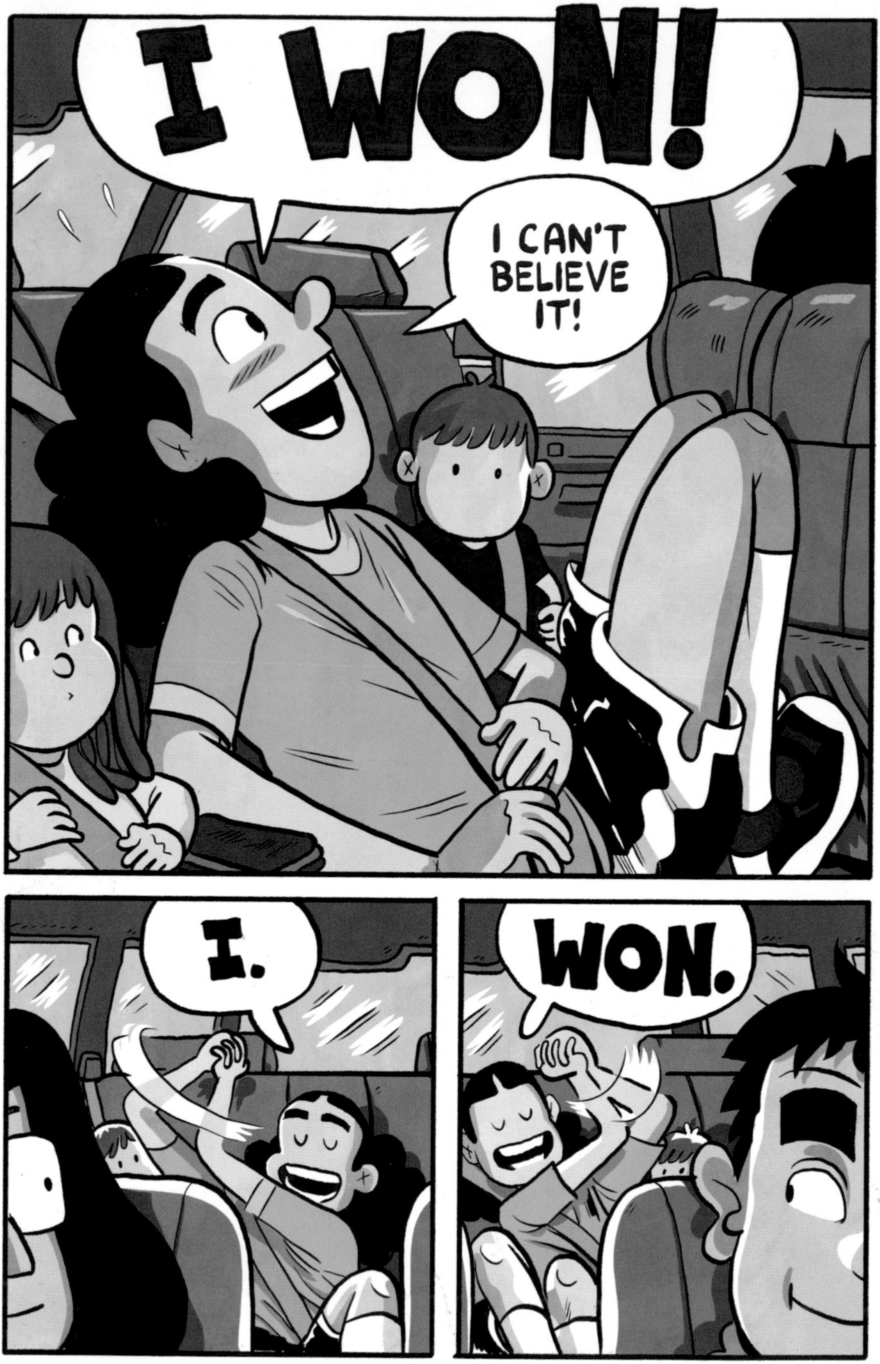
I WON!
I CAN'T BELIEVE IT!
I.
WON.

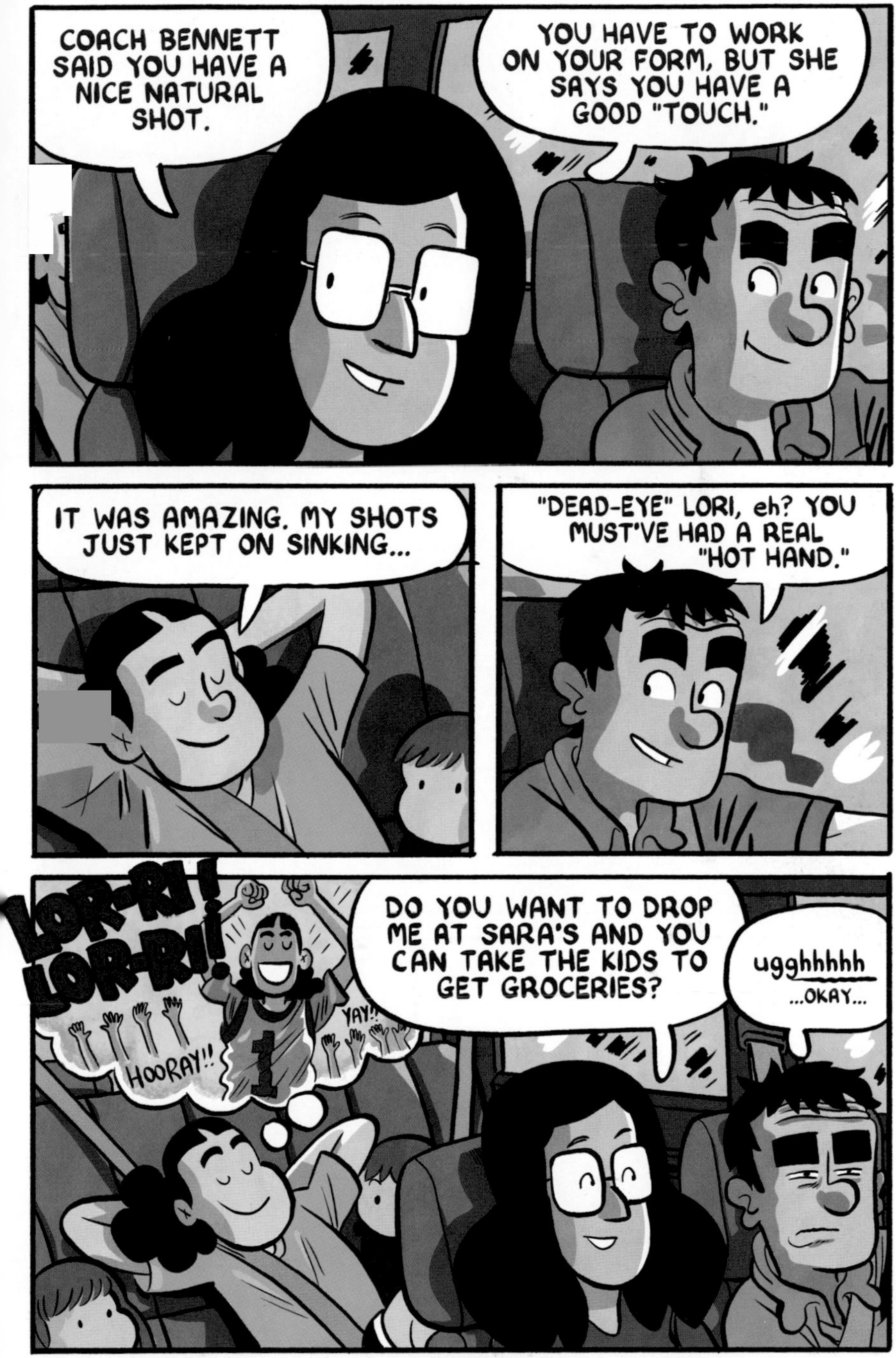
COACH BENNETT SAID YOU HAVE A NICE NATURAL SHOT.
YOU HAVE TO WORK ON YOUR FORM, BUT SHE SAYS YOU HAVE A GOOD "TOUCH."
IT WAS AMAZING. MY SHOTS JUST KEPT ON SINKING...
"DEAD-EYE" LORI, eh? YOU MUST'VE HAD A REAL "HOT HAND."
LOR-RI! LOR-RI!
YAY!!
HOORAY!!
DO YOU WANT TO DROP ME AT SARA'S AND YOU CAN TAKE THE KIDS TO GET GROCERIES?
ugghhhhh
...OKAY...

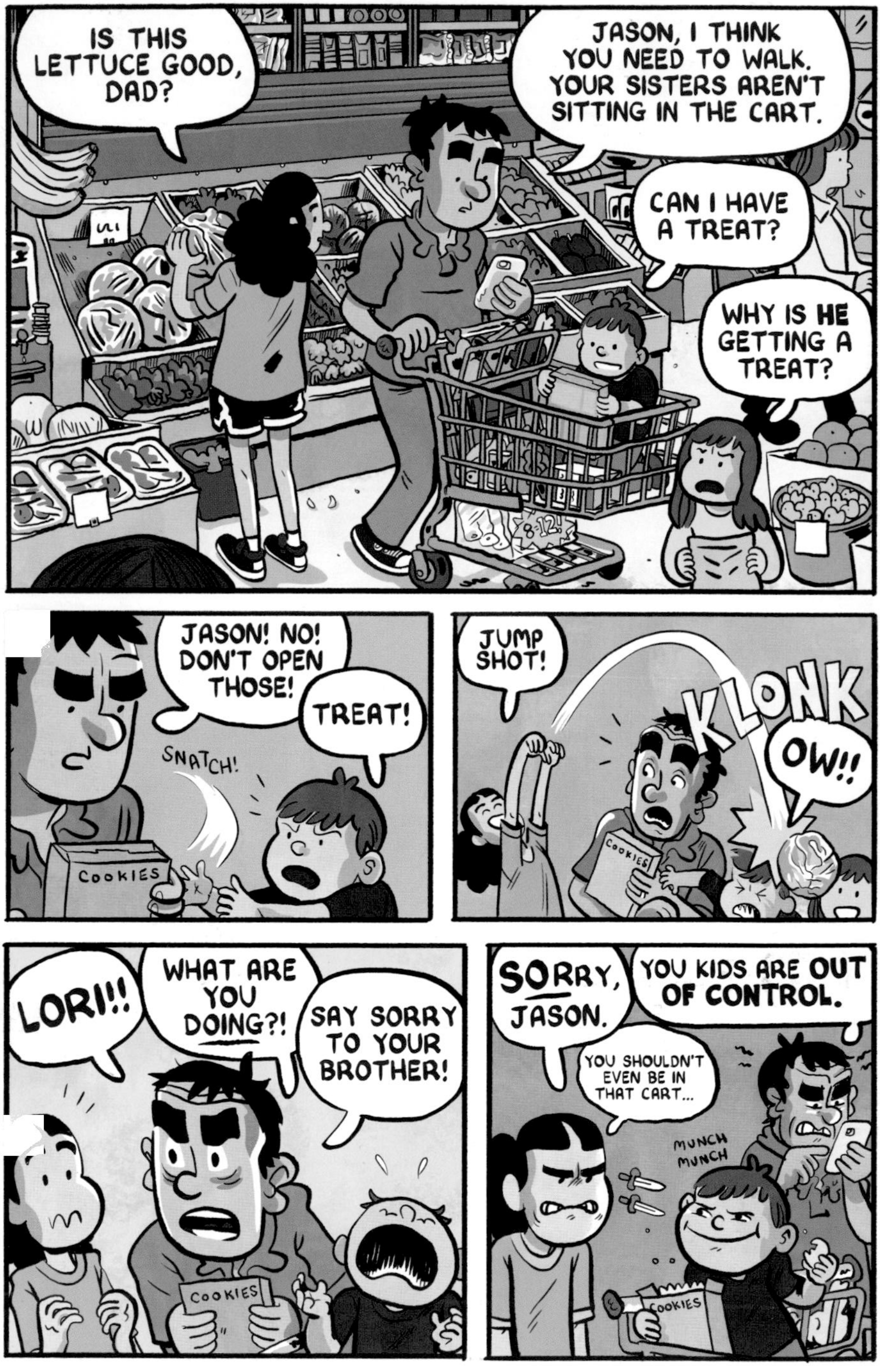
IS THIS LETTUCE GOOD, DAD?
JASON, I THINK YOU NEED TO WALK. YOUR SISTERS AREN'T SITTING IN THE CART.
CAN I HAVE A TREAT?
WHY IS HE GETTING A TREAT?
JASON! NO! DON'T OPEN THOSE!
TREAT!
SNATCH!
COOKIES
JUMP SHOT!
KLONK
OW!!
COOKIES
LORI!!
WHAT ARE YOU DOING?!
SAY SORRY TO YOUR BROTHER!
COOKIES
SORRY, JASON.
YOU KIDS ARE OUT OF CONTROL.
YOU SHOULDN'T EVEN BE IN THAT CART...
MUNCH MUNCH
COOKIES

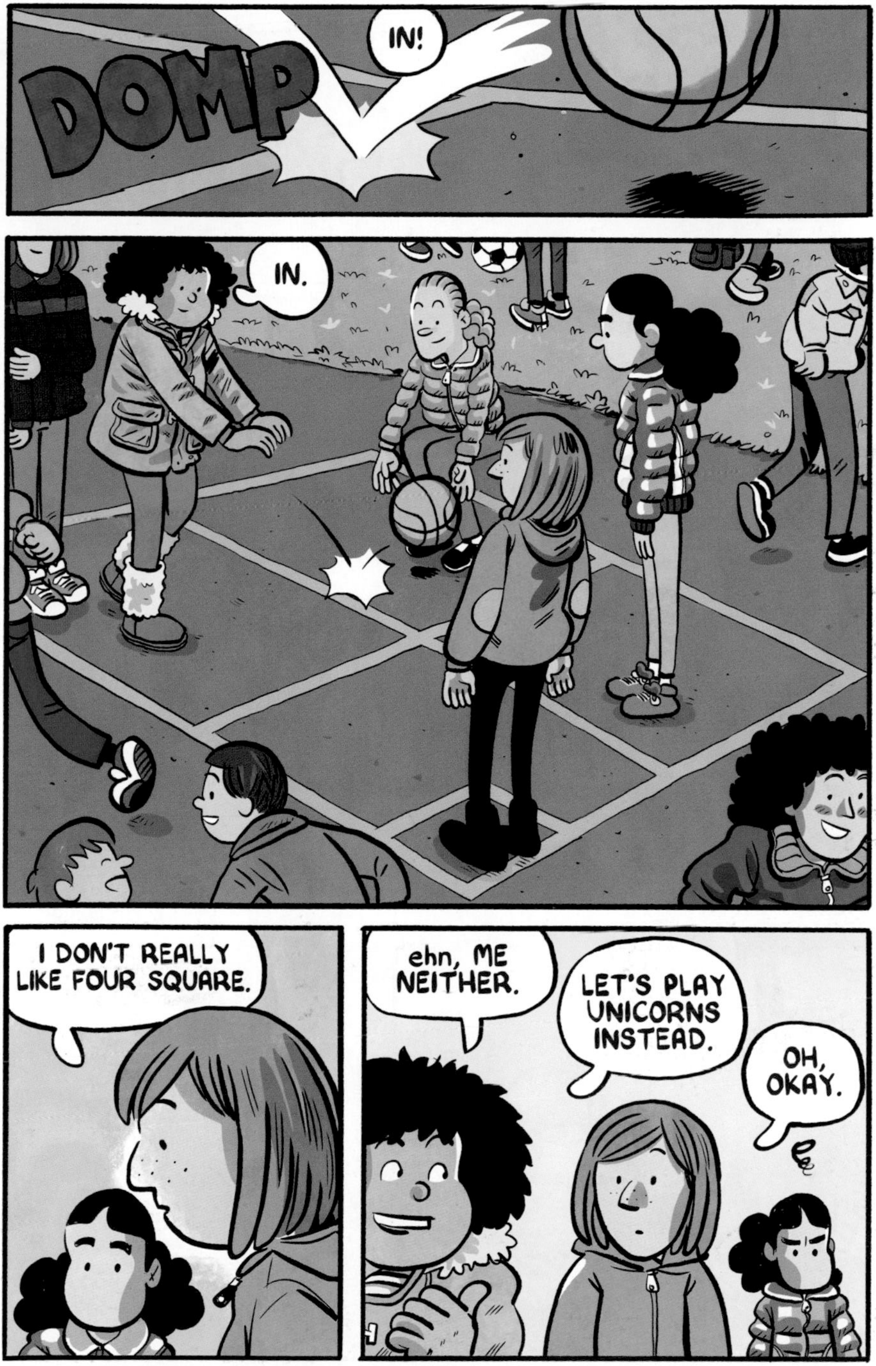
DOMP
IN!
IN.
I DON'T REALLY LIKE FOUR SQUARE.
ehn, ME NEITHER.
LET'S PLAY UNICORNS INSTEAD.
OH, OKAY.

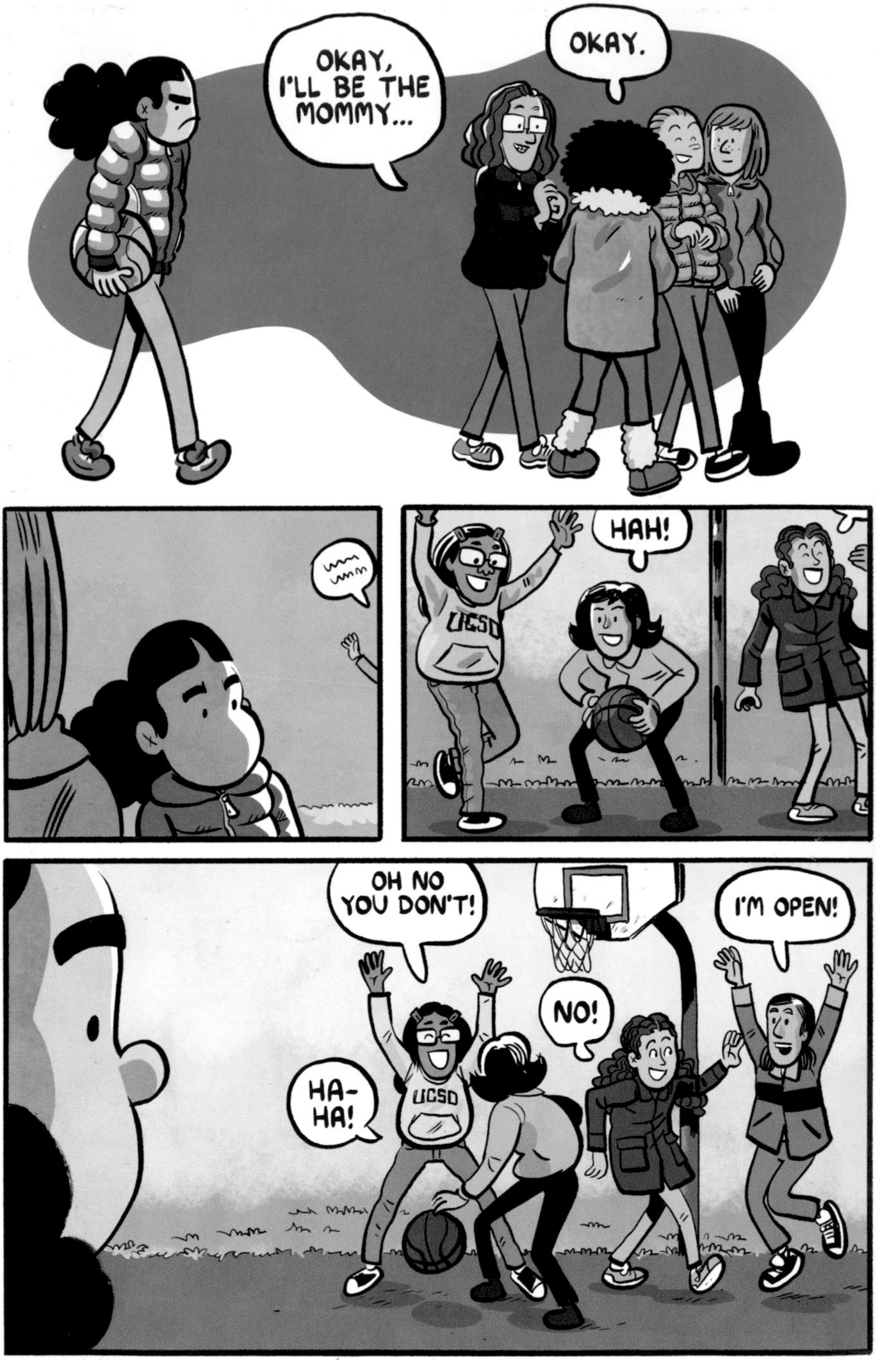
OKAY, I'LL BE THE MOMMY...
OKAY.
HAH!
OH NO YOU DON'T!
I'M OPEN!
NO!
HA-HA!

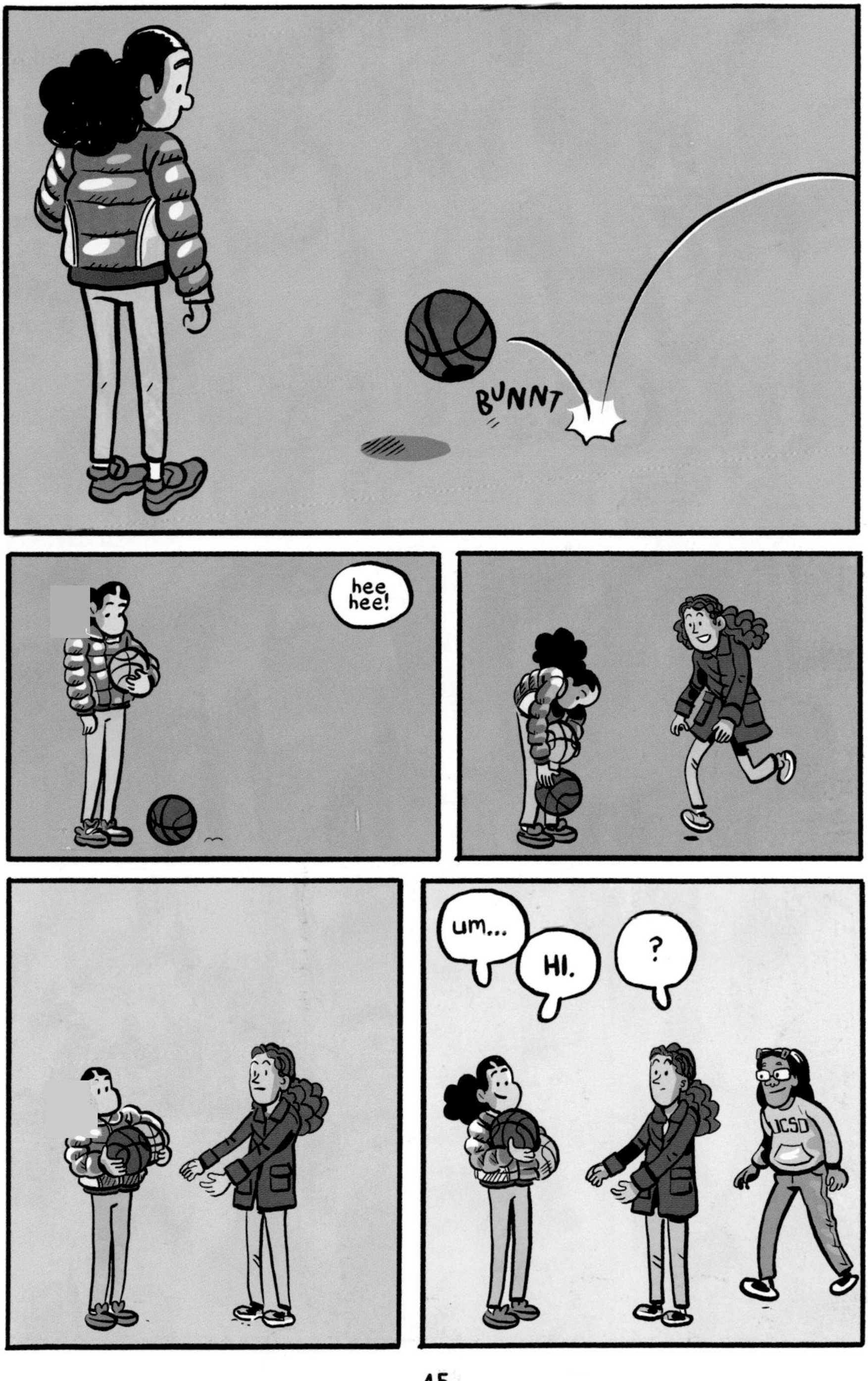
BUNNT
hee hee!
um...
HI.
?

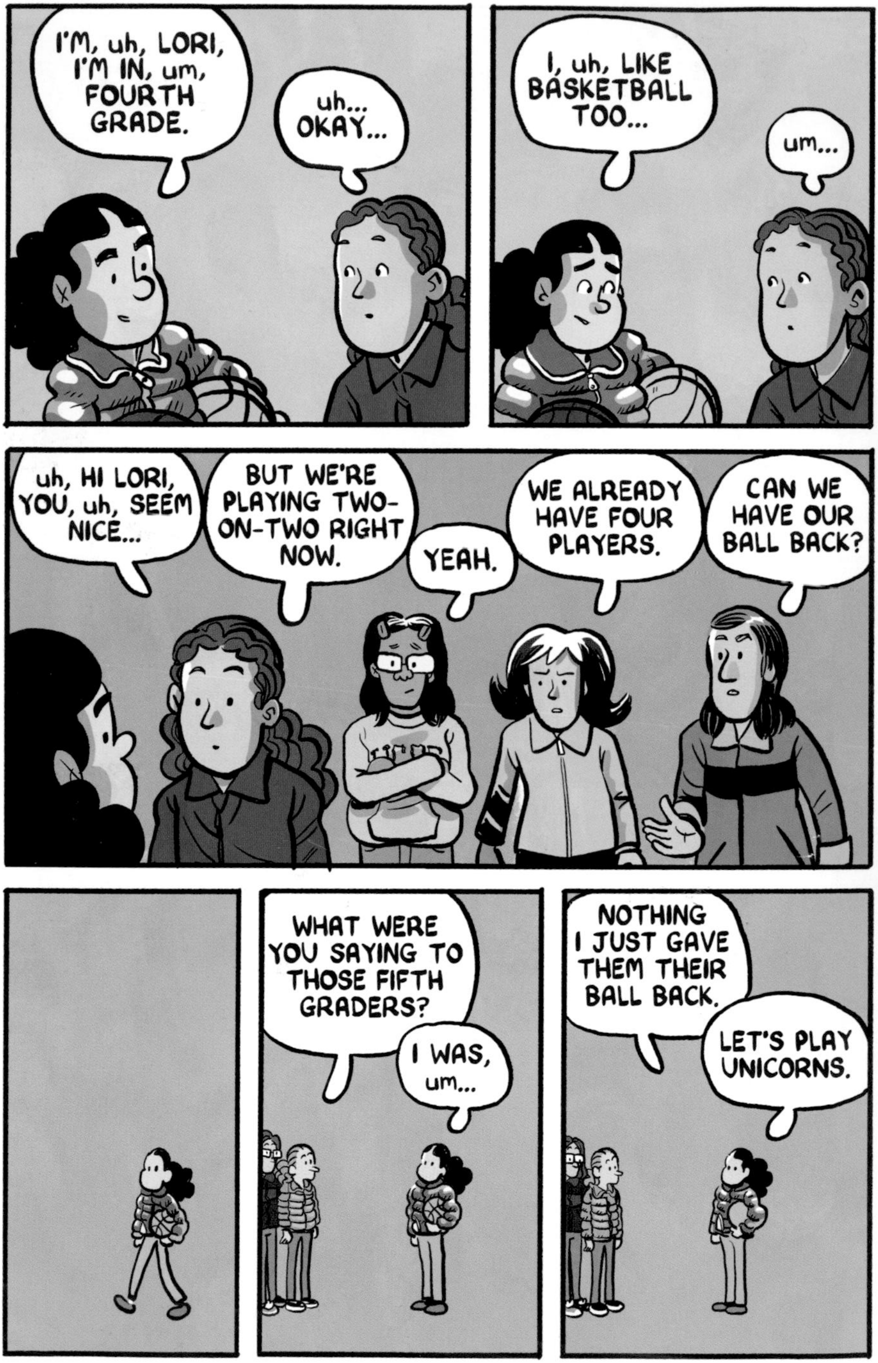
I'M, uh, LORI, I'M IN, um, FOURTH GRADE.
uh... OKAY...
I, uh, LIKE BASKETBALL TOO...
um...
uh, HI LORI, YOU, uh, SEEM NICE...
BUT WE'RE PLAYING TWO-ON-TWO RIGHT NOW.
YEAH.
WE ALREADY HAVE FOUR PLAYERS.
CAN WE HAVE OUR BALL BACK?
WHAT WERE YOU SAYING TO THOSE FIFTH GRADERS?
I WAS, um...
NOTHING I JUST GAVE THEM THEIR BALL BACK.
LET'S PLAY UNICORNS.

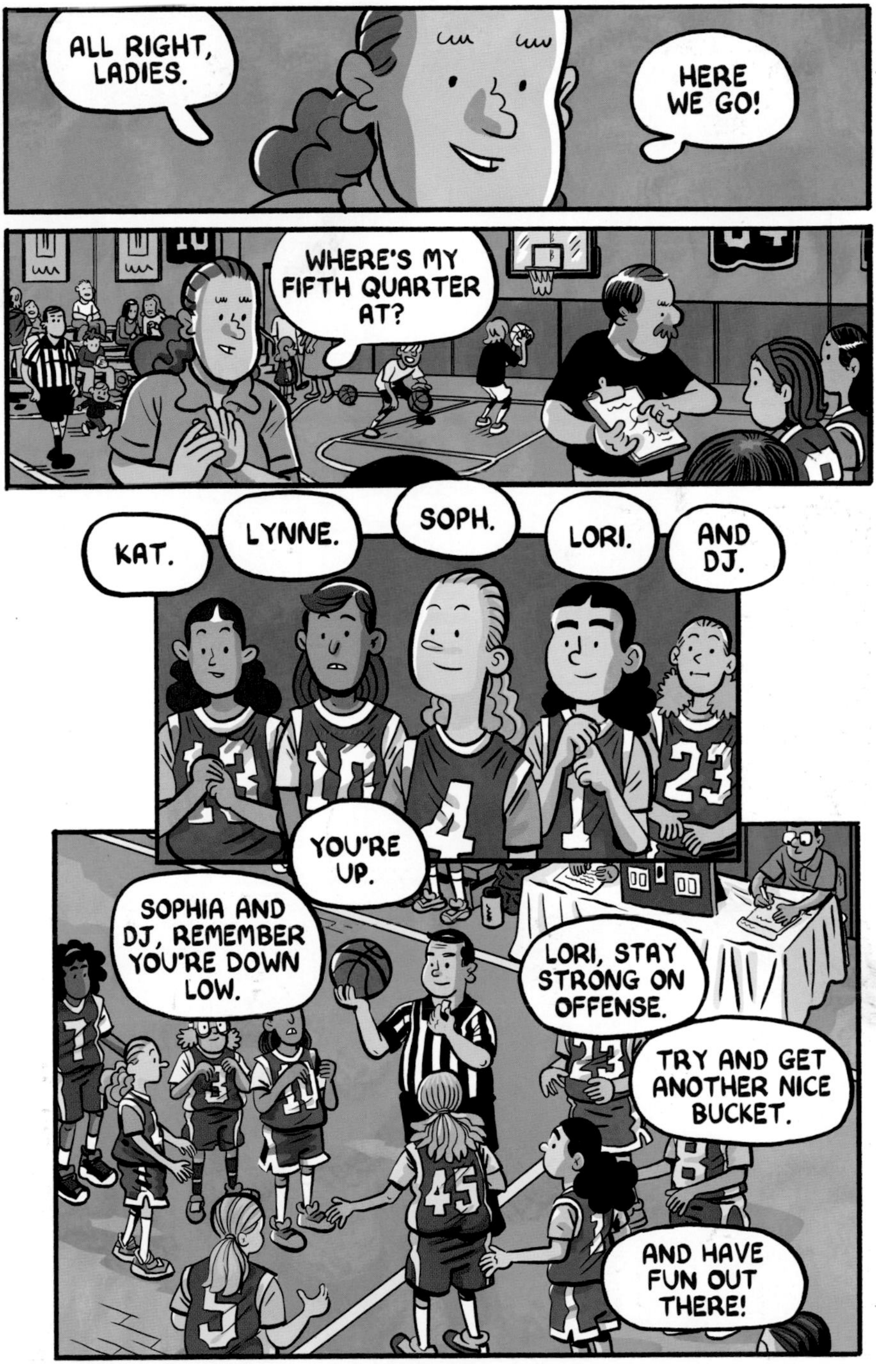
ALL RIGHT, LADIES.
HERE WE GO!
WHERE'S MY FIFTH QUARTER AT?
KAT.
LYNNE.
SOPH.
LORI.
AND DJ.
YOU'RE UP.
SOPHIA AND DJ, REMEMBER YOU'RE DOWN LOW.
LORI, STAY STRONG ON OFFENSE.
TRY AND GET ANOTHER NICE BUCKET.
AND HAVE FUN OUT THERE!

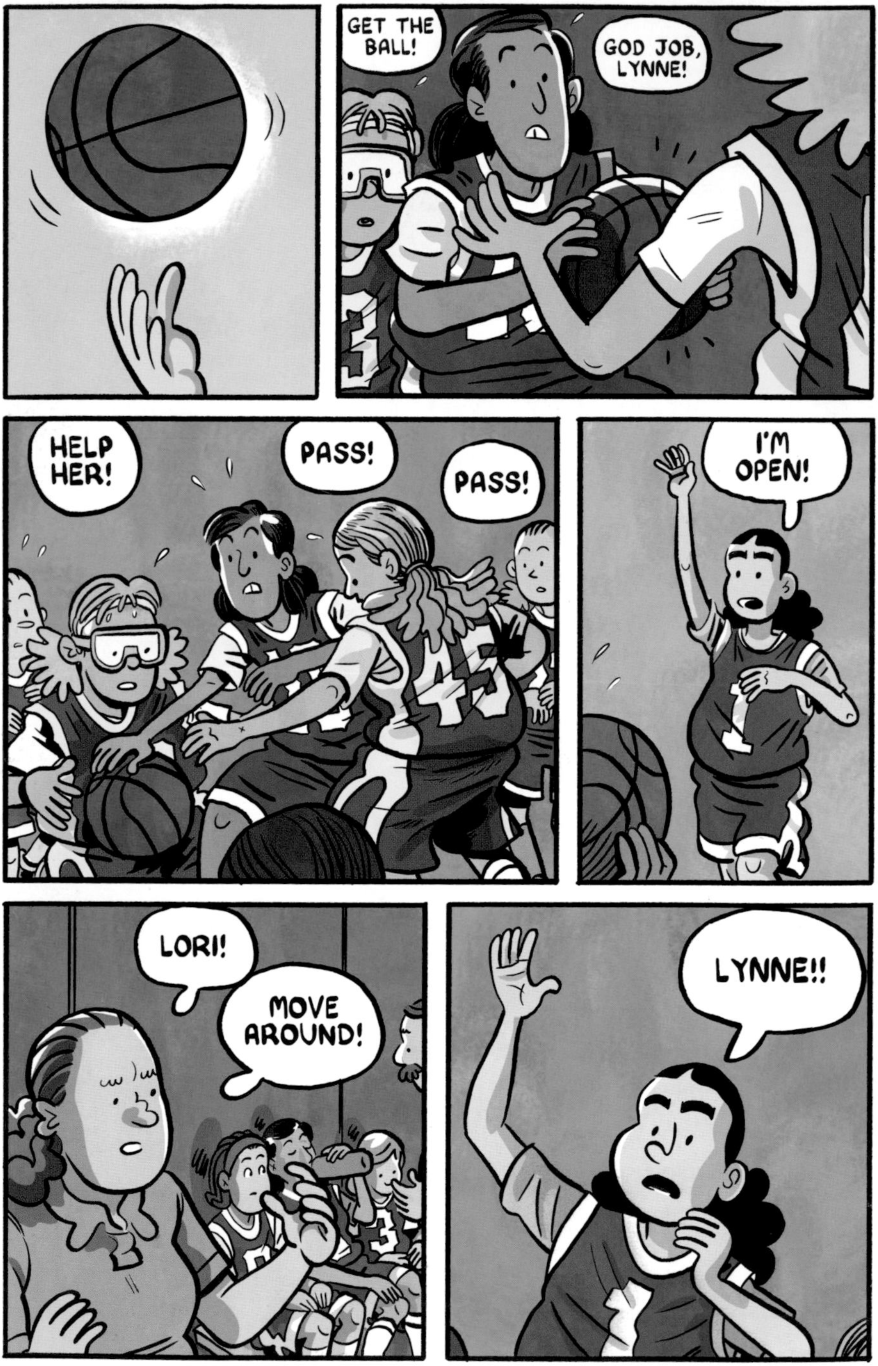
GET THE BALL!
GOD JOB, LYNNE!
HELP HER!
PASS!
PASS!
I'M OPEN!
LORI!
MOVE AROUND!
LYNNE!!

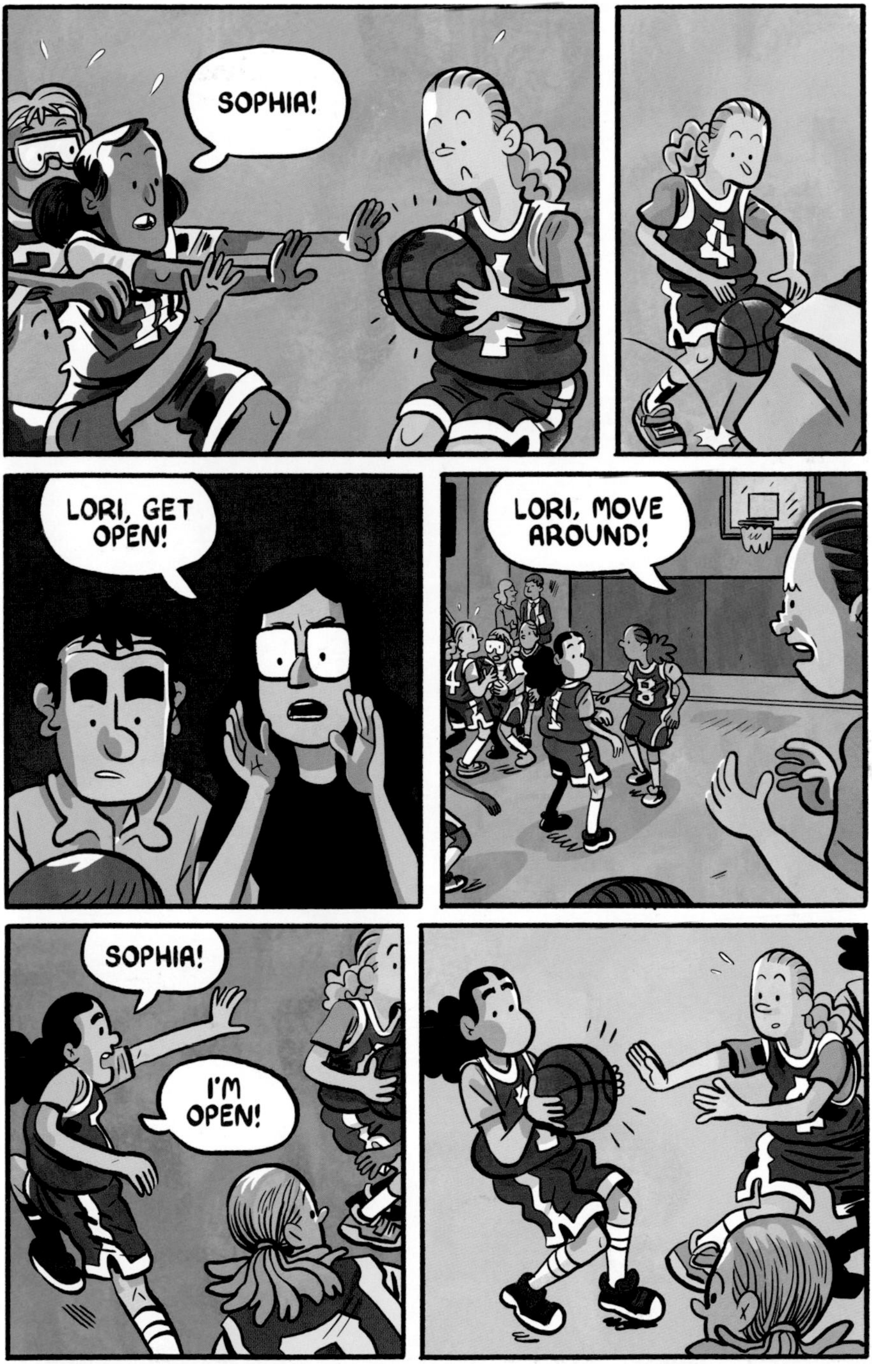
SOPHIA!
LORI, GET OPEN!
LORI, MOVE AROUND!
SOPHIA!
I'M OPEN!

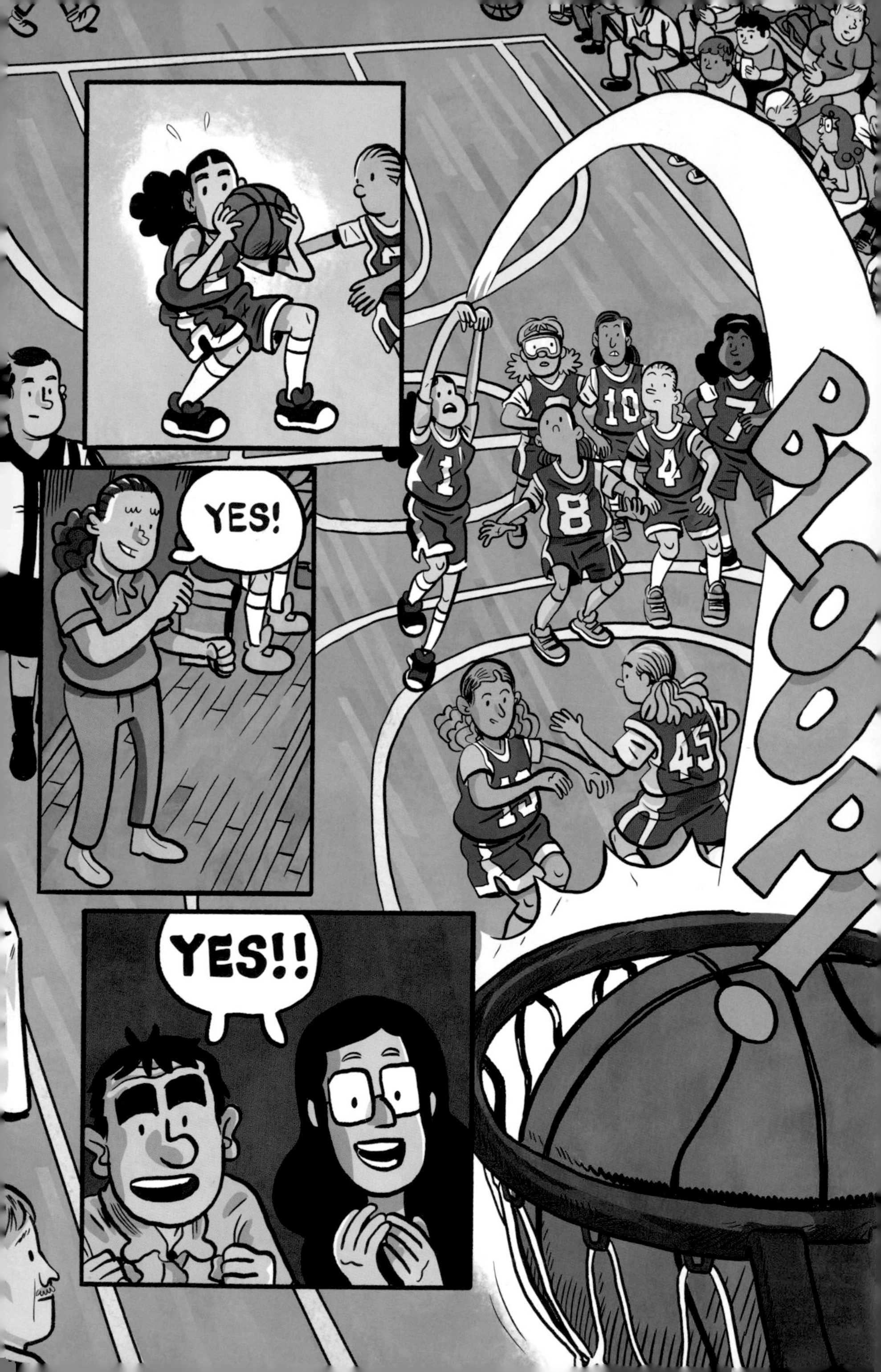
YES!
YES!!
BLOOP!

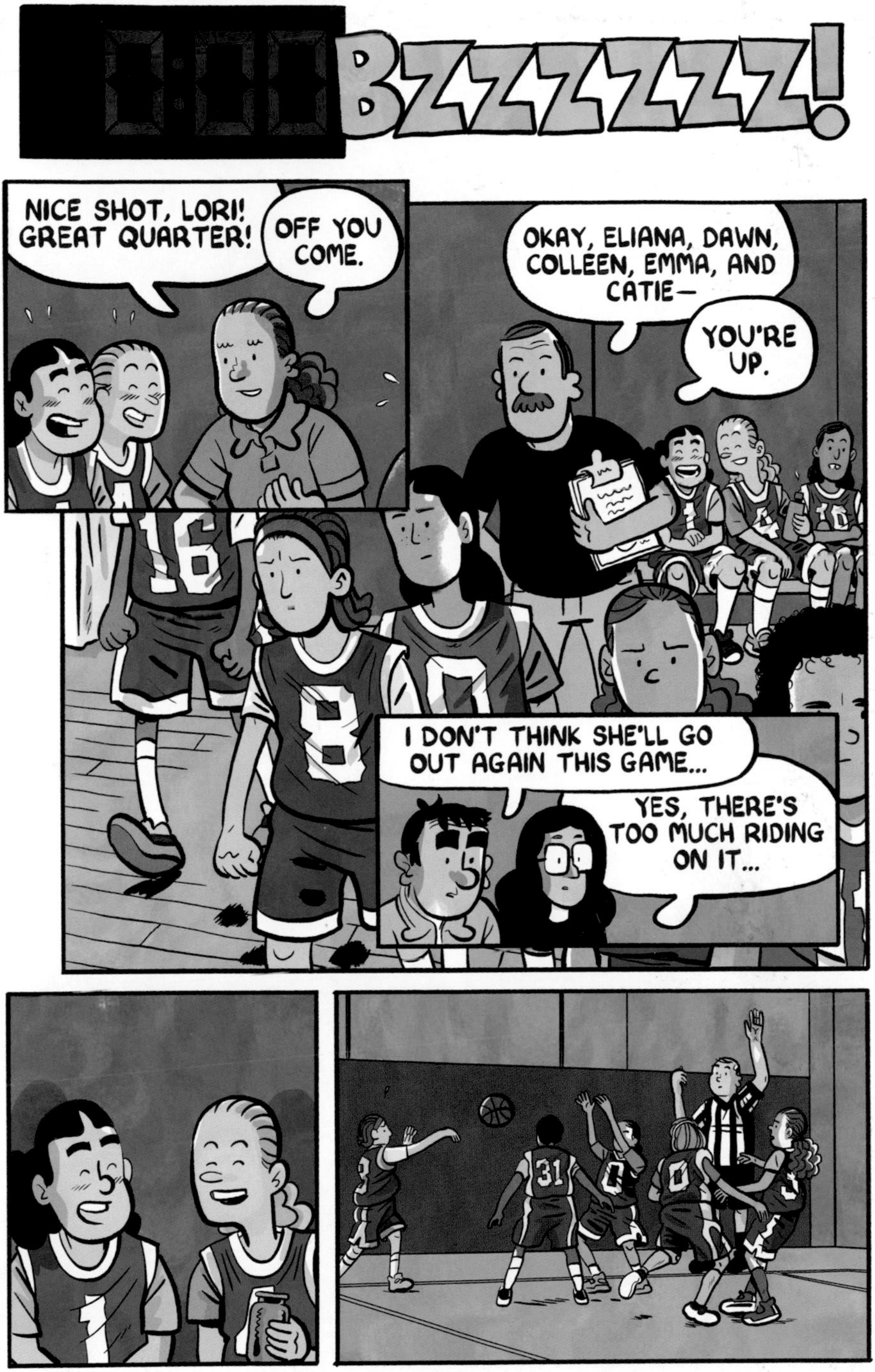
0:00
BZZZZZZZZ!
NICE SHOT, LORI! GREAT QUARTER!
OFF YOU COME.
OKAY, ELIANA, DAWN, COLLEEN, EMMA, AND CATIE—
YOU'RE UP.
I DON'T THINK SHE'LL GO OUT AGAIN THIS GAME...
YES, THERE'S TOO MUCH RIDING ON IT...

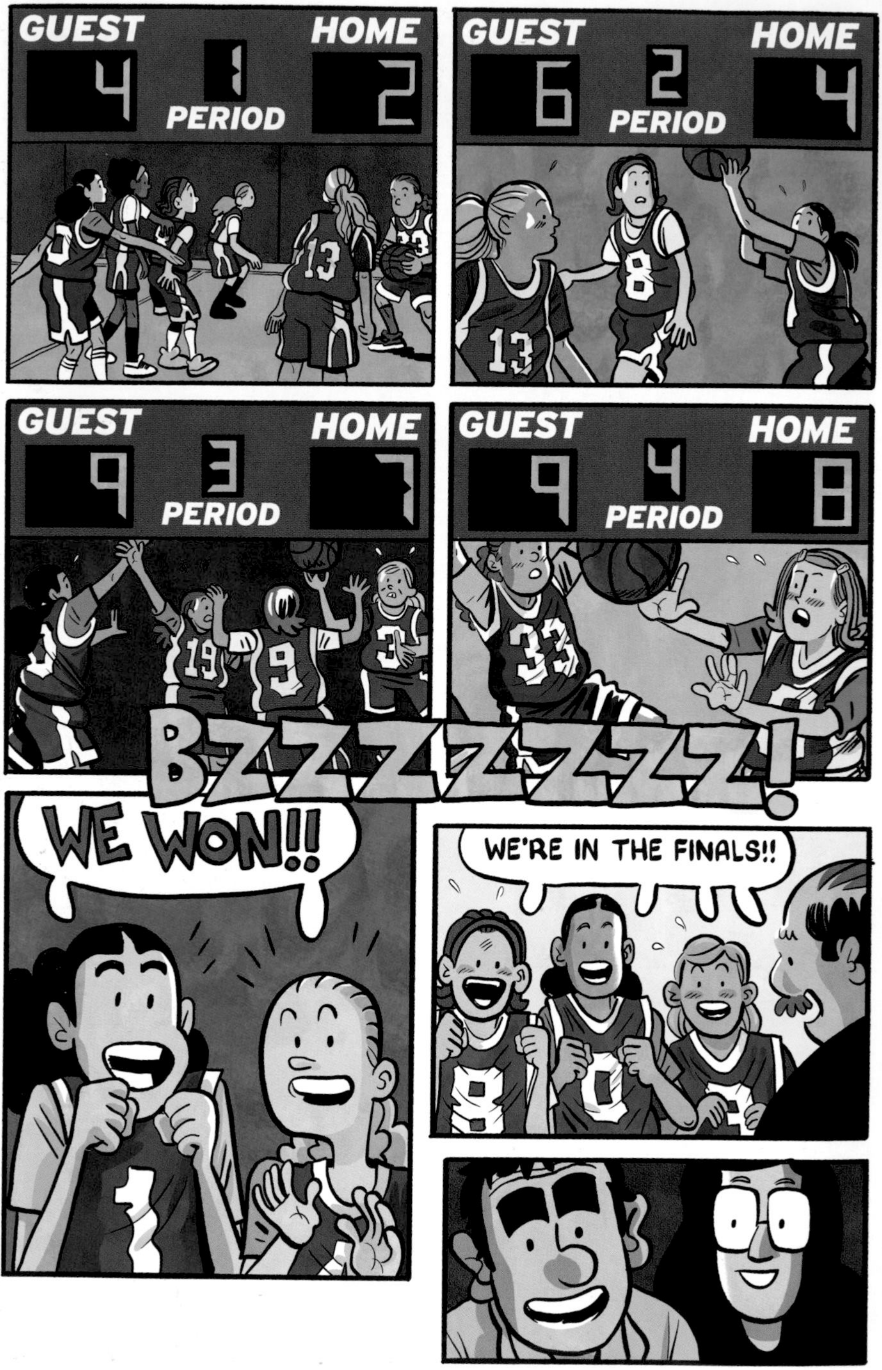
GUEST 4 1 PERIOD HOME 2
GUEST 6 2 PERIOD HOME 4
GUEST 9 3 PERIOD HOME 7
GUEST 9 4 PERIOD HOME 8
BZZZZZZZ!
WE WON!!
WE'RE IN THE FINALS!!

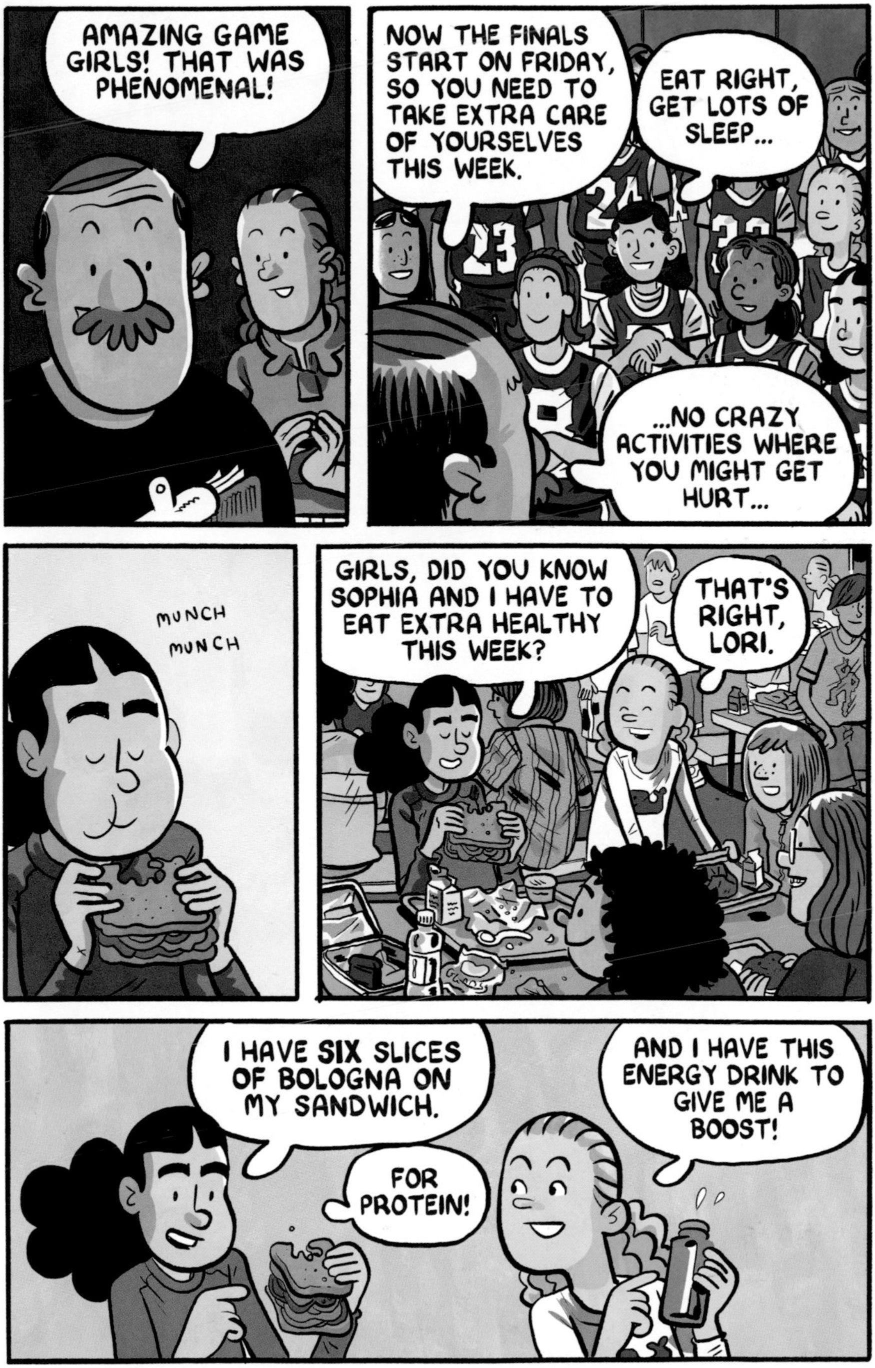
AMAZING GAME GIRLS! THAT WAS PHENOMENAL!
NOW THE FINALS START ON FRIDAY, SO YOU NEED TO TAKE EXTRA CARE OF YOURSELVES THIS WEEK.
EAT RIGHT, GET LOTS OF SLEEP...
...NO CRAZY ACTIVITIES WHERE YOU MIGHT GET HURT...
MUNCH
MUNCH
GIRLS, DID YOU KNOW SOPHIA AND I HAVE TO EAT EXTRA HEALTHY THIS WEEK?
THAT'S RIGHT, LORI.
I HAVE **SIX** SLICES OF BOLOGNA ON MY SANDWICH.
FOR PROTEIN!
AND I HAVE THIS ENERGY DRINK TO GIVE ME A BOOST!

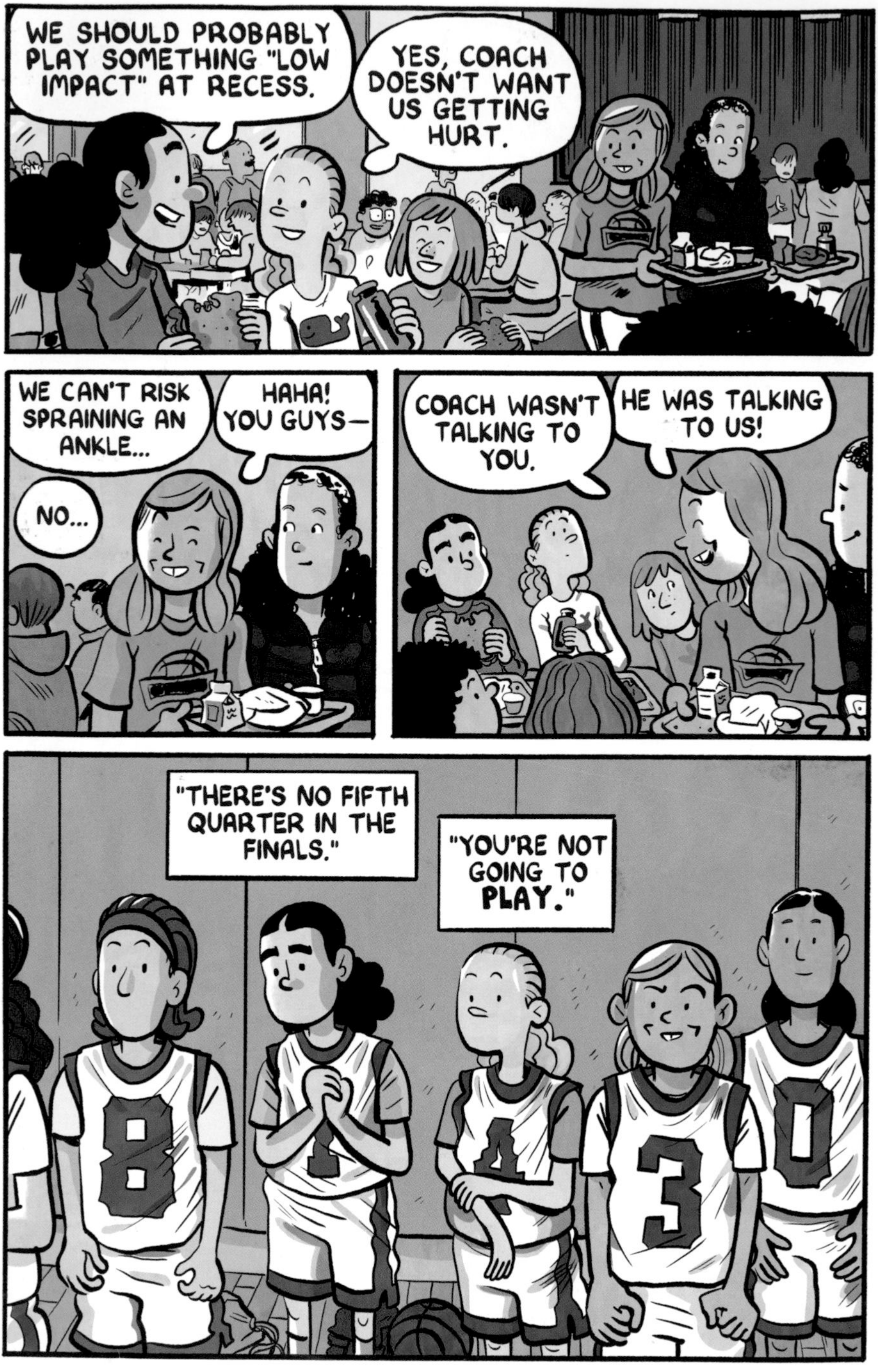
WE SHOULD PROBABLY PLAY SOMETHING "LOW IMPACT" AT RECESS.
YES, COACH DOESN'T WANT US GETTING HURT.
WE CAN'T RISK SPRAINING AN ANKLE...
HAHA! YOU GUYS—
NO...
COACH WASN'T TALKING TO YOU.
HE WAS TALKING TO US!
"THERE'S NO FIFTH QUARTER IN THE FINALS."
"YOU'RE NOT GOING TO PLAY."

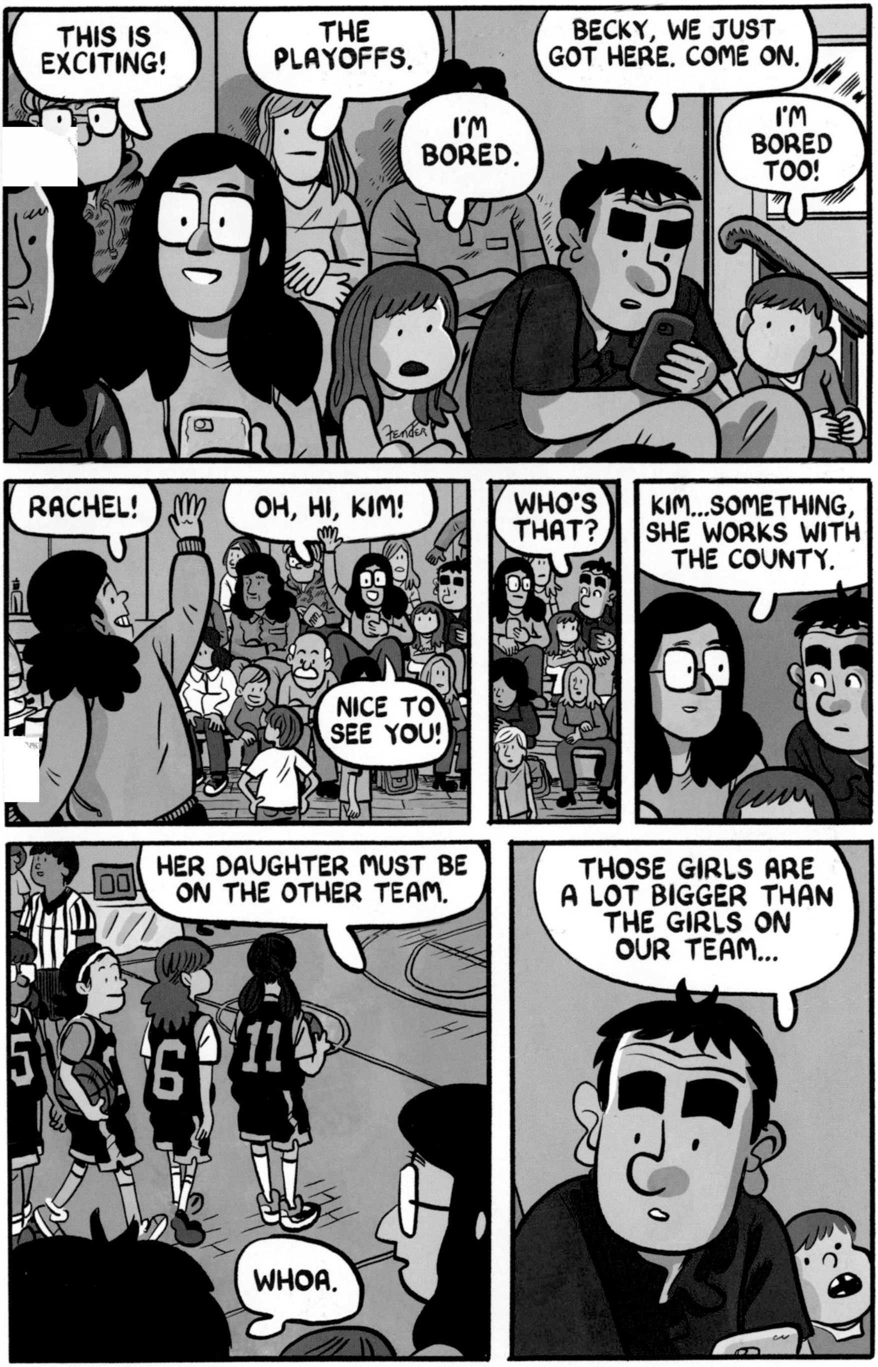
THIS IS EXCITING!
THE PLAYOFFS.
I'M BORED.
BECKY, WE JUST GOT HERE. COME ON.
I'M BORED TOO!
RACHEL!
OH, HI, KIM!
NICE TO SEE YOU!
WHO'S THAT?
KIM...SOMETHING, SHE WORKS WITH THE COUNTY.
HER DAUGHTER MUST BE ON THE OTHER TEAM.
WHOA.
THOSE GIRLS ARE A LOT BIGGER THAN THE GIRLS ON OUR TEAM...

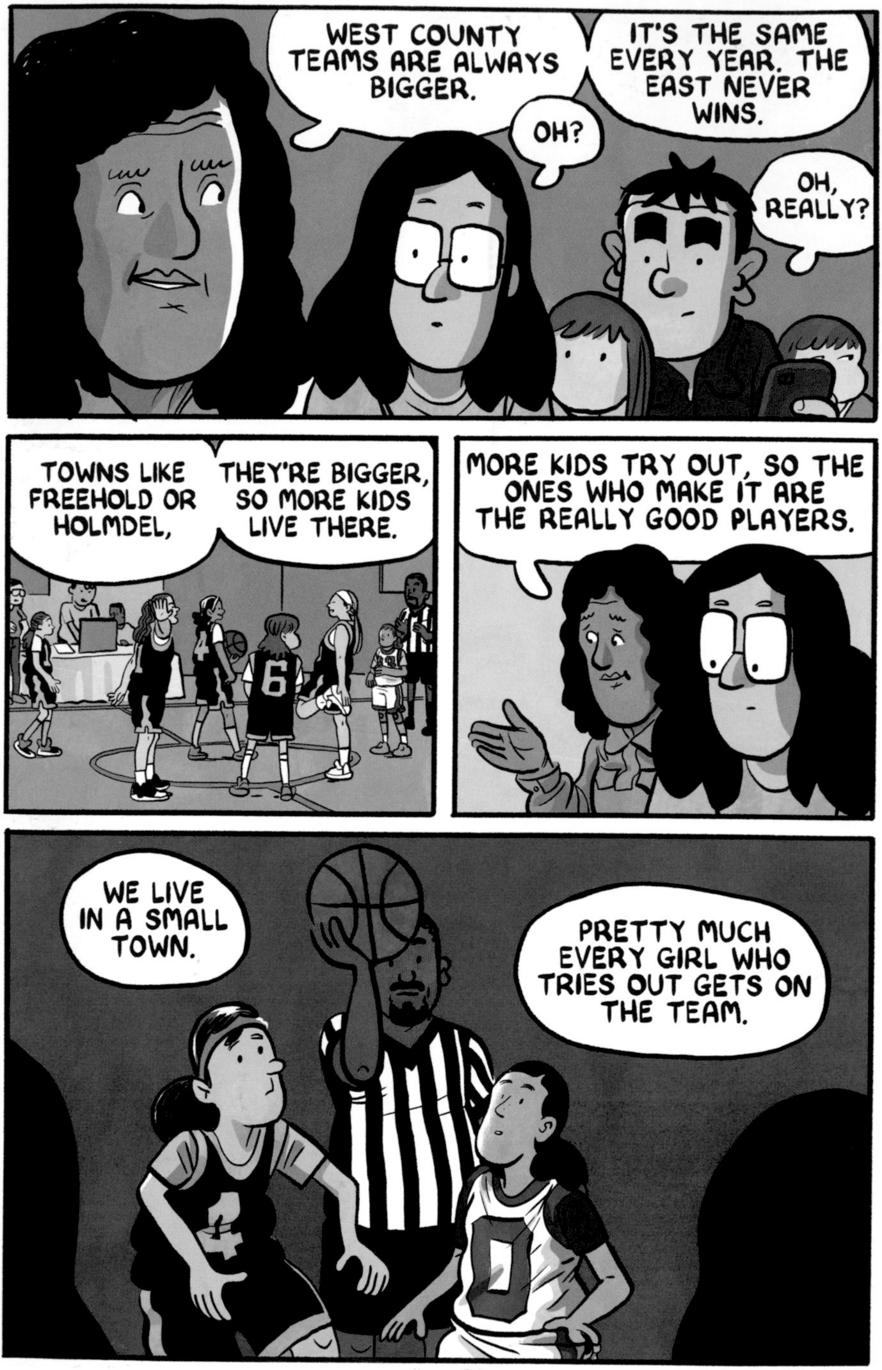
WEST COUNTY TEAMS ARE ALWAYS BIGGER.
OH?
IT'S THE SAME EVERY YEAR. THE EAST NEVER WINS.
OH, REALLY?
TOWNS LIKE FREEHOLD OR HOLMDEL,
THEY'RE BIGGER, SO MORE KIDS LIVE THERE.
MORE KIDS TRY OUT, SO THE ONES WHO MAKE IT ARE THE REALLY GOOD PLAYERS.
WE LIVE IN A SMALL TOWN.
PRETTY MUCH EVERY GIRL WHO TRIES OUT GETS ON THE TEAM.

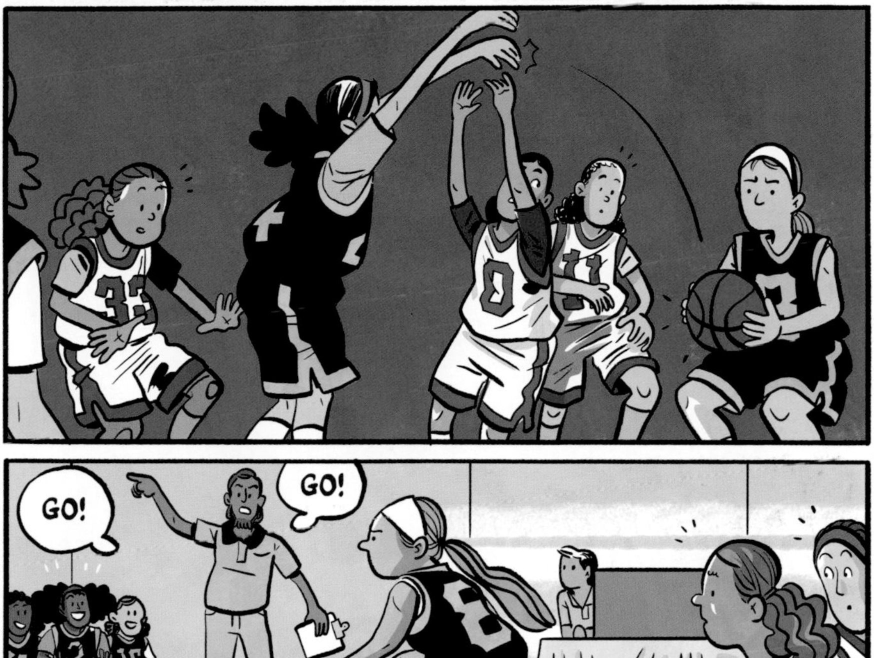
GO!
GO!
OKAY! REGROUP! COLLEEN, YOU TAKE IT UP!
WHOA.

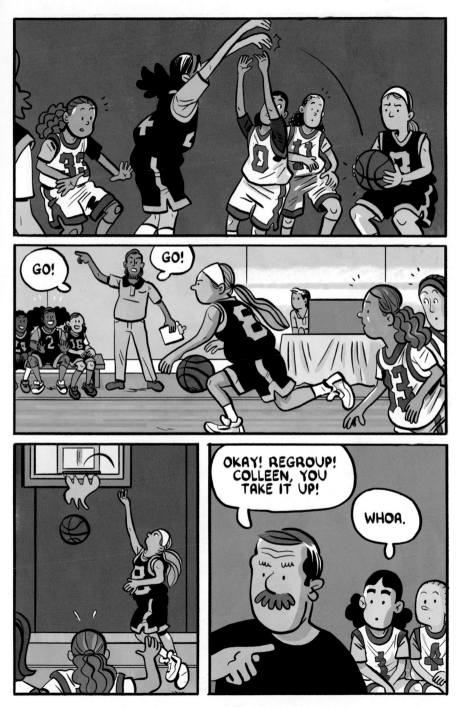

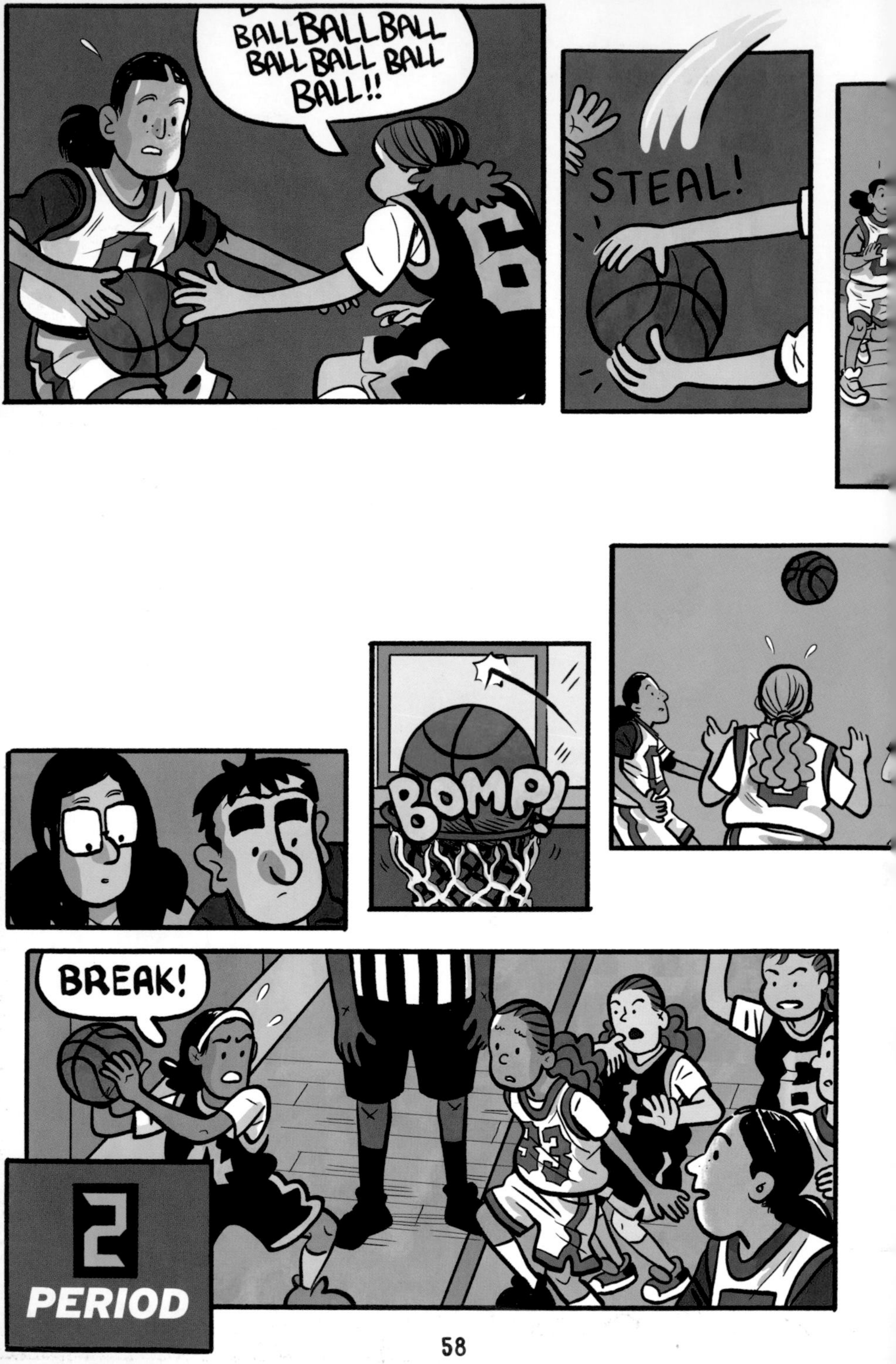
BALL BALL BALL BALL
BALL BALL BALL
BALL!!
STEAL!
BOMP!
BREAK!
2
PERIOD

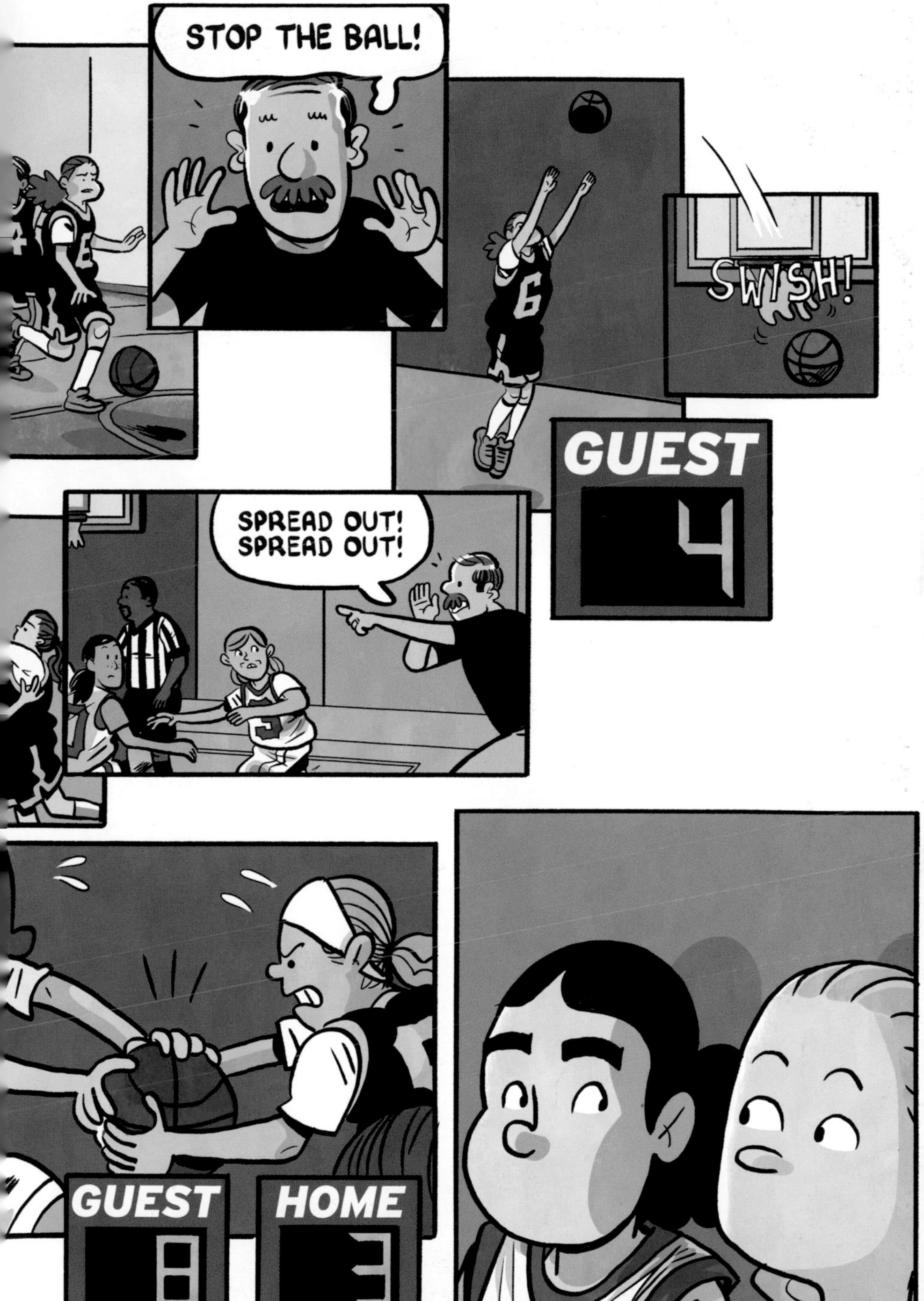
STOP THE BALL!
SWISH!
GUEST
4
SPREAD OUT! SPREAD OUT!
GUEST
8
HOME
3

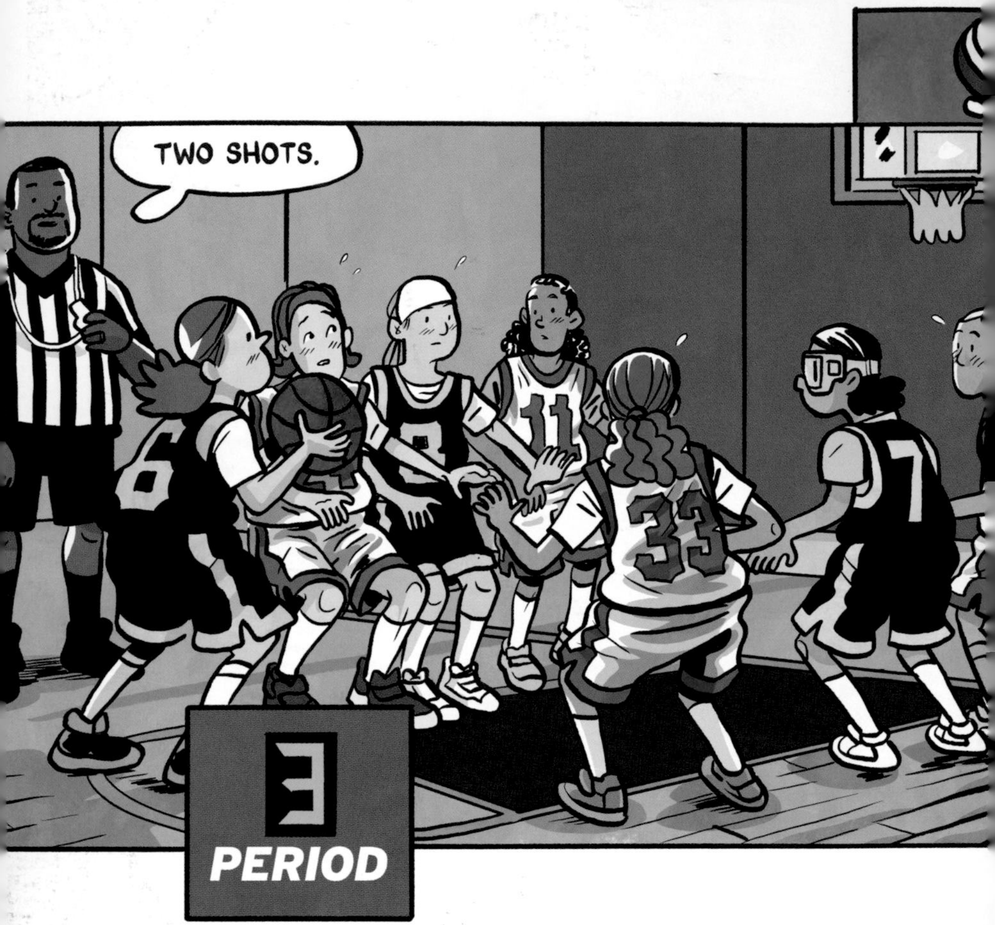
TWO SHOTS.
3
PERIOD

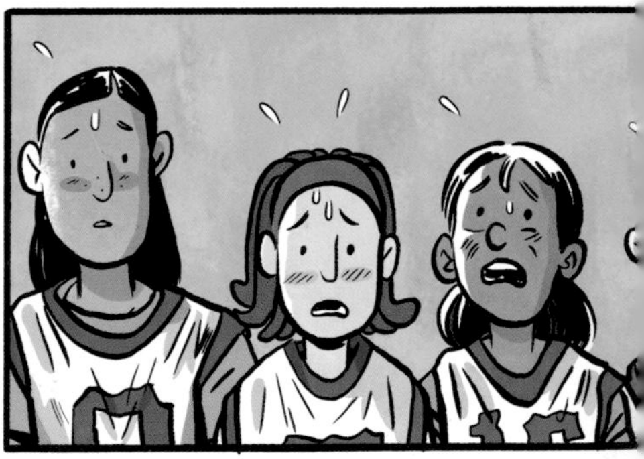

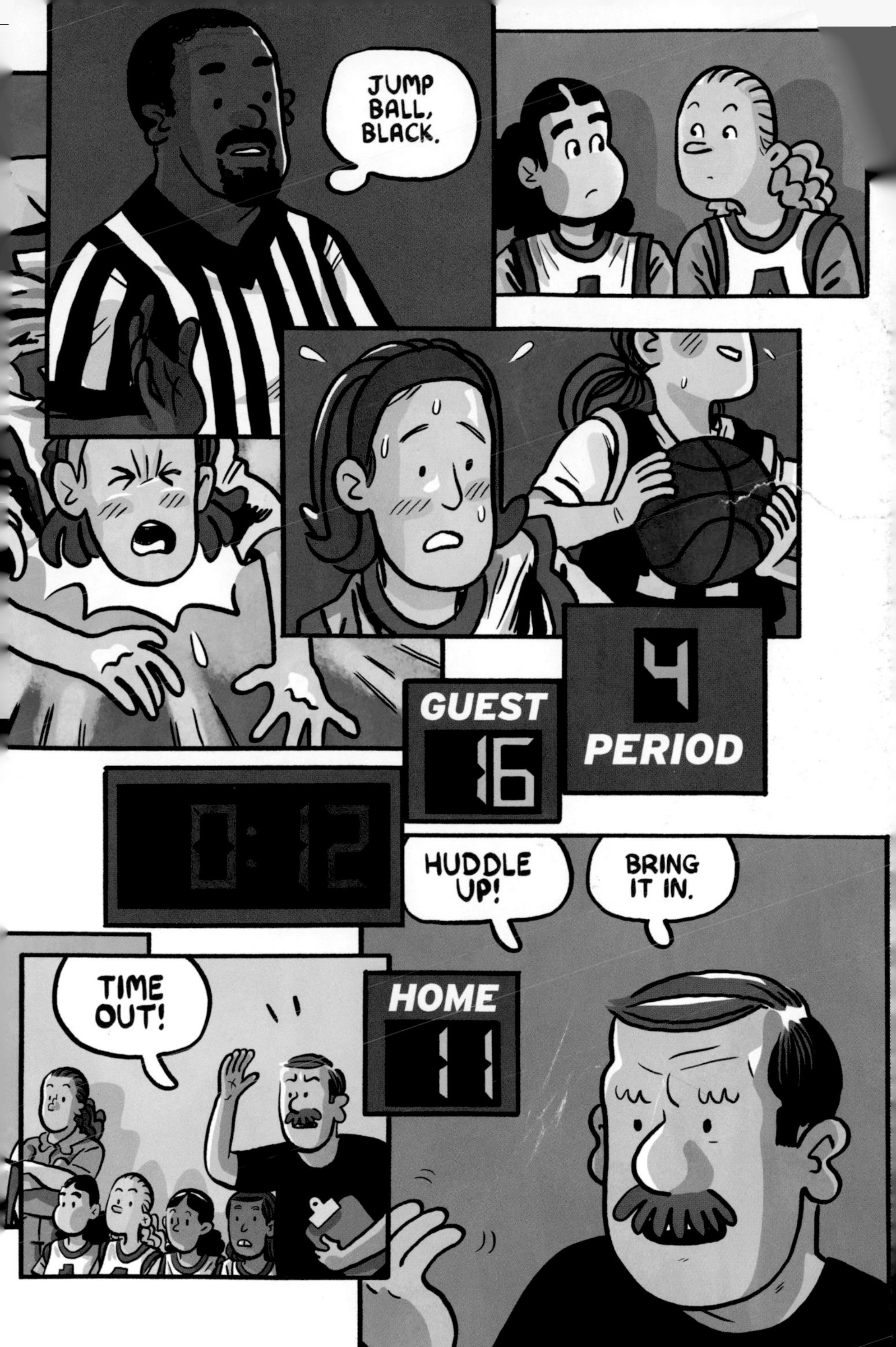
JUMP BALL, BLACK.
GUEST
16
4
PERIOD
0:12
HUDDLE UP!
BRING IT IN.
TIME OUT!
HOME
11

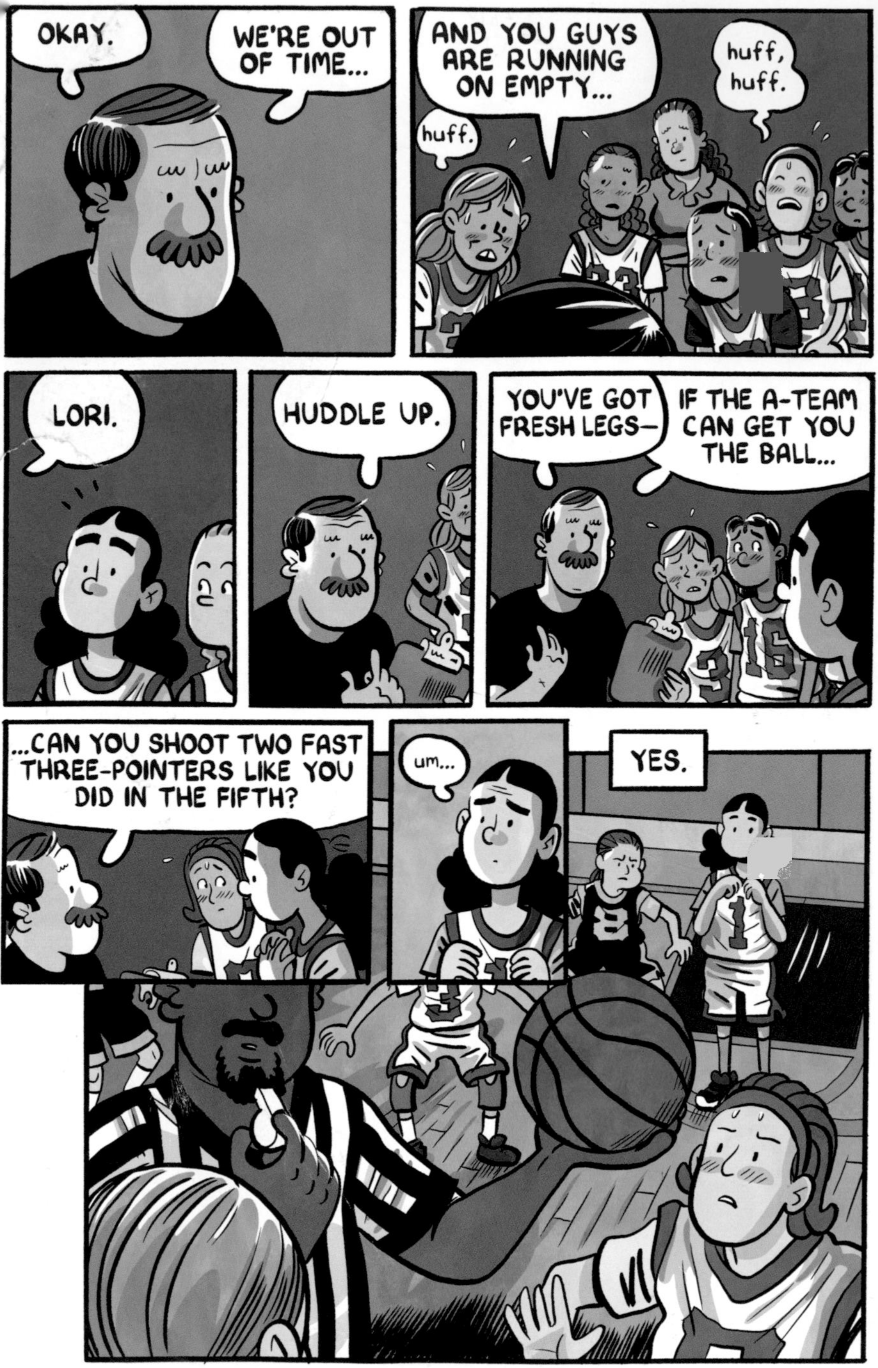
OKAY.
WE'RE OUT OF TIME...
AND YOU GUYS ARE RUNNING ON EMPTY...
huff.
huff, huff.
LORI.
HUDDLE UP.
YOU'VE GOT FRESH LEGS—
IF THE A-TEAM CAN GET YOU THE BALL...
...CAN YOU SHOOT TWO FAST THREE-POINTERS LIKE YOU DID IN THE FIFTH?
um...
YES.

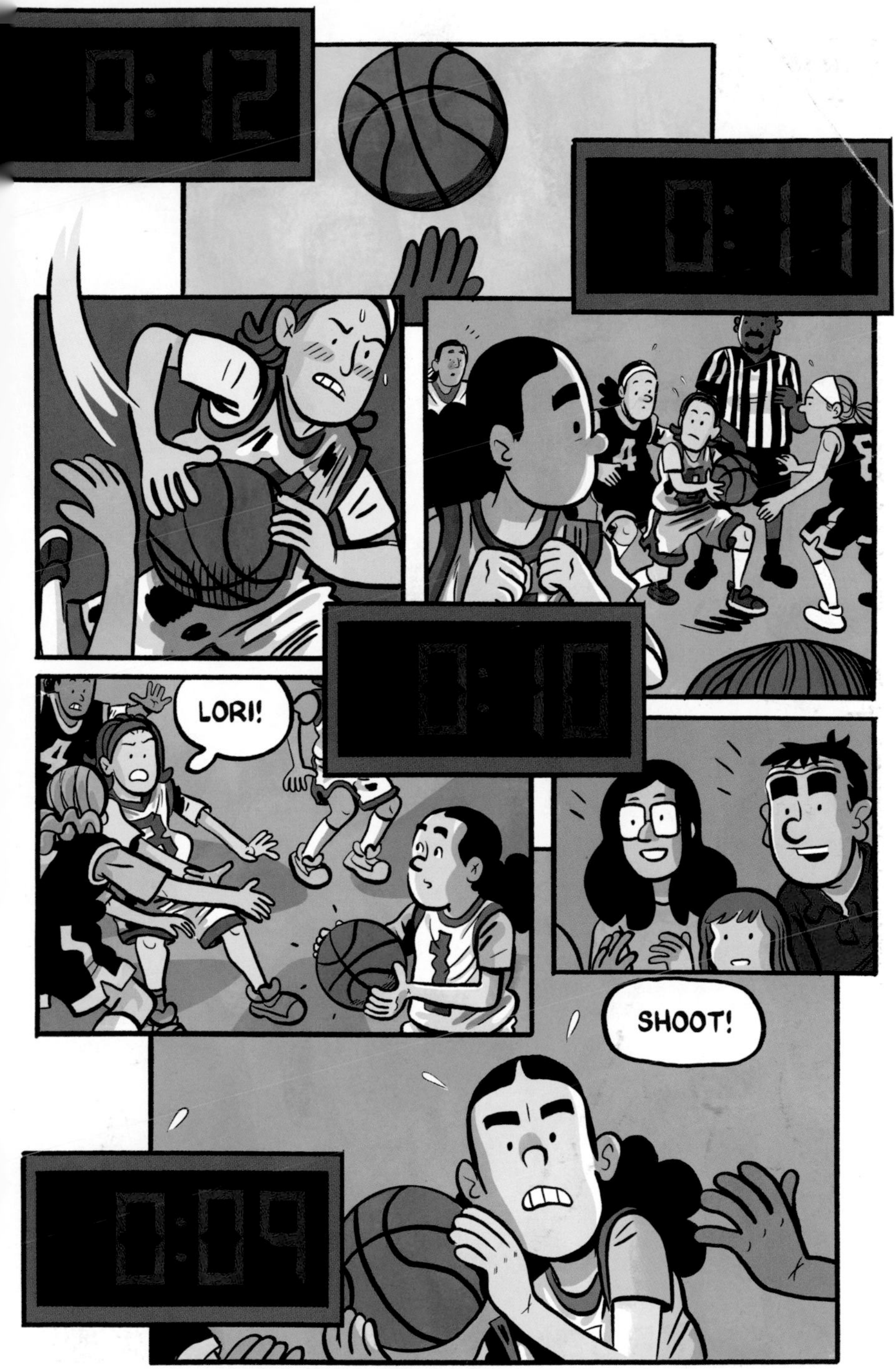
0:12
0:11
0:10
LORI!
SHOOT!
0:09

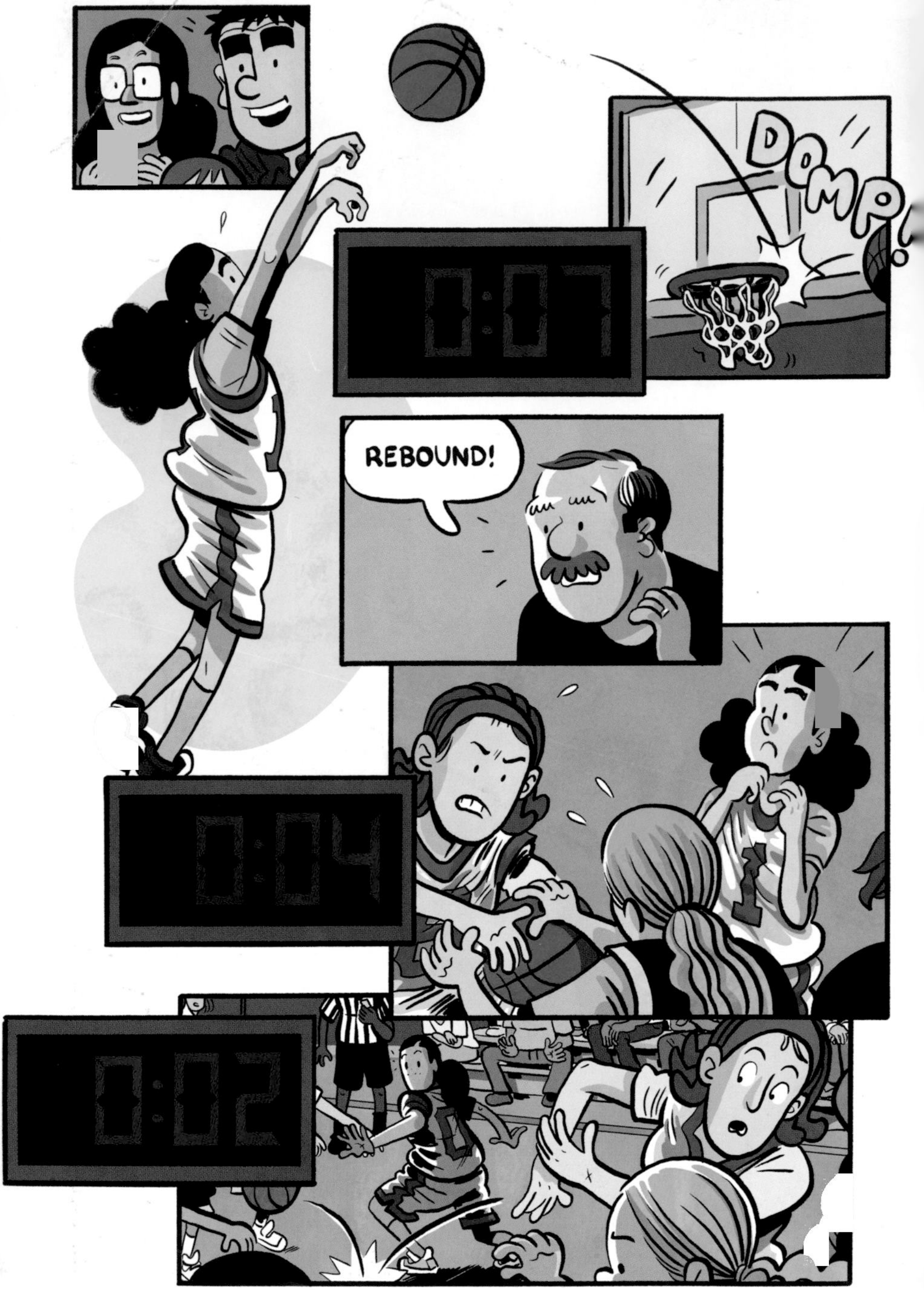
DOMP!
0:07
REBOUND!
0:04
0:02

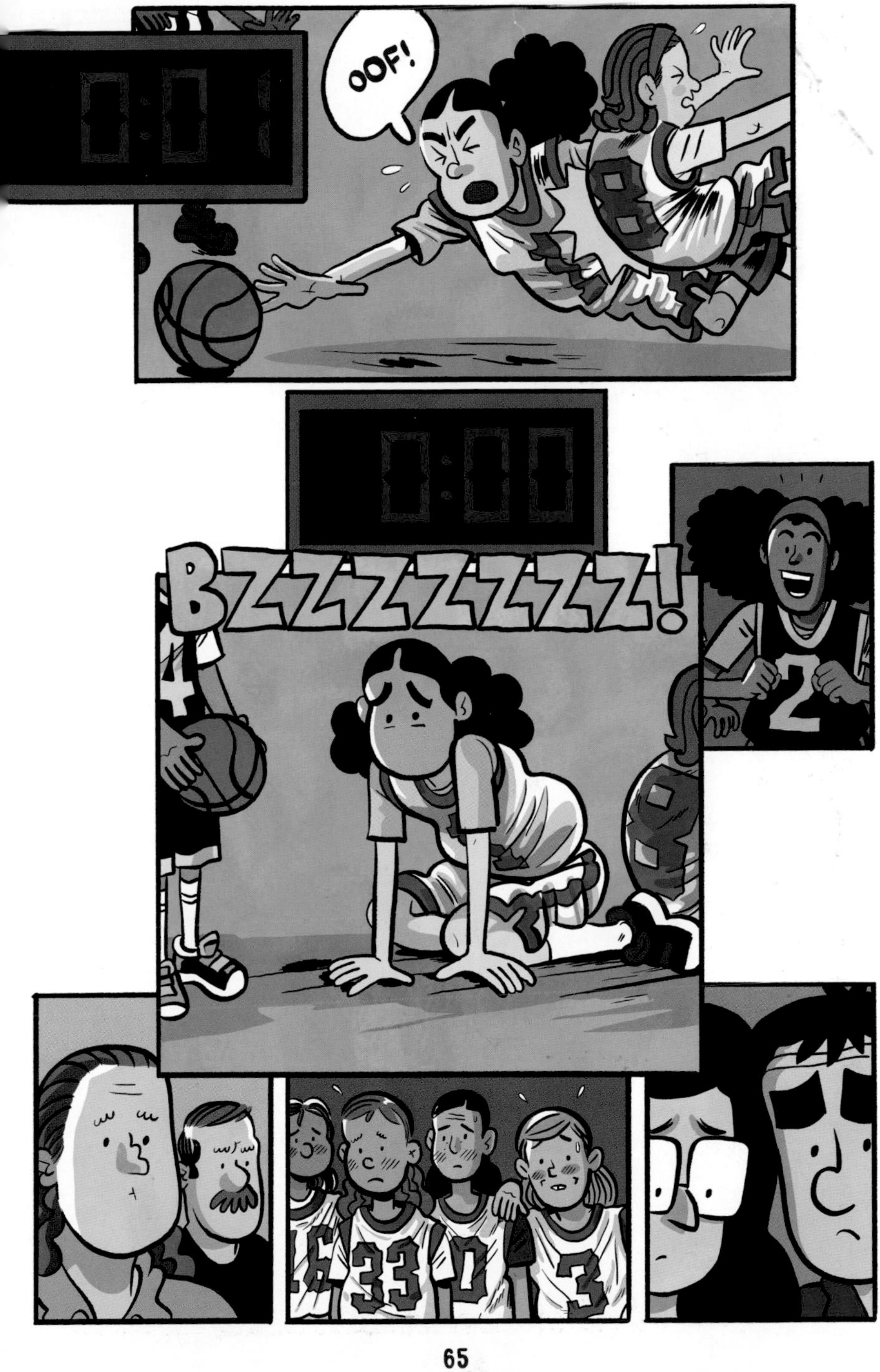
0:01
OOF!
0:00
BZZZZZZZ!

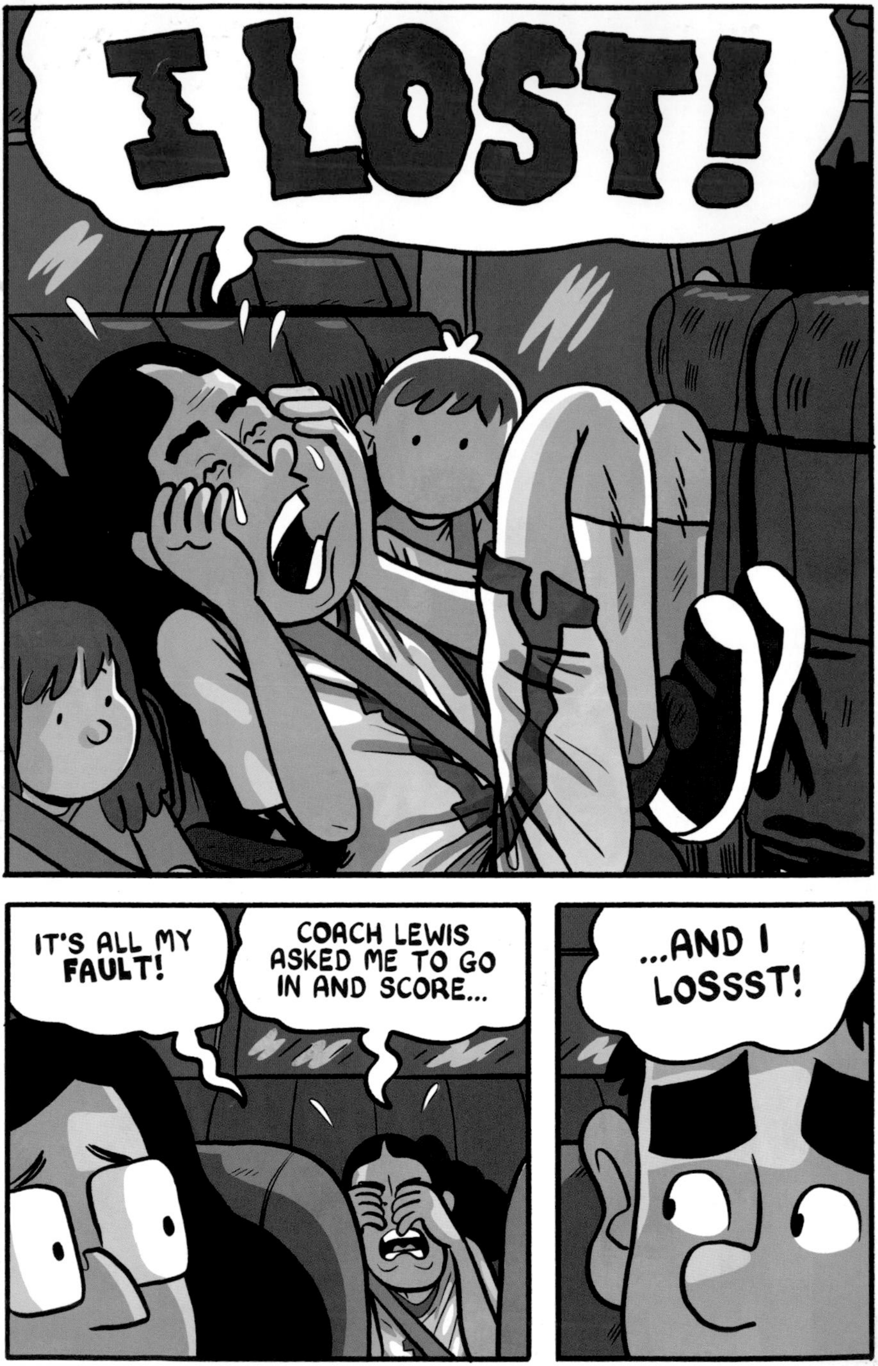
I LOST!
IT'S ALL MY FAULT!
COACH LEWIS ASKED ME TO GO IN AND SCORE...
...AND I LOSSST!

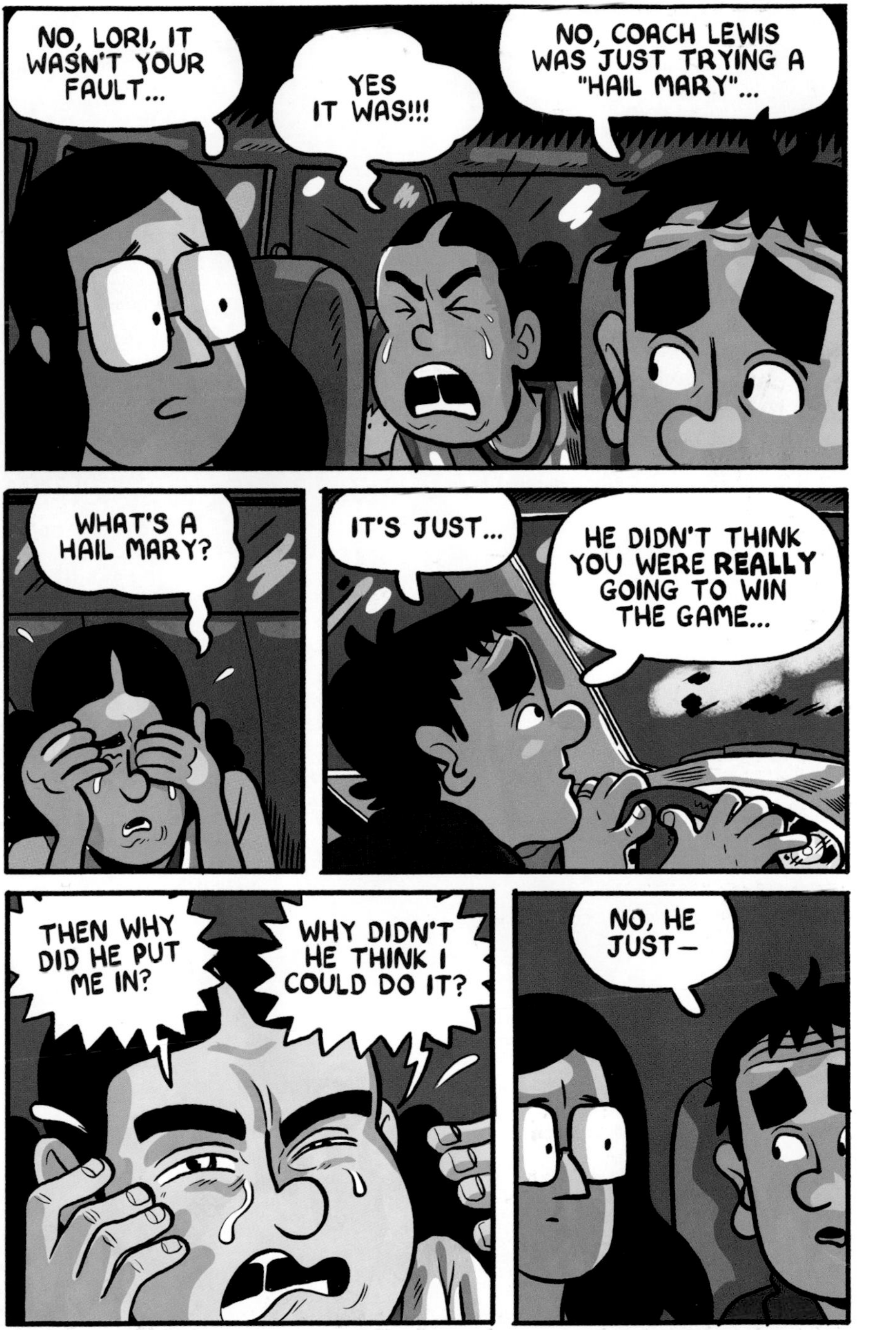
NO, LORI, IT WASN'T YOUR FAULT...
YES IT WAS!!!
NO, COACH LEWIS WAS JUST TRYING A "HAIL MARY"...
WHAT'S A HAIL MARY?
IT'S JUST...
HE DIDN'T THINK YOU WERE REALLY GOING TO WIN THE GAME...
THEN WHY DID HE PUT ME IN?
WHY DIDN'T HE THINK I COULD DO IT?
NO, HE JUST—

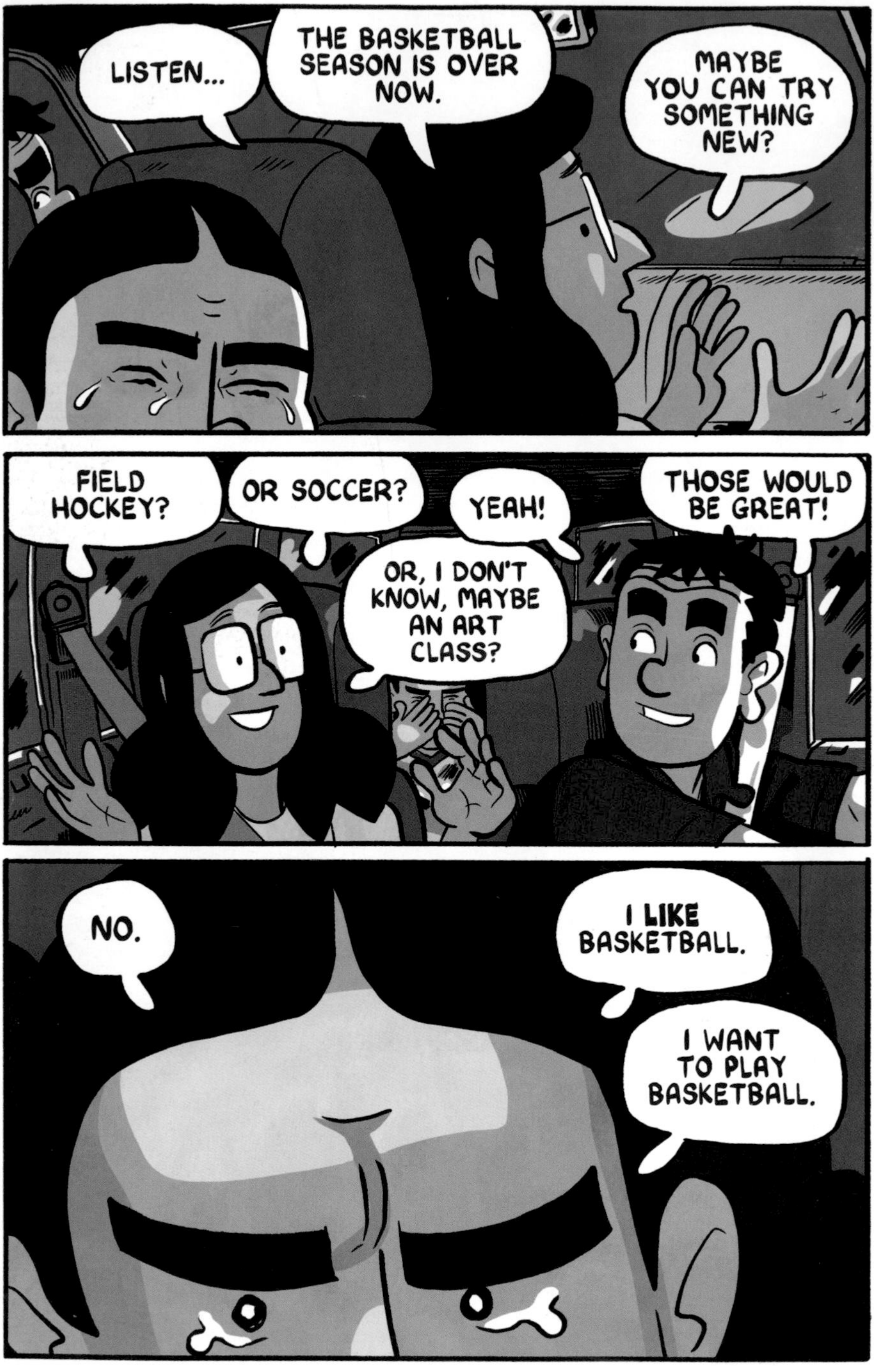
LISTEN...
THE BASKETBALL SEASON IS OVER NOW.
MAYBE YOU CAN TRY SOMETHING NEW?
FIELD HOCKEY?
OR SOCCER?
YEAH!
OR, I DON'T KNOW, MAYBE AN ART CLASS?
THOSE WOULD BE GREAT!
NO.
I LIKE BASKETBALL.
I WANT TO PLAY BASKETBALL.

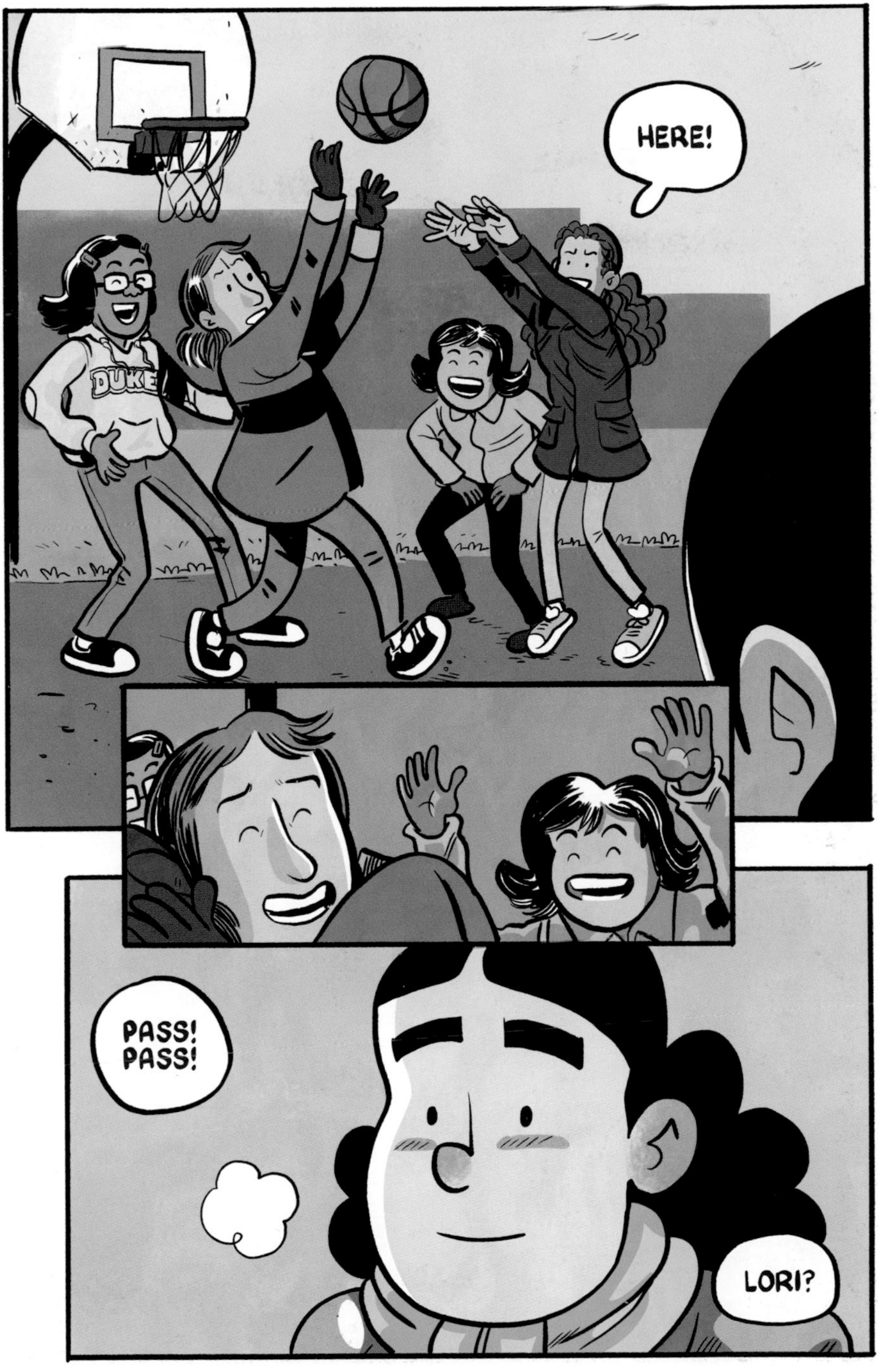
DUKE
HERE!
PASS! PASS!
LORI?

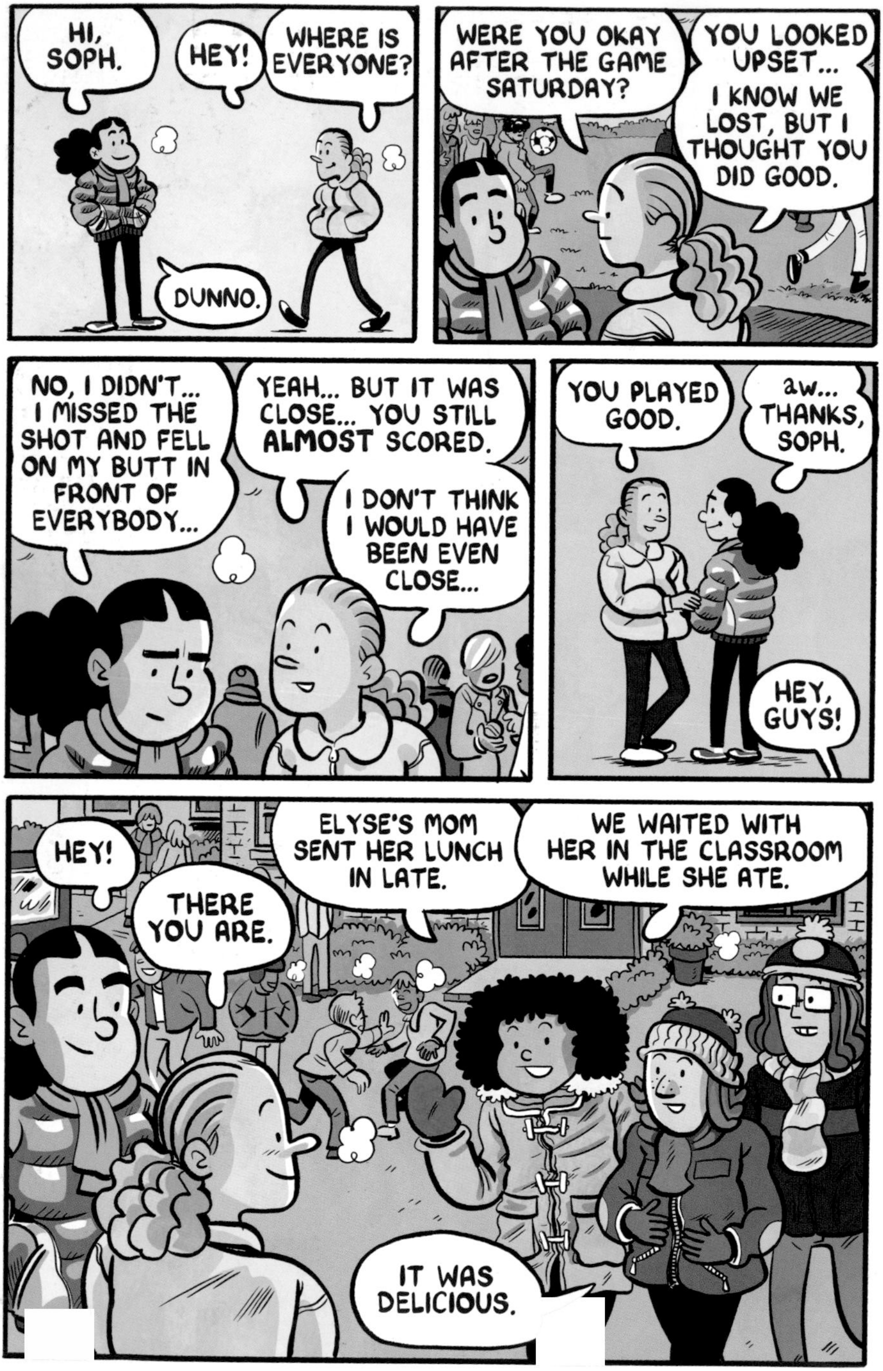
HI, SOPH.
HEY!
WHERE IS EVERYONE?
DUNNO.
WERE YOU OKAY AFTER THE GAME SATURDAY?
YOU LOOKED UPSET...
I KNOW WE LOST, BUT I THOUGHT YOU DID GOOD.
NO, I DIDN'T... I MISSED THE SHOT AND FELL ON MY BUTT IN FRONT OF EVERYBODY...
YEAH... BUT IT WAS CLOSE... YOU STILL ALMOST SCORED.
I DON'T THINK I WOULD HAVE BEEN EVEN CLOSE...
YOU PLAYED GOOD.
aw... THANKS, SOPH.
HEY, GUYS!
HEY!
THERE YOU ARE.
ELYSE'S MOM SENT HER LUNCH IN LATE.
WE WAITED WITH HER IN THE CLASSROOM WHILE SHE ATE.
IT WAS DELICIOUS.

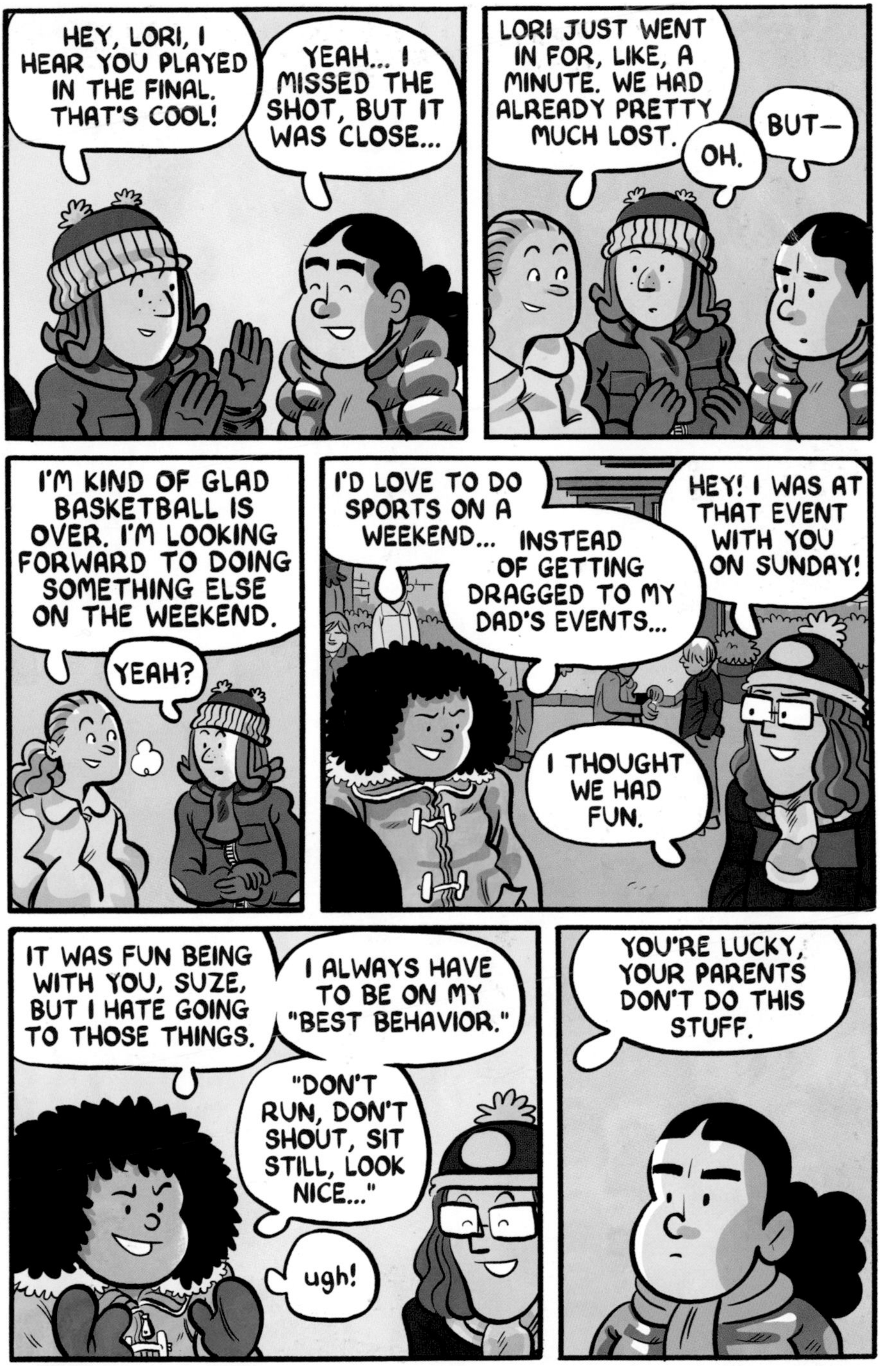
HEY, LORI, I HEAR YOU PLAYED IN THE FINAL. THAT'S COOL!
YEAH... I MISSED THE SHOT, BUT IT WAS CLOSE...
LORI JUST WENT IN FOR, LIKE, A MINUTE. WE HAD ALREADY PRETTY MUCH LOST.
OH.
BUT—
I'M KIND OF GLAD BASKETBALL IS OVER. I'M LOOKING FORWARD TO DOING SOMETHING ELSE ON THE WEEKEND.
YEAH?
I'D LOVE TO DO SPORTS ON A WEEKEND...
INSTEAD OF GETTING DRAGGED TO MY DAD'S EVENTS...
HEY! I WAS AT THAT EVENT WITH YOU ON SUNDAY!
I THOUGHT WE HAD FUN.
IT WAS FUN BEING WITH YOU, SUZE, BUT I HATE GOING TO THOSE THINGS.
I ALWAYS HAVE TO BE ON MY "BEST BEHAVIOR."
"DON'T RUN, DON'T SHOUT, SIT STILL, LOOK NICE..."
ugh!
YOU'RE LUCKY, YOUR PARENTS DON'T DO THIS STUFF.

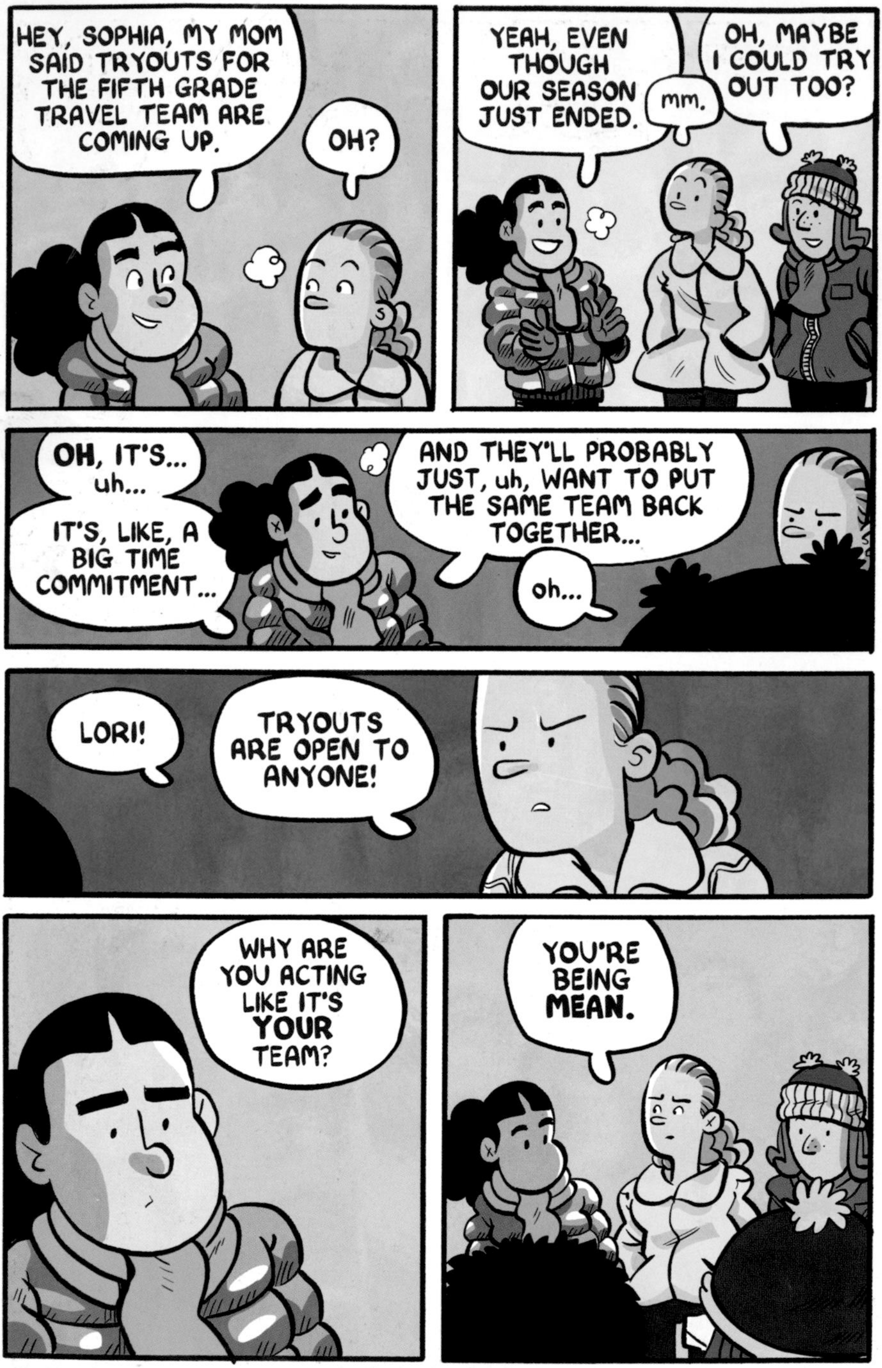

HEY, SOPHIA, MY MOM SAID TRYOUTS FOR THE FIFTH GRADE TRAVEL TEAM ARE COMING UP.
OH?
YEAH, EVEN THOUGH OUR SEASON JUST ENDED.
mm.
OH, MAYBE I COULD TRY OUT TOO?
OH, IT'S... uh...
IT'S, LIKE, A BIG TIME COMMITMENT...
AND THEY'LL PROBABLY JUST, uh, WANT TO PUT THE SAME TEAM BACK TOGETHER...
oh...
LORI!
TRYOUTS ARE OPEN TO ANYONE!
WHY ARE YOU ACTING LIKE IT'S **YOUR** TEAM?
YOU'RE BEING **MEAN.**

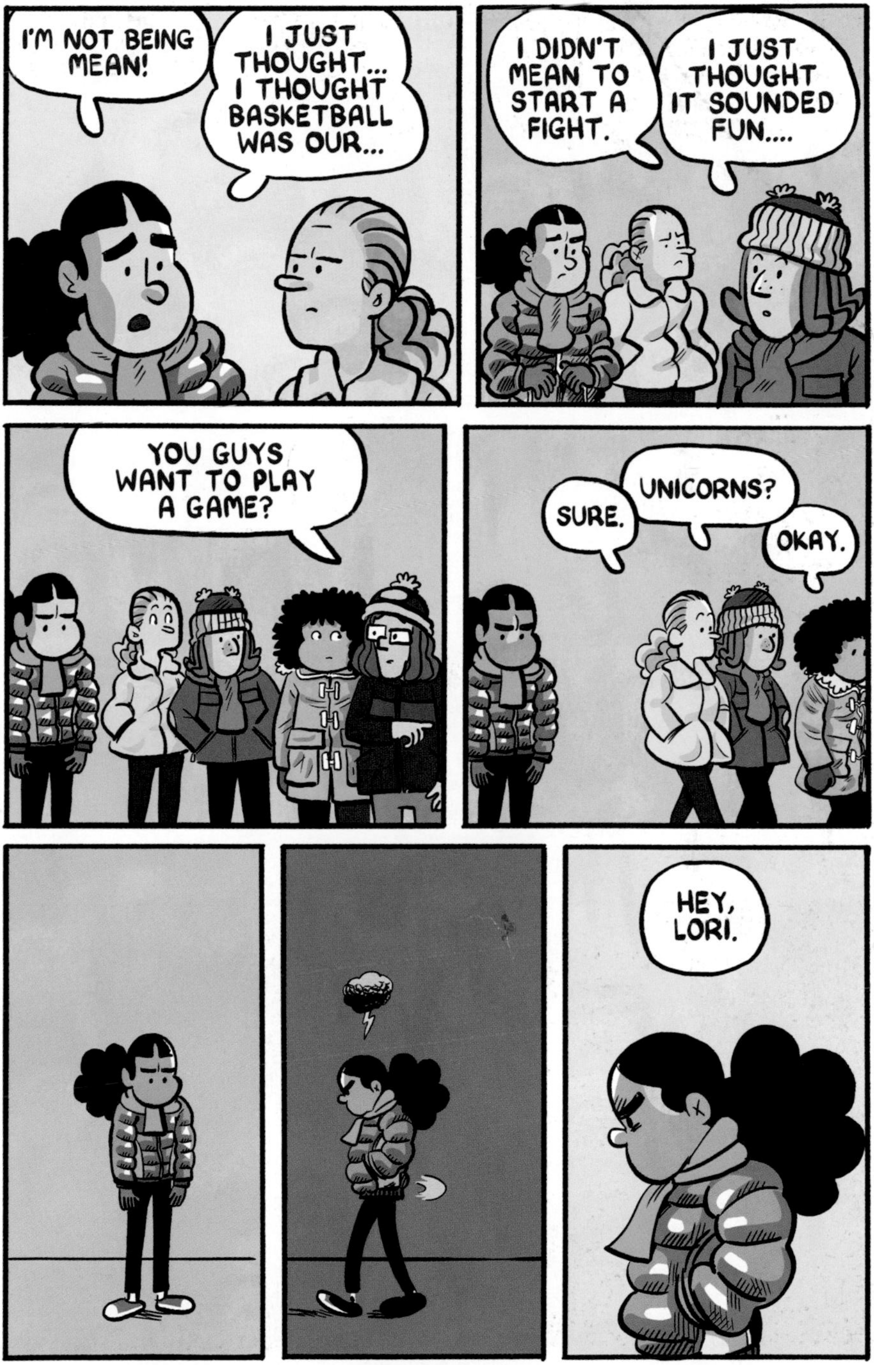
I'M NOT BEING MEAN!
I JUST THOUGHT... I THOUGHT BASKETBALL WAS OUR...
I DIDN'T MEAN TO START A FIGHT.
I JUST THOUGHT IT SOUNDED FUN....
YOU GUYS WANT TO PLAY A GAME?
SURE.
UNICORNS?
OKAY.
HEY, LORI.

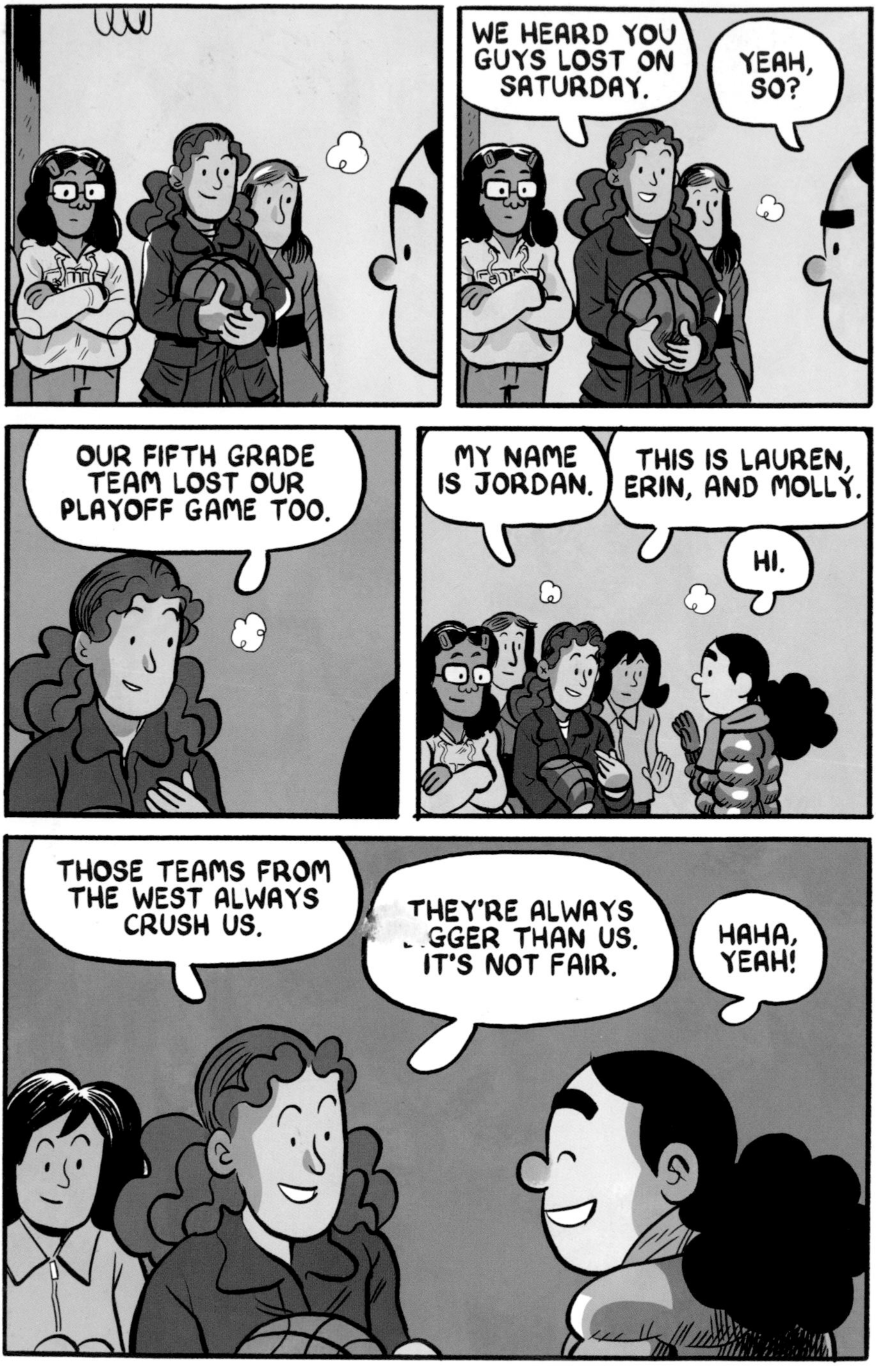
WE HEARD YOU GUYS LOST ON SATURDAY.
YEAH, SO?
OUR FIFTH GRADE TEAM LOST OUR PLAYOFF GAME TOO.
MY NAME IS JORDAN.
THIS IS LAUREN, ERIN, AND MOLLY.
HI.
THOSE TEAMS FROM THE WEST ALWAYS CRUSH US.
THEY'RE ALWAYS BIGGER THAN US. IT'S NOT FAIR.
HAHA, YEAH!

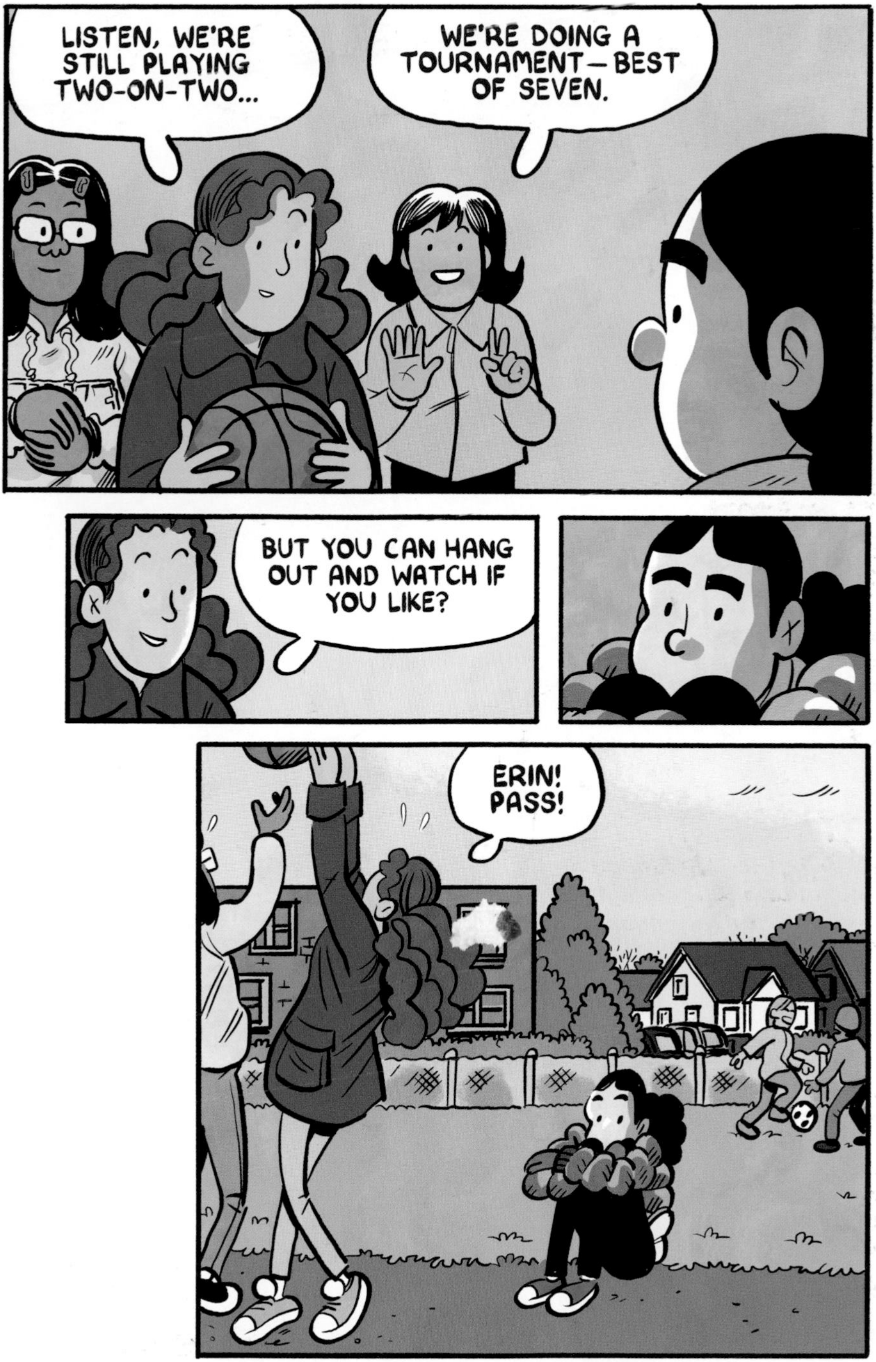
LISTEN, WE'RE STILL PLAYING TWO-ON-TWO...
WE'RE DOING A TOURNAMENT—BEST OF SEVEN.
BUT YOU CAN HANG OUT AND WATCH IF YOU LIKE?
ERIN! PASS!

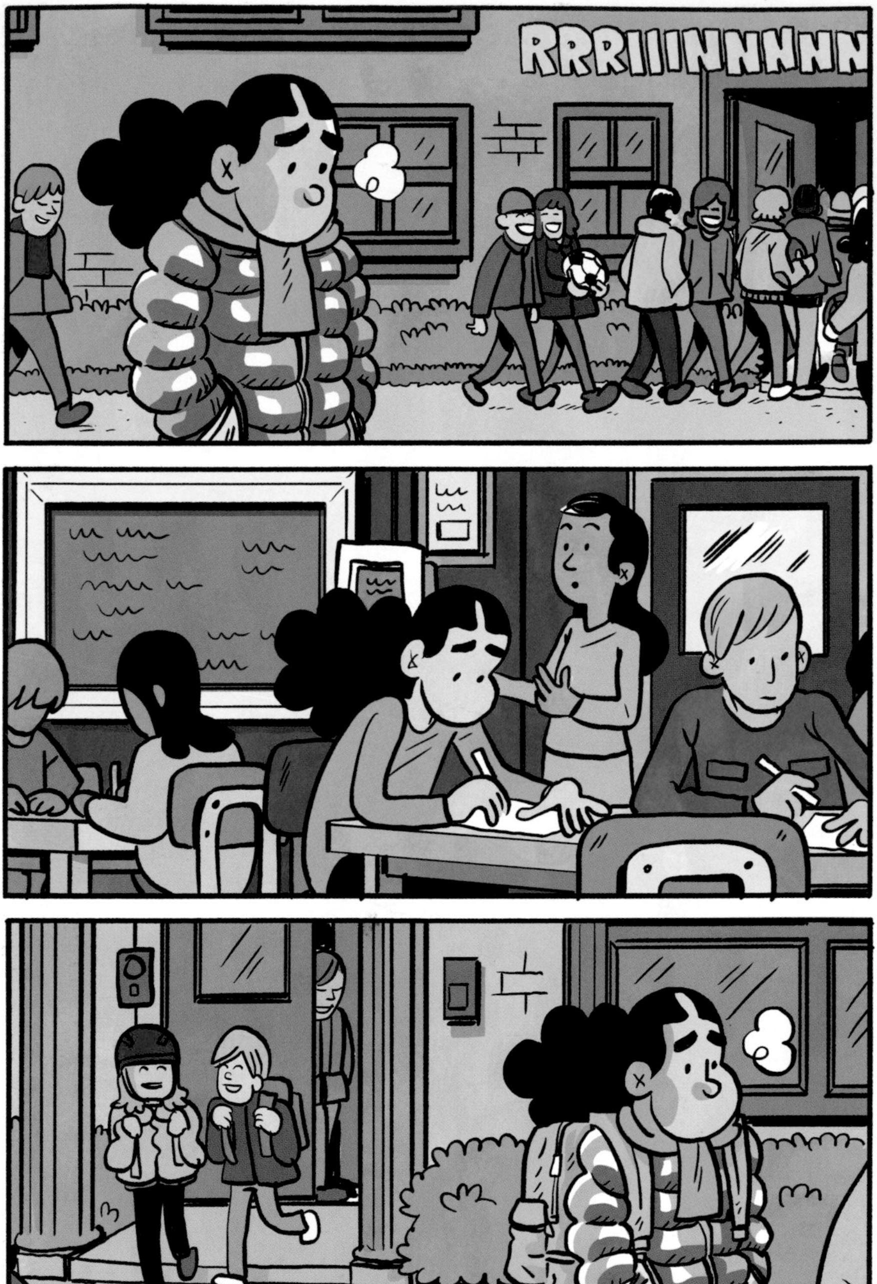
RRRIIINNNNN

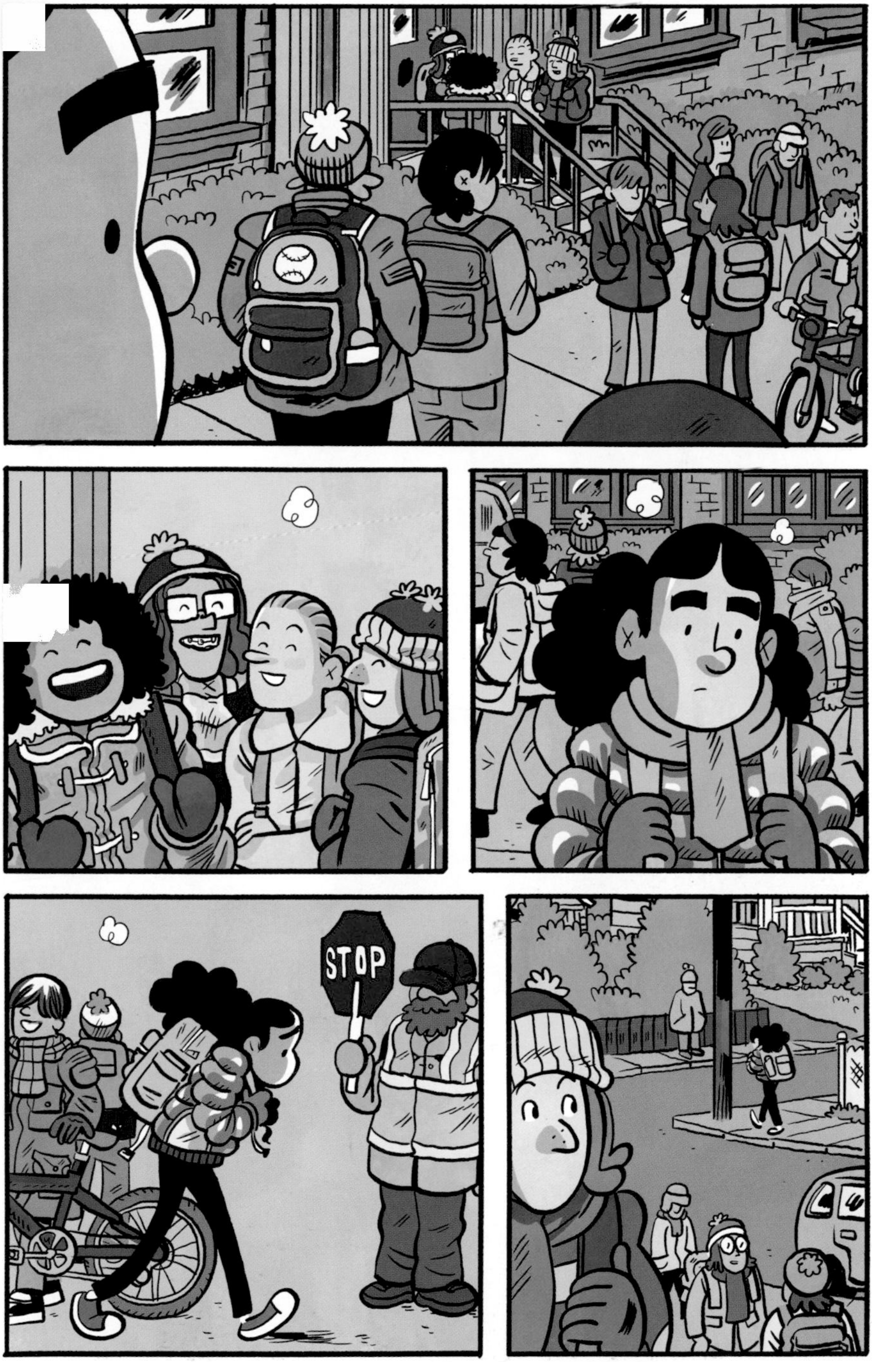
STOP

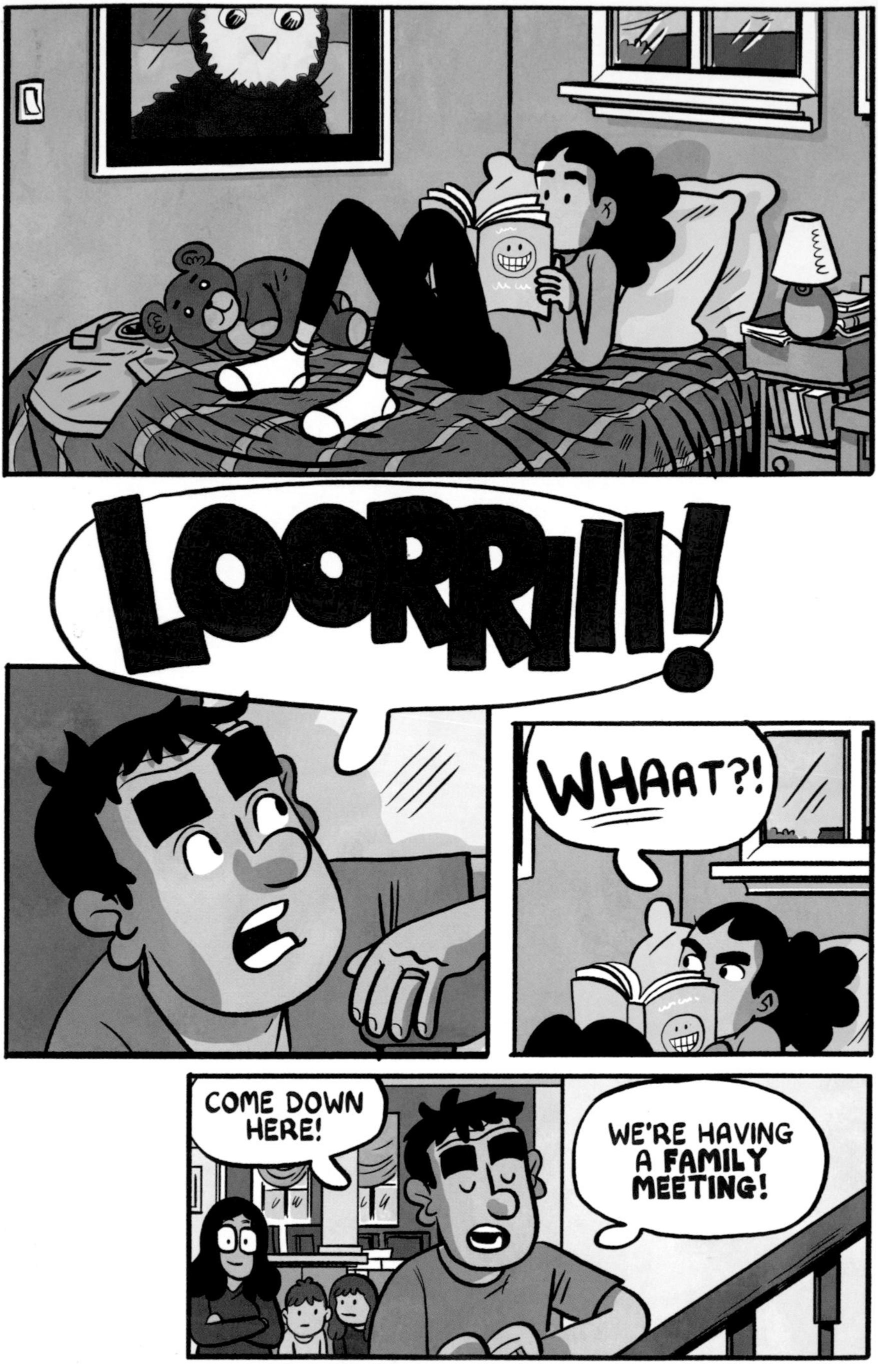
LOORRIII!
WHAAT?!
COME DOWN HERE!
WE'RE HAVING A **FAMILY MEETING**!

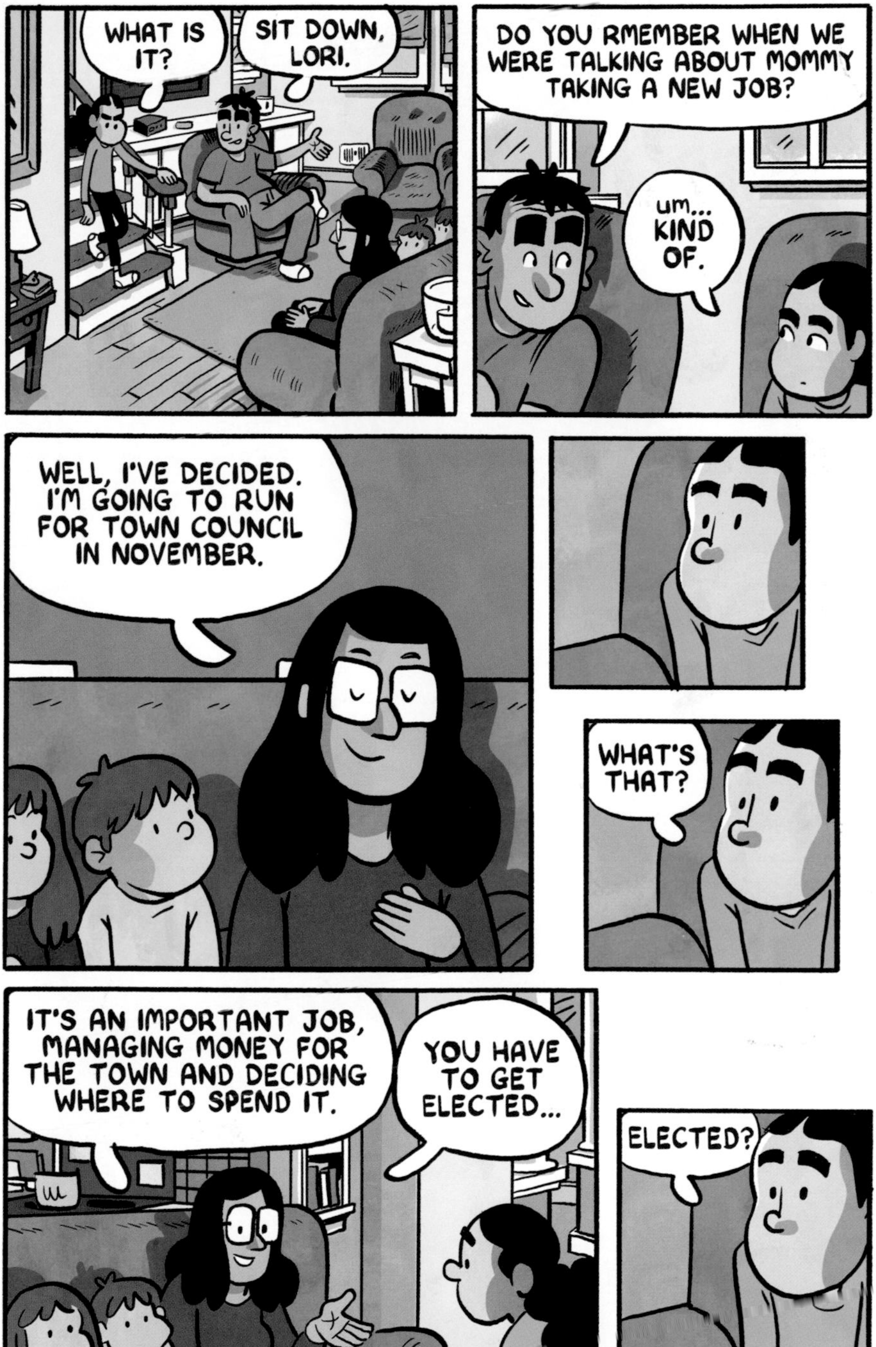
WHAT IS IT?
SIT DOWN, LORI.
DO YOU RMEMBER WHEN WE WERE TALKING ABOUT MOMMY TAKING A NEW JOB?
um... KIND OF.
WELL, I'VE DECIDED. I'M GOING TO RUN FOR TOWN COUNCIL IN NOVEMBER.
WHAT'S THAT?
IT'S AN IMPORTANT JOB, MANAGING MONEY FOR THE TOWN AND DECIDING WHERE TO SPEND IT.
YOU HAVE TO GET ELECTED...
ELECTED?

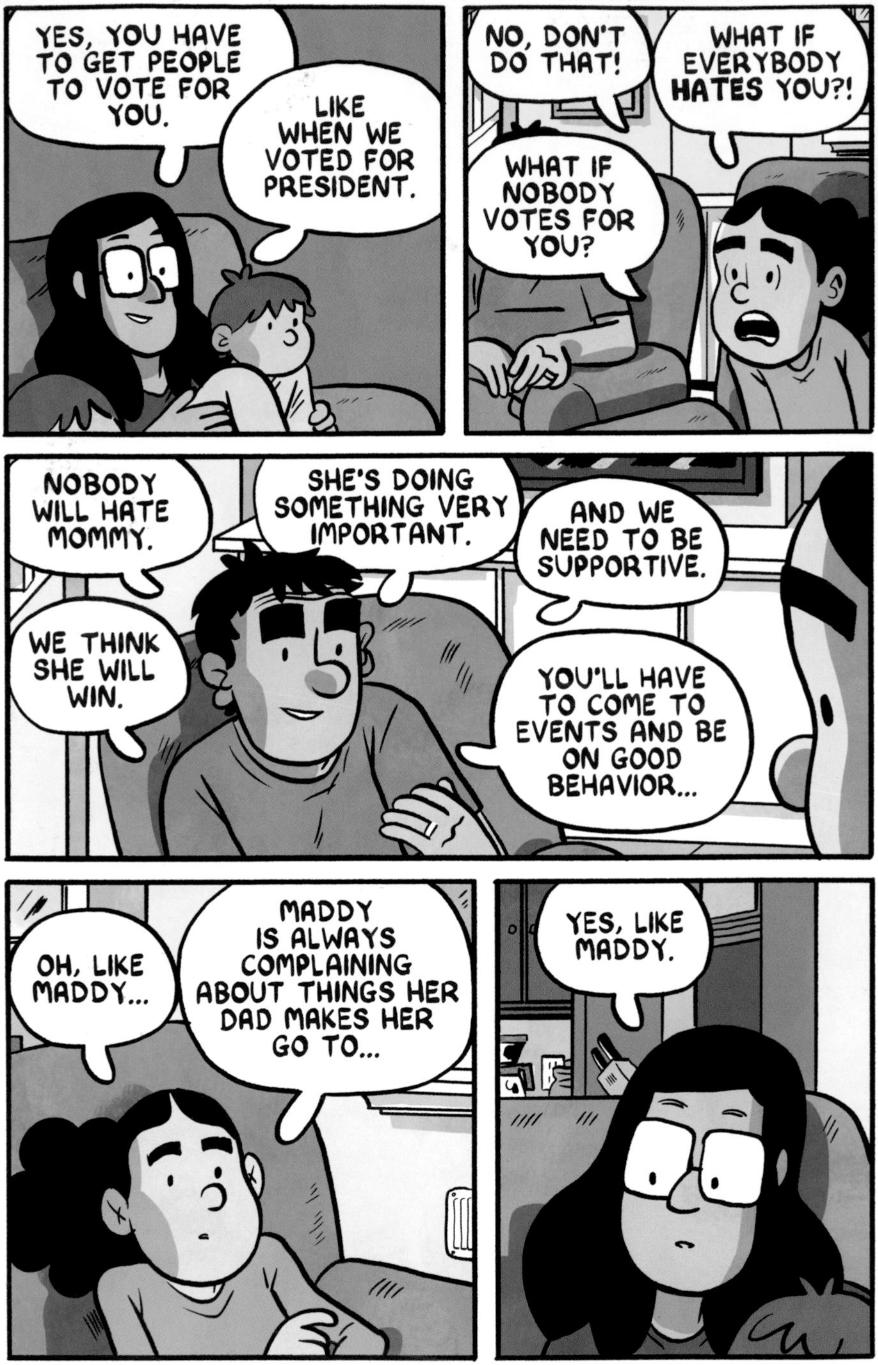
YES, YOU HAVE TO GET PEOPLE TO VOTE FOR YOU.
LIKE WHEN WE VOTED FOR PRESIDENT.
NO, DON'T DO THAT!
WHAT IF EVERYBODY **HATES** YOU?!
WHAT IF NOBODY VOTES FOR YOU?
NOBODY WILL HATE MOMMY.
SHE'S DOING SOMETHING VERY IMPORTANT.
AND WE NEED TO BE SUPPORTIVE.
WE THINK SHE WILL WIN.
YOU'LL HAVE TO COME TO EVENTS AND BE ON GOOD BEHAVIOR...
OH, LIKE MADDY...
MADDY IS ALWAYS COMPLAINING ABOUT THINGS HER DAD MAKES HER GO TO...
YES, LIKE MADDY.

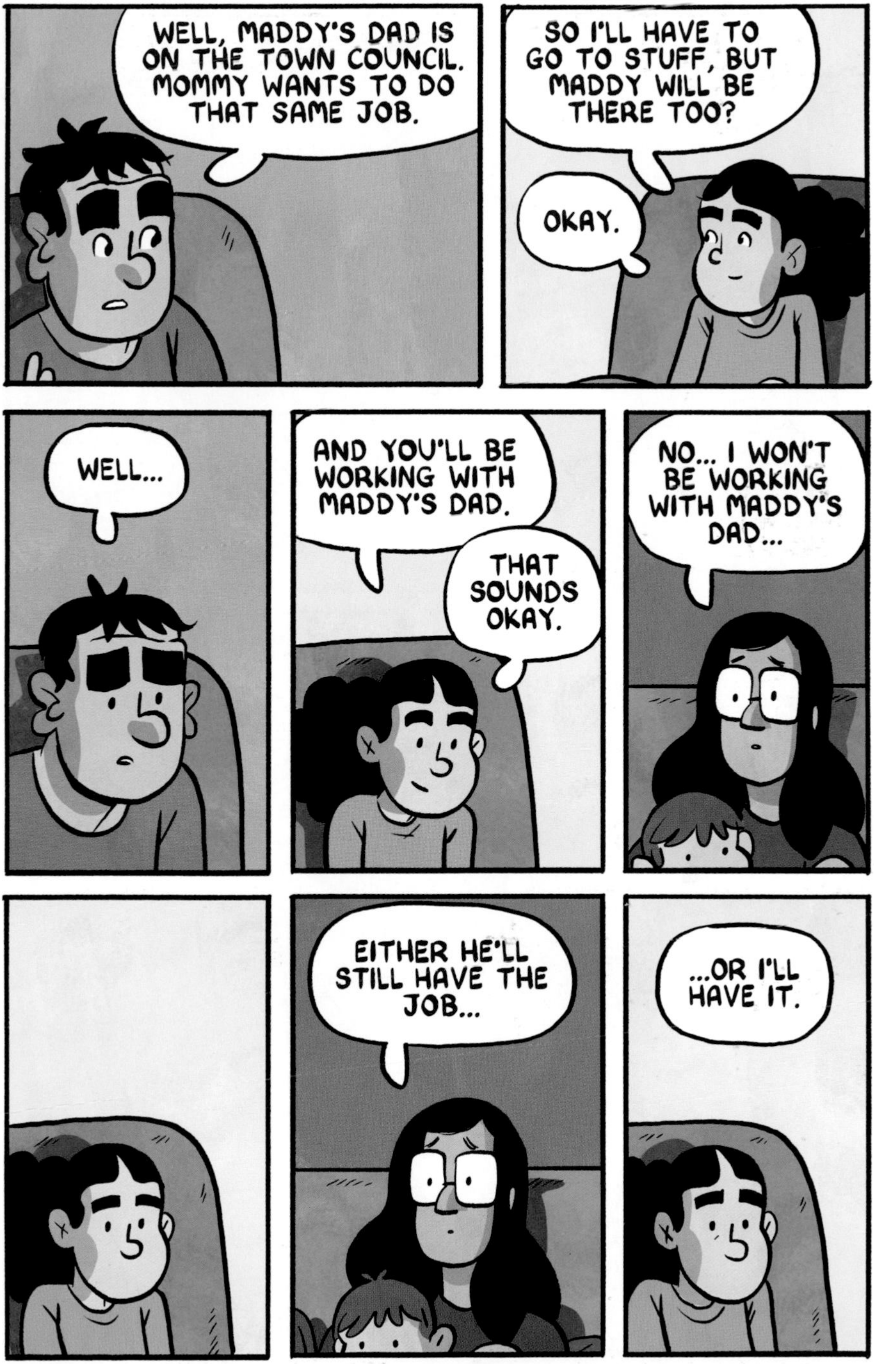
WELL, MADDY'S DAD IS ON THE TOWN COUNCIL. MOMMY WANTS TO DO THAT SAME JOB.
SO I'LL HAVE TO GO TO STUFF, BUT MADDY WILL BE THERE TOO?
OKAY.
WELL...
AND YOU'LL BE WORKING WITH MADDY'S DAD.
THAT SOUNDS OKAY.
NO... I WON'T BE WORKING WITH MADDY'S DAD...
EITHER HE'LL STILL HAVE THE JOB...
...OR I'LL HAVE IT.

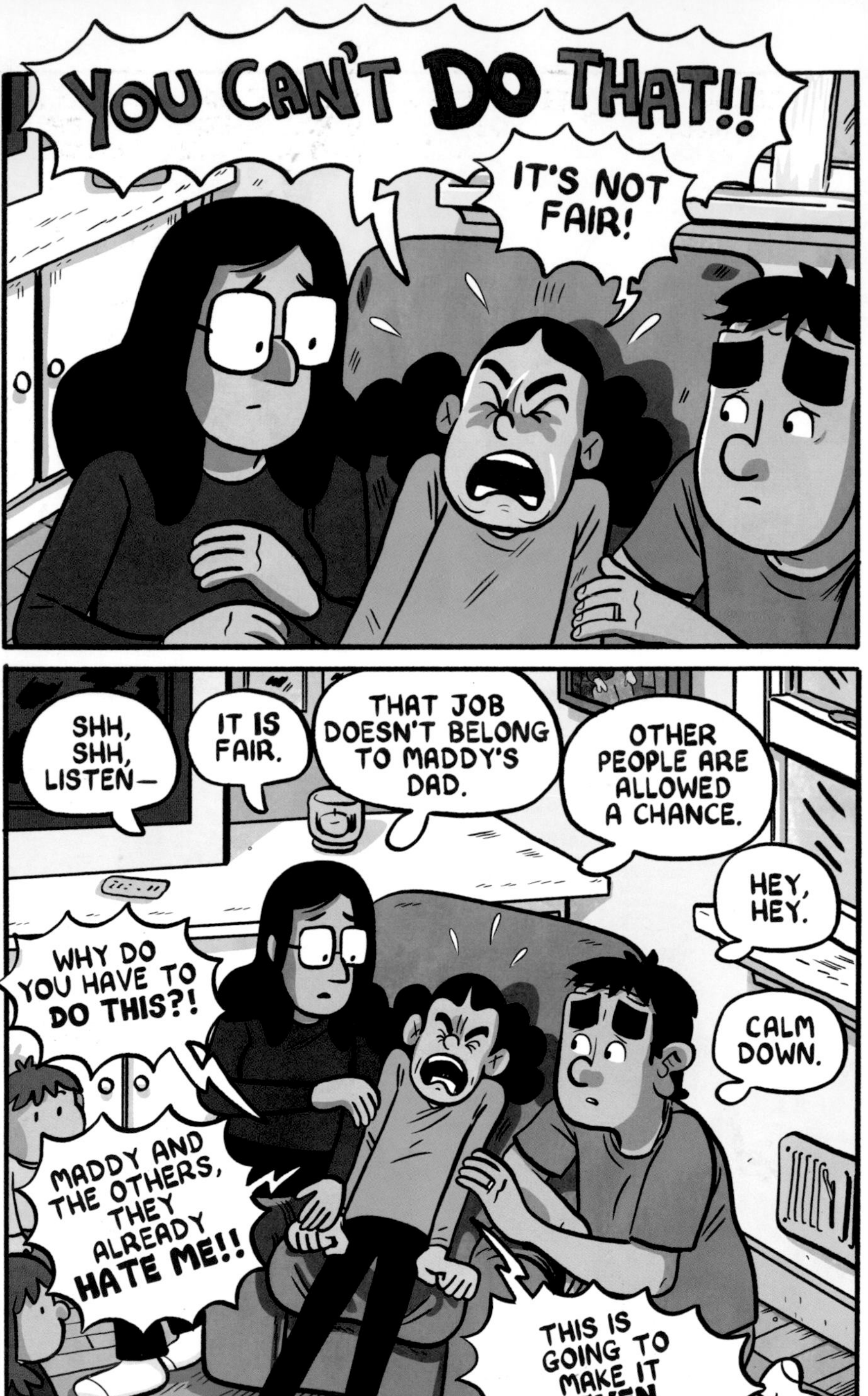
YOU CAN'T DO THAT!!
IT'S NOT FAIR!
SHH, SHH, LISTEN—
IT IS FAIR.
THAT JOB DOESN'T BELONG TO MADDY'S DAD.
OTHER PEOPLE ARE ALLOWED A CHANCE.
HEY, HEY.
WHY DO YOU HAVE TO DO THIS?!
CALM DOWN.
MADDY AND THE OTHERS, THEY ALREADY HATE ME!!
THIS IS GOING TO MAKE IT EVEN WORSE!

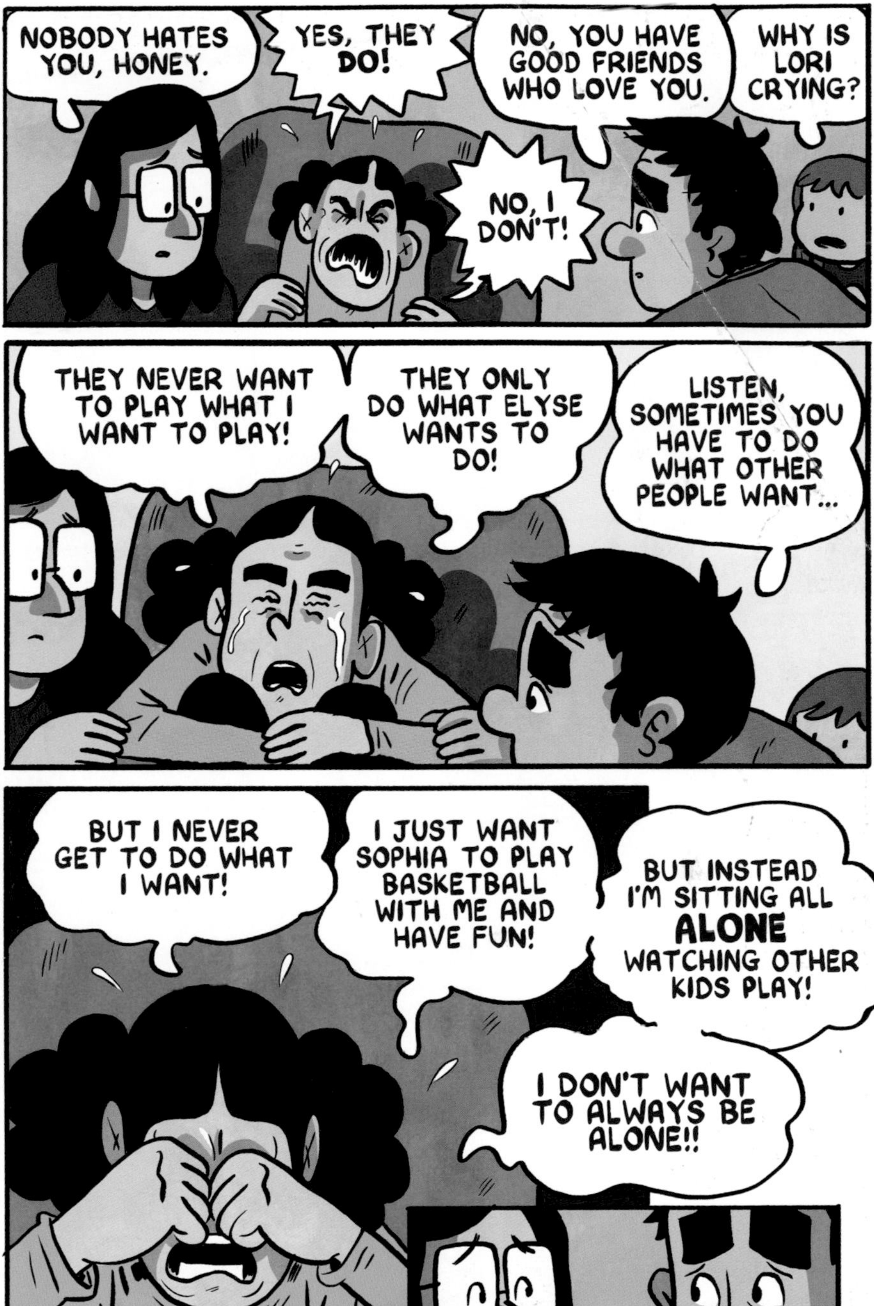
NOBODY HATES YOU, HONEY.
YES, THEY DO!
NO, YOU HAVE GOOD FRIENDS WHO LOVE YOU.
NO, I DON'T!
WHY IS LORI CRYING?
THEY NEVER WANT TO PLAY WHAT I WANT TO PLAY!
THEY ONLY DO WHAT ELYSE WANTS TO DO!
LISTEN, SOMETIMES YOU HAVE TO DO WHAT OTHER PEOPLE WANT...
BUT I NEVER GET TO DO WHAT I WANT!
I JUST WANT SOPHIA TO PLAY BASKETBALL WITH ME AND HAVE FUN!
BUT INSTEAD I'M SITTING ALL ALONE WATCHING OTHER KIDS PLAY!
I DON'T WANT TO ALWAYS BE ALONE!!

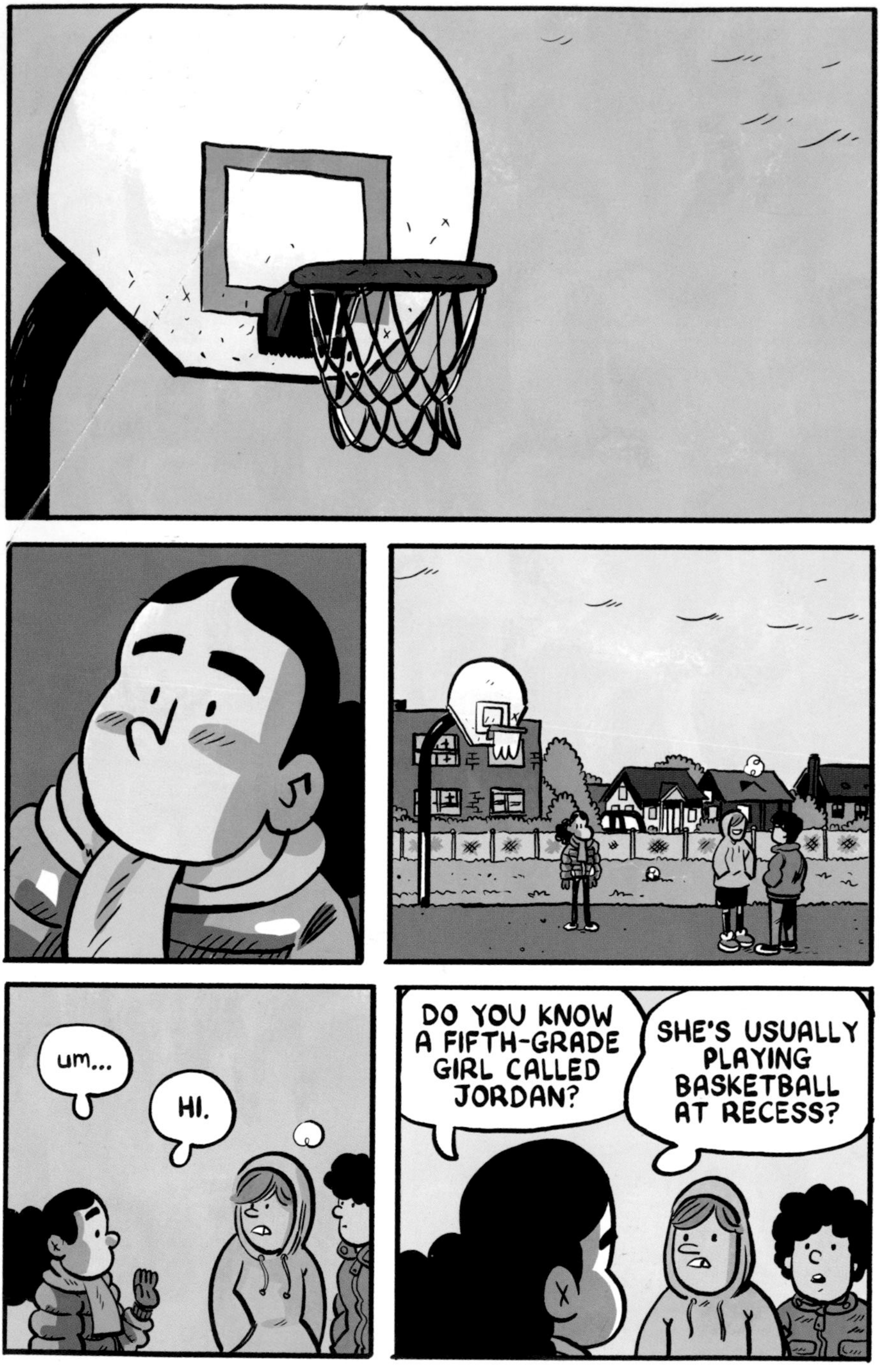
um...
HI.
DO YOU KNOW A FIFTH-GRADE GIRL CALLED JORDAN?
SHE'S USUALLY PLAYING BASKETBALL AT RECESS?

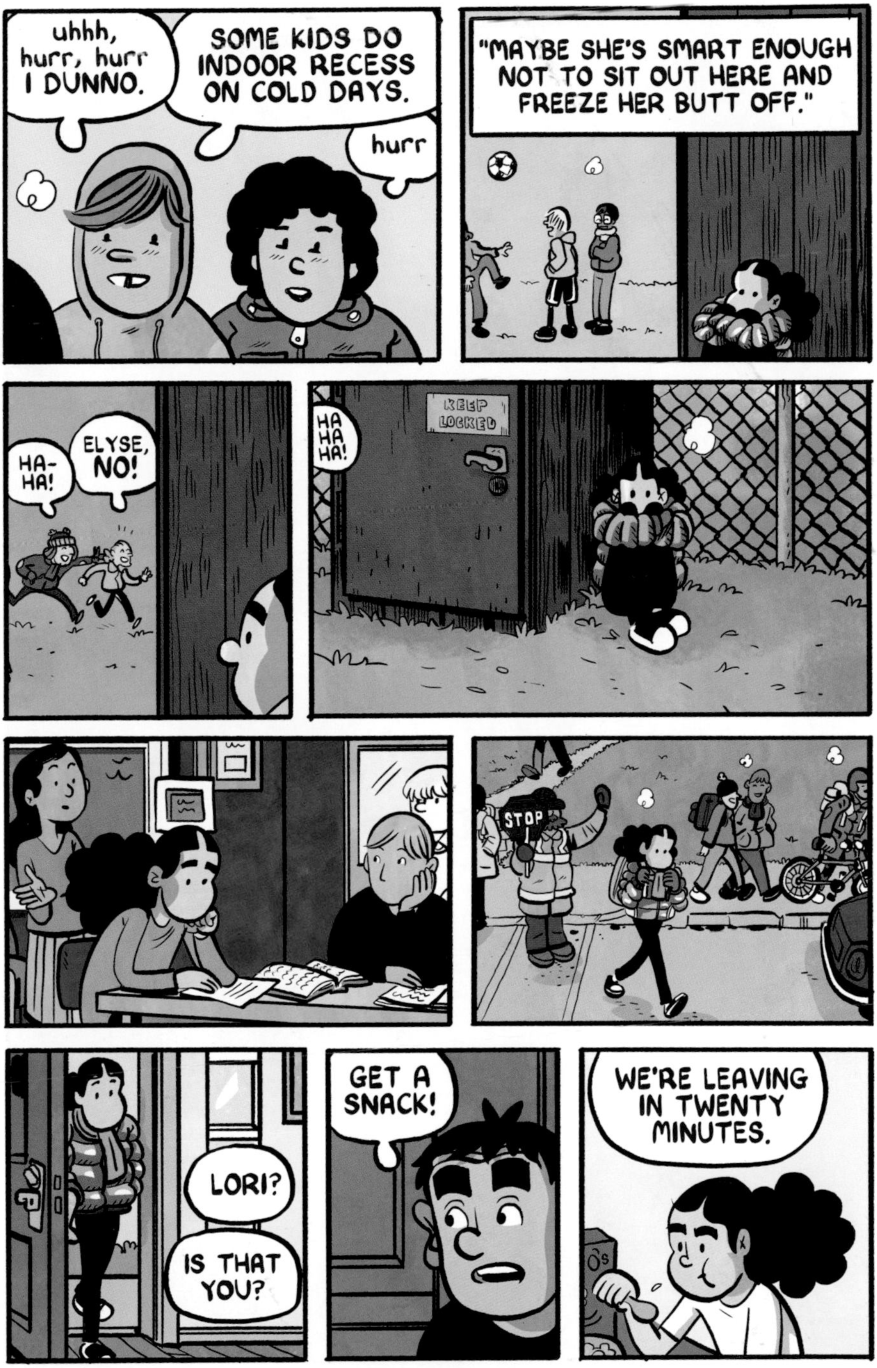
uhhh, hurr, hurr I DUNNO.
SOME KIDS DO INDOOR RECESS ON COLD DAYS.
hurr
"MAYBE SHE'S SMART ENOUGH NOT TO SIT OUT HERE AND FREEZE HER BUTT OFF."
HA-HA!
ELYSE, NO!
KEEP LOCKED
HA HA HA!
STOP
LORI?
IS THAT YOU?
GET A SNACK!
WE'RE LEAVING IN TWENTY MINUTES.

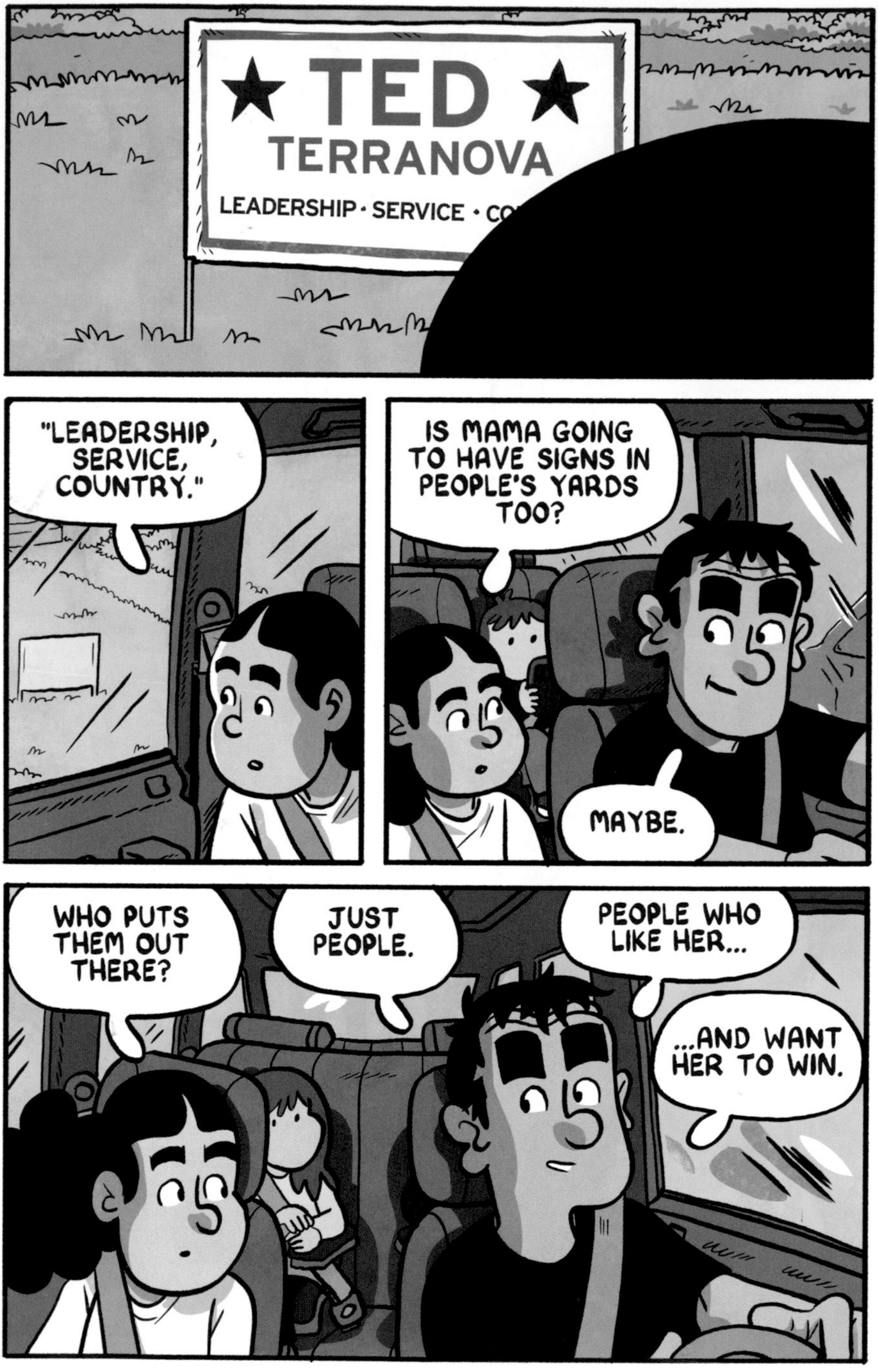
★ TED ★
TERRANOVA
LEADERSHIP · SERVICE · CO
"LEADERSHIP, SERVICE, COUNTRY."
IS MAMA GOING TO HAVE SIGNS IN PEOPLE'S YARDS TOO?
MAYBE.
WHO PUTS THEM OUT THERE?
JUST PEOPLE.
PEOPLE WHO LIKE HER...
...AND WANT HER TO WIN.

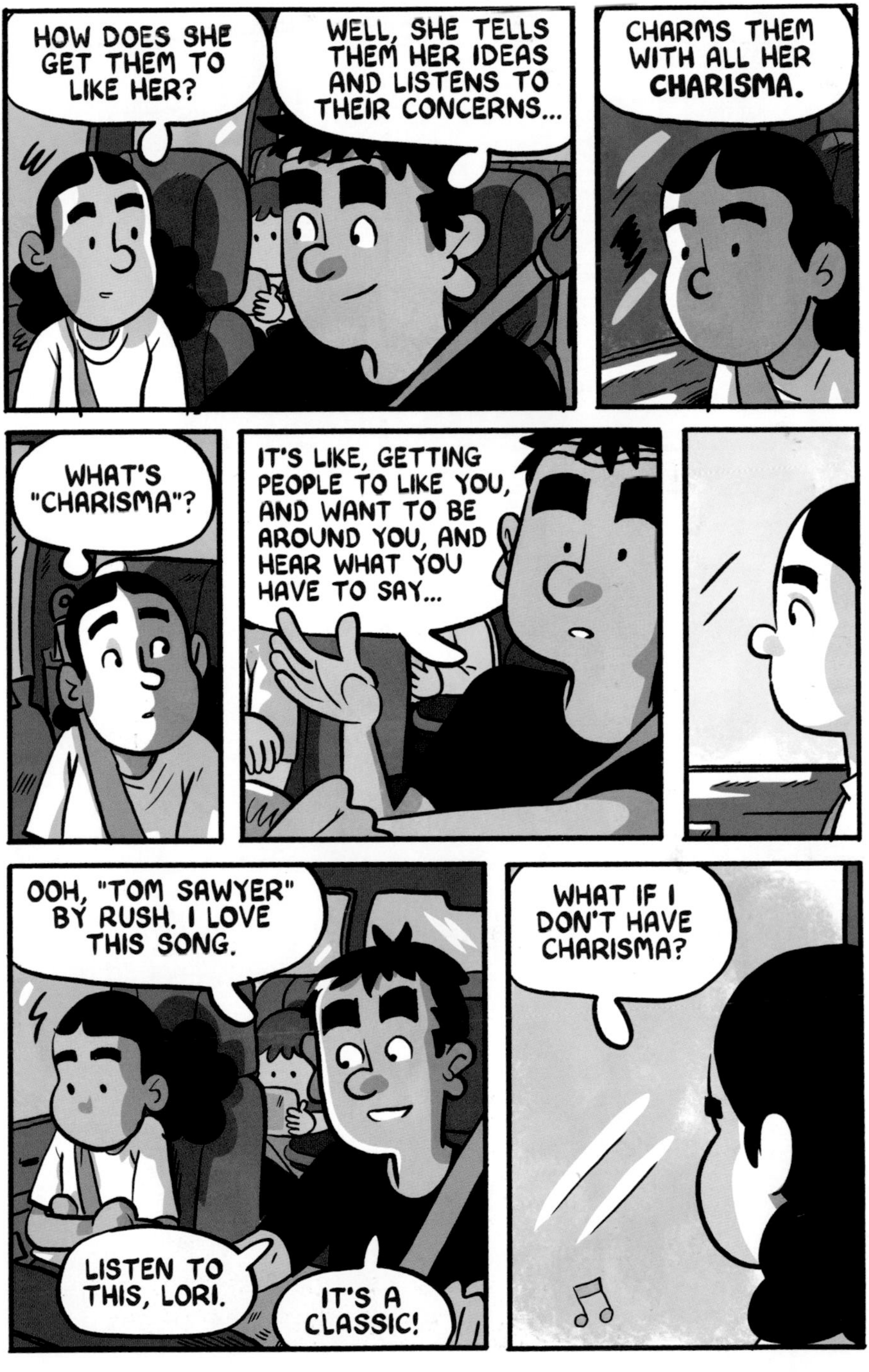
HOW DOES SHE GET THEM TO LIKE HER?
WELL, SHE TELLS THEM HER IDEAS AND LISTENS TO THEIR CONCERNS...
CHARMS THEM WITH ALL HER **CHARISMA.**
WHAT'S "CHARISMA"?
IT'S LIKE, GETTING PEOPLE TO LIKE YOU, AND WANT TO BE AROUND YOU, AND HEAR WHAT YOU HAVE TO SAY...
OOH, "TOM SAWYER" BY RUSH. I LOVE THIS SONG.
LISTEN TO THIS, LORI.
IT'S A CLASSIC!
WHAT IF I DON'T HAVE CHARISMA?

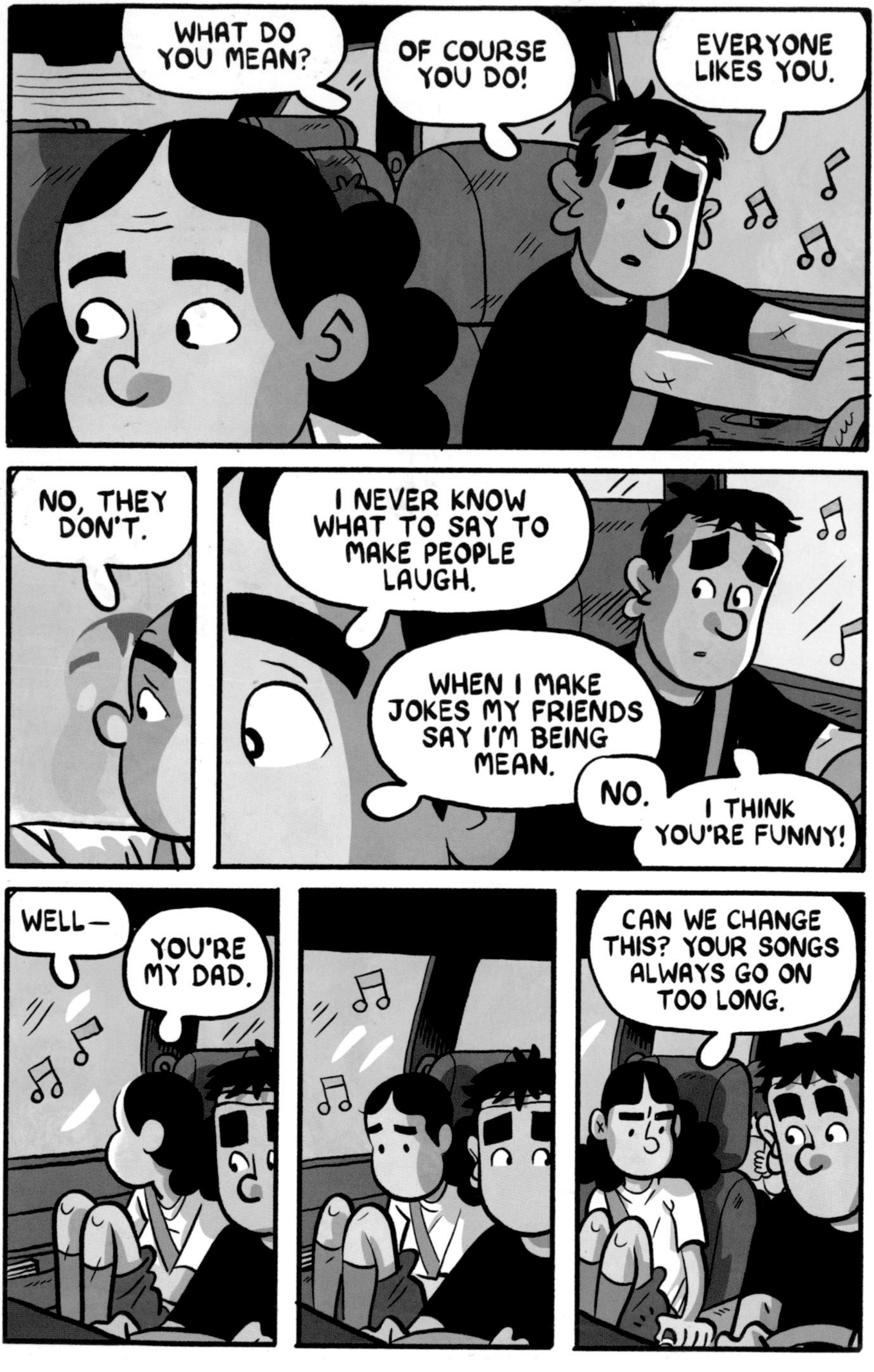
WHAT DO YOU MEAN?
OF COURSE YOU DO!
EVERYONE LIKES YOU.
NO, THEY DON'T.
I NEVER KNOW WHAT TO SAY TO MAKE PEOPLE LAUGH.
WHEN I MAKE JOKES MY FRIENDS SAY I'M BEING MEAN.
NO.
I THINK YOU'RE FUNNY!
WELL—
YOU'RE MY DAD.
CAN WE CHANGE THIS? YOUR SONGS ALWAYS GO ON TOO LONG.

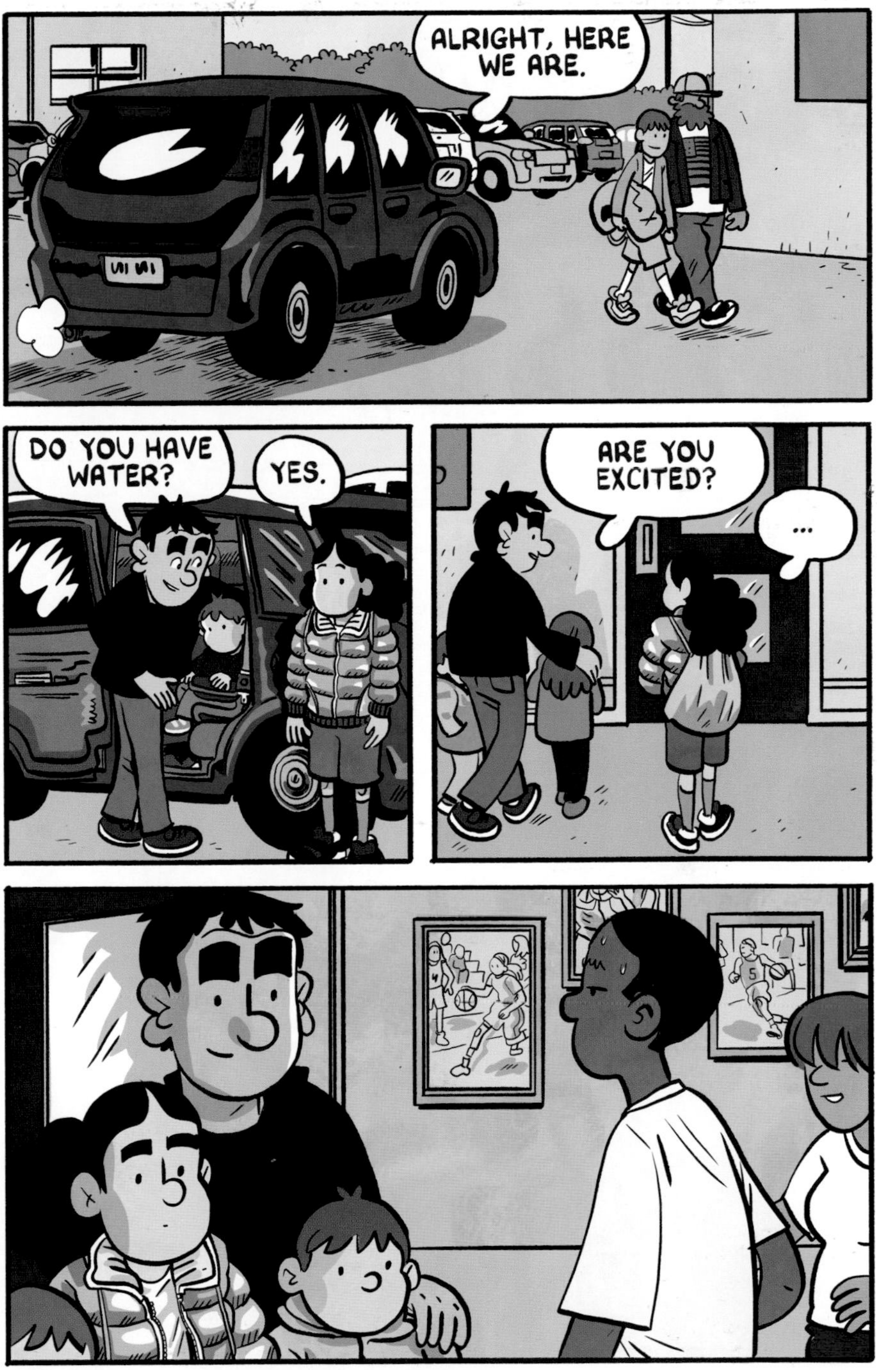
ALRIGHT, HERE WE ARE.
DO YOU HAVE WATER?
YES.
ARE YOU EXCITED?
...

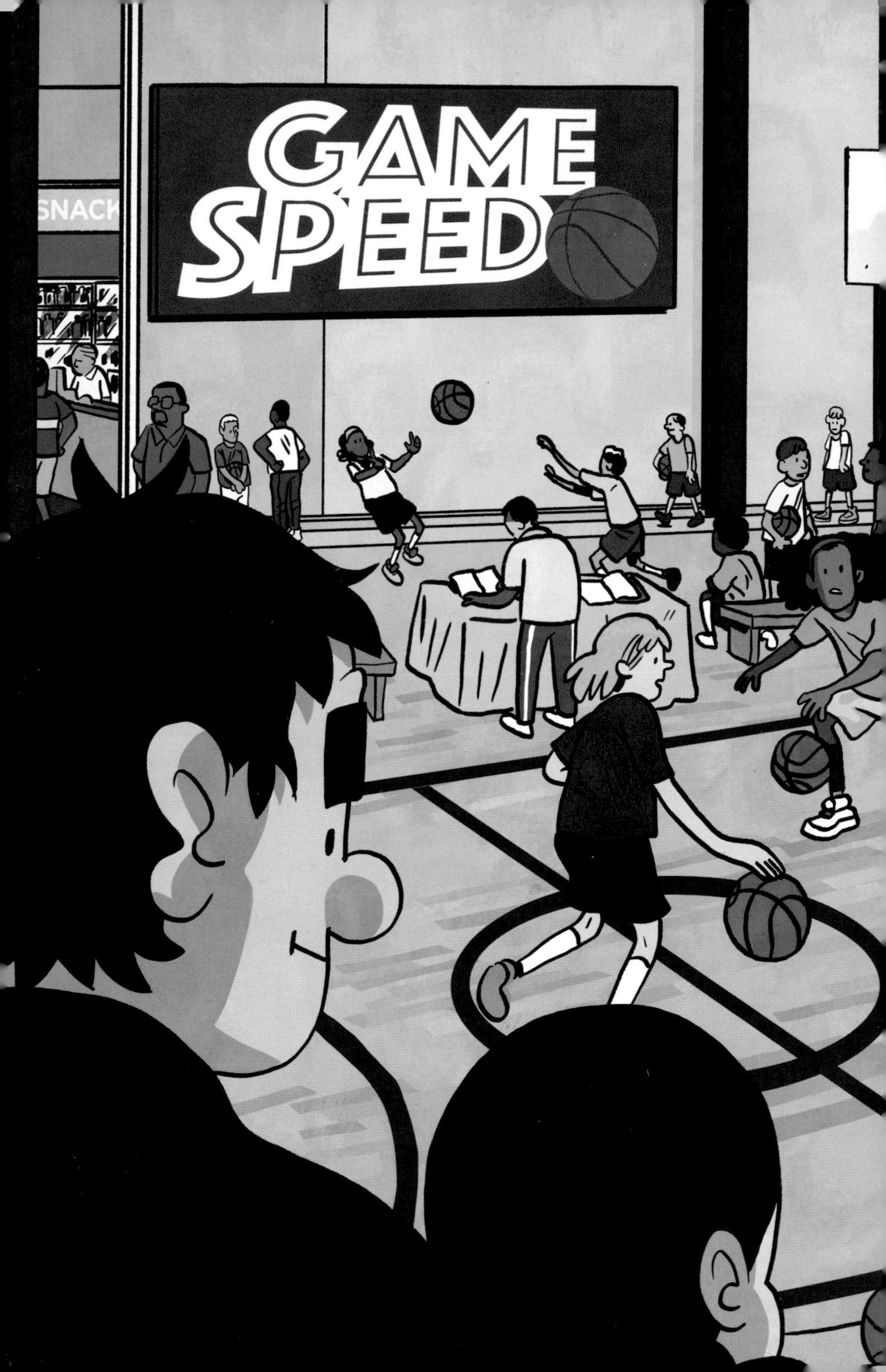
GAME SPEED
SNACK

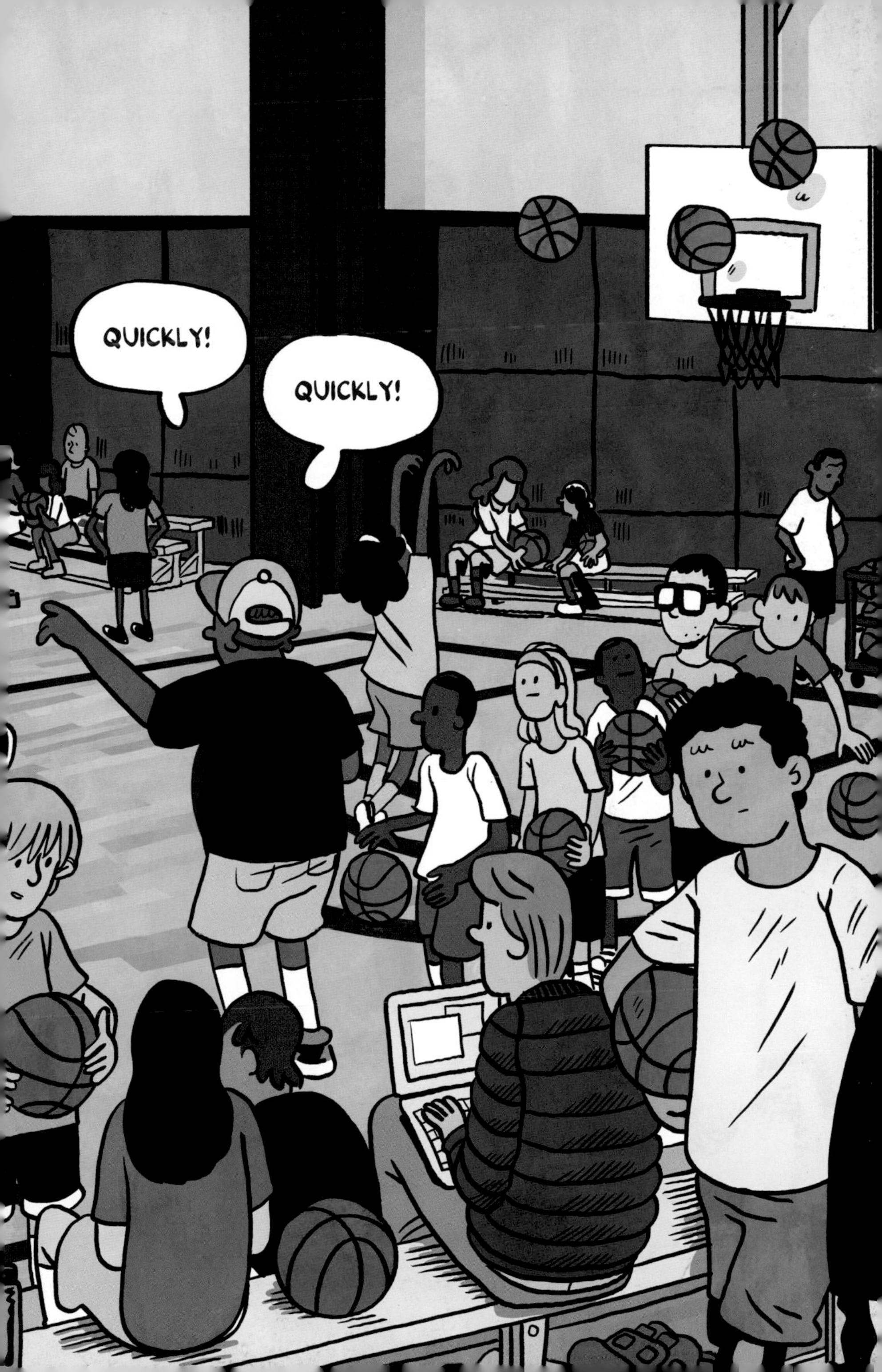
QUICKLY!
QUICKLY!

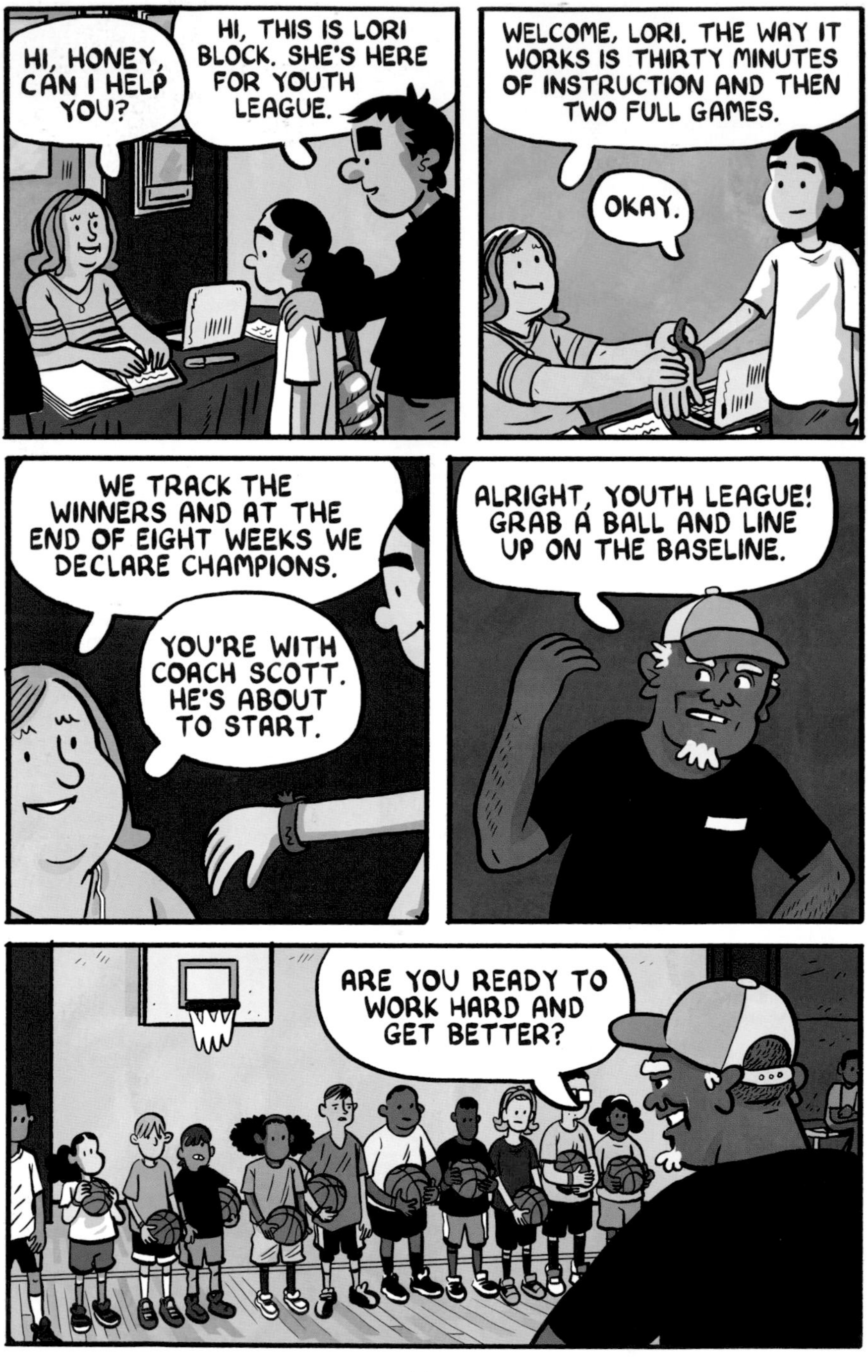
HI, HONEY, CAN I HELP YOU?
HI, THIS IS LORI BLOCK. SHE'S HERE FOR YOUTH LEAGUE.
WELCOME, LORI. THE WAY IT WORKS IS THIRTY MINUTES OF INSTRUCTION AND THEN TWO FULL GAMES.
OKAY.
WE TRACK THE WINNERS AND AT THE END OF EIGHT WEEKS WE DECLARE CHAMPIONS.
YOU'RE WITH COACH SCOTT. HE'S ABOUT TO START.
ALRIGHT, YOUTH LEAGUE! GRAB A BALL AND LINE UP ON THE BASELINE.
ARE YOU READY TO WORK HARD AND GET BETTER?

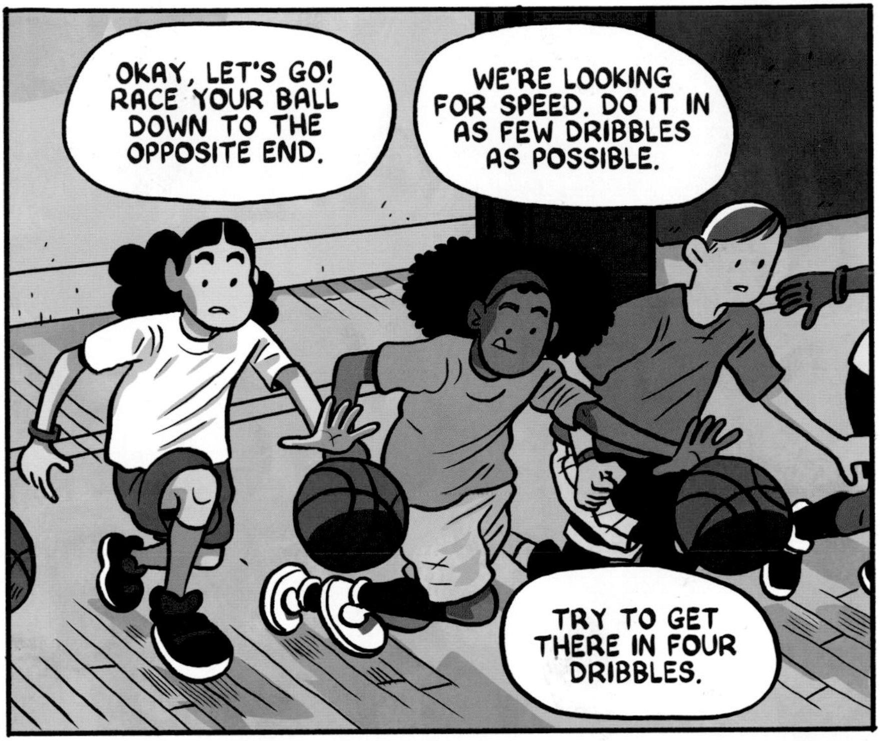
OKAY, LET'S GO! RACE YOUR BALL DOWN TO THE OPPOSITE END.
WE'RE LOOKING FOR SPEED. DO IT IN AS FEW DRIBBLES AS POSSIBLE.
TRY TO GET THERE IN FOUR DRIBBLES.

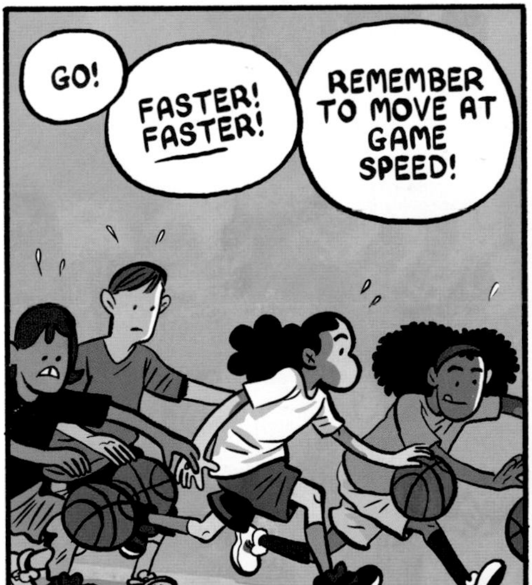
GO!
FASTER! FASTER!
REMEMBER TO MOVE AT GAME SPEED!

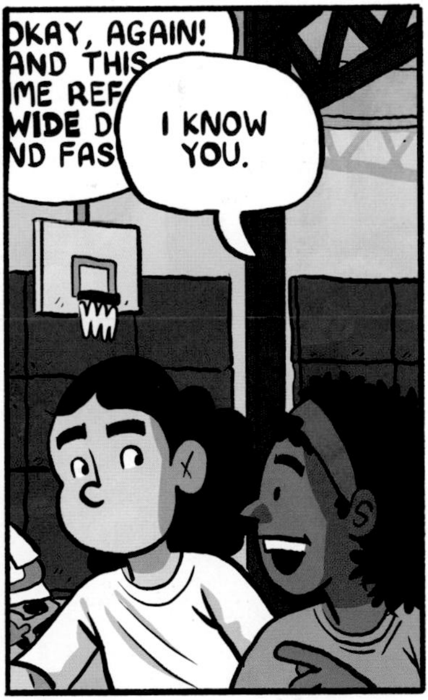
I KNOW YOU.

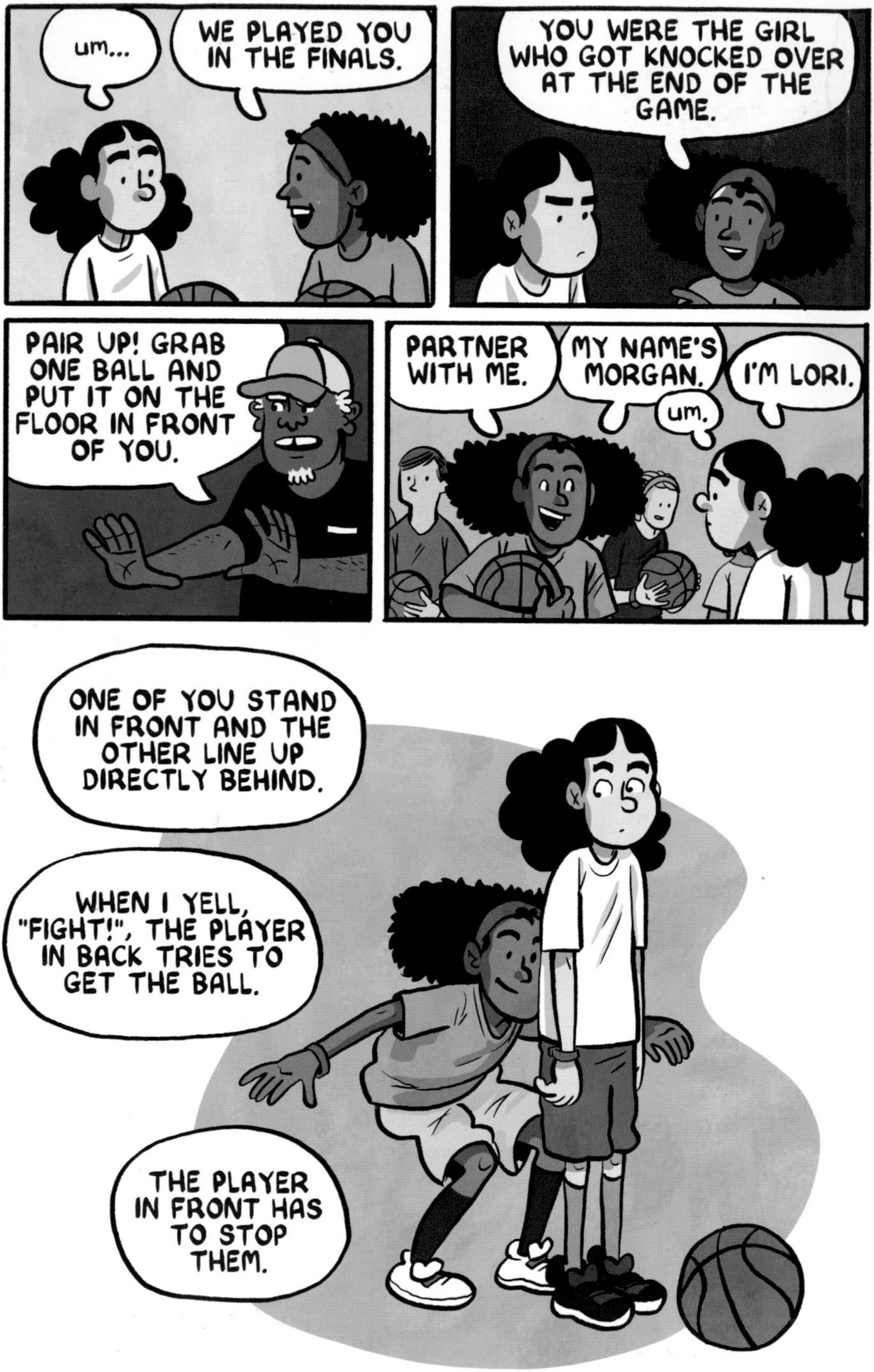
um...
WE PLAYED YOU IN THE FINALS.
YOU WERE THE GIRL WHO GOT KNOCKED OVER AT THE END OF THE GAME.
PAIR UP! GRAB ONE BALL AND PUT IT ON THE FLOOR IN FRONT OF YOU.
PARTNER WITH ME.
MY NAME'S MORGAN.
um.
I'M LORI.
ONE OF YOU STAND IN FRONT AND THE OTHER LINE UP DIRECTLY BEHIND.
WHEN I YELL, "FIGHT!", THE PLAYER IN BACK TRIES TO GET THE BALL.
THE PLAYER IN FRONT HAS TO STOP THEM.

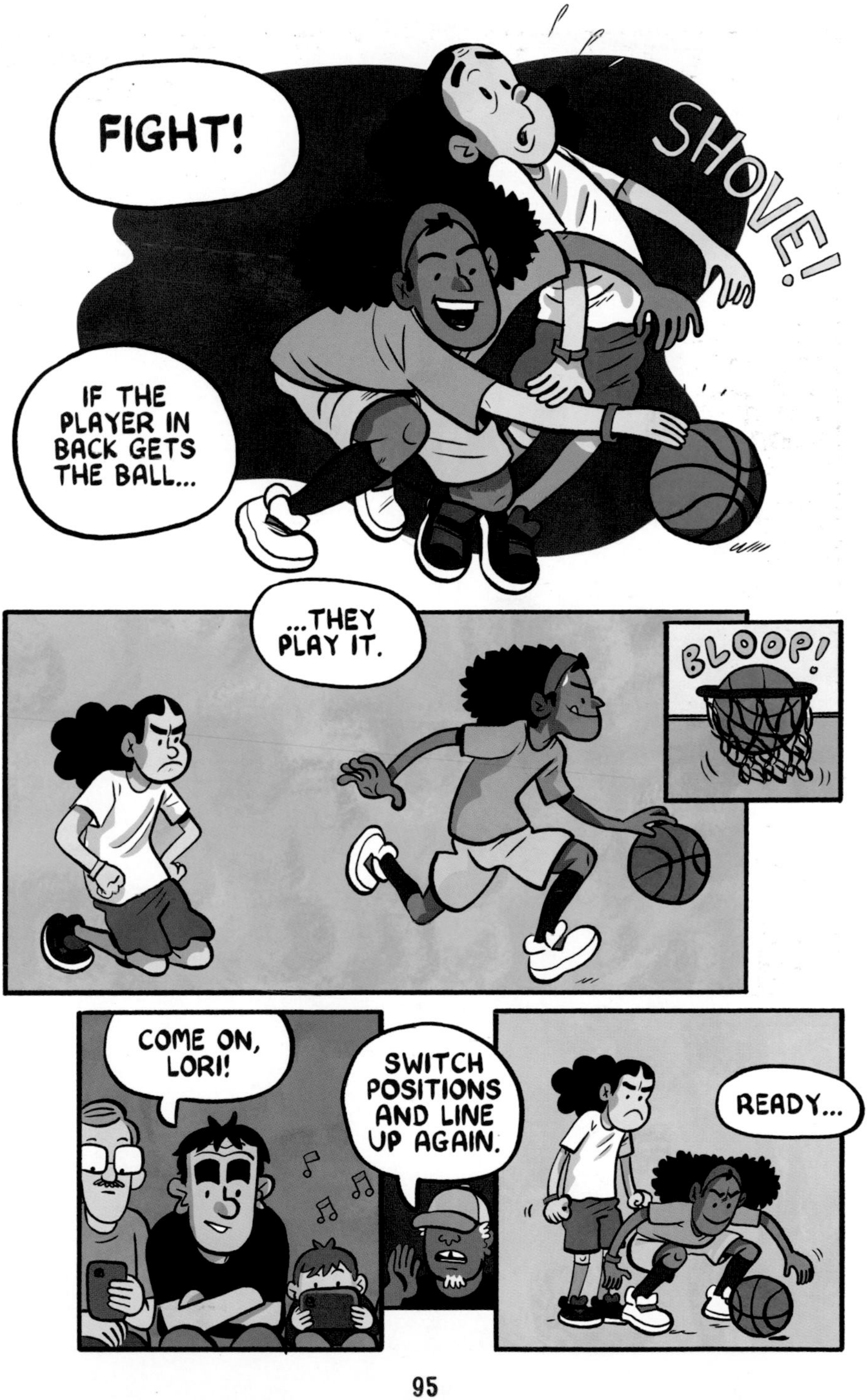
FIGHT!
SHOVE!
IF THE PLAYER IN BACK GETS THE BALL...
...THEY PLAY IT.
BLOOP!
COME ON, LORI!
SWITCH POSITIONS AND LINE UP AGAIN.
READY...

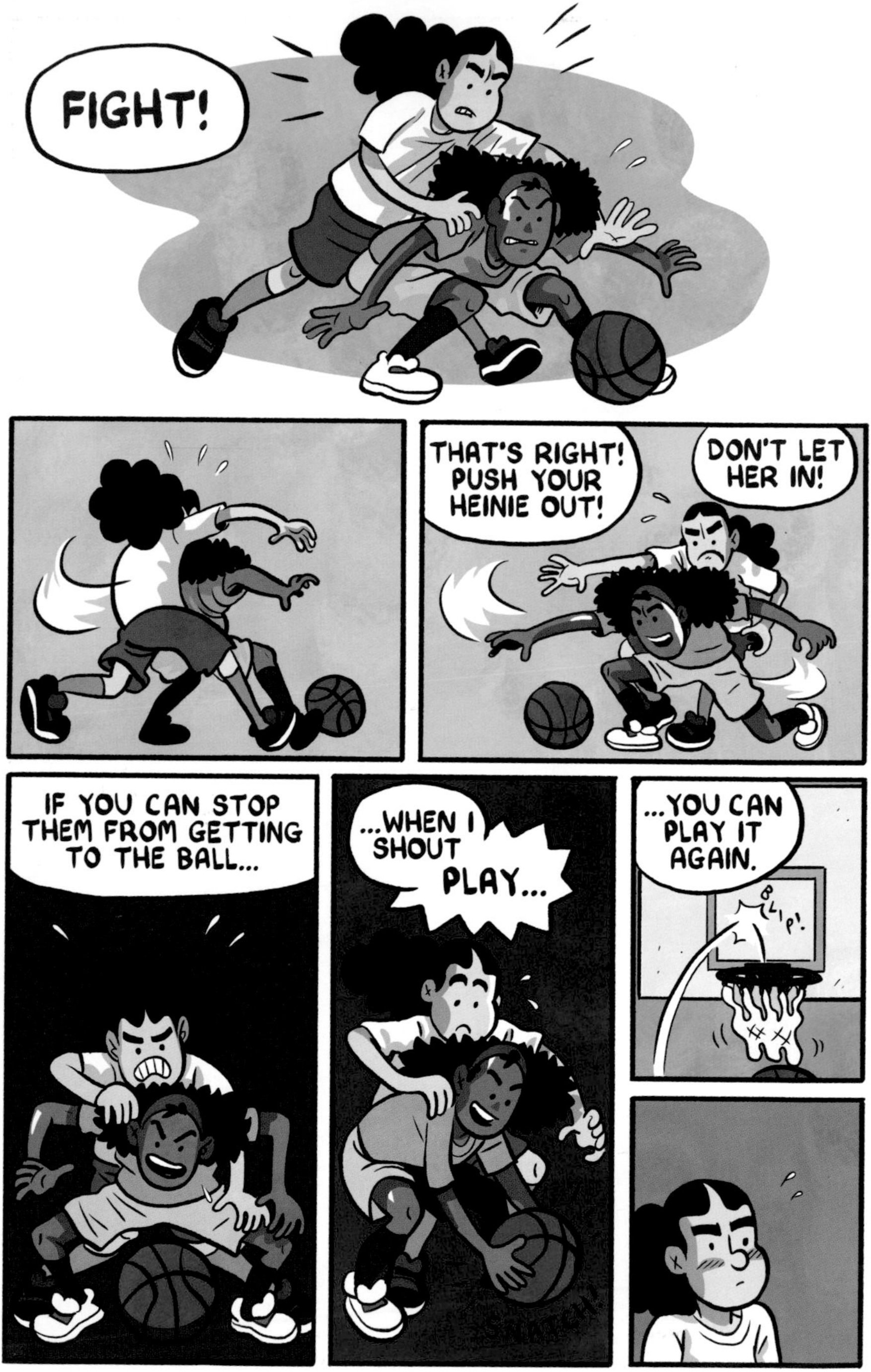
FIGHT!
THAT'S RIGHT! PUSH YOUR HEINIE OUT!
DON'T LET HER IN!
IF YOU CAN STOP THEM FROM GETTING TO THE BALL...
...WHEN I SHOUT PLAY...
...YOU CAN PLAY IT AGAIN.
BLIP!

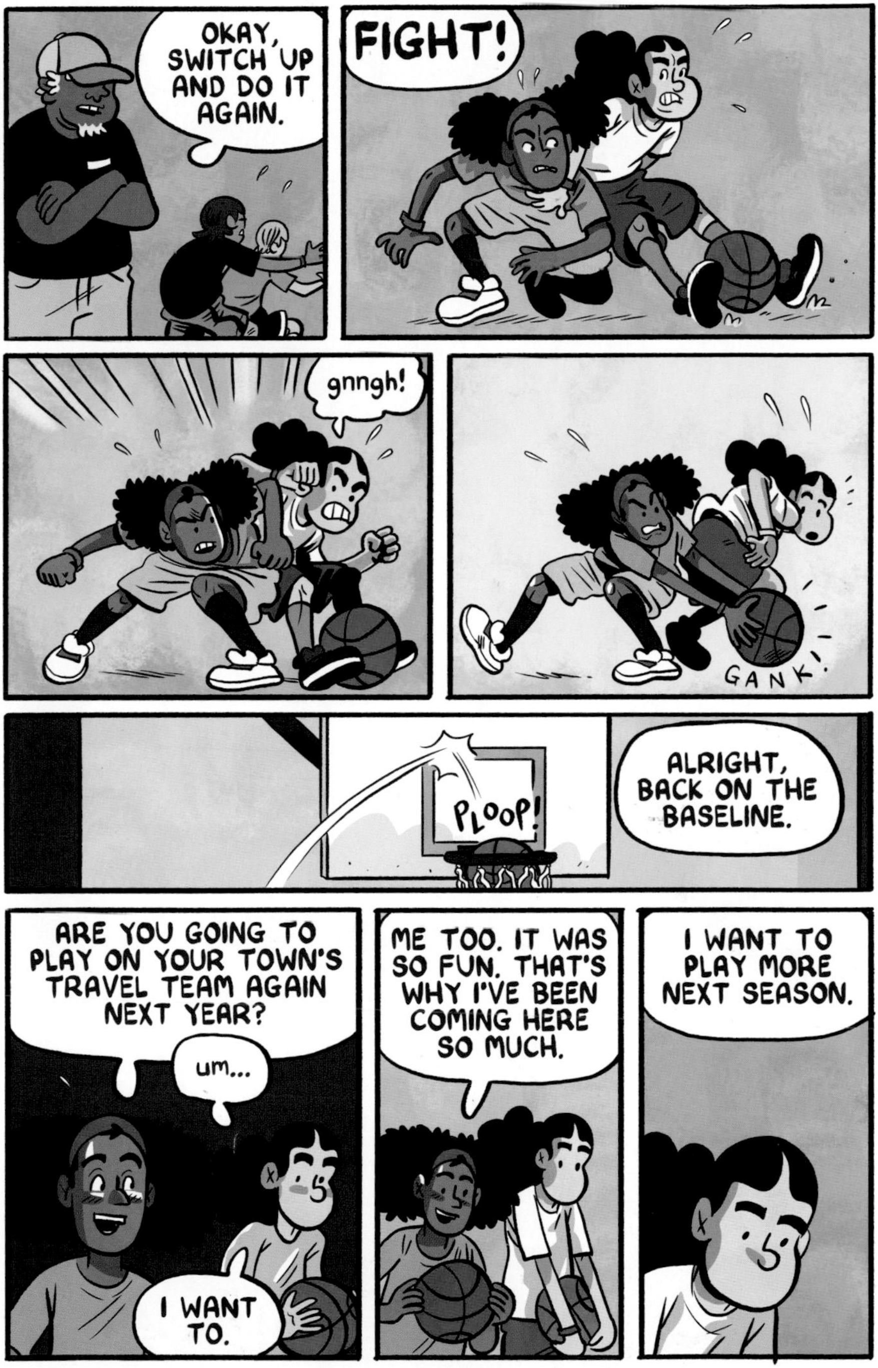
OKAY, SWITCH UP AND DO IT AGAIN.
FIGHT!
gnngh!
GANK!
PLOOP!
ALRIGHT, BACK ON THE BASELINE.
ARE YOU GOING TO PLAY ON YOUR TOWN'S TRAVEL TEAM AGAIN NEXT YEAR?
um...
I WANT TO.
ME TOO. IT WAS SO FUN. THAT'S WHY I'VE BEEN COMING HERE SO MUCH.
I WANT TO PLAY MORE NEXT SEASON.

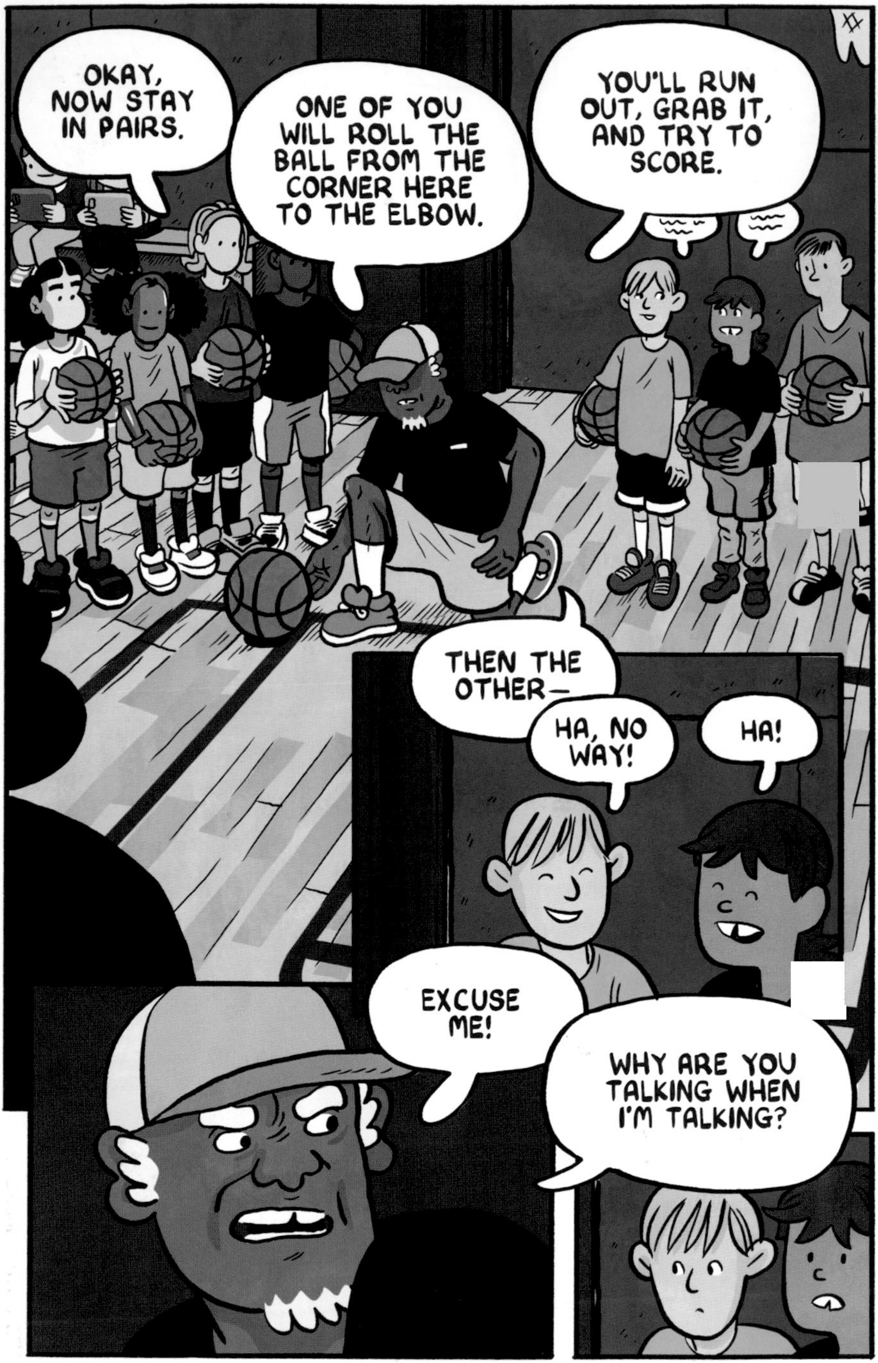
OKAY, NOW STAY IN PAIRS.
ONE OF YOU WILL ROLL THE BALL FROM THE CORNER HERE TO THE ELBOW.
YOU'LL RUN OUT, GRAB IT, AND TRY TO SCORE.
THEN THE OTHER—
HA, NO WAY!
HA!
EXCUSE ME!
WHY ARE YOU TALKING WHEN I'M TALKING?

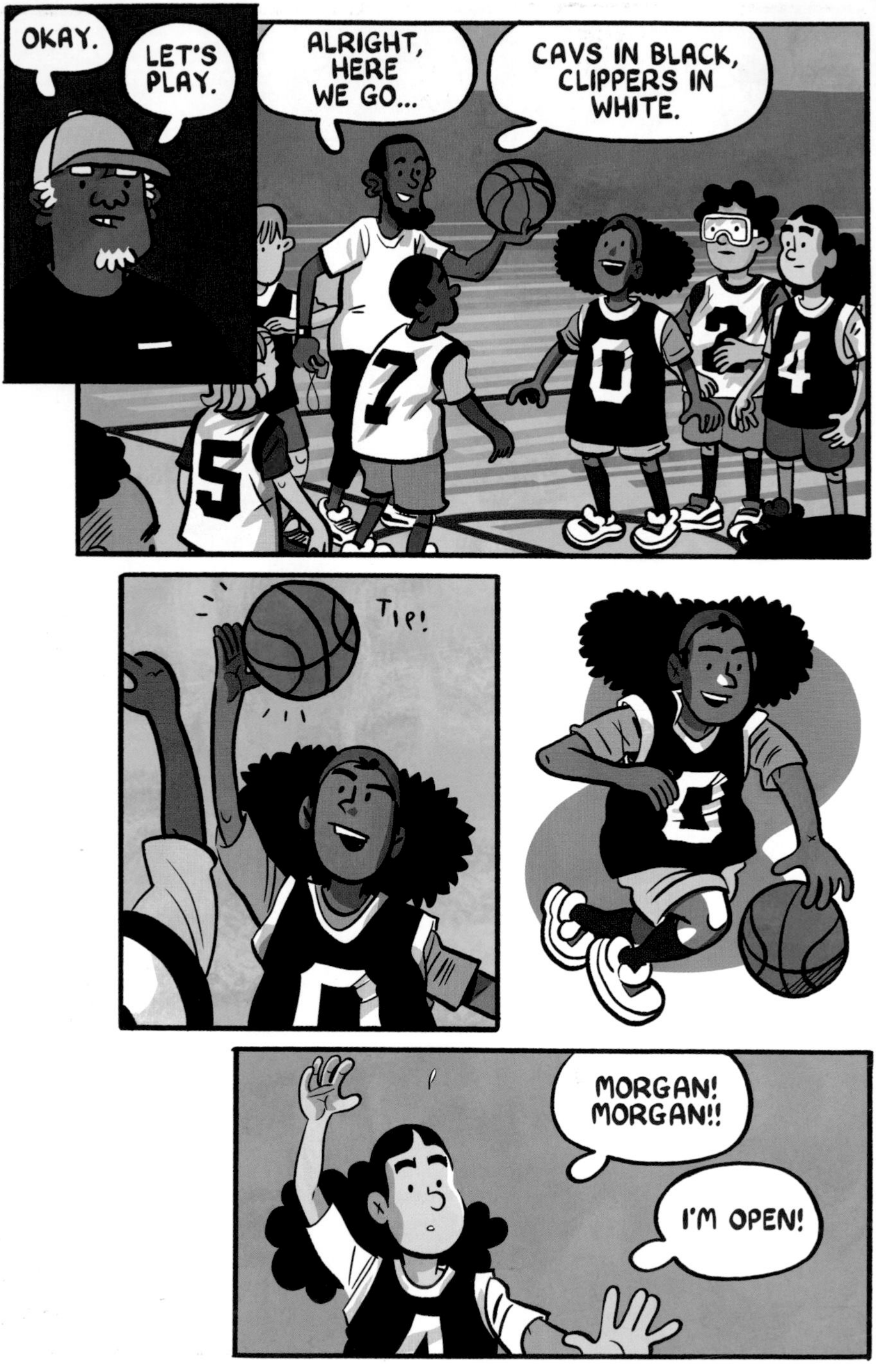
OKAY.
LET'S PLAY.
ALRIGHT, HERE WE GO...
CAVS IN BLACK, CLIPPERS IN WHITE.
TIP!
MORGAN! MORGAN!!
I'M OPEN!

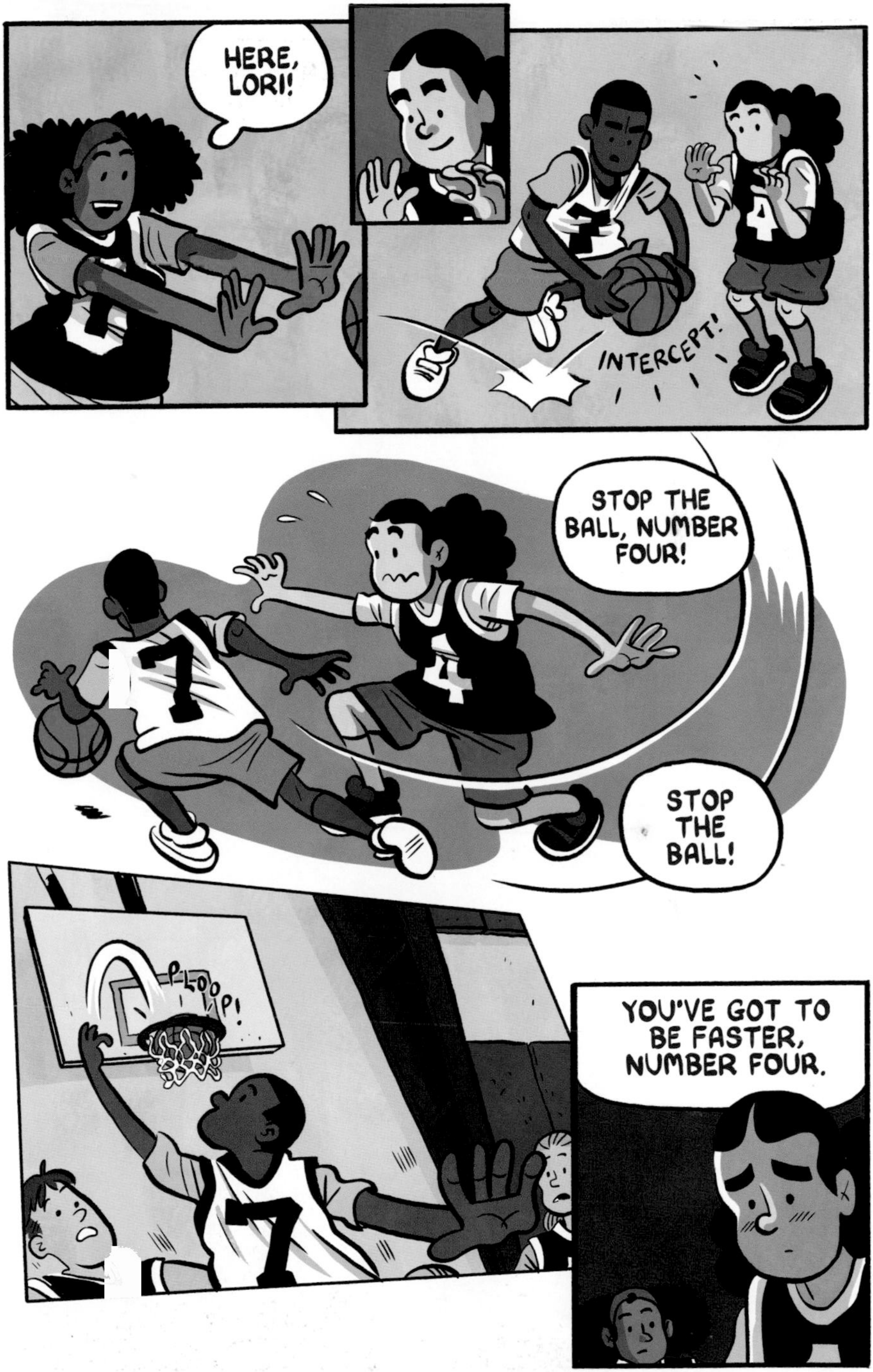
HERE, LORI!
INTERCEPT!
STOP THE BALL, NUMBER FOUR!
STOP THE BALL!
PLOOP!
YOU'VE GOT TO BE FASTER, NUMBER FOUR.

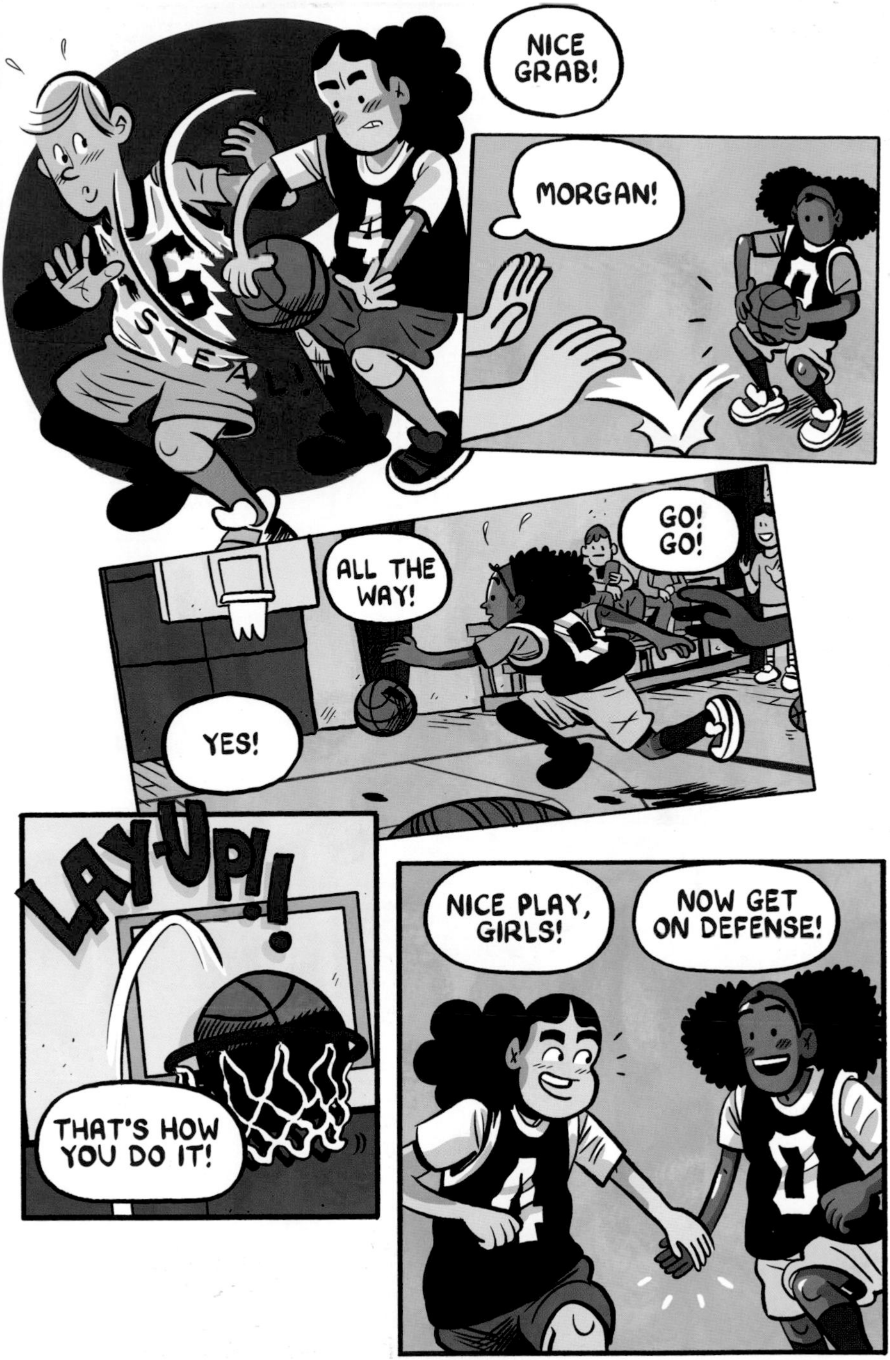
STEAL!
NICE GRAB!
MORGAN!
ALL THE WAY!
GO! GO!
YES!
LAY-UP!!
THAT'S HOW YOU DO IT!
NICE PLAY, GIRLS!
NOW GET ON DEFENSE!

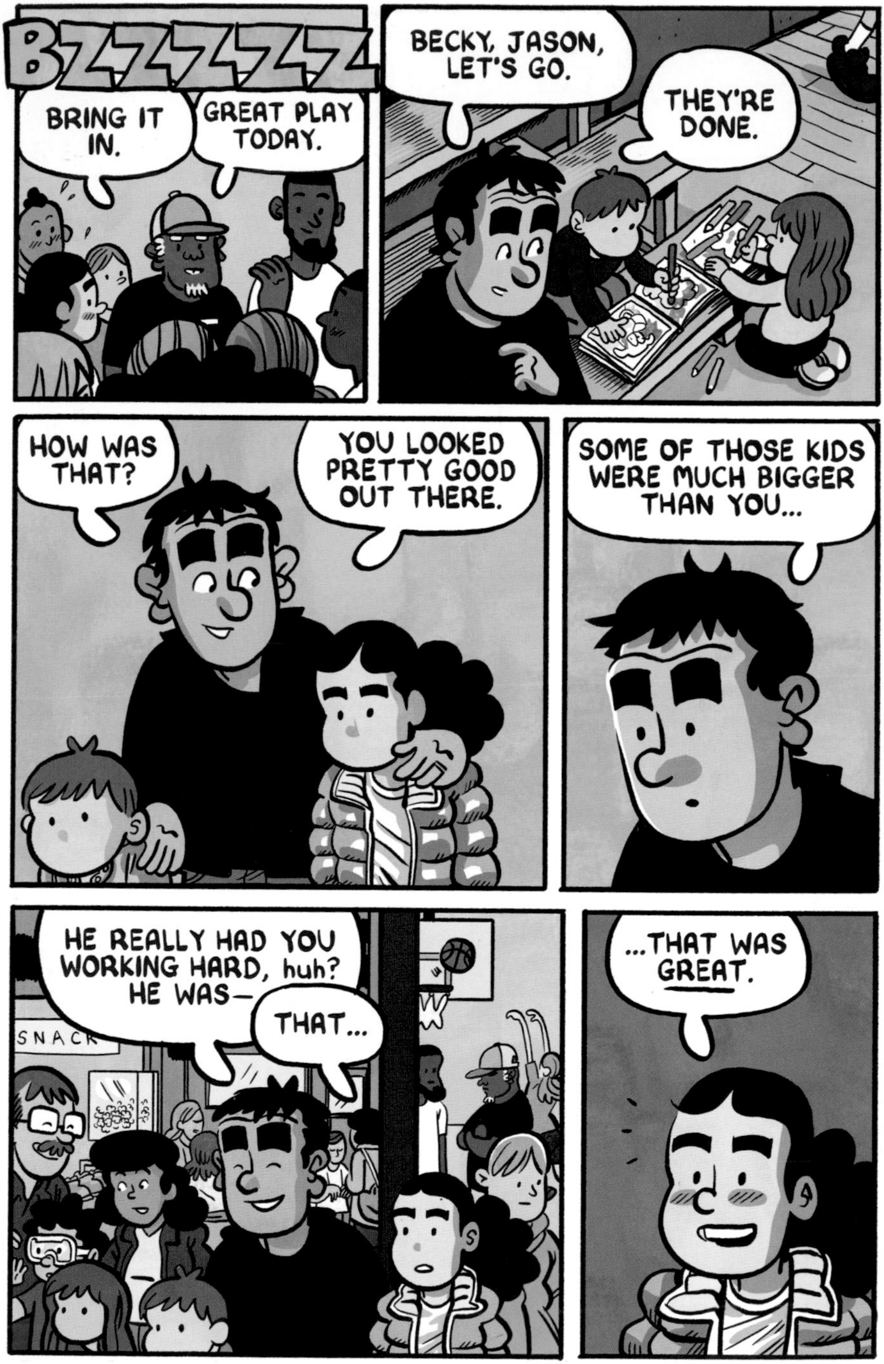
BZZZZZZZ
BRING IT IN.
GREAT PLAY TODAY.
BECKY, JASON, LET'S GO.
THEY'RE DONE.
HOW WAS THAT?
YOU LOOKED PRETTY GOOD OUT THERE.
SOME OF THOSE KIDS WERE MUCH BIGGER THAN YOU...
HE REALLY HAD YOU WORKING HARD, huh? HE WAS—
THAT...
SNACK
...THAT WAS GREAT.

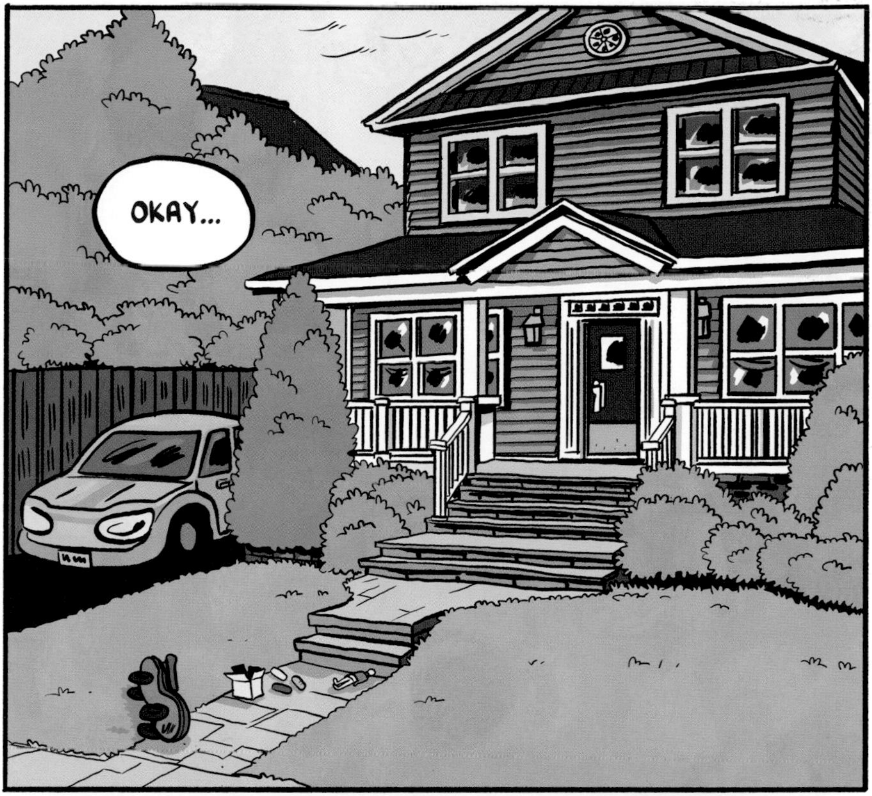
OKAY...

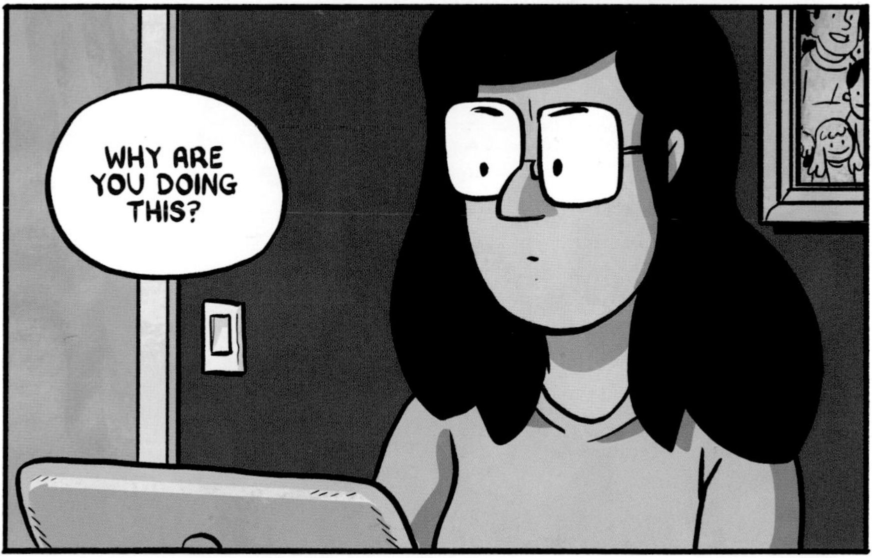
WHY ARE YOU DOING THIS?

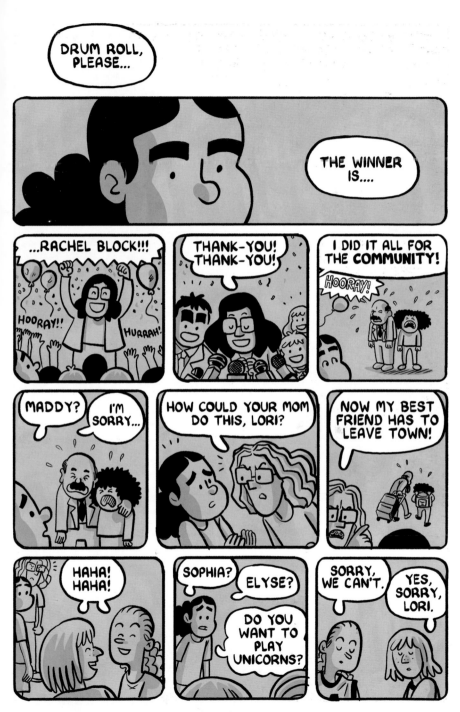

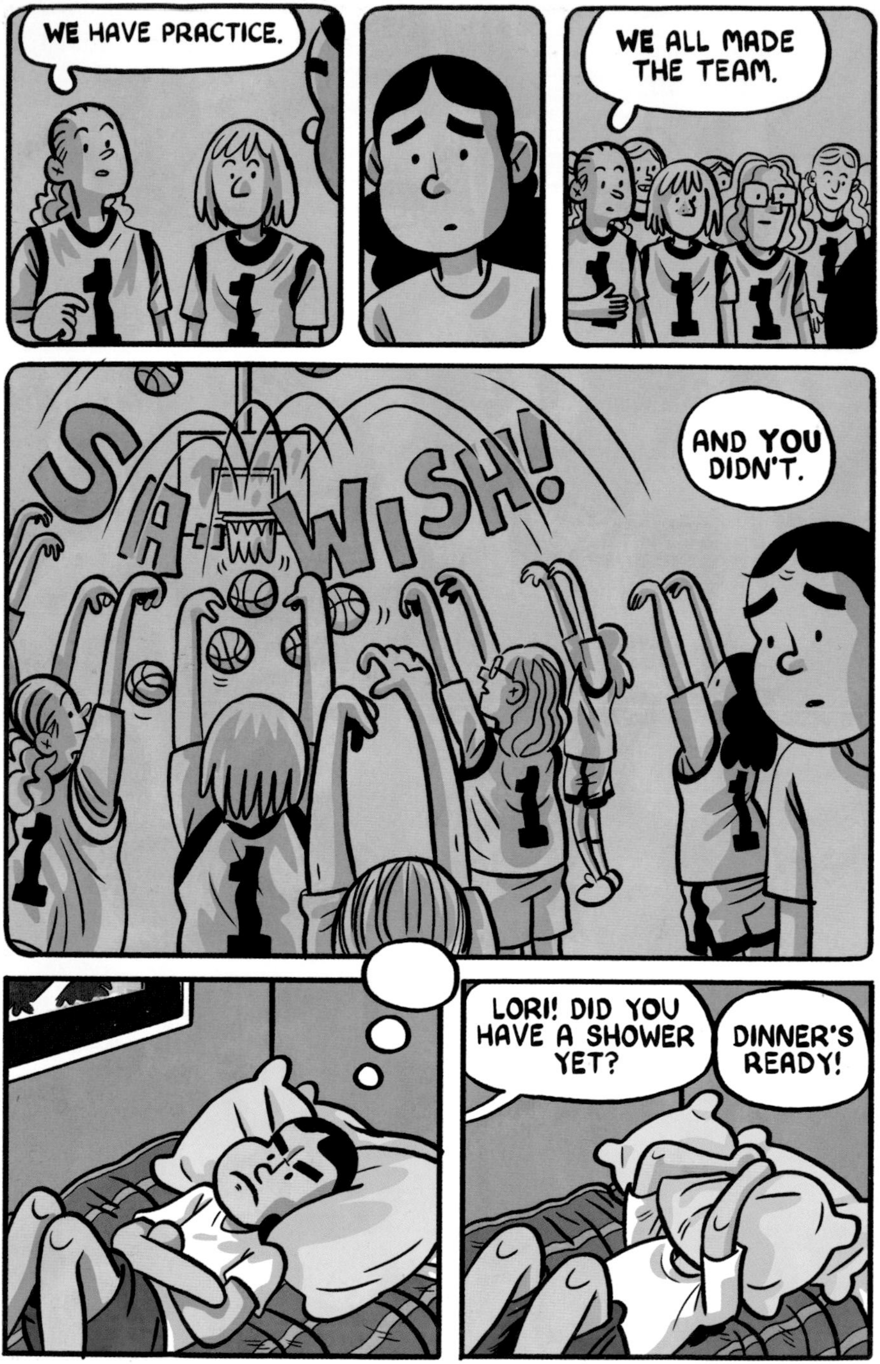

WE HAVE PRACTICE.
WE ALL MADE THE TEAM.
SA-WISH!
AND YOU DIDN'T.
LORI! DID YOU HAVE A SHOWER YET?
DINNER'S READY!

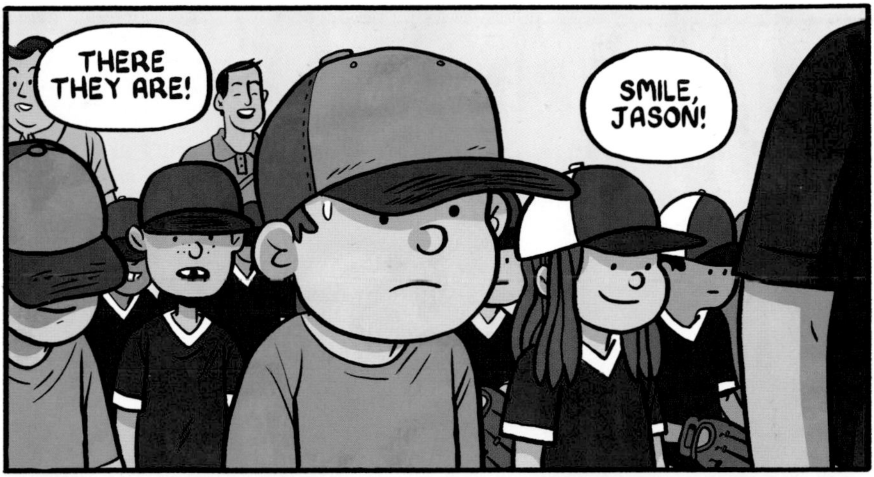
THERE THEY ARE!
SMILE, JASON!

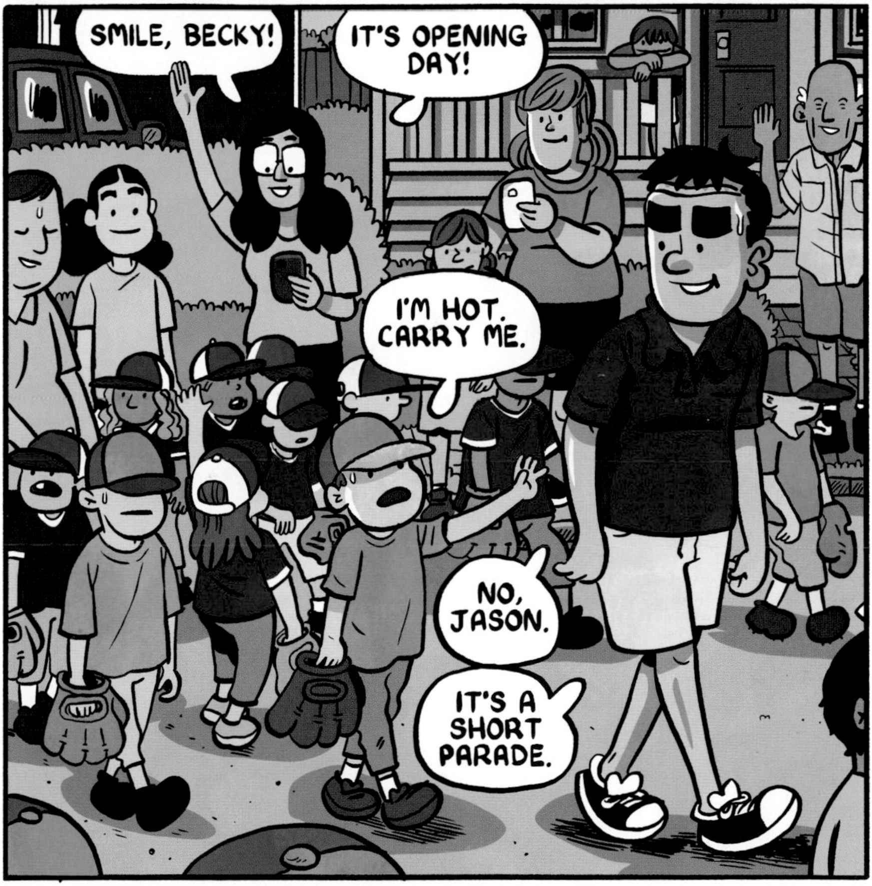
SMILE, BECKY!
IT'S OPENING DAY!
I'M HOT. CARRY ME.
NO, JASON.
IT'S A SHORT PARADE.

112

113

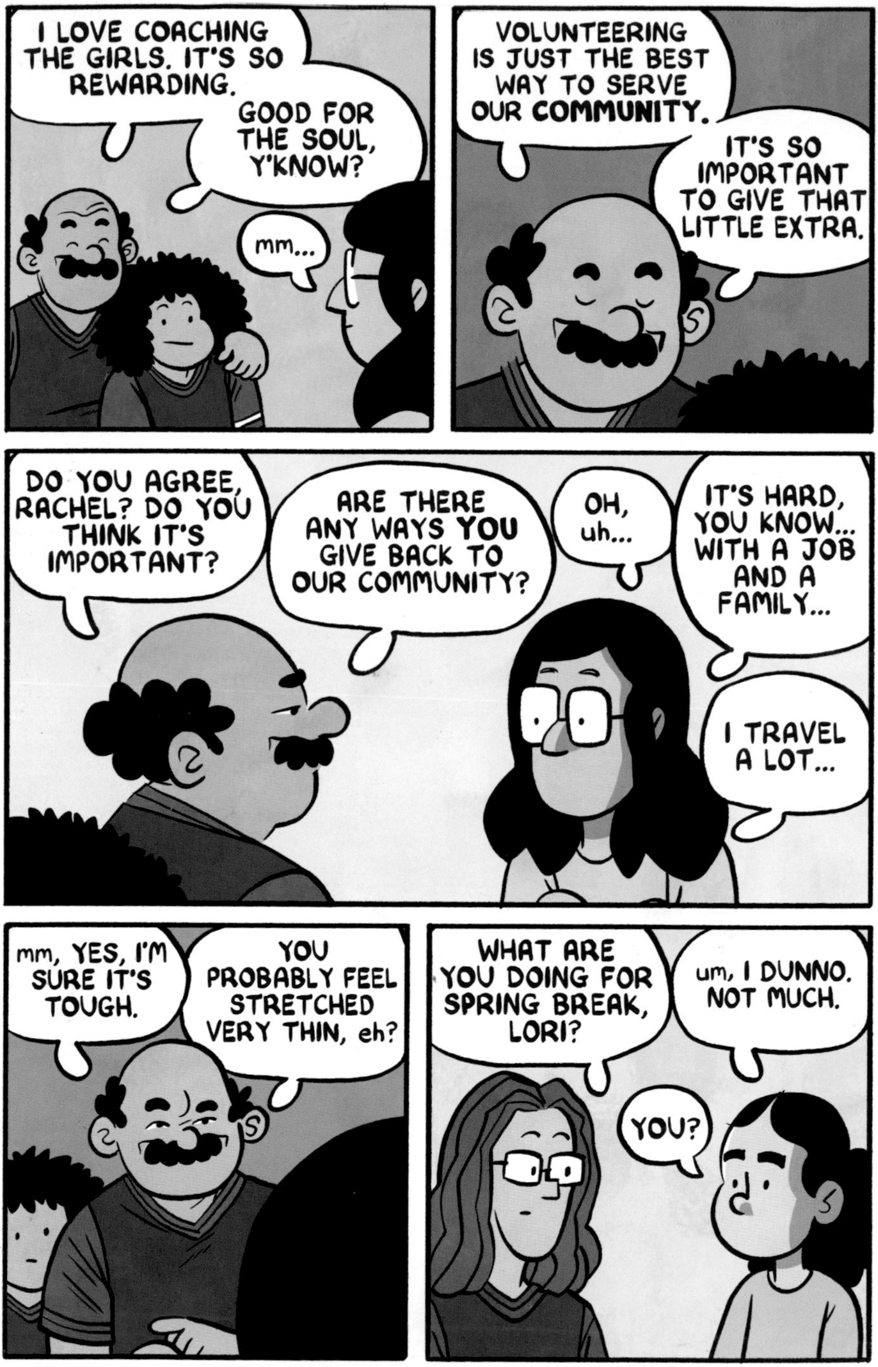
I LOVE COACHING THE GIRLS. IT'S SO REWARDING.
GOOD FOR THE SOUL, Y'KNOW?
mm...
VOLUNTEERING IS JUST THE BEST WAY TO SERVE OUR **COMMUNITY**.
IT'S SO IMPORTANT TO GIVE THAT LITTLE EXTRA.
DO YOU AGREE, RACHEL? DO YOU THINK IT'S IMPORTANT?
ARE THERE ANY WAYS **YOU** GIVE BACK TO OUR COMMUNITY?
OH, uh...
IT'S HARD, YOU KNOW... WITH A JOB AND A FAMILY...
I TRAVEL A LOT...
mm, YES, I'M SURE IT'S TOUGH.
YOU PROBABLY FEEL STRETCHED VERY THIN, eh?
WHAT ARE YOU DOING FOR SPRING BREAK, LORI?
um, I DUNNO. NOT MUCH.
YOU?

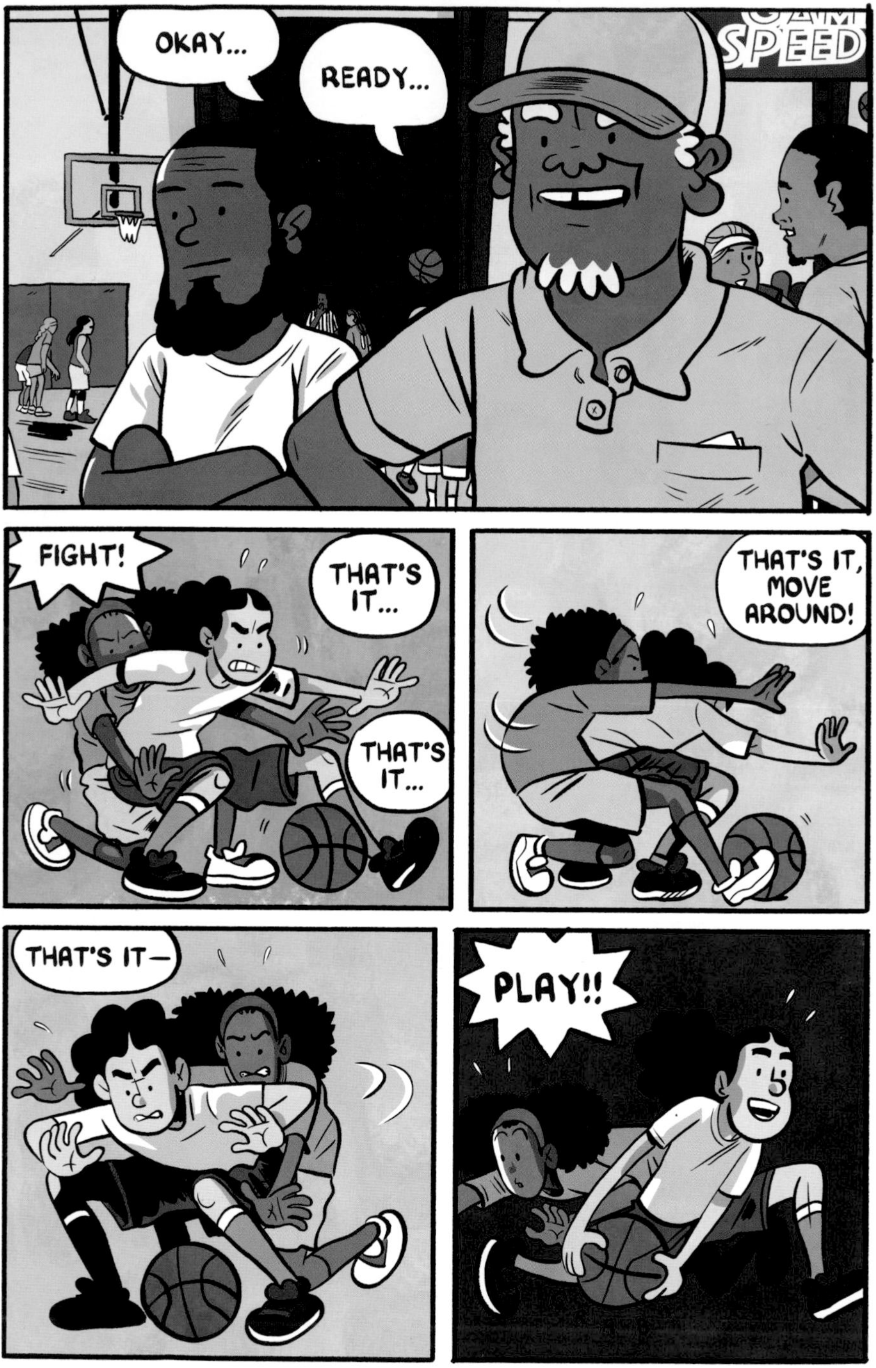
SPEED
OKAY...
READY...
FIGHT!
THAT'S IT...
THAT'S IT...
THAT'S IT, MOVE AROUND!
THAT'S IT—
PLAY!!

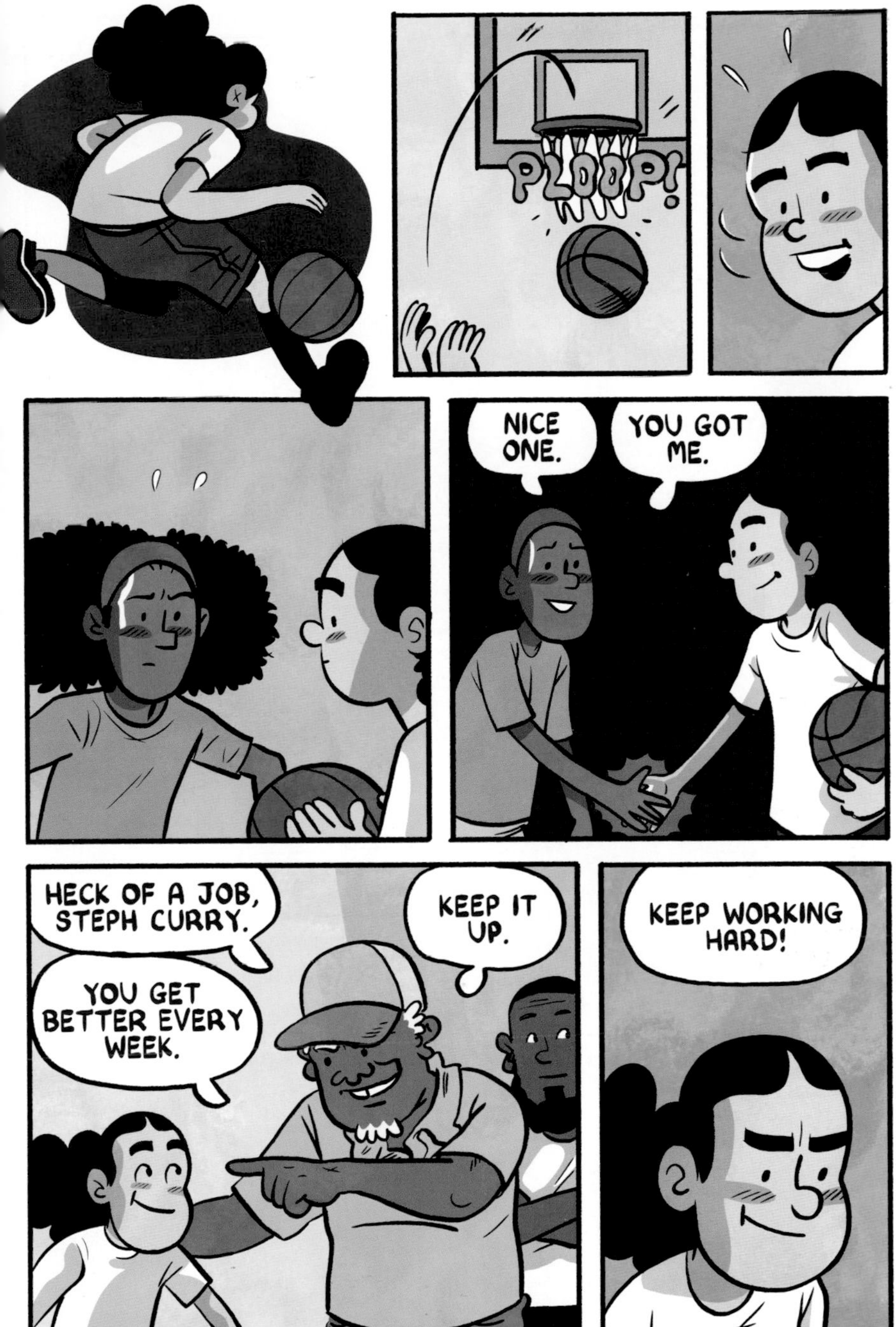
PLOOP!
NICE ONE.
YOU GOT ME.
HECK OF A JOB, STEPH CURRY.
YOU GET BETTER EVERY WEEK.
KEEP IT UP.
KEEP WORKING HARD!

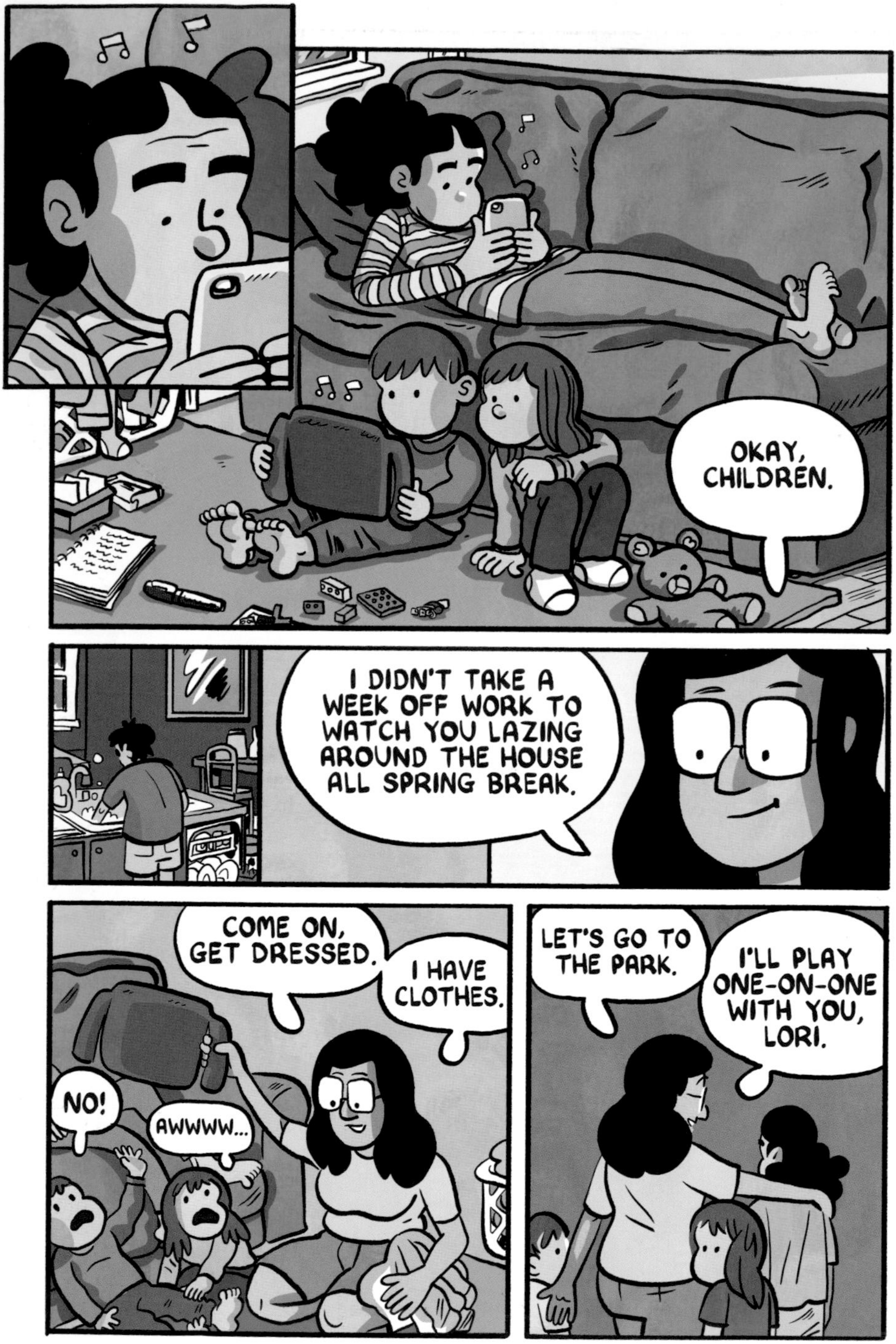
OKAY, CHILDREN.
I DIDN'T TAKE A WEEK OFF WORK TO WATCH YOU LAZING AROUND THE HOUSE ALL SPRING BREAK.
COME ON, GET DRESSED.
I HAVE CLOTHES.
NO!
AWWWW...
LET'S GO TO THE PARK.
I'LL PLAY ONE-ON-ONE WITH YOU, LORI.

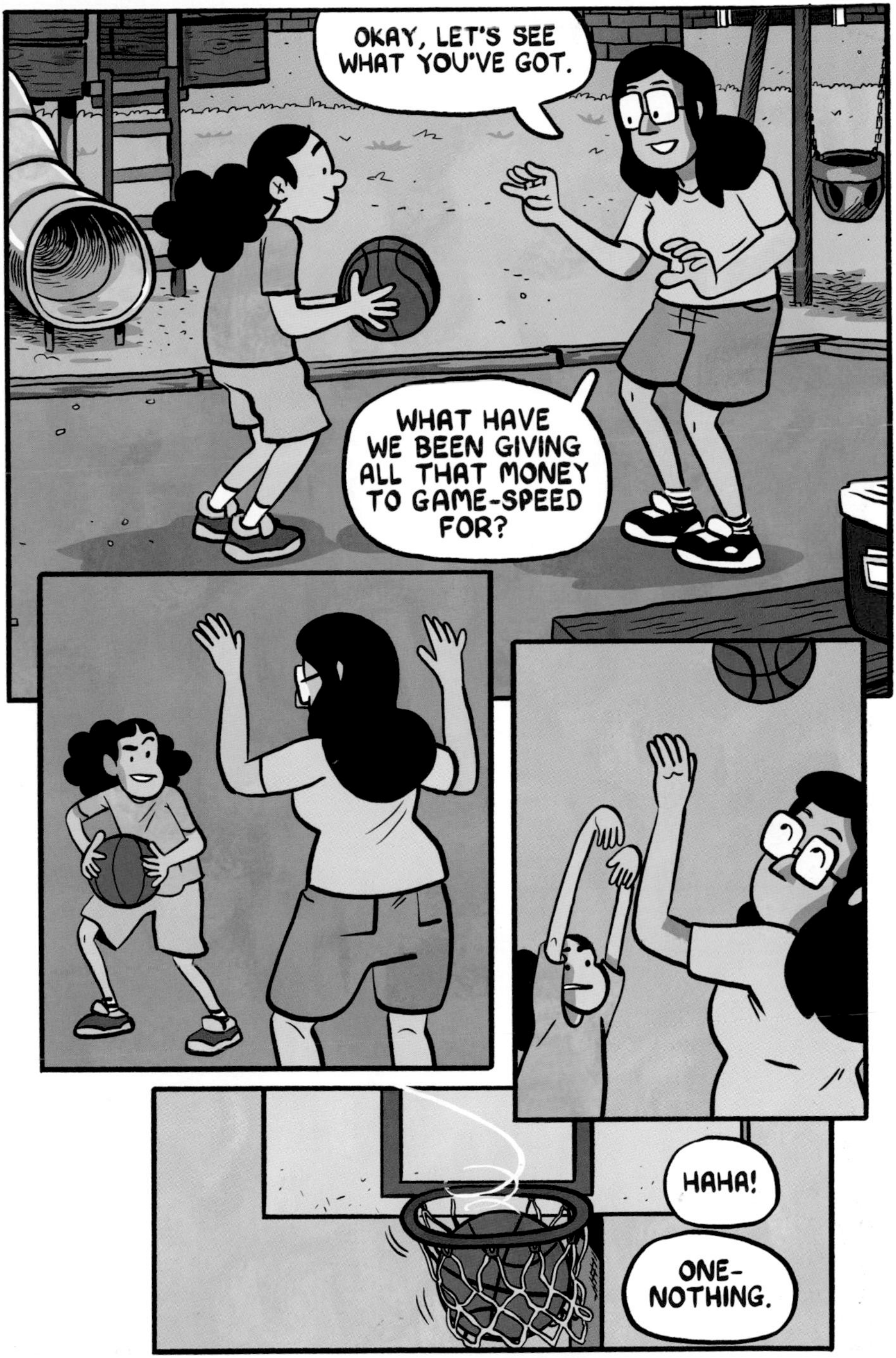
OKAY, LET'S SEE WHAT YOU'VE GOT.
WHAT HAVE WE BEEN GIVING ALL THAT MONEY TO GAME-SPEED FOR?
HAHA!
ONE-NOTHING.

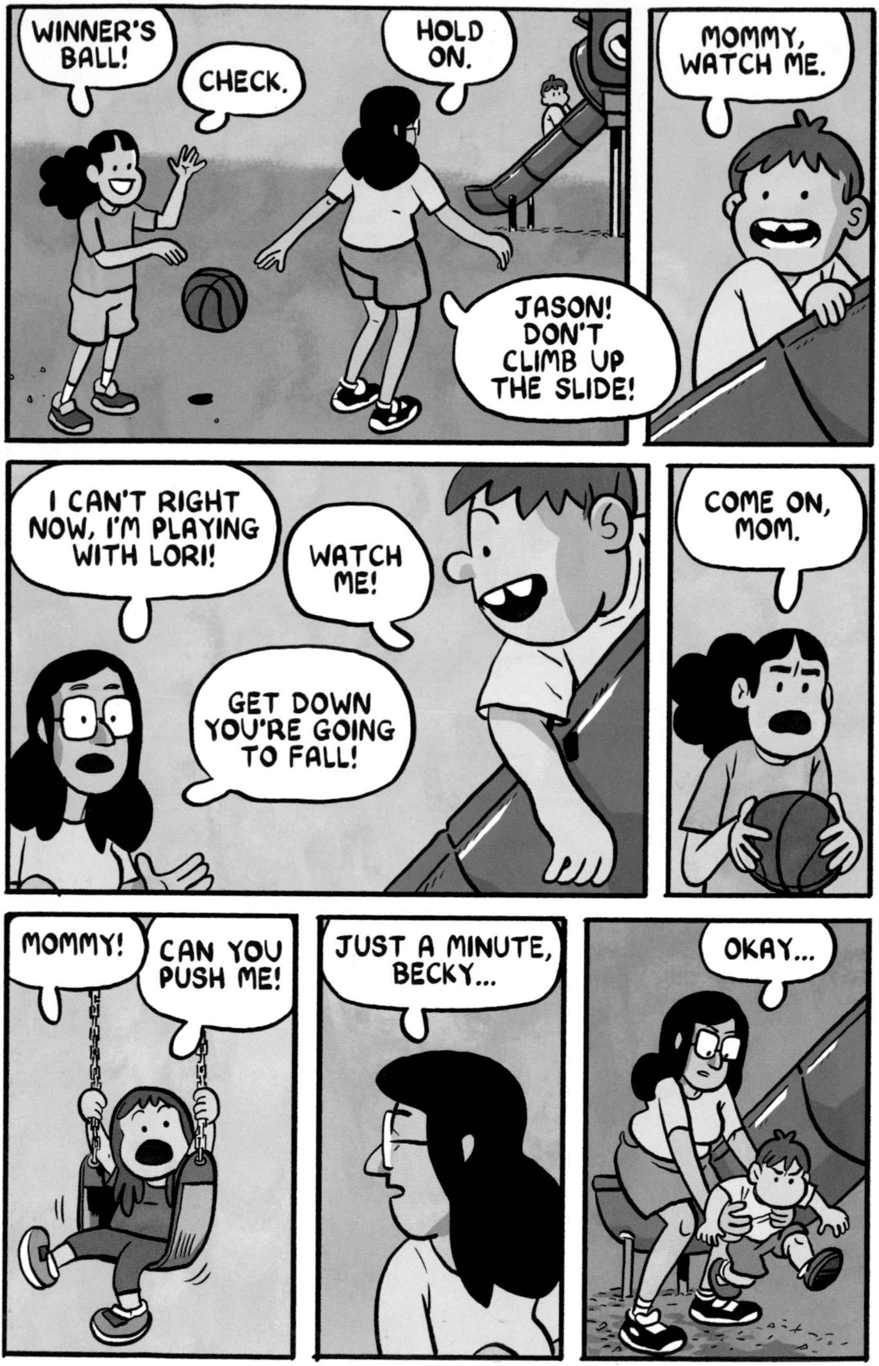
WINNER'S BALL!
CHECK.
HOLD ON.
JASON! DON'T CLIMB UP THE SLIDE!
MOMMY, WATCH ME.
I CAN'T RIGHT NOW, I'M PLAYING WITH LORI!
WATCH ME!
GET DOWN YOU'RE GOING TO FALL!
COME ON, MOM.
MOMMY!
CAN YOU PUSH ME!
JUST A MINUTE, BECKY...
OKAY...

121

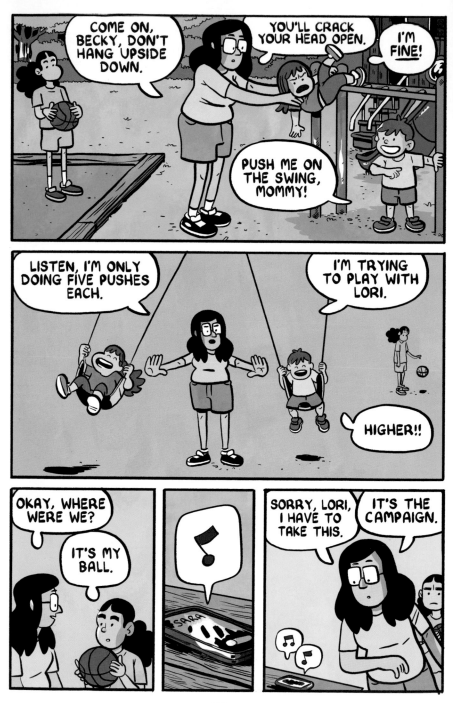

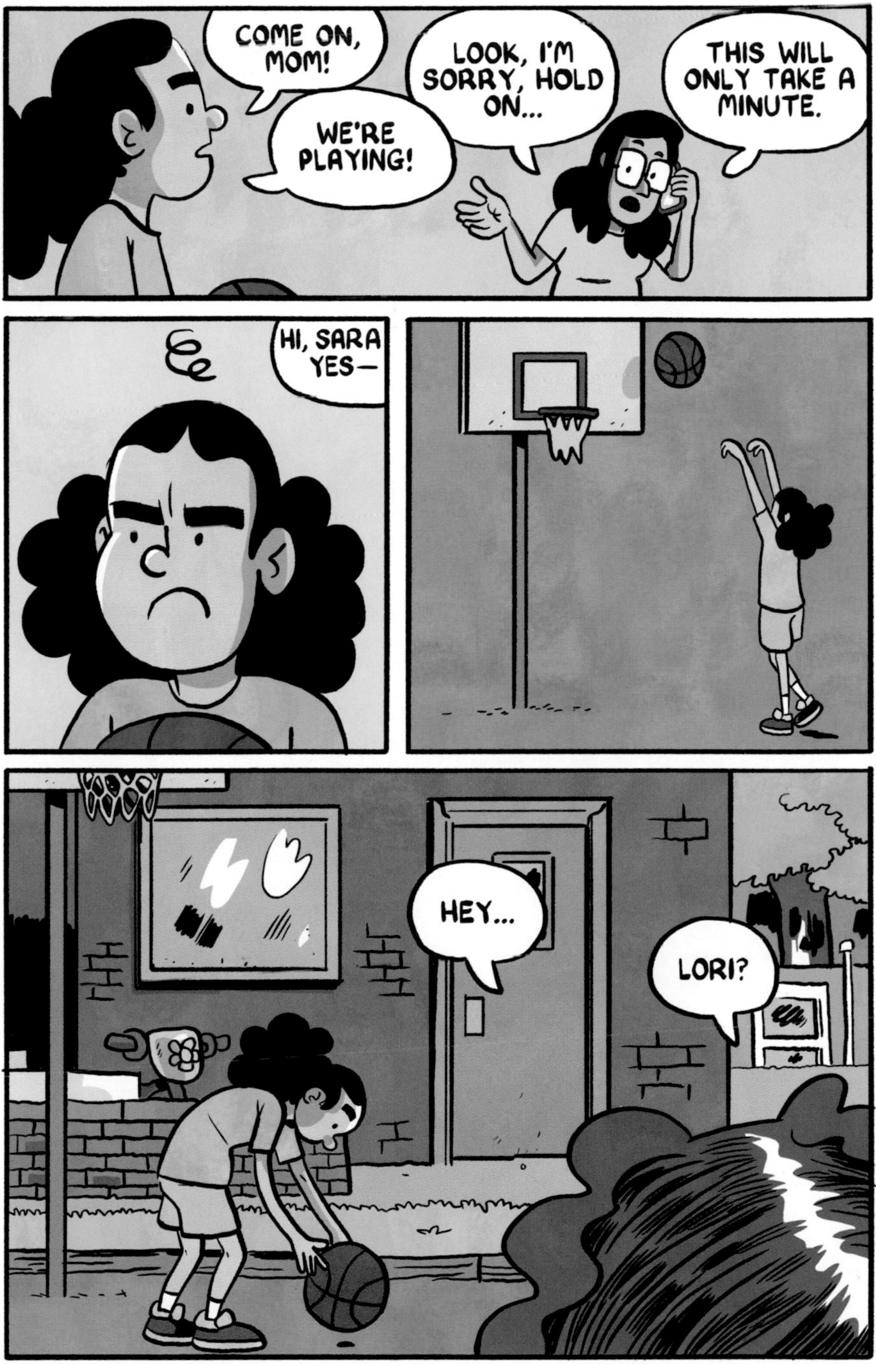
COME ON, MOM!
WE'RE PLAYING!
LOOK, I'M SORRY, HOLD ON...
THIS WILL ONLY TAKE A MINUTE.
HI, SARA YES—
HEY...
LORI?

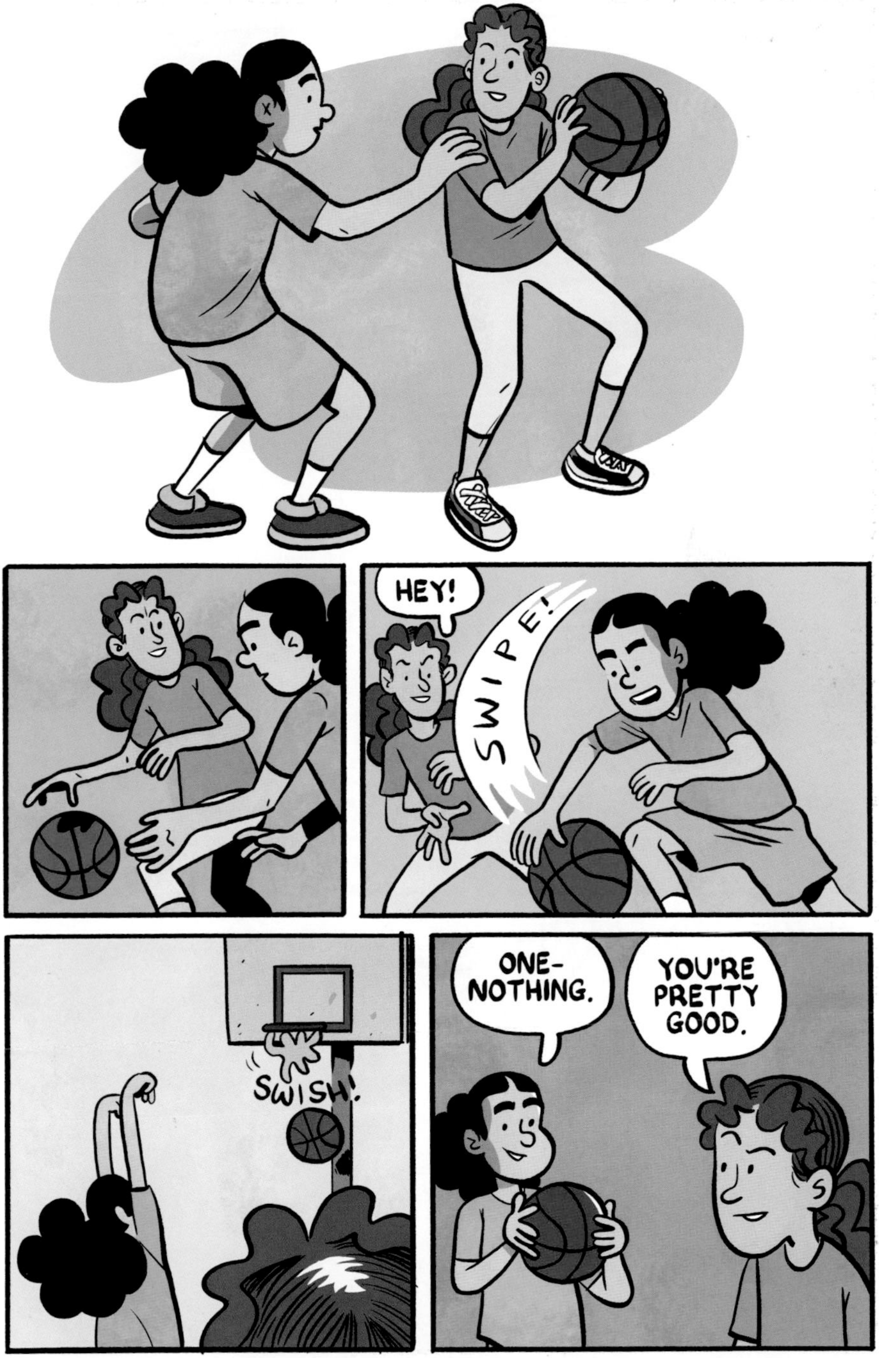
HEY!
SWIPE!
SWISH!
ONE-NOTHING.
YOU'RE PRETTY GOOD.

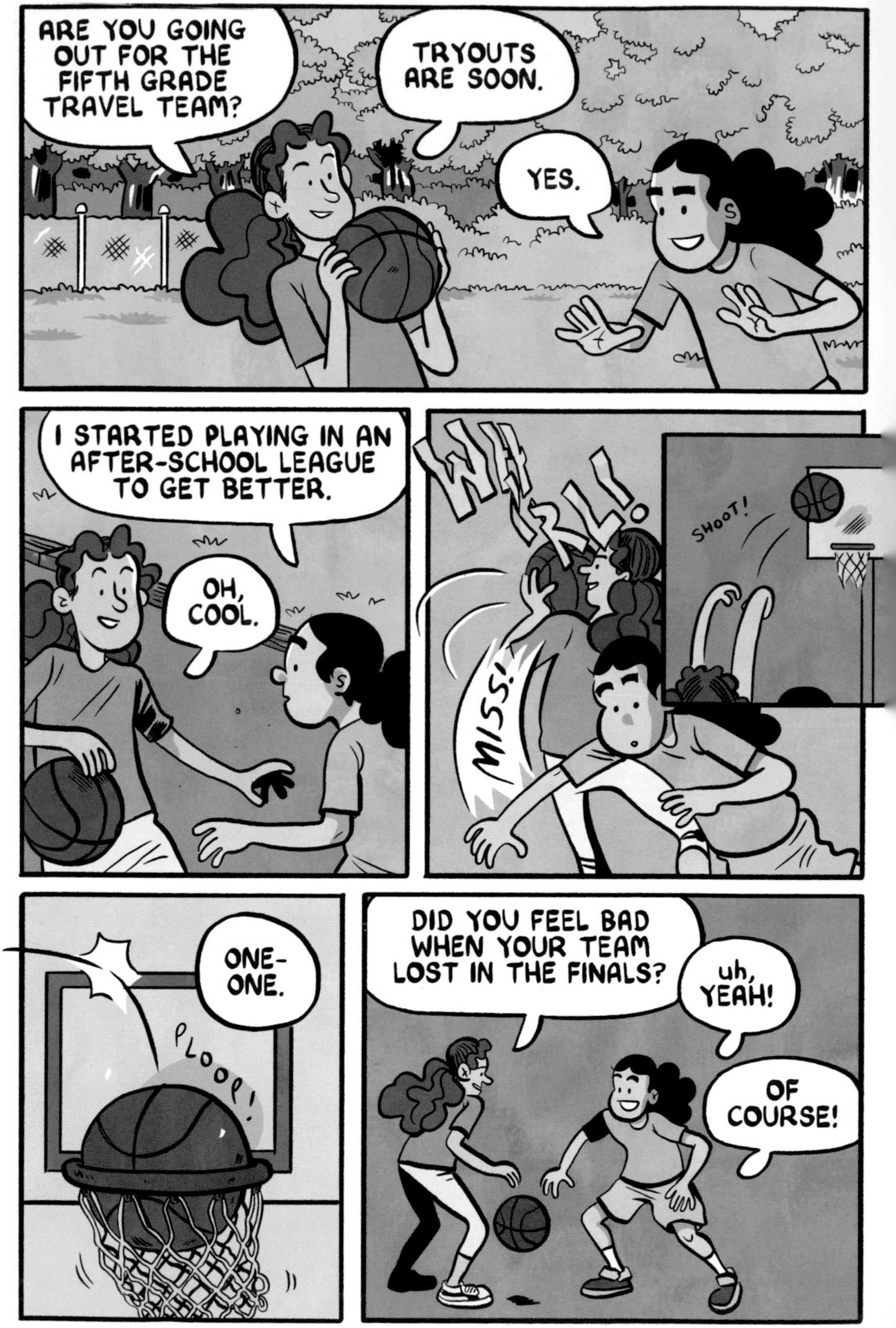

ARE YOU GOING OUT FOR THE FIFTH GRADE TRAVEL TEAM?
TRYOUTS ARE SOON.
YES.
I STARTED PLAYING IN AN AFTER-SCHOOL LEAGUE TO GET BETTER.
OH, COOL.
SHOOT!
MISS!
ONE-ONE.
PLOOP!
DID YOU FEEL BAD WHEN YOUR TEAM LOST IN THE FINALS?
uh, YEAH!
OF COURSE!

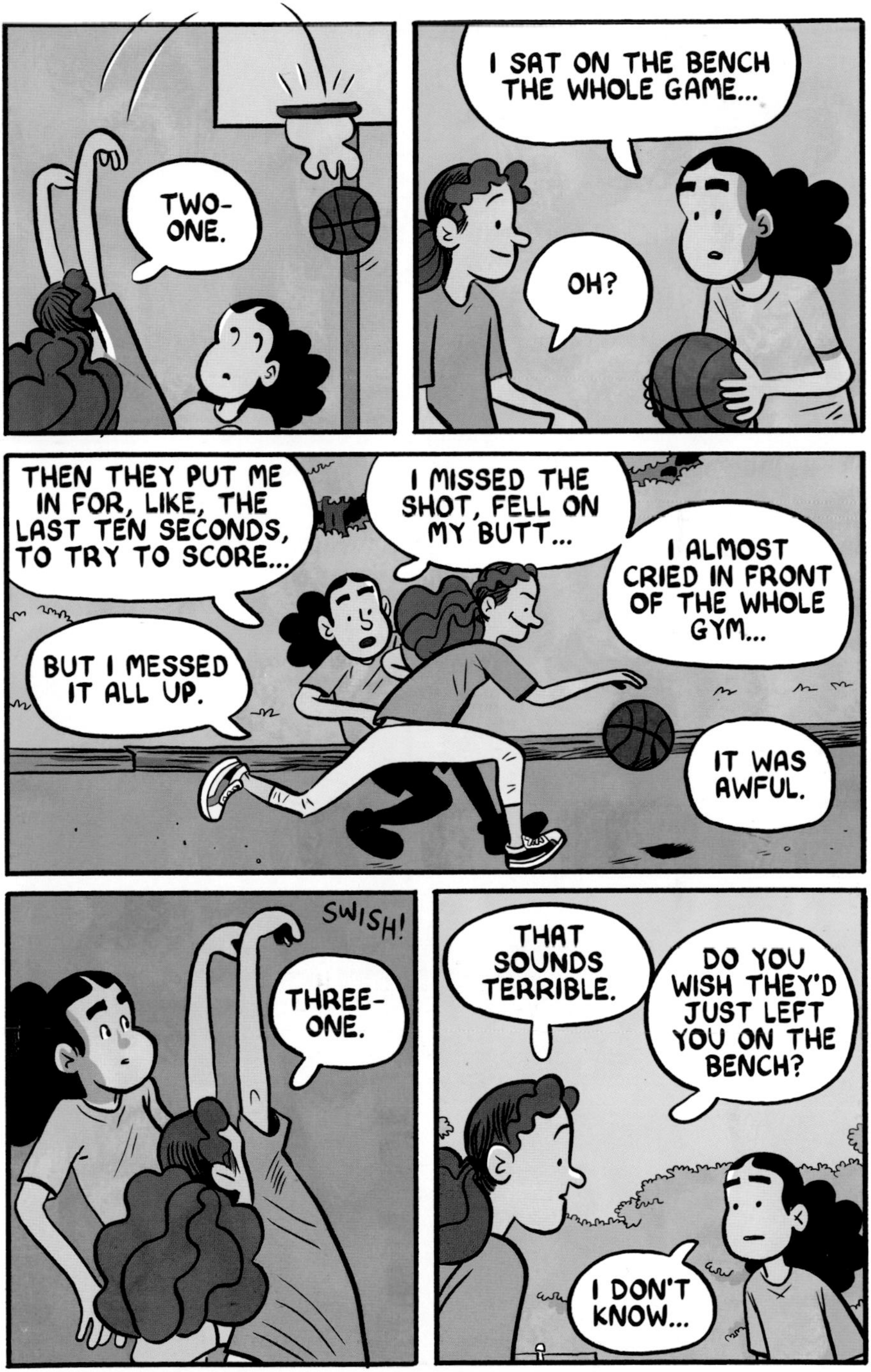
TWO-ONE.
I SAT ON THE BENCH THE WHOLE GAME...
OH?
THEN THEY PUT ME IN FOR, LIKE, THE LAST TEN SECONDS, TO TRY TO SCORE...
I MISSED THE SHOT, FELL ON MY BUTT...
I ALMOST CRIED IN FRONT OF THE WHOLE GYM...
BUT I MESSED IT ALL UP.
IT WAS AWFUL.
SWISH!
THREE-ONE.
THAT SOUNDS TERRIBLE.
DO YOU WISH THEY'D JUST LEFT YOU ON THE BENCH?
I DON'T KNOW...

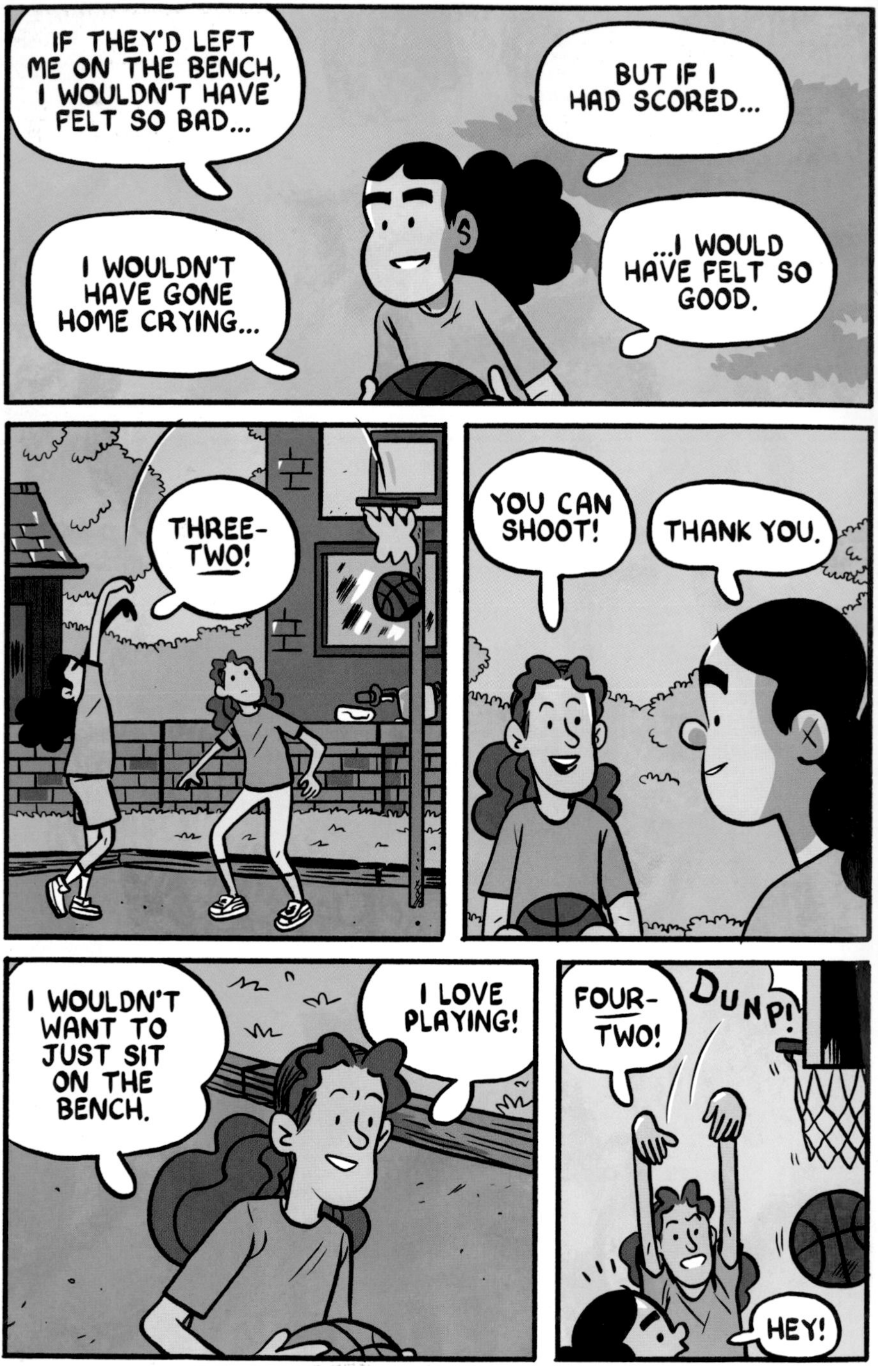
IF THEY'D LEFT ME ON THE BENCH, I WOULDN'T HAVE FELT SO BAD...
BUT IF I HAD SCORED...
I WOULDN'T HAVE GONE HOME CRYING...
...I WOULD HAVE FELT SO GOOD.
THREE-TWO!
YOU CAN SHOOT!
THANK YOU.
I WOULDN'T WANT TO JUST SIT ON THE BENCH.
I LOVE PLAYING!
FOUR-TWO!
DUNP!
HEY!

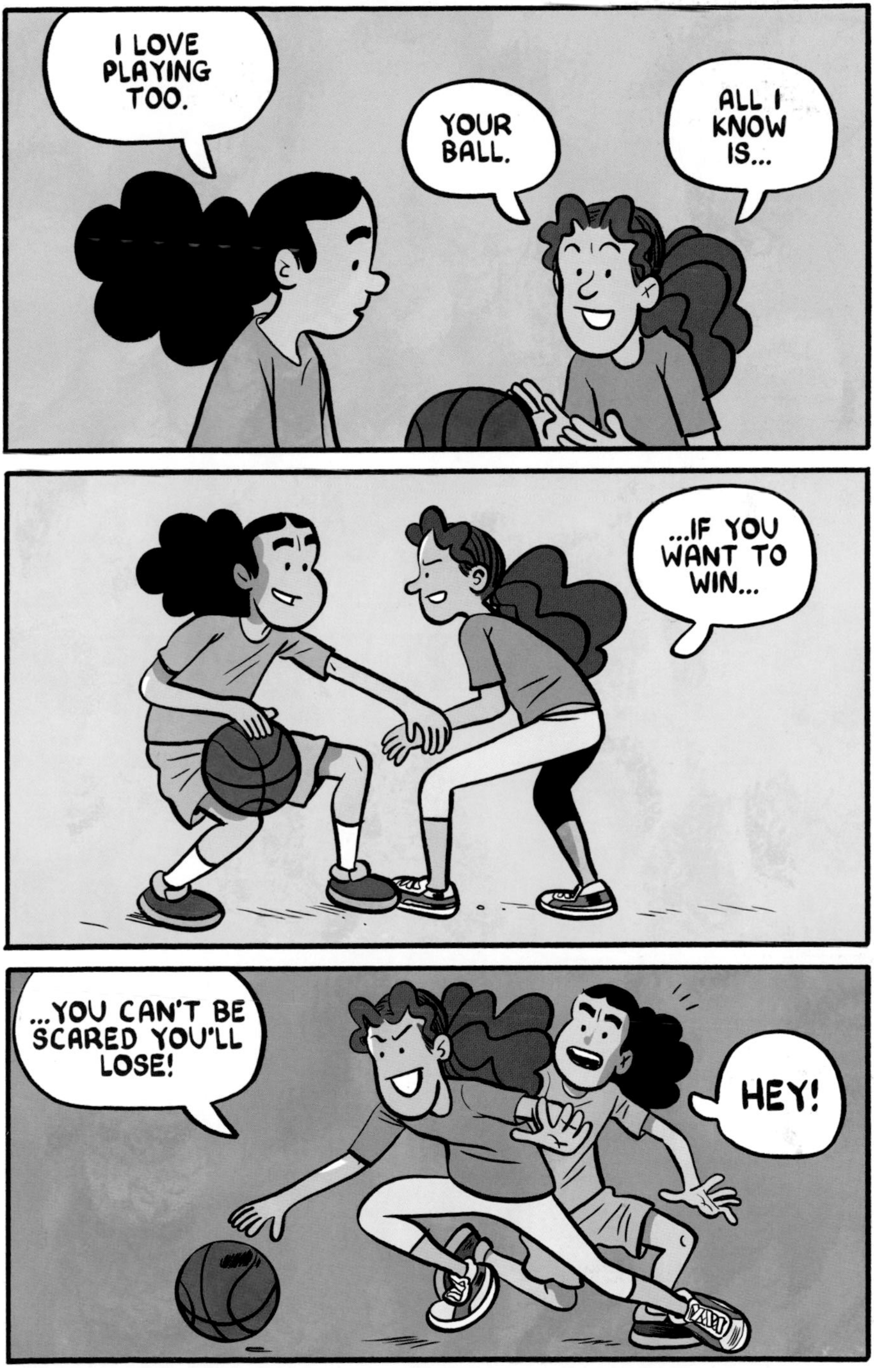
I LOVE PLAYING TOO.
ALL I KNOW IS...
YOUR BALL.
...IF YOU WANT TO WIN...
...YOU CAN'T BE SCARED YOU'LL LOSE!
HEY!

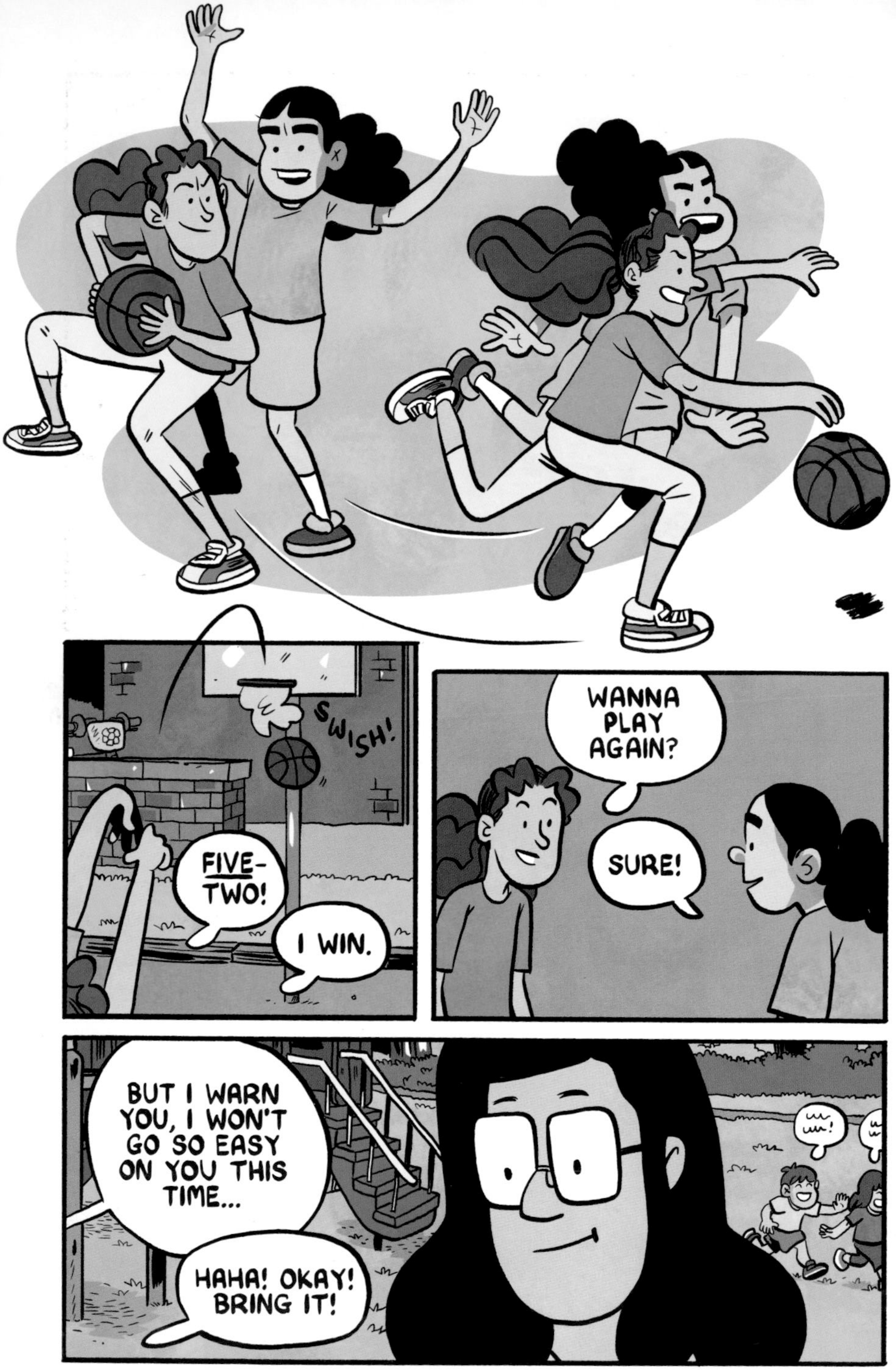
SWISH!
FIVE-TWO!
I WIN.
WANNA PLAY AGAIN?
SURE!
BUT I WARN YOU, I WON'T GO SO EASY ON YOU THIS TIME...
HAHA! OKAY! BRING IT!

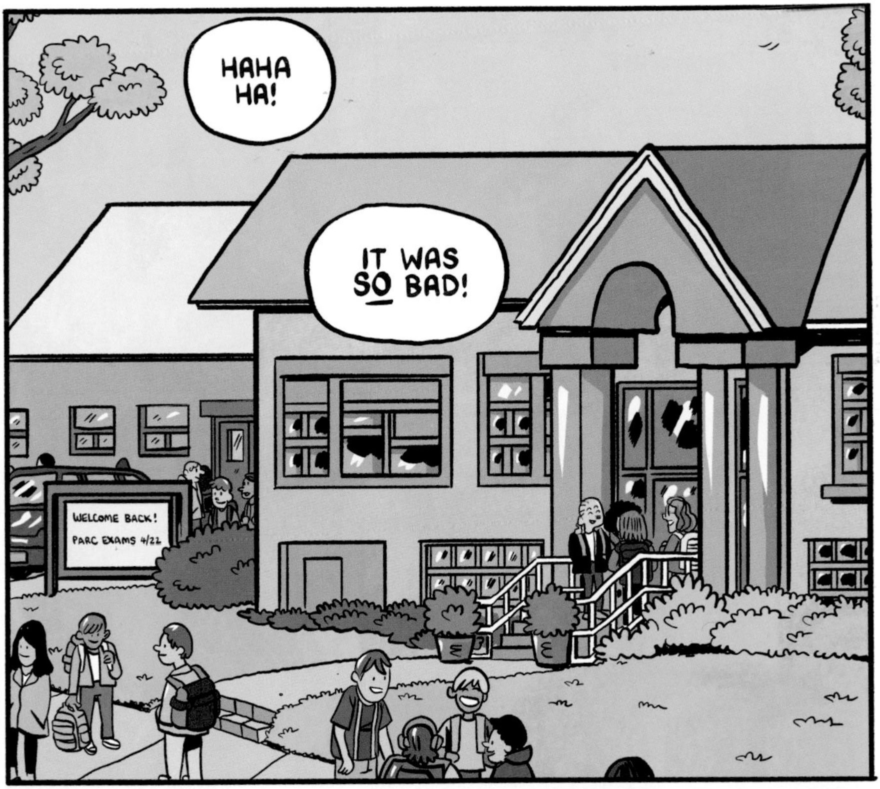
HAHA HA!
IT WAS SO BAD!
WELCOME BACK!
PARC EXAMS 4/22

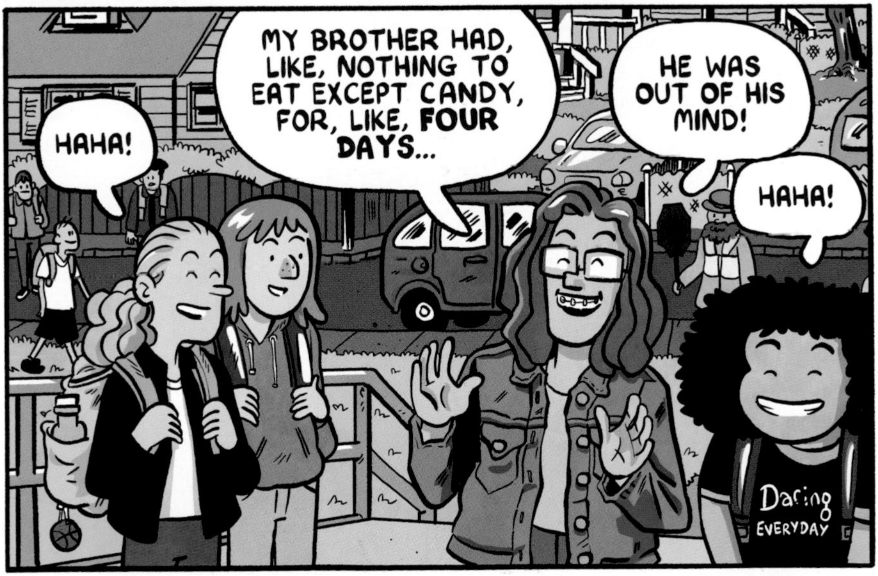
HAHA!
MY BROTHER HAD, LIKE, NOTHING TO EAT EXCEPT CANDY, FOR, LIKE, **FOUR DAYS**...
HE WAS OUT OF HIS MIND!
HAHA!
Daring EVERYDAY

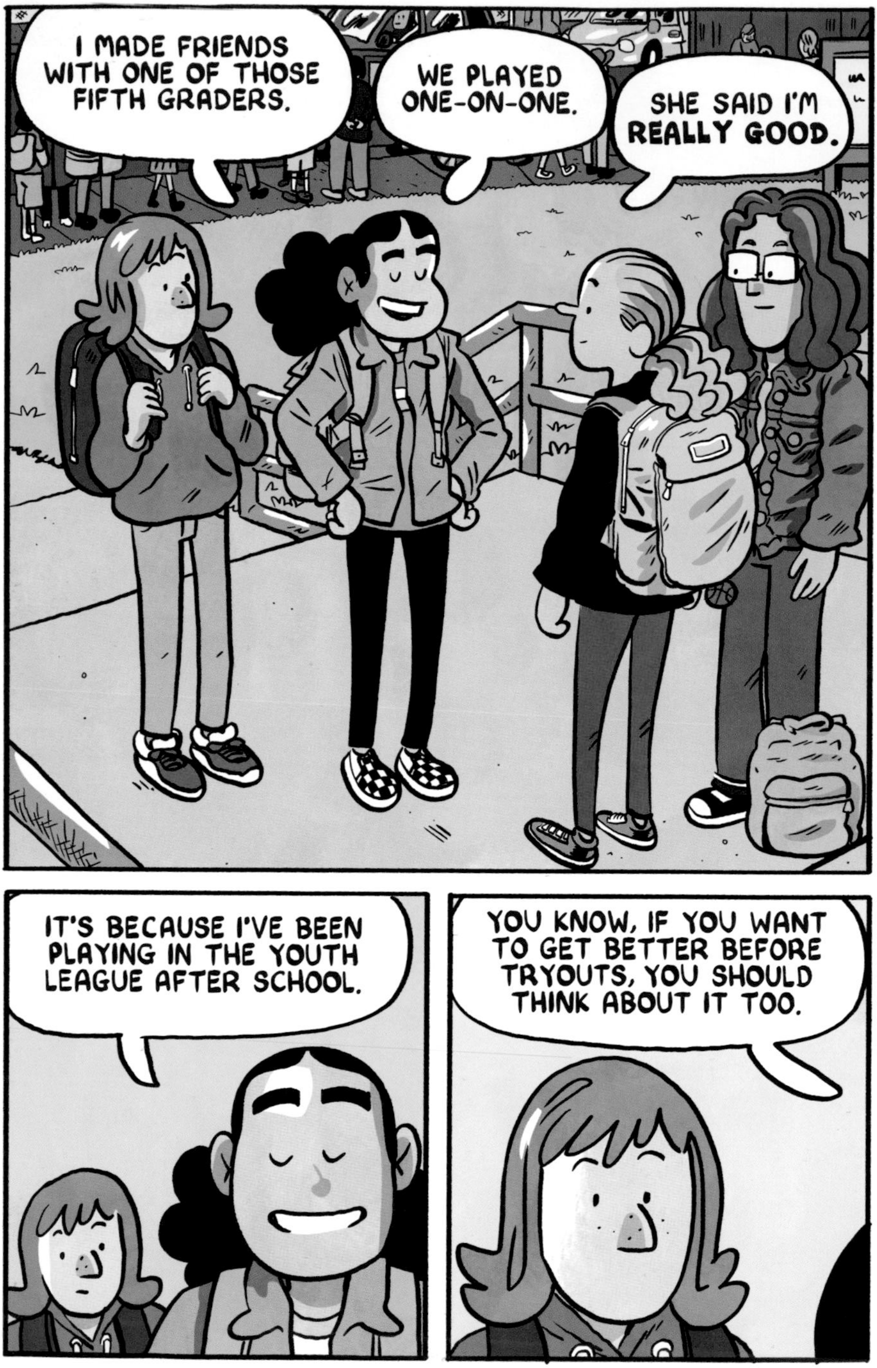
I MADE FRIENDS WITH ONE OF THOSE FIFTH GRADERS.
WE PLAYED ONE-ON-ONE.
SHE SAID I'M **REALLY GOOD.**
IT'S BECAUSE I'VE BEEN PLAYING IN THE YOUTH LEAGUE AFTER SCHOOL.
YOU KNOW, IF YOU WANT TO GET BETTER BEFORE TRYOUTS, YOU SHOULD THINK ABOUT IT TOO.

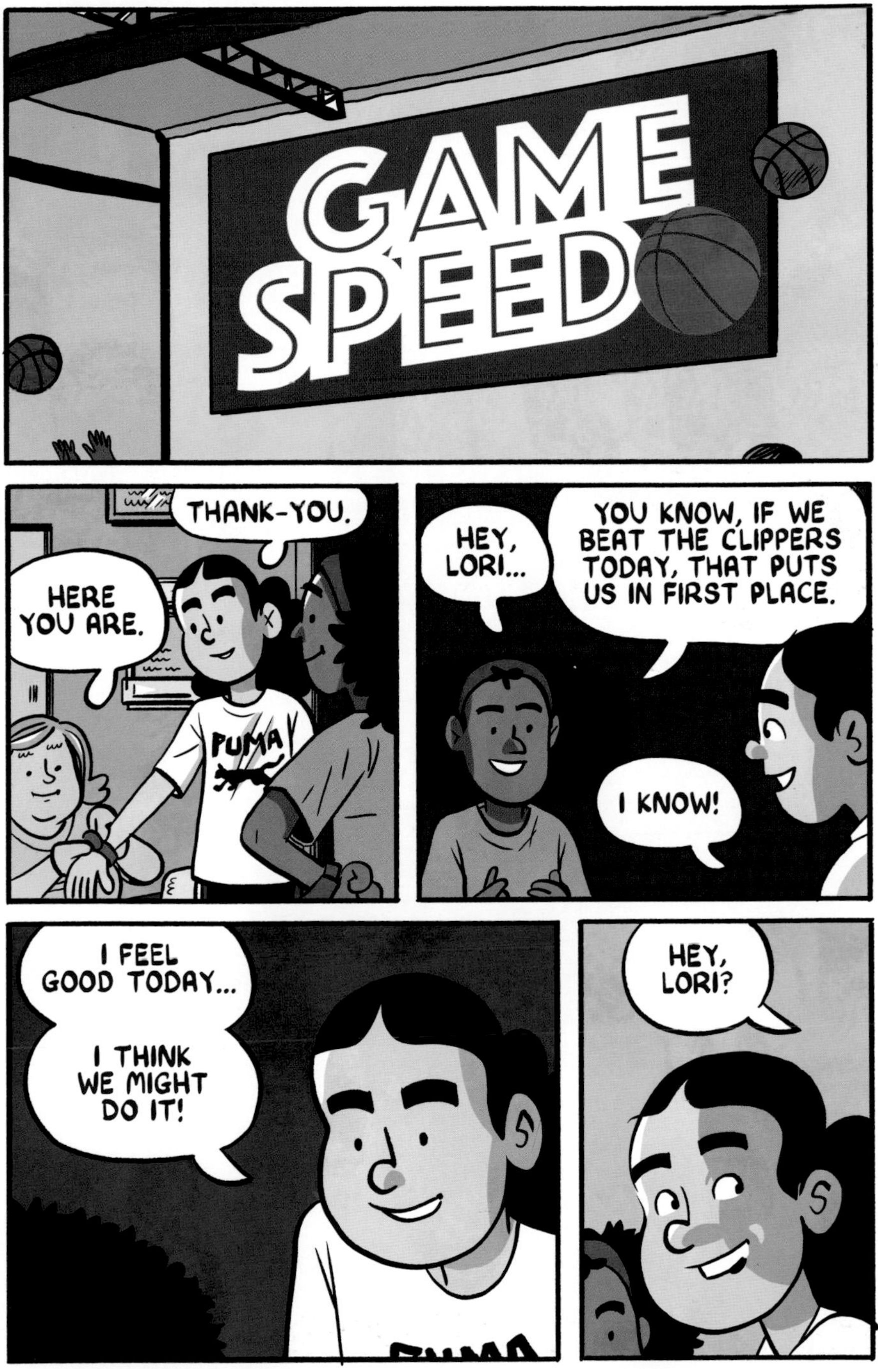
GAME SPEED
THANK-YOU.
HERE YOU ARE.
HEY, LORI...
YOU KNOW, IF WE BEAT THE CLIPPERS TODAY, THAT PUTS US IN FIRST PLACE.
I KNOW!
I FEEL GOOD TODAY...
I THINK WE MIGHT DO IT!
HEY, LORI?

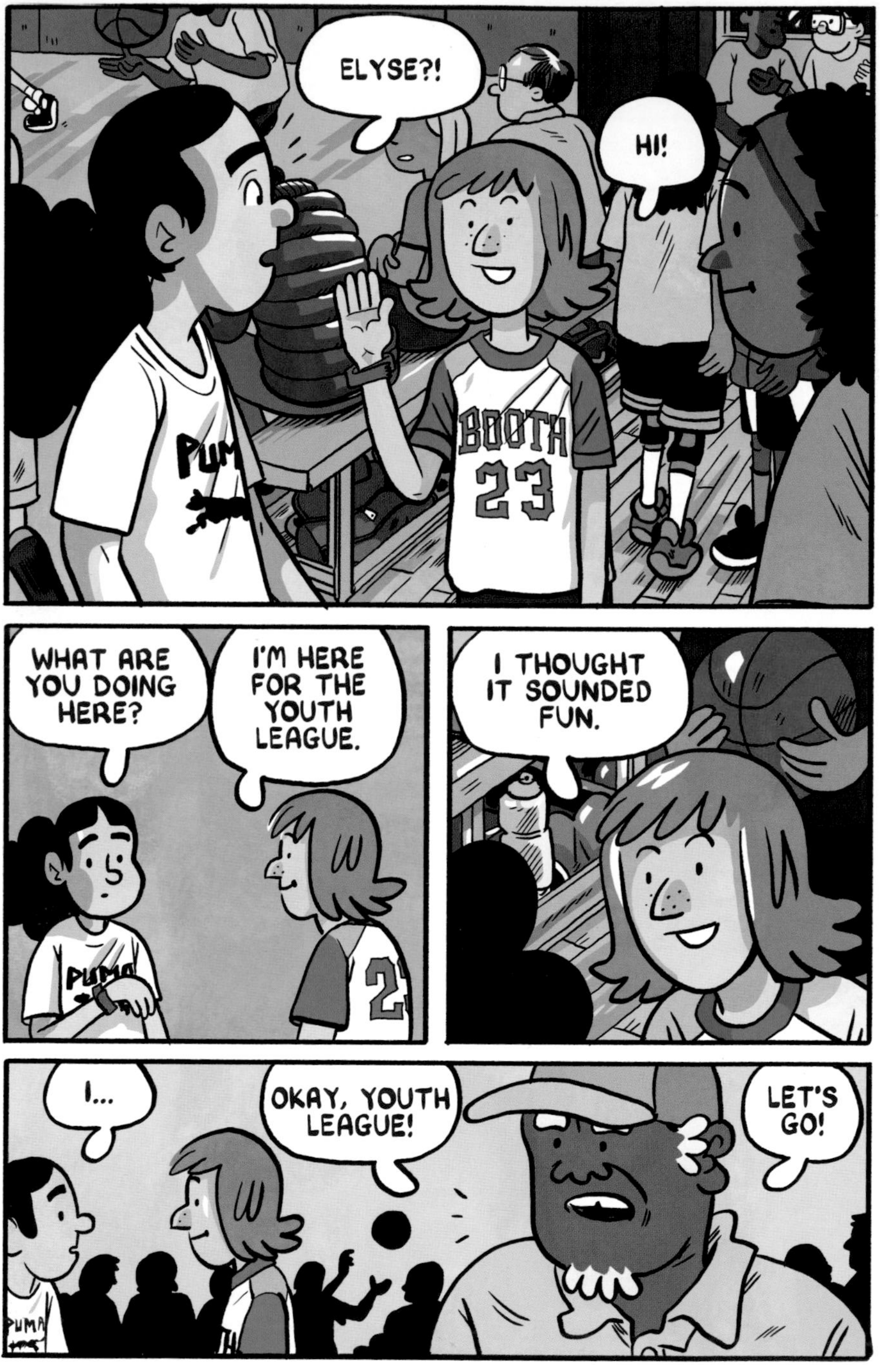
ELYSE?!
HI!
BOOTH 23
PUMA
WHAT ARE YOU DOING HERE?
I'M HERE FOR THE YOUTH LEAGUE.
I THOUGHT IT SOUNDED FUN.
I...
OKAY, YOUTH LEAGUE!
LET'S GO!

137

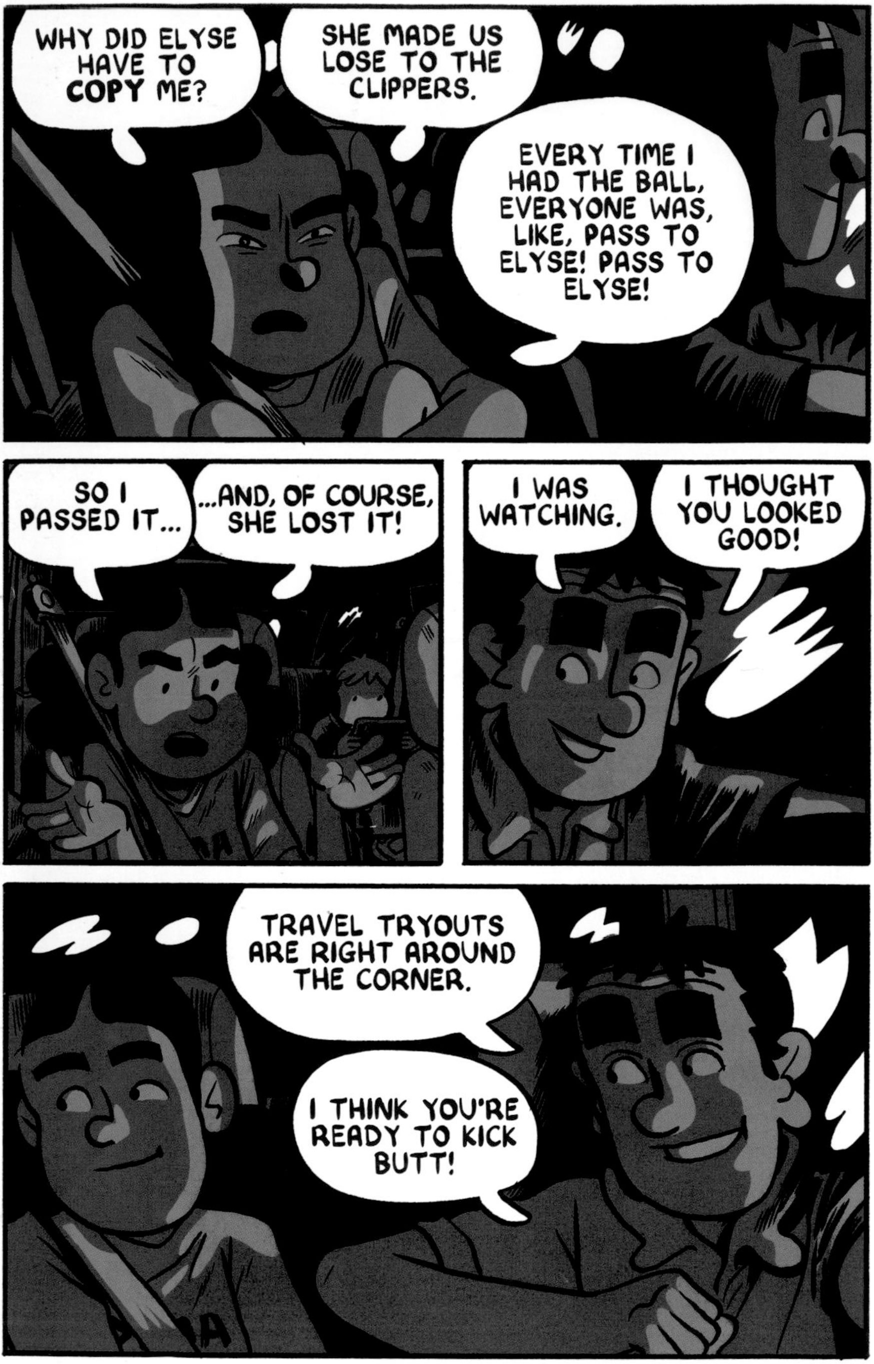
WHY DID ELYSE HAVE TO **COPY** ME?
SHE MADE US LOSE TO THE CLIPPERS.
EVERY TIME I HAD THE BALL, EVERYONE WAS, LIKE, PASS TO ELYSE! PASS TO ELYSE!
SO I PASSED IT...
...AND, OF COURSE, SHE LOST IT!
I WAS WATCHING.
I THOUGHT YOU LOOKED GOOD!
TRAVEL TRYOUTS ARE RIGHT AROUND THE CORNER.
I THINK YOU'RE READY TO KICK BUTT!

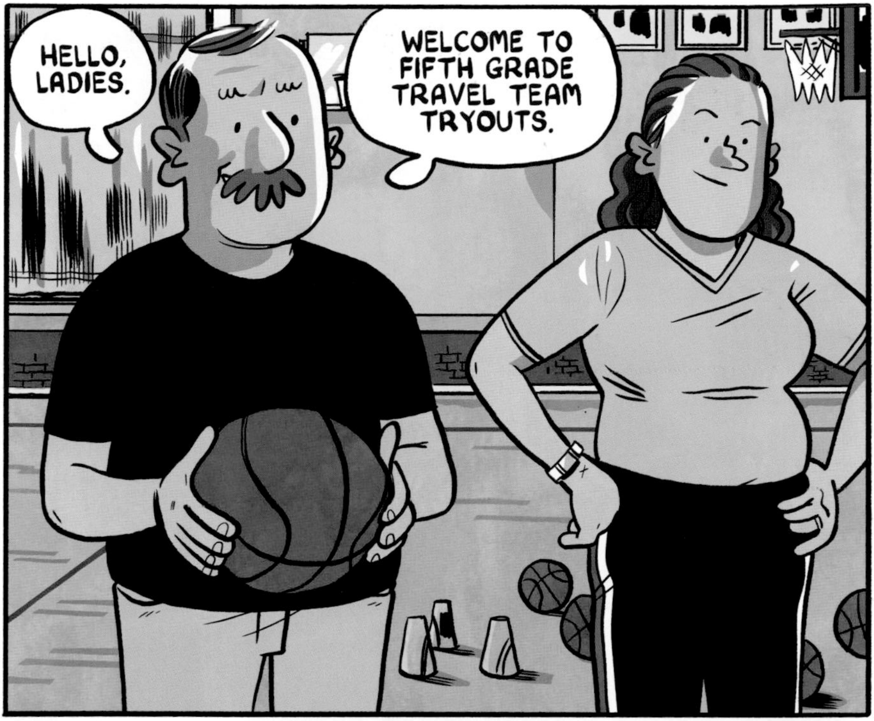
HELLO, LADIES.
WELCOME TO FIFTH GRADE TRAVEL TEAM TRYOUTS.

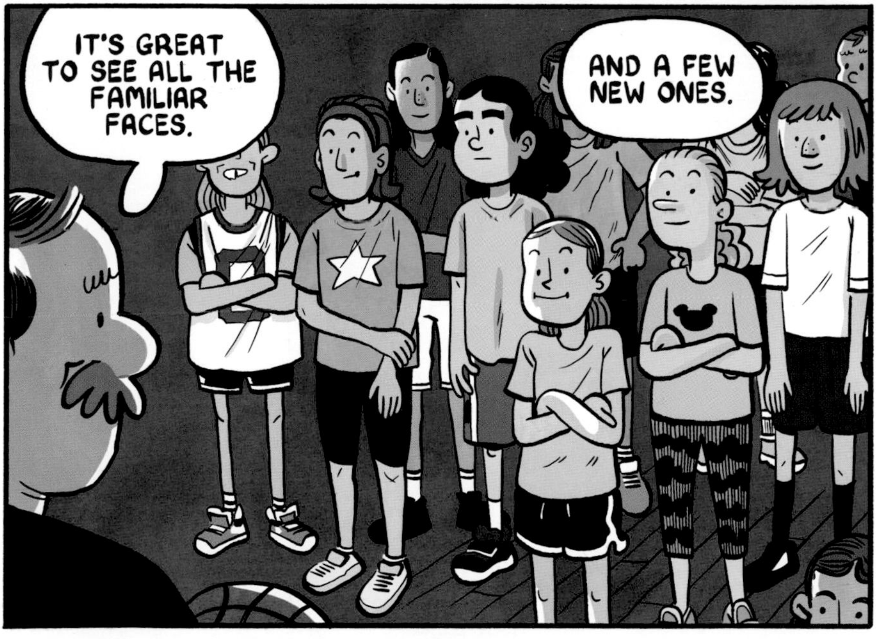
IT'S GREAT TO SEE ALL THE FAMILIAR FACES.
AND A FEW NEW ONES.

140

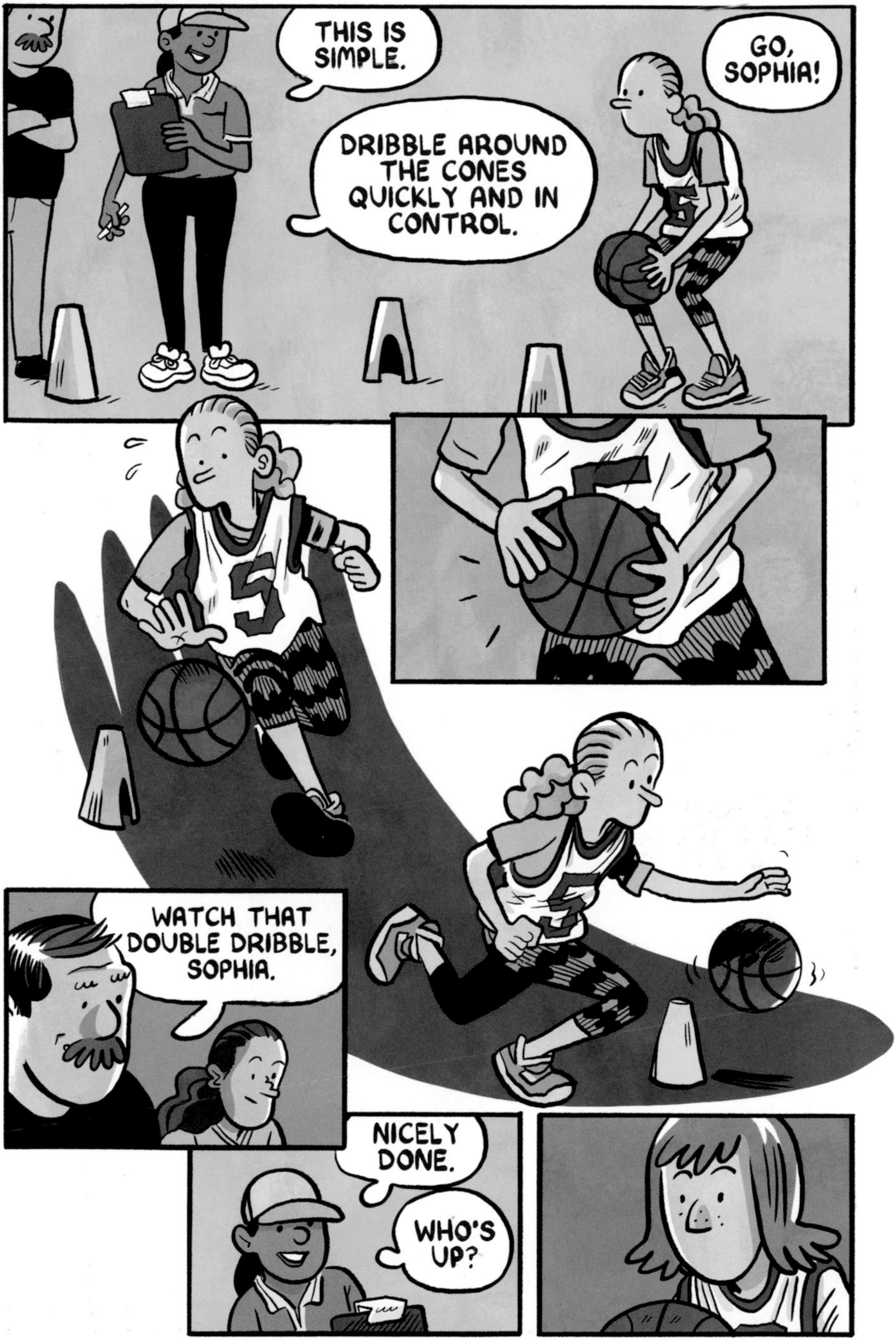
THIS IS SIMPLE.
DRIBBLE AROUND THE CONES QUICKLY AND IN CONTROL.
GO, SOPHIA!
WATCH THAT DOUBLE DRIBBLE, SOPHIA.
NICELY DONE.
WHO'S UP?

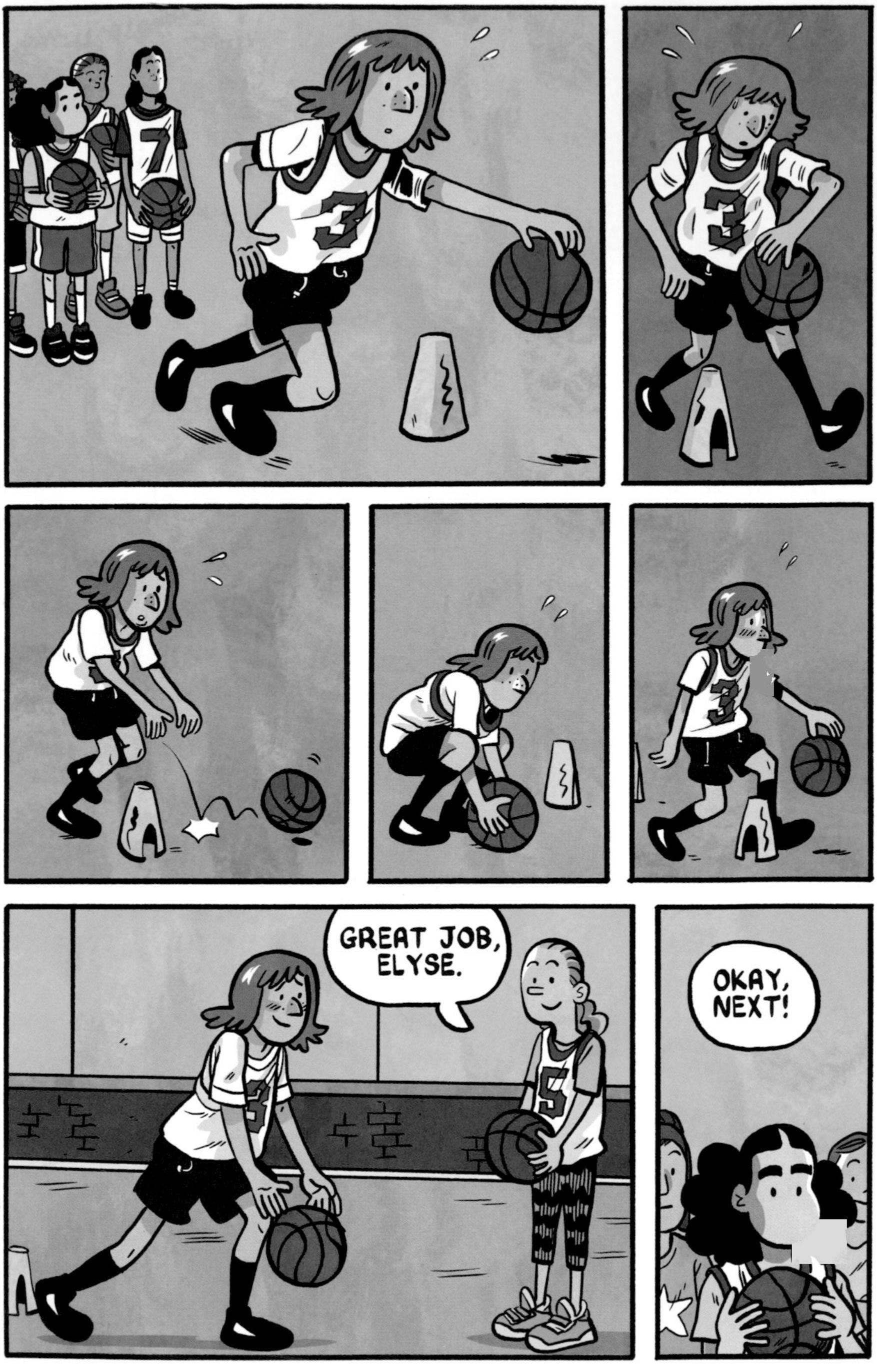
GREAT JOB, ELYSE.
OKAY, NEXT!

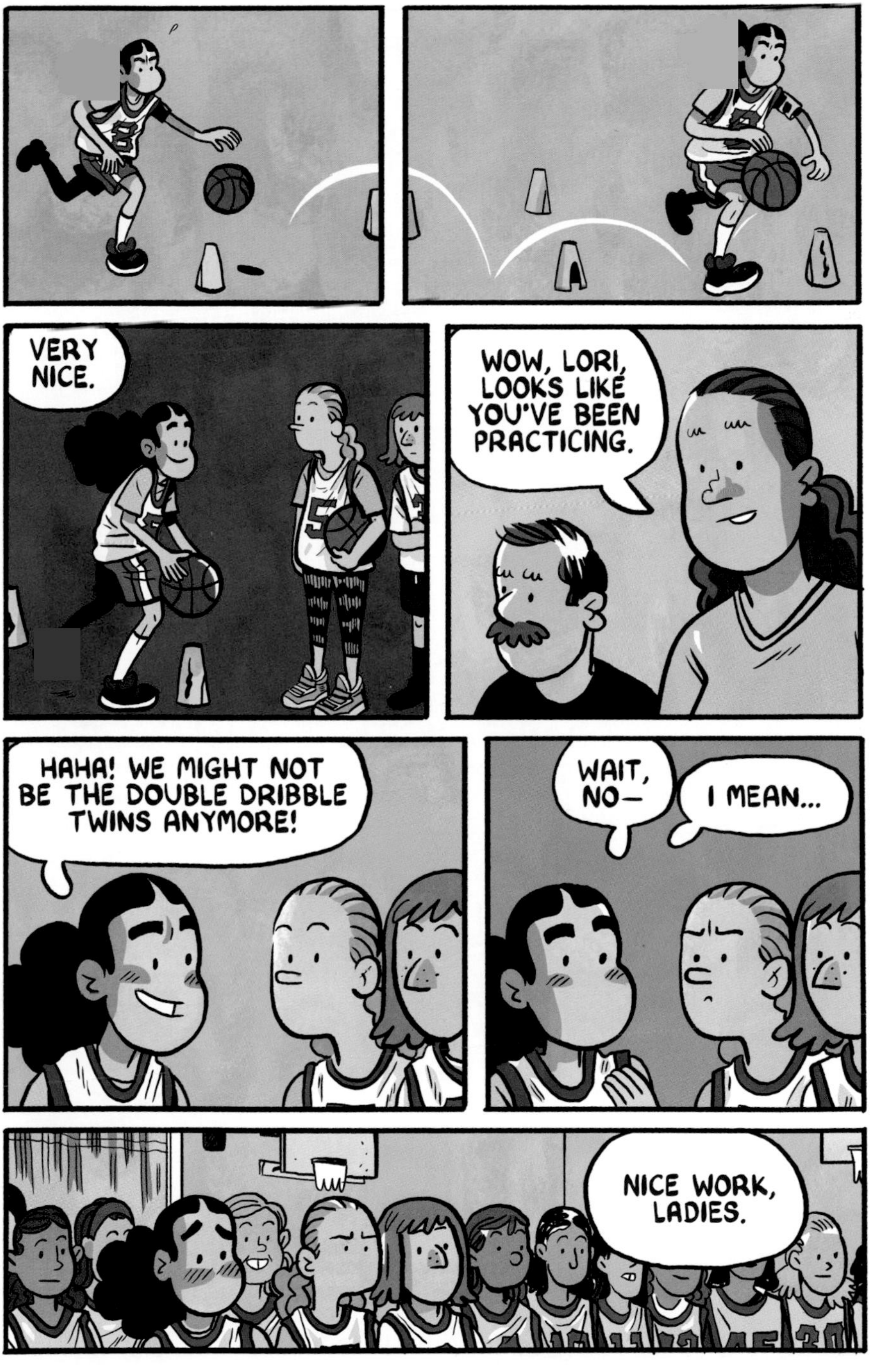
VERY NICE.
WOW, LORI, LOOKS LIKE YOU'VE BEEN PRACTICING.
HAHA! WE MIGHT NOT BE THE DOUBLE DRIBBLE TWINS ANYMORE!
WAIT, NO—
I MEAN...
NICE WORK, LADIES.

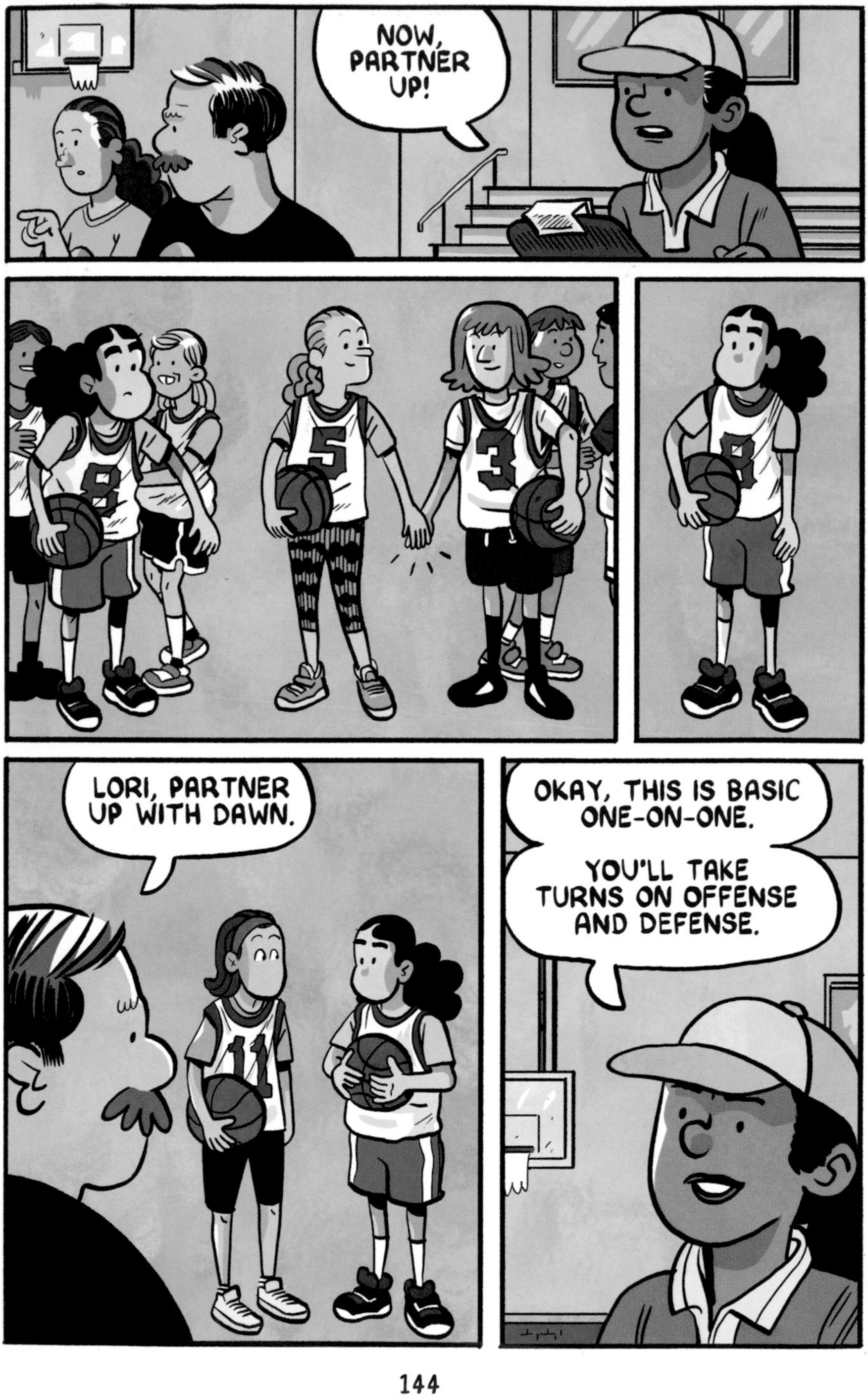
NOW, PARTNER UP!
LORI, PARTNER UP WITH DAWN.
OKAY, THIS IS BASIC ONE-ON-ONE.
YOU'LL TAKE TURNS ON OFFENSE AND DEFENSE.

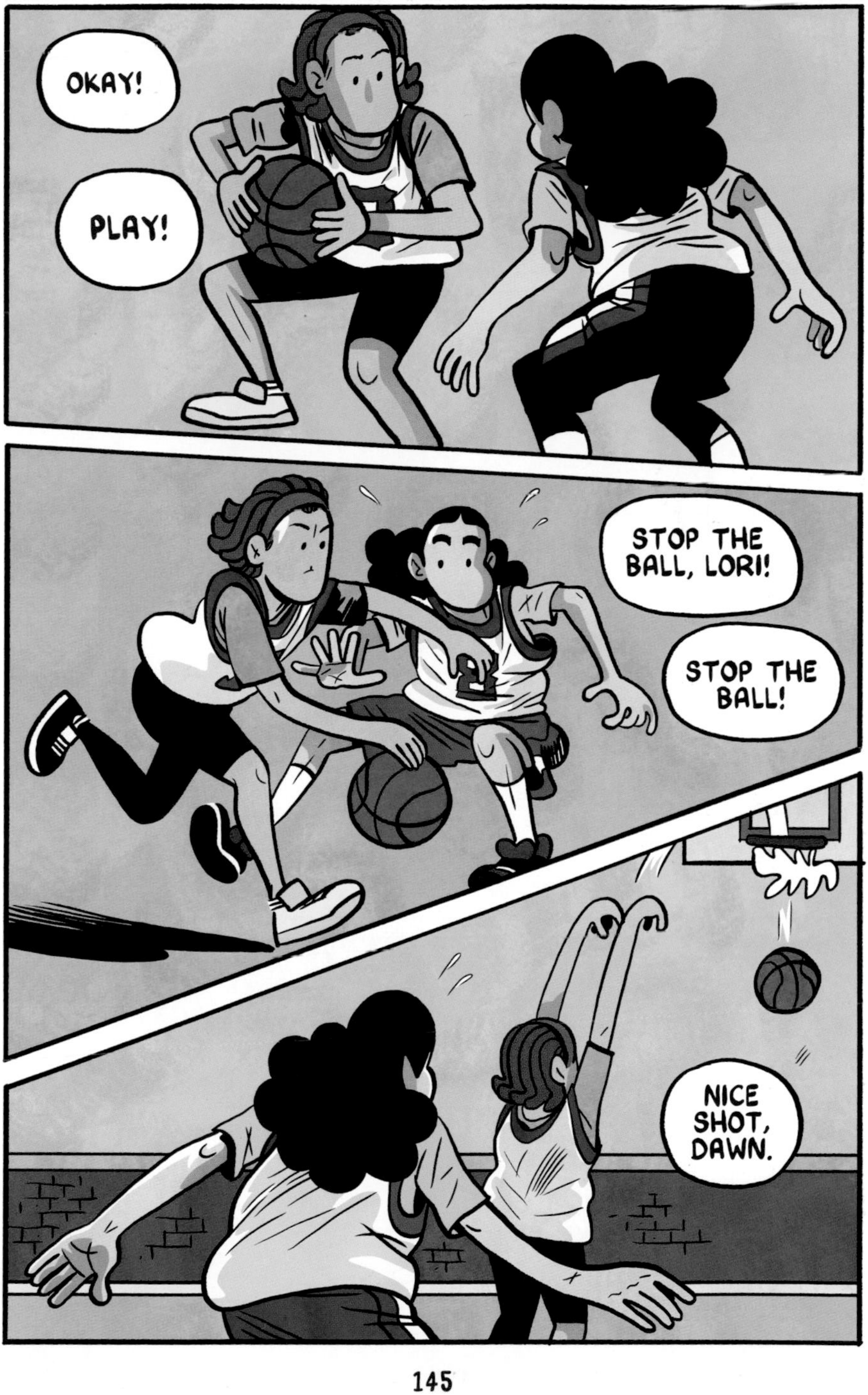
OKAY!
PLAY!
STOP THE BALL, LORI!
STOP THE BALL!
NICE SHOT, DAWN.

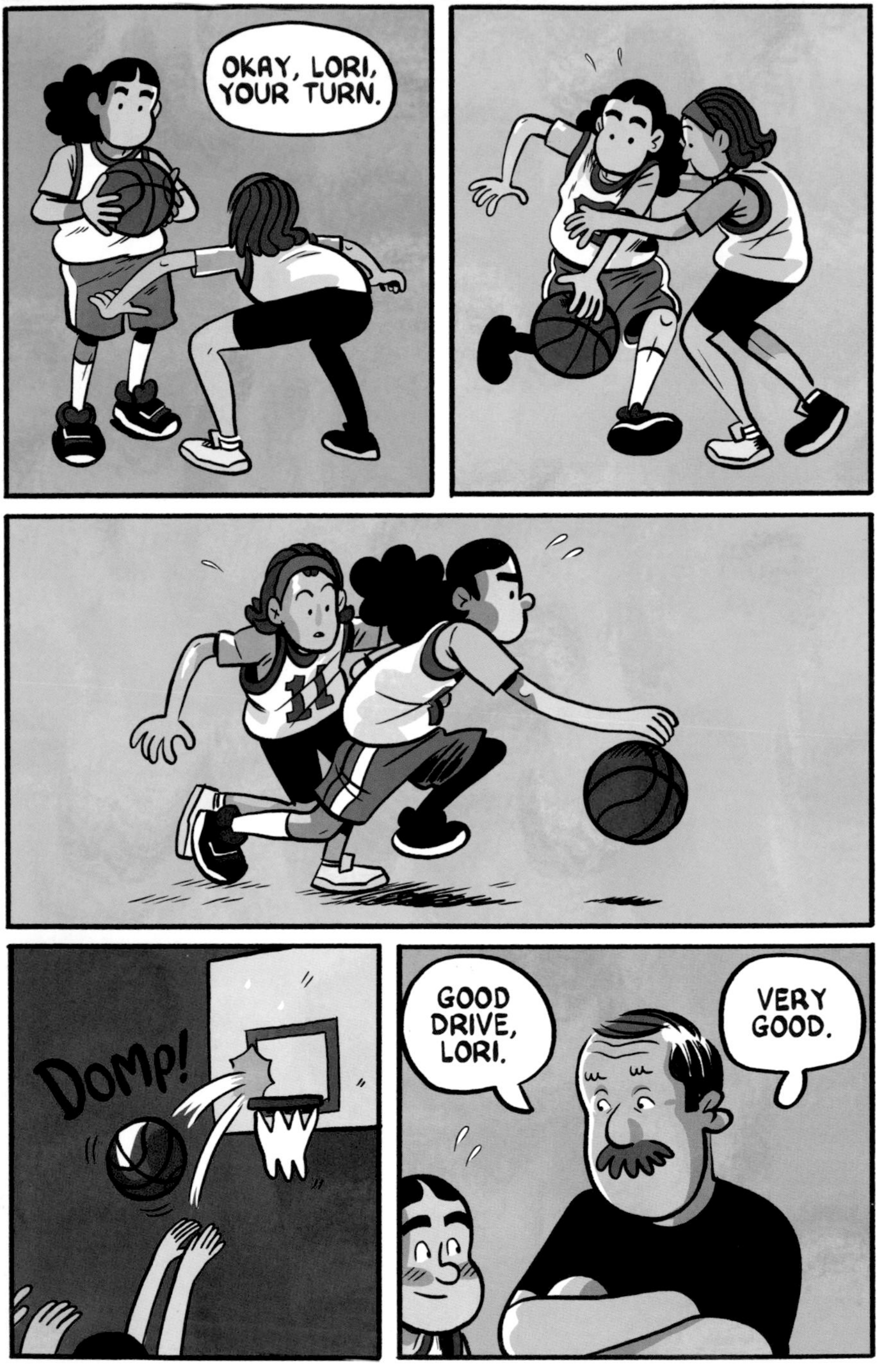
OKAY, LORI, YOUR TURN.
DOMP!
GOOD DRIVE, LORI.
VERY GOOD.

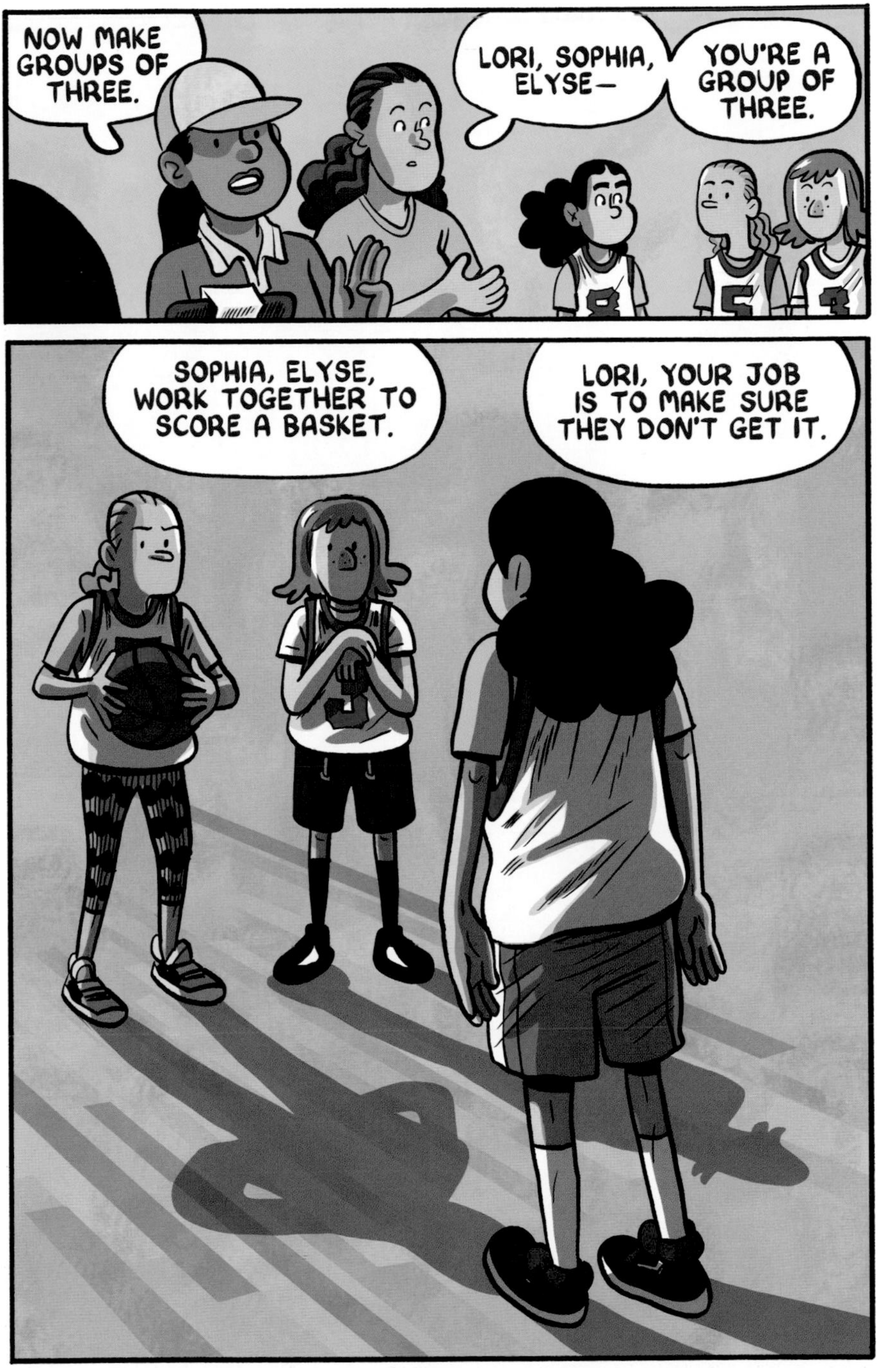
NOW MAKE GROUPS OF THREE.
LORI, SOPHIA, ELYSE—
YOU'RE A GROUP OF THREE.
SOPHIA, ELYSE, WORK TOGETHER TO SCORE A BASKET.
LORI, YOUR JOB IS TO MAKE SURE THEY DON'T GET IT.

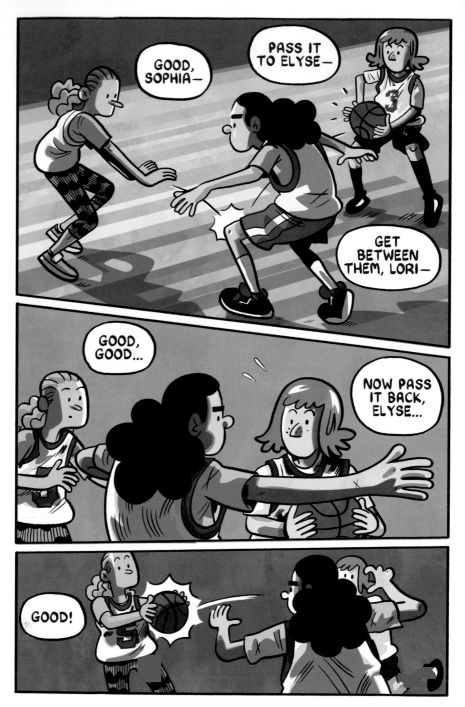

149

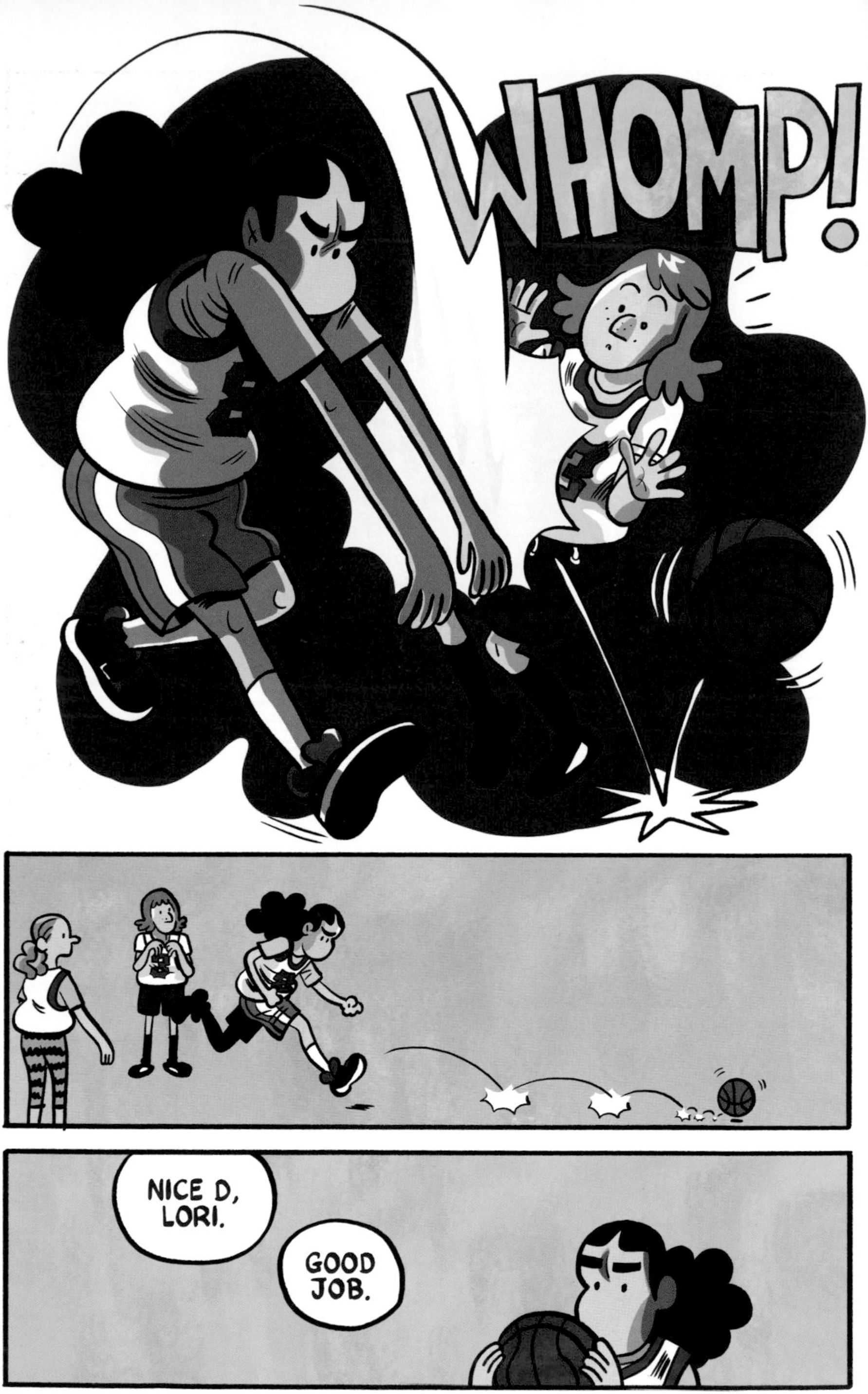
WHOMP!
NICE D, LORI.
GOOD JOB.

154

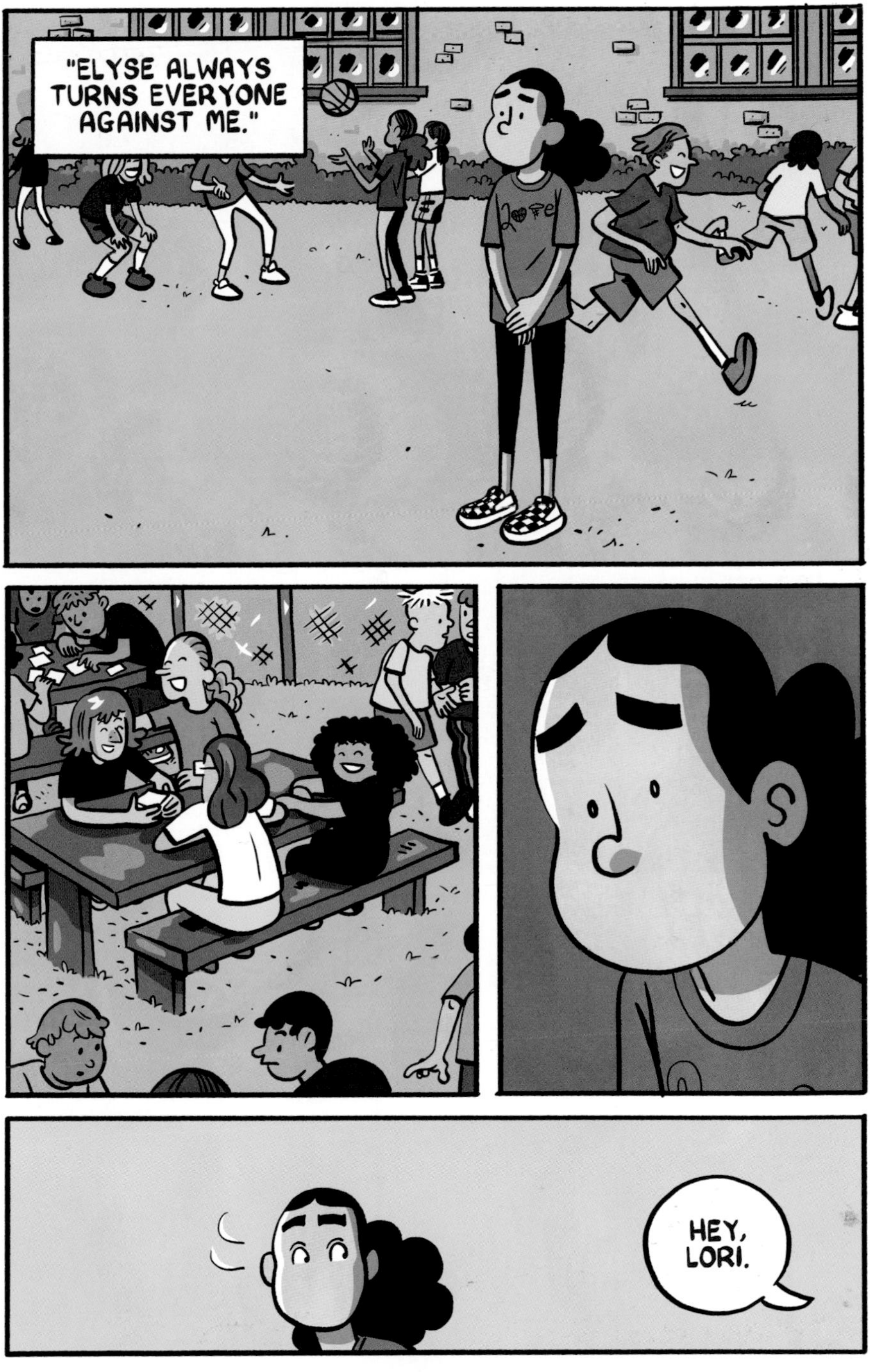
"ELYSE ALWAYS TURNS EVERYONE AGAINST ME."
HEY, LORI.

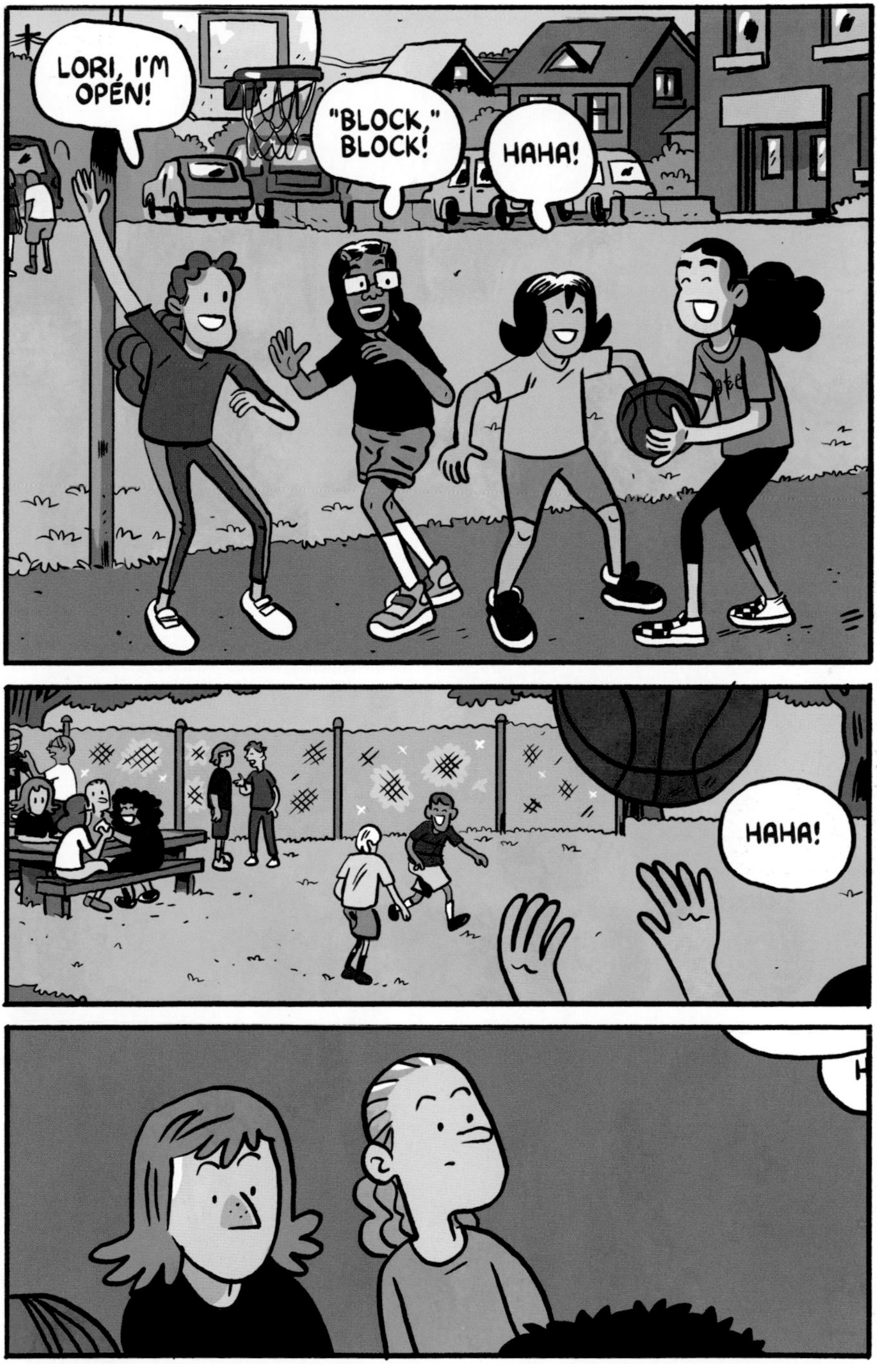
LORI, I'M OPEN!
"BLOCK," BLOCK!
HAHA!
HAHA!

159

160

163

164

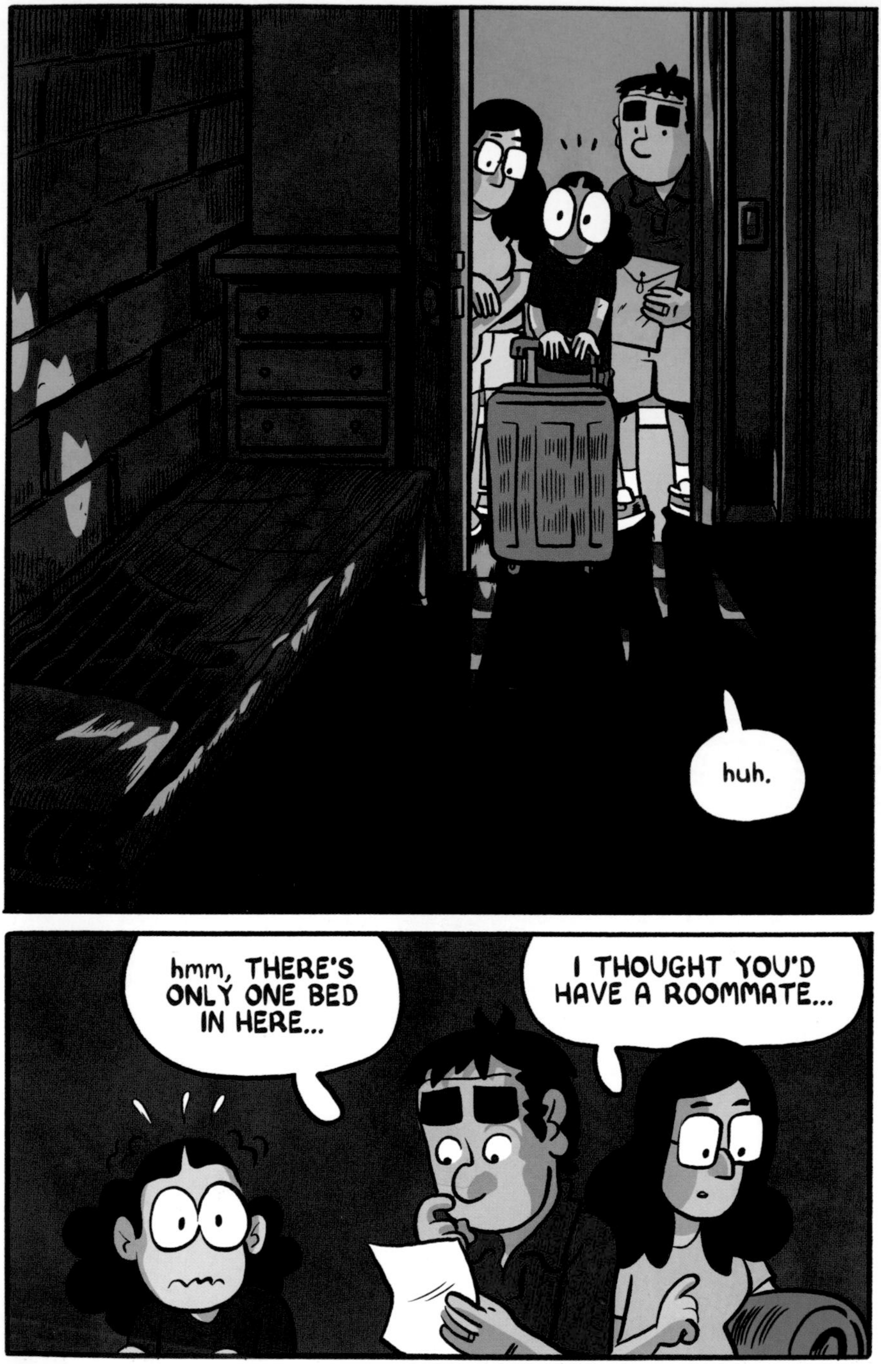
huh.
hmm, THERE'S ONLY ONE BED IN HERE...
I THOUGHT YOU'D HAVE A ROOMMATE...

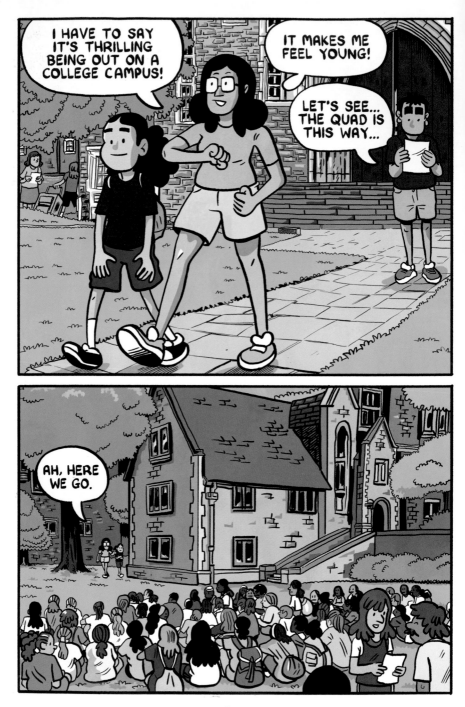

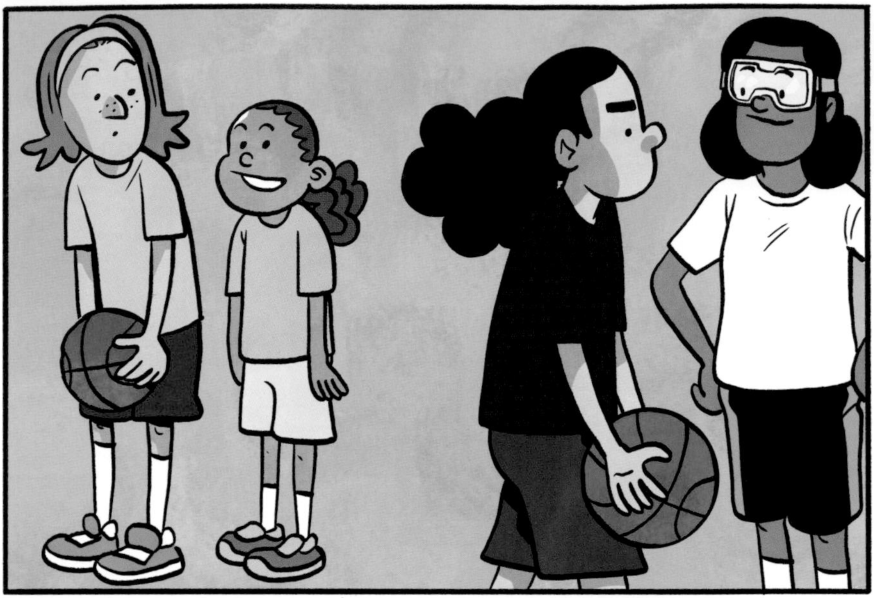

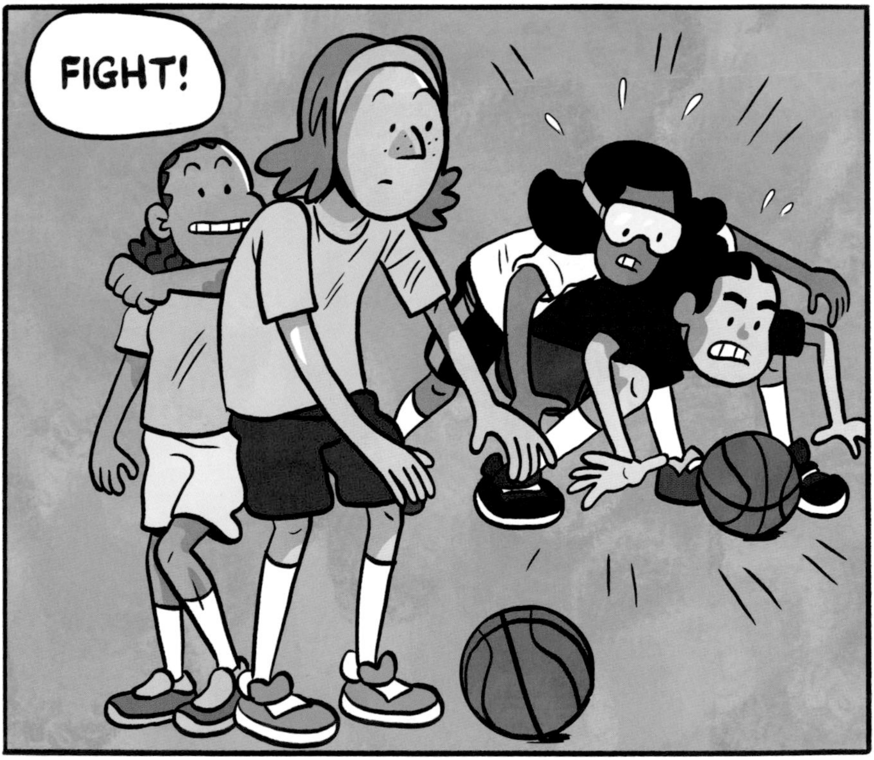
FIGHT!

184

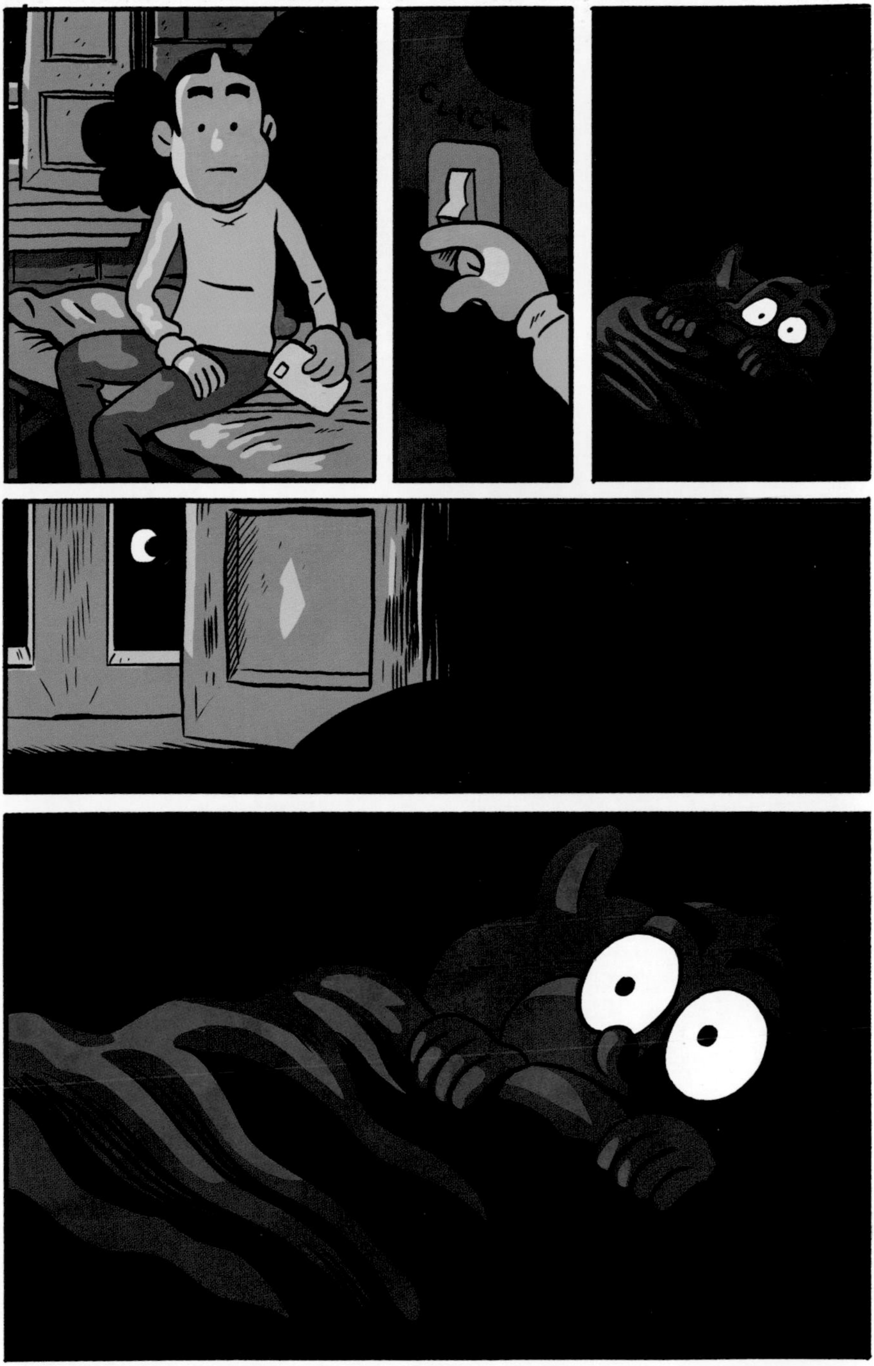
CLICK

186

187

188

189

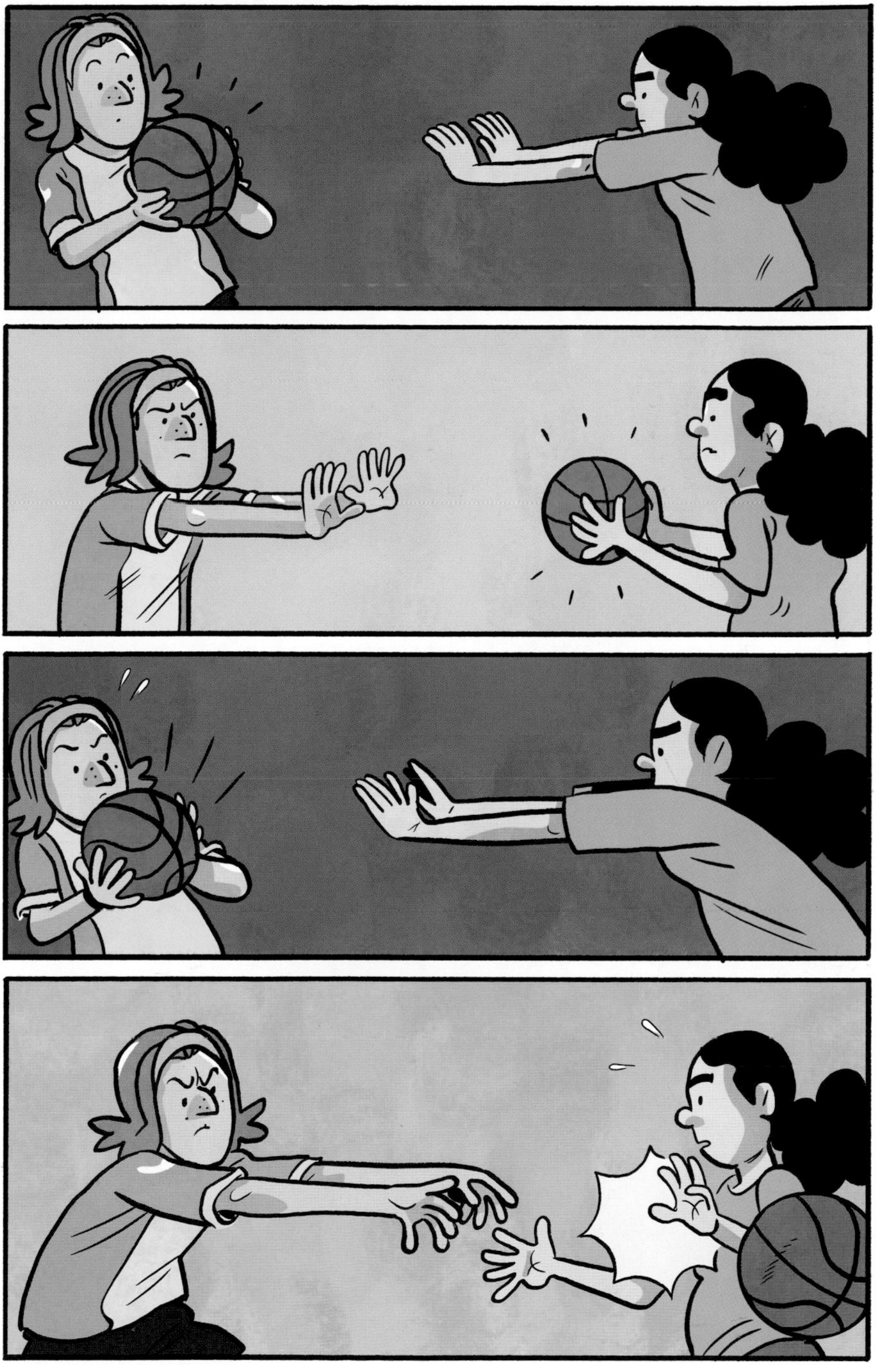

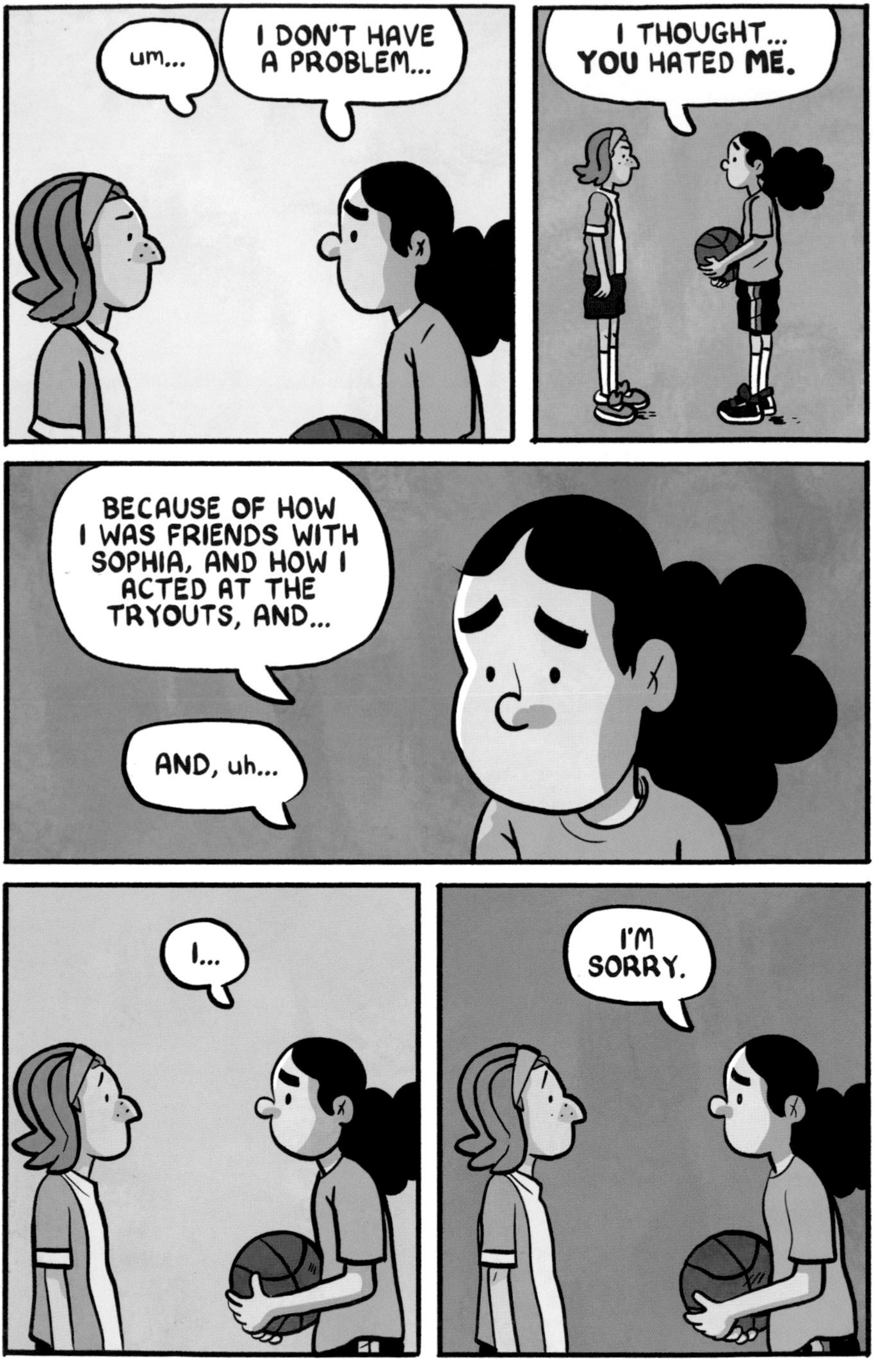
um...
I DON'T HAVE A PROBLEM...
I THOUGHT... YOU HATED ME.
BECAUSE OF HOW I WAS FRIENDS WITH SOPHIA, AND HOW I ACTED AT THE TRYOUTS, AND...
AND, uh...
I...
I'M SORRY.

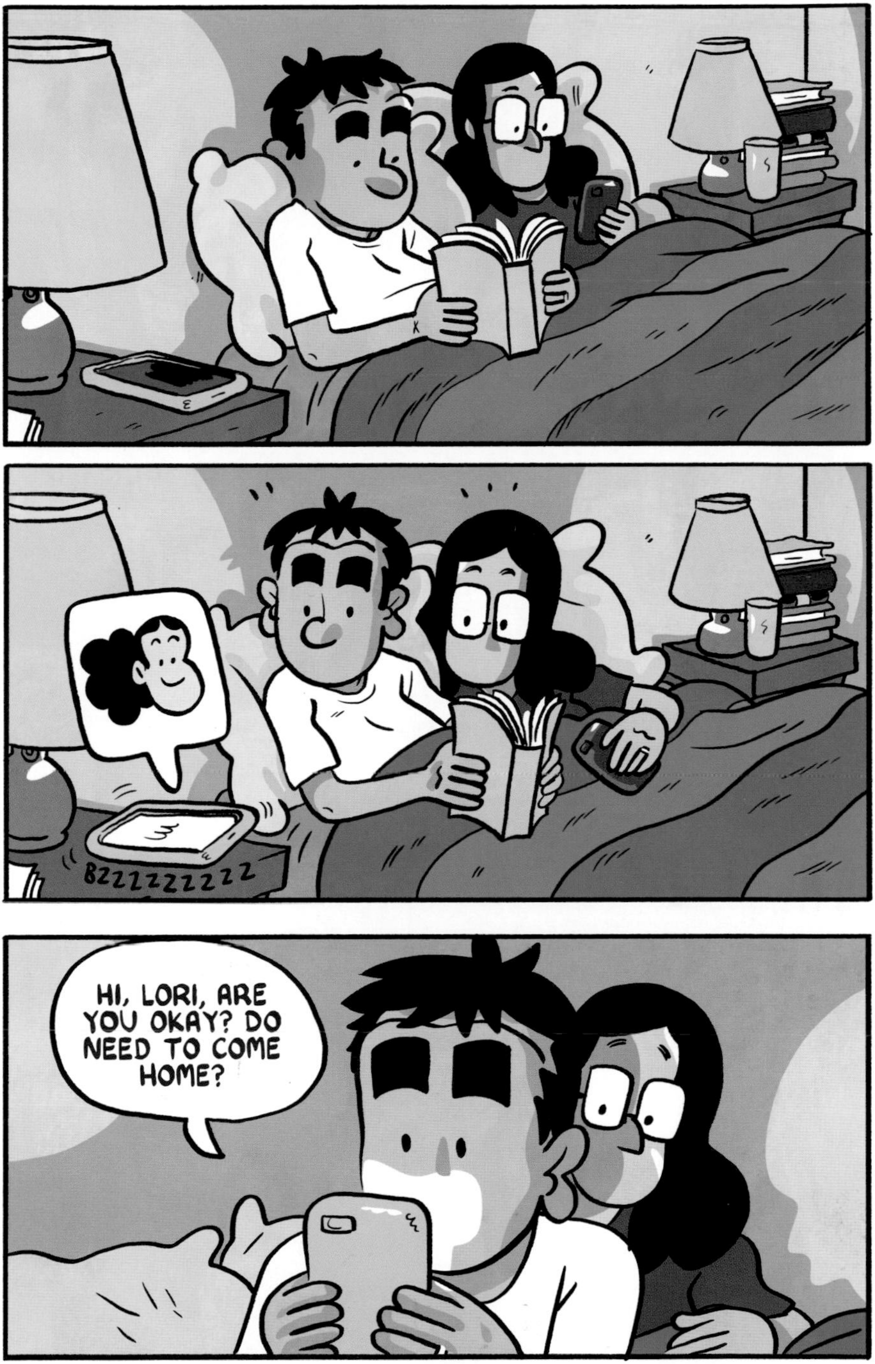
BZZZZZZZZZZ
HI, LORI, ARE YOU OKAY? DO NEED TO COME HOME?

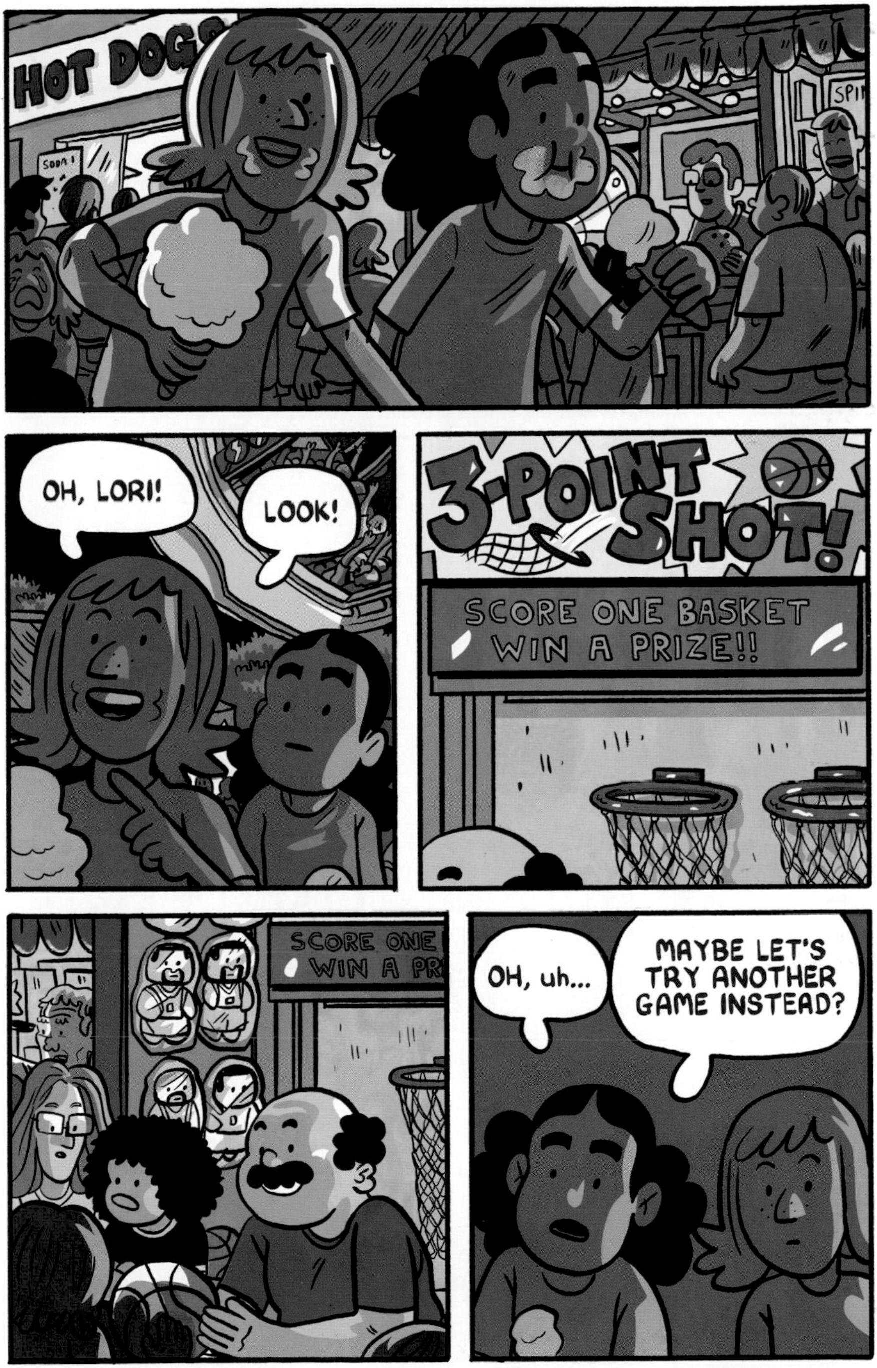
HOT DOGS
SODA
SPIN
OH, LORI!
LOOK!
3-POINT SHOT!
SCORE ONE BASKET
WIN A PRIZE!!
SCORE ONE
WIN A PR
OH, uh...
MAYBE LET'S TRY ANOTHER GAME INSTEAD?

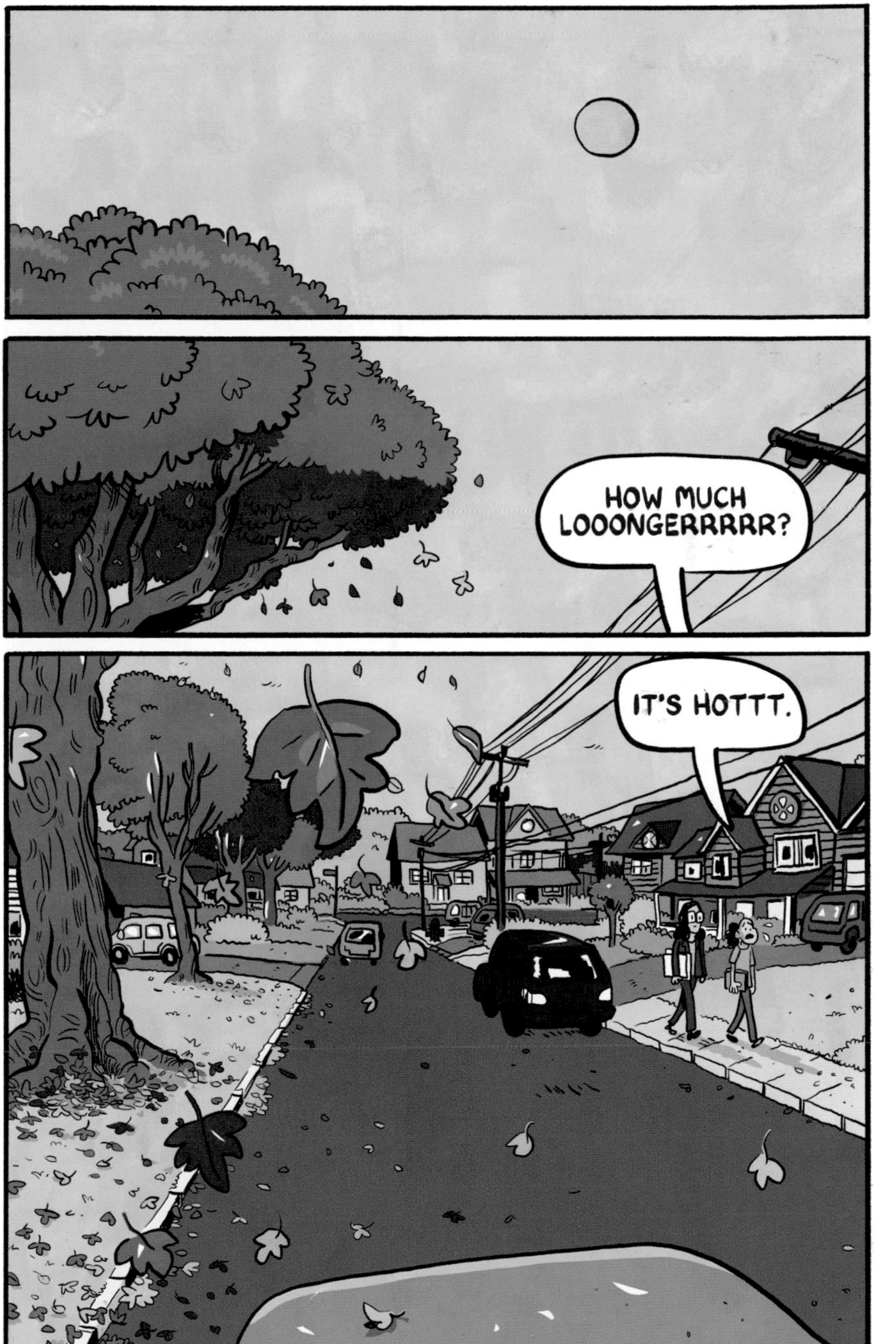
HOW MUCH LOOONGERRRRR?
IT'S HOTTT.

205

206

211

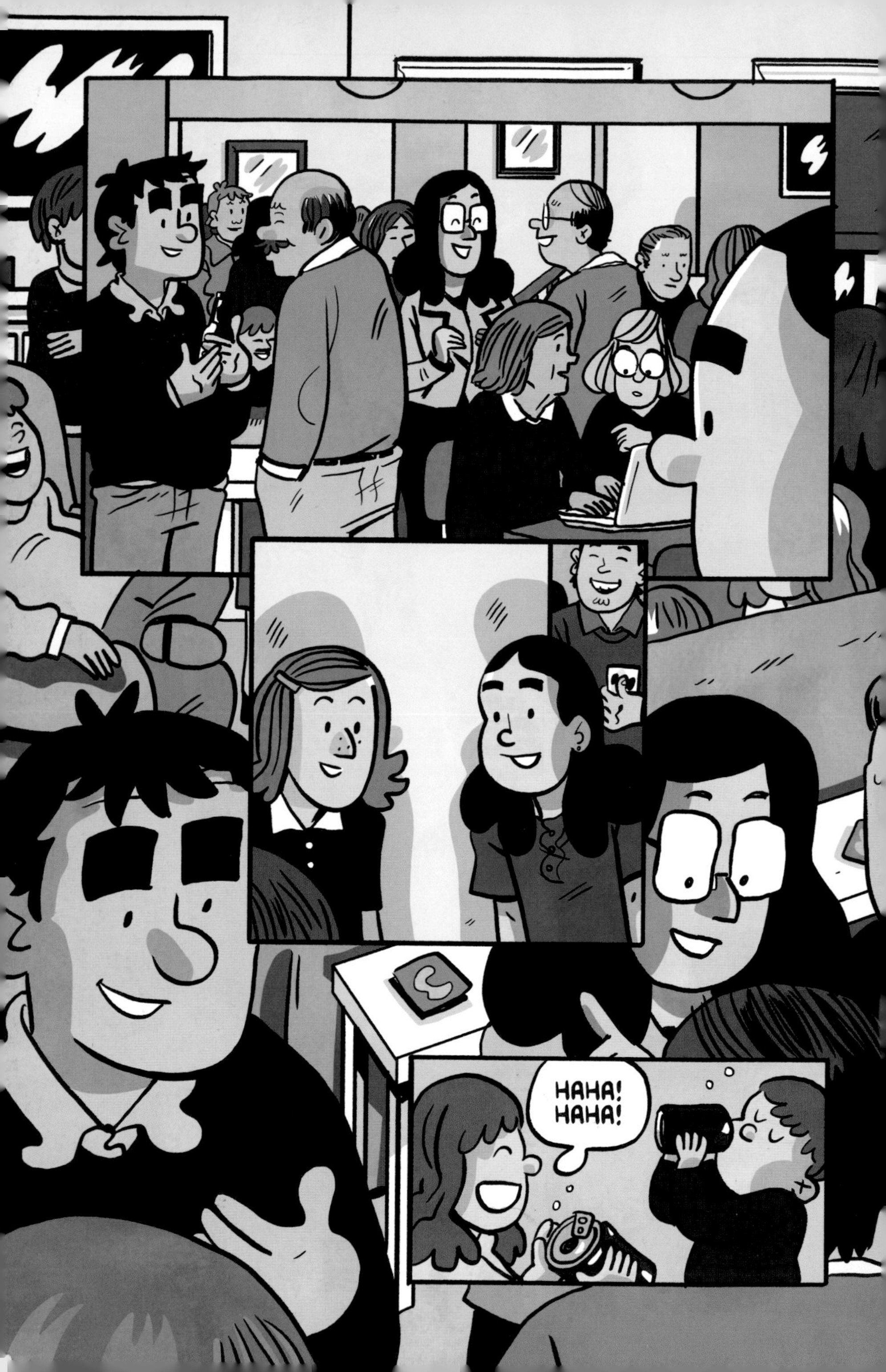
HAHA!
HAHA!

216

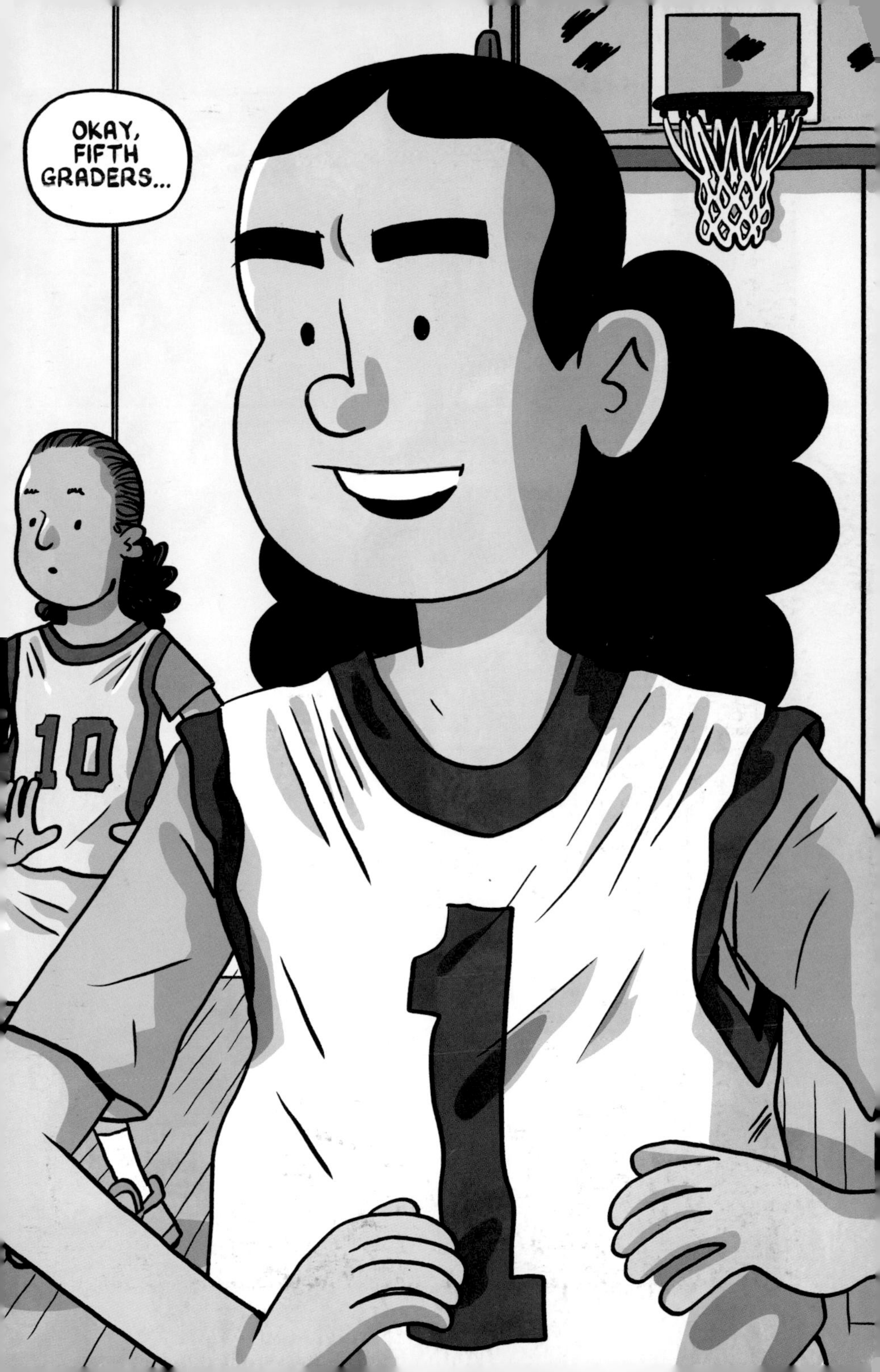
OKAY, FIFTH GRADERS...
10
1

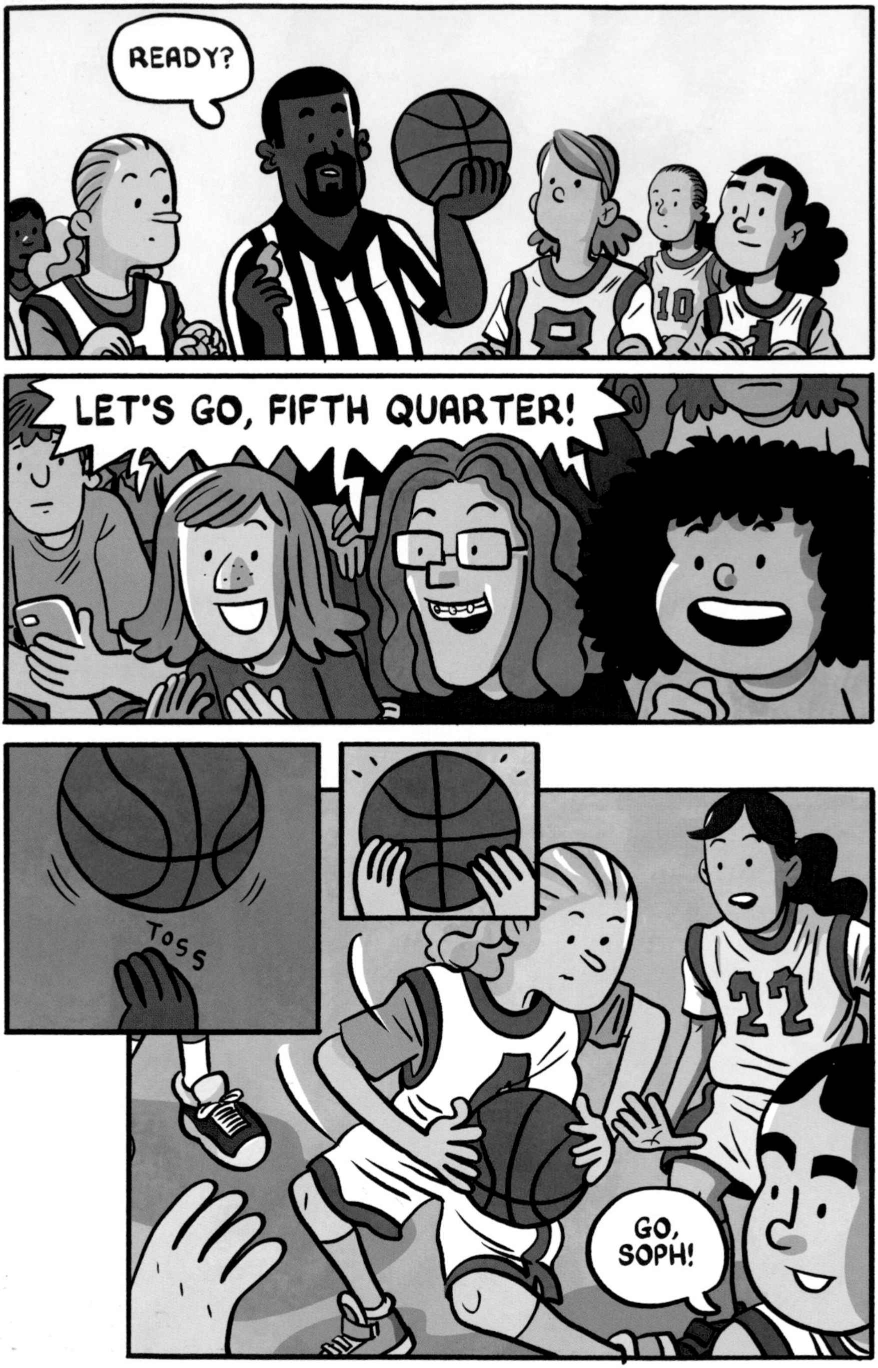
READY?
LET'S GO, FIFTH QUARTER!
TOSS
GO, SOPH!

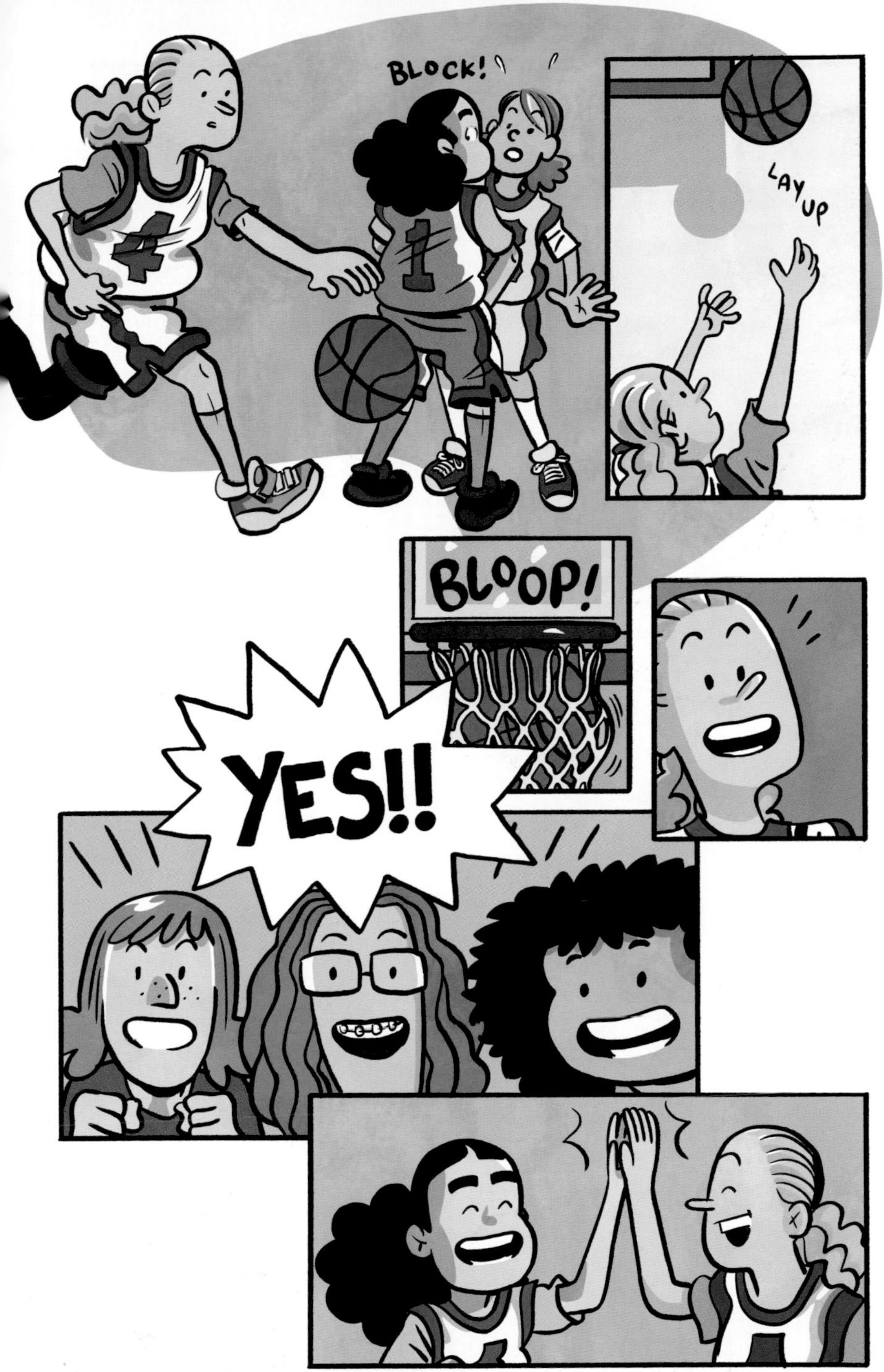
BLOCK!
LAYUP
BLOOP!
YES!!

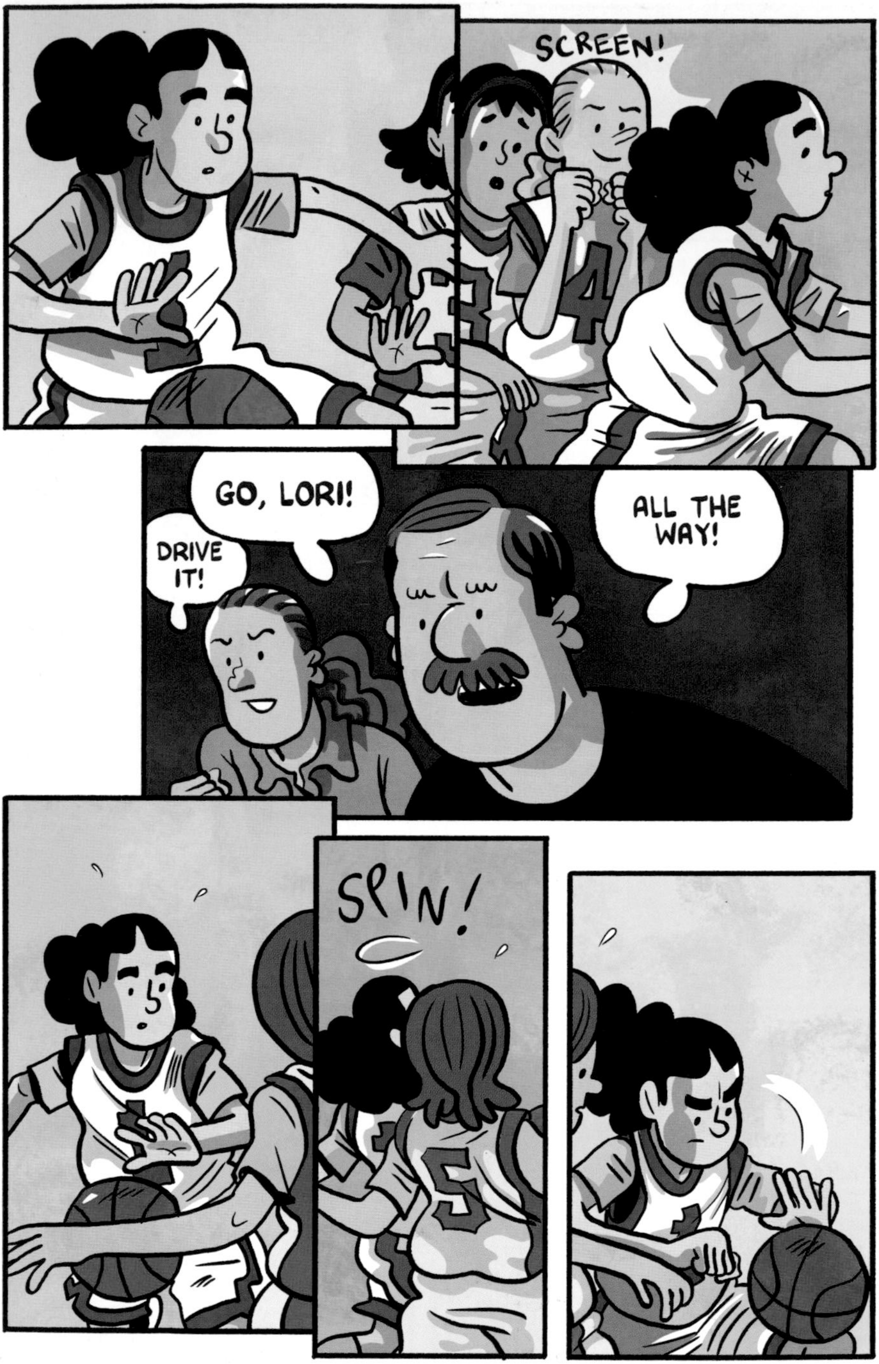
SCREEN!
GO, LORI!
DRIVE IT!
ALL THE WAY!
SPIN!

229

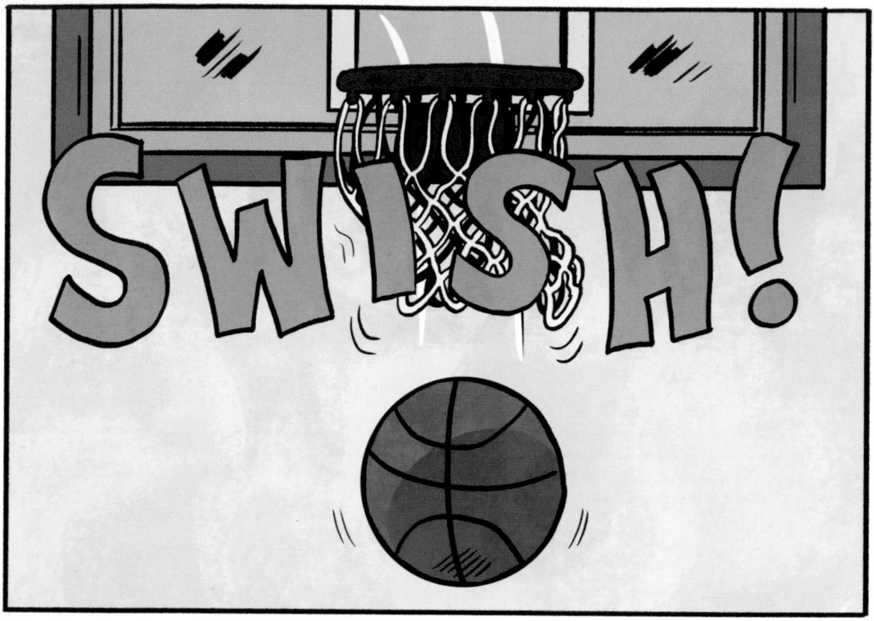
SWISH!

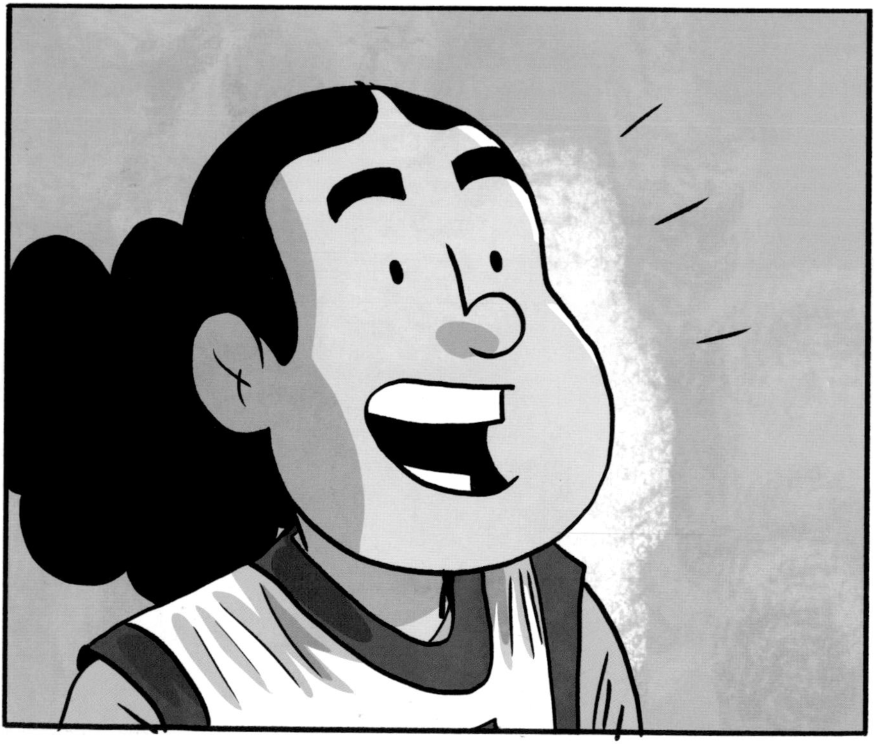

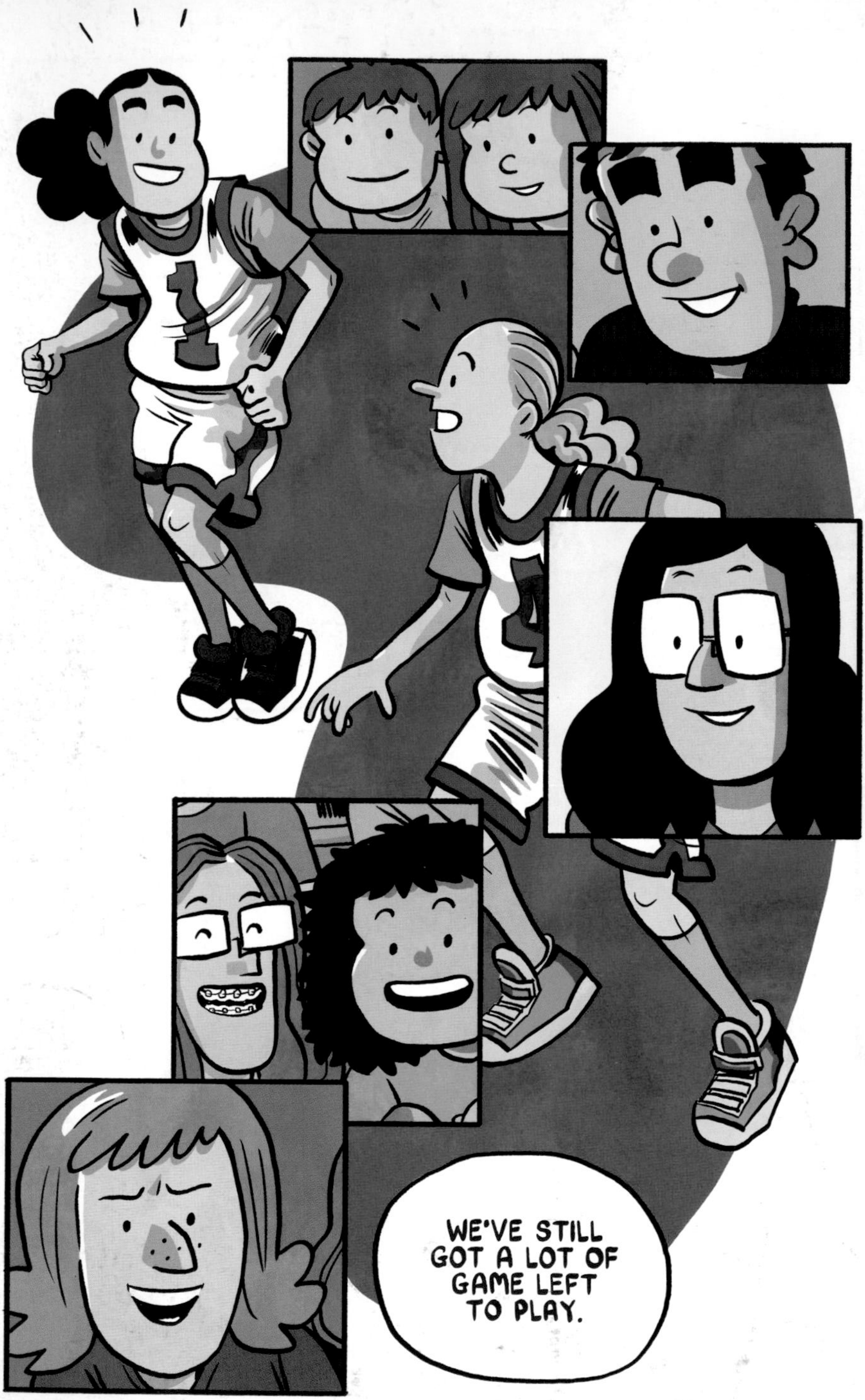
WE'VE STILL GOT A LOT OF GAME LEFT TO PLAY.

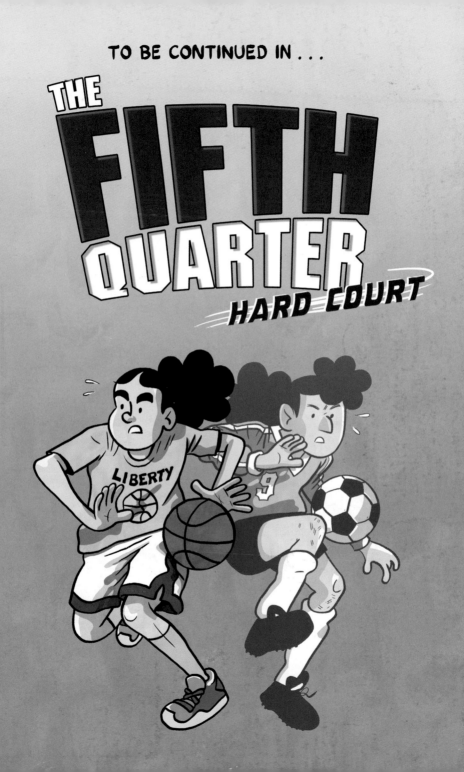

Acknowledgments

All of my love and gratitude to Aliza, Orli, and Ewan for their immense support and inspiration. Without you none of this would have been possible.

Thank-you to Greg Hunter, who provided the spark, Dan Kois, Hazel Newlevant, MariNaomi, Mark Siegel, and Gordon Warnock.

Special thanks to Jess Patel. Thanks also to Erin Howard, Liz DeBeer, Chris Rodriguez, Meghan Chrisner-Keefe, Michael McCue, and everybody willing to put themselves out there and run for something.

Thank-you to the coaches, Tiny Green, Jenny Liggio, Tracey Sabino and the incredible team at Hoop Group, Eugene Curran, John Reid, Jason Corrigan, and anybody who volunteers their time helping kids build confidence and get better.

Additional thanks to Brian Jensen, Zoe Arhanic, Annie Lachanski, and the talented players of the Lady Knights for their many exciting games.